All of a sudden she was fighting to keep her distance from him, and it was getting harder and harder.

She wasn't sure when it had happened. Perhaps in those first moments after the crash, when he'd given her that extra bit of support.... An embrace.

Or maybe the big moment had been when he'd suggested she walk behind him, to shade herself from the sun, and that he carry her bag. The idea was sweet and thoughtful. And she admittedly enjoyed the constant view of sinewy ripples of muscle in his shoulders through his shirt, and of strong, determined thighs in his jeans as he'd walked ahead of her.

And just now, when he'd reached down with those big, capable hands. He was supposed to be city-soft and reliant on her, but she knew if she let him he'd lift her to the top of the rock with no effort. Yes, *that* was when she'd got scared. When she'd started to realize he was occupying too much of her mind.

Dear Reader,

This is the second of my far-north Australia books. As I said in *Midwife in a Million,* I loved the scenery in Baz Luhrmann's *Australia.* I watched the movie and wondered why I'd never made it to the Kimberley region of Western Australia—apart from the fact it's nearly two and a half thousand miles from my house. Naturally, when the opportunity arose to attend a midwifery conference in Darwin there was enough serendipity in that for me to make the leap.

So followed a glorious week in the top end of Australia and a magical day when I flew almost to the edge of the Tanami Desert and the magnificent Purnululu National Park. The Bungle Bungles are a maze of black-and-orange-striped domes shaped like beehives that soar three hundred meters out of the arid plain and have been there for twenty million years. On landing we walked the secret trails into the center, past silent rock pools and fan palms that hang out of crevices and under overhangs. Later we flew low over the domes in a helicopter, and on that flight I couldn't help but wonder what would happen if we were forced to land in that desolate but beautiful landscape.

From that adventure blossomed the story of Sophie and Levi, two people I grew to love. Their journey is a tribute to the strength, courage and humor of the people who live all year round at the top end of Australia. I hope that within these pages you can glimpse the incredible beauty of the Kimberleys that thrilled me.

I wish you happy reading!

Fiona McArthur

THE MIDWIFE AND THE MILLIONAIRE
Fiona McArthur

TORONTO • NEW YORK • LONDON
AMSTERDAM • PARIS • SYDNEY • HAMBURG
STOCKHOLM • ATHENS • TOKYO • MILAN • MADRID
PRAGUE • WARSAW • BUDAPEST • AUCKLAND

Recycling programs
for this product may
not exist in your area.

ISBN-13: 978-0-373-06744-2

THE MIDWIFE AND THE MILLIONAIRE

First North American Publication 2010.

Copyright © 2010 by Fiona McArthur.

www.eHarlequin.com

Printed in U.S.A.

THE MIDWIFE AND THE MILLIONAIRE

With thanks to:
Glenn at Heliworks, for his help with helicopters
and moments of unusual interest.
To Fiona, the guide at the Bungle Bungles,
who shared her knowledge and enthusiasm
for an amazing place.
And Annie, for being a natural-born teacher and
one of my wonderful Maytone friends.

CHAPTER ONE

ANOTHER squat boab tree dropped its leaves as Sophie Sullivan drove past, a sure sign the wet season was nearly over. She sounded her car horn at the frilled-neck lizard basking in the middle of the dirt track and he reared on hind legs, spread his neck frill and hissed until he seemed much more than he really was.

Typical male.

At least the craggy red mountains that embraced her were true, she thought, as she drove towards the boulder-strewn river—that range was a dear part of home.

Home: far north Western Australia, the Kimberleys and a place blissfully away from the city and men who shed lies like the boab shed leaves.

Even the dusty Gibb River Road looked attractive until she saw the vehicle parked by the Pentecost and the motionless man beside the sluggish water.

More crocodile fodder. She sighed—travellers caused her no end of concern, especially ones who hovered for long periods at the edge of the crocodile-inhabited rivers.

The tourists parked by the river because of the view to the Cockburn Range across the ochre plains. Locals used the designated parking area at the top of the hill, well away from the water.

She pulled up next to the expensive all-terrain vehicle and wound down her window. 'You OK, there?'

The man didn't answer. He must've heard her truck. She was ten feet away from him. Careless *and* rude, she thought and narrowed her eyes. Finally he turned his head and glanced at her dismissively. 'Fine, thanks.'

He was big—Sophie couldn't help but notice—bigger than her brother, Smiley, who topped six-two, and this guy was very nicely muscled so he'd be a mouthful for any croc, but he was too close and too stationary in a dangerous spot. It would be a shame to waste the body, she thought dispassionately, and with the new knowledge from Brand-name Brad she could have done without, it would be a waste of the designer jeans and Rolex watch.

Congratulations were in order for her immunity from the male species. A hard-won but valuable lesson.

Sophie bit back another sigh. How did you tell someone to get back in their vehicle when they blatantly ignored you?

'You've seen the warnings?' She looked at the sign herself, read it under her breath even. 'Crocodiles Inhabit This Area. Keep Away from the Edge. Do Not Enter the Water.' But her reading it didn't make him face her. In fact, no further response to her at all.

Grrr. Spare me from arrogant males. Despite the flags that waved from the man to say go away, she tried one more time. 'About the crocodiles here?'

'Yes, thanks.' Far less cordial and this time he shifted his feet so he faced her. 'I'm just passing through.'

'You'll pass right through a croc,' she said drily. 'I lost my darling dog in a spot like this once.' And still had nightmares about the tragedy her lack of concentration had caused.

Then he looked directly at her. He wasn't to-die-for handsome, really, but he had those dark, dark lashes and an intense gaze that held her, effortlessly, until he dropped the connection as easily as he'd reeled her in. The trumpet call. *Danger*, and not from crocodiles. Her skin prickled.

'I'm sorry to hear about your pet.' He glanced back at the river before he looked again at her, to assess if she'd be a nuisance by the look of it, and Sophie could feel the warmth of the sun beat in the window, or she hoped that explained the heat.

Best not to become entangled in another look so she concentrated on a small scar on his chin that made him less imposing—more vulnerable, which was a funny thing to think about a stranger, but his mouth… She had a sudden ridiculous urge to see those lips smile.

Sophie searched for the question she'd asked.

He coughed and she looked up in time to see him roll his eyes, obviously used to stunned mullet expressions on passing females, and he didn't bother to hide the sigh. 'If I get attacked by a croc because I had to talk to you I'm going to be extremely unhappy.'

Sophie blinked. What the heck was she doing? So much for immunity! She obviously needed a booster shot against this guy, so leaving was a great idea. 'Right, then. Your funeral.' For the first time in ten years Sophie crunched the gears as she slipped her vehicle into reverse.

Levi Pearson turned back to contemplate the spot where his father had been taken five months ago. Or had he been pushed and the crocodile only secondary to his demise? He'd find out.

That tiny whiff of suspicion, something only he seemed to have sniffed, was the reason he'd flown up here after the wet season and why he'd asked his stubbornly determined sister not to mention their proper connection to Xanadu. That and the fact the other consultant he worked with had recommended a holiday for the tenth time in the past two years.

As soon as he'd confirmed or dismissed the concept of foul play he'd get her the hell out of downtown nowheresville and back to Sydney. The manager here was more than capable of running Xanadu, and Levi didn't need another burden, but he'd discovered a motive he couldn't dismiss.

Lord knew the original owners of the station had enough reason to hate his family if the stories of his father were true.

He took his eye off the bank and risked a glance at the blonde woman's four-wheel-drive vehicle as it ploughed through the river away from him. Nothing else mattered. Hadn't for a long while. Definitely not a pair of concerned blue eyes under two stern eyebrows. Above a lush little mouth. He frowned. She'd been an officious little thing but strangely intriguing.

Still, he'd read the population of the Kimberley region was about thirty thousand people in an area slightly bigger than Germany and it was the last place he'd ever settle. So, he should be safe from bumping into her again. He didn't need the complication of fleeting sexual attraction to a cowgirl.

A stealthy splash to the left of where he stood had his attention firmly back on the water and Levi took a few steps towards the vehicle he'd borrowed from the resort. Probably better not to get eaten and give her the chance to say *I told you so*.

He could feel the twitch of his lips at the thought, along with surprise at the idea of smiling, something he hadn't done much of in the past year or two, and climbed back into his vehicle.

Nearly two hours later Sophie swerved around another pothole and the old four-wheel drive bounced off the thousandth corrugation on her way to Jabiru Station Township. They'd grade the road soon now the rain had stopped. She gritted her teeth to stop the jarring. Almost home.

Funnily enough, she wasn't tired. Hadn't been since the Pentecost. She didn't want to think about the man at the river any more. It had been one of those moments in time when you catch another person's eye and, for a second or two, glances tangle and reverberate, and then you both look away and the moment passes.

Except the moment seemed to last an eternity and she was still waiting for it to pass.

It had been one of those moments. Just a stranger. With great eyes. And a great body. And a great mouth. Even in the firm line, she remembered, his mouth had hinted at a fullness and dangerous curve that made her wonder how he'd got the scar. She hoped some hot-blooded woman had thrown a plate at him. Her lips twitched but she pulled them back into line. He'd looked like everything she didn't want in a man.

Rude, definitely.

Stupid, obviously. She frowned. He didn't look stupid; actually, he'd looked fearsomely intelligent. So not stupid, maybe reckless. She didn't want that either, did she? No way.

Worst of all, he'd had the trappings of her ex. Stinking, selfishly, blatantly wealthy. Like Dr Brad Gale. The liar. She was finished with doctors and liars and people who thought they could buy you. And serve you a prenuptial at the same time.

She was glad to be home, in a place where people said what they meant and didn't string you along. Where she could be useful to those who needed her, and not as some decorative arm hanging, and definitely not confined to answering only when spoken to.

Sophie did wonder if her poor brother had become used to his bachelor ways while she'd been away. He'd looked surprised when she'd arrived to move back into her own room, even if 'Shortest engagement in history,' was all he'd said.

She drove through the tiny Jabiru Station Township— mostly pubs and boarded buildings—to their house, a modest timber residence with bull-nosed verandas on all sides and a tiny dry garden. Neat and comfortable, in the same state of disrepair as they'd inherited it from their parents, who'd inherited it from her father's parents after Granddad did that bad thing.

A place where Smiley could save every cent for his dream station, like the one his grandfather had been tricked out of in a card game all those years ago. Against a man who'd lied.

Not that Smiley lusted after Xanadu. He'd his own plans for a different station that accounted for his cattle having to be lodged all over the Kimberley while he saved for the land, but it irked Sophie that her own father and now Smiley had to scrimp so hard to make their way in the place they were born.

'You must've loaded the cattle early, because I didn't see the road train on the way in,' she said as she rounded the veranda, then stopped. He had someone with him.

Her brother's drawl seemed more noticeable, which was saying something, as his normal speech defined the word *leisurely*. 'Sophie.' He looked at her, and then indicated the petite dark-haired woman beside him. 'This is Odette. From Sydney. She's having a baby, and in the area for a week or so, and wanted to meet a midwife in case she had any problems.'

Sophie held out her hand and shook the young woman's perfectly manicured fingers. Nice expensive watch. Brad had bought her one just like it. She'd left it in Perth.

Sophie bit back the thought. He'd made her judgemental and that wasn't like her—or hadn't been before she'd tripped off to Perth for her midwifery. She needed to get her new prejudice under control. Wealthy tourists kept a lot of people in jobs around here.

'Nice to meet you, Odette. Welcome to Jabiru Station Township. You been waiting long?'

'I flew in an hour ago.' Her coral-coloured lips tilted as she smiled. She had a sweet face, Sophie thought, and well made up, which was interesting as the heat usually melted foundation around here. 'Guess I should have rung first but I thought the clinic was open.'

Sophie looked across the street to the old homestead that'd been turned into the clinic. 'I've been visiting an Aboriginal community. It's "women's health" day. Just takes a few hours to cover the distance around here.'

'So Smiley was explaining.' She looked shyly up at Sophie's brother. Goofily, Smiley actually smiled back, an occurrence that was so rare it had derived his nickname. Sophie felt herself frown. She'd never seen him look like that. Or be much into explaining anything. She'd be lucky to get a dozen words out of him on a normal morning.

'Odette flew herself in a chopper,' he said.

Impressive. 'You're a pilot? Wow.' And very pregnant, but she didn't say it.

Odette shrugged with a smile. 'I do it for fun. You're a midwife. Wow.'

Sophie had to laugh. 'I do that for fun too. My friend, Kate, the other midwife, flies her own plane from Jabiru Homestead.'

Odette exuded good nature and Sophie couldn't help liking her. 'So you're having a baby? And want a check-up? Come across to the clinic. Was there something you were worried about?'

Odette turned and smiled at Sophie's brother. 'Thanks, Smiley. I hope I get to see you again.'

He nodded and tipped his hat. The two women crossed the road and Odette looked back. 'Your brother's a handsome man.'

Sophie blinked. She'd never thought about it. He was just…Smiley. 'If he's not in the house he's got an Akubra on so I don't often see his face. I guess I still see skinned knees and freckles.'

'I didn't see any of those.' Odette sounded almost dreamy and Sophie grimaced. City-rich women and Smiley did not mix.

'Is it your husband's helicopter?' Not very subtle.

'I don't have a husband.' Odette was no fool and she

met Sophie's eyes without a flicker. 'The father of my baby is dead.'

Bummer, for more reasons than one, Sophie thought. Was she being judgemental again? 'Sorry for being nosy.'

'That's OK. Better to get it out in the open anyway. He wasn't a nice man,' Odette went on. 'And the chopper belongs to the resort where I'm staying.'

'That would be Xanadu, then.' It wasn't a question. Xanadu. Now an ultra-high-end resort a hundred kilometres away, as the chopper flew, that catered for a Kimberley adventure in five-star luxury. Private suites, fine wine and cuisine, and escorted tours with private sittings in the hot springs and gorges. They'd turned it into a wilderness park with a few token cattle. Not like in Grandfather's day. 'I've never known them to lend the chopper before.'

Odette shrugged. 'I just asked the manager.' She looked across at Sophie. 'I could take you and Smiley up for a fly if you want.'

'Thanks, but maybe another time. Should you be flying when you're pregnant?'

'You sound like my brother.'

Now why did she suddenly think of the man at the river? 'Don't suppose he's a big bloke, scar on his chin, not into smiling.' The one who was 'just passing through.'

'You've met Levi?'

'Levi?' It seemed he was another person who was happy to bend the truth. As opposed to the straightforward people from around here who didn't lie. 'Yep. Guess I have. He was at the Pentecost River crossing.' Sophie didn't say *a little too close to the water* because she didn't want to worry Odette. She shrugged. 'I warned him about the crocodiles.'

Odette pursed her lips for a moment, then visibly pushed away whatever had caused the look. 'He knows about the crocodiles. But thank you. Levi is a good guy, just forgotten how to have fun.'

And too attractive, and Sophie needed to talk about something new because she had the feeling anything else she learnt about him wouldn't help her forget.

'So when's your baby due, Odette?'

'A month.'

Sophie fought to keep her jaw from dropping but she had another look. Surely too small. Maybe Odette had it all tucked away. 'I'd say your brother was right and you shouldn't be flying. Where's your mother?'

'She died when I was a kid.' Oops, Sophie thought. Another foot-in-mouth question.

Luckily Odette didn't seem worried. 'Levi brought me up. Our father ran off with another woman when I was young. That's why Levi's serious. He's been the man of the house for a lot of years.'

Too much information. Not hearing this. 'OK.' Sophie pushed open the door and they went into the small exam room. 'How about I check your blood pressure, feel your tummy and have a listen to your baby's heart rate? If it's OK with you I'll photocopy your antenatal card. Then if you have any worries I can talk you through most of it on the phone.'

Odette grinned. 'This is like booking into a spare hospital.'

Sophie smiled back. 'Except we don't deliver babies here, only the unexpected ones.' She gestured to the chair beside her desk. 'Have a seat.'

Odette settled herself and held out her arm. 'That's OK. We'll probably be back in Sydney in a few days anyway.'

Maybe that justifies as passing through and he didn't technically lie. Though what the heck was he doing bringing someone this pregnant away from home?

Sophie wrapped the cuff around Odette's arm and pumped it up, then let it down. She unhooked the stethoscope from her ears and smiled. 'Blood pressure's perfect. One ten on sixty.' She indicated the footstool beside the examination table. 'If you can climb up there we'll see where this baby of yours is hiding.'

Odette chuckled. 'Everyone says I'm small but I was only five pounds when I was born. The ultrasound said it's a boy.'

Sophie draped a thin sheet over the lower half of Odette's body and Odette lifted her shirt. 'A boy. Wow. Nice tummy.' Sophie was serious. Odette's abdomen curved up in a perfect small hill, brown and smooth, and the baby shifted a body part into a small point as Sophie laughed. 'He's waving.'

Odette slid her hand over the point and the baby

subsided as if trained. 'My baby's no sloth. Moves heaps, especially at night.'

'Women tend to feel their babies at night because they're not busy like they are in the daytime. They say the baby already has a rhythm so if he's awake a lot at night you might be in for some sleep deprivation.'

'I don't mind.' Odette smiled dreamily. 'I can't wait.'

I hope you do, Sophie thought, as she measured the mound of Odette's belly and, taking into account the petite mother, the measurements confirmed Odette's estimated due date.

She slid the hand-held Doppler over the area she'd palpated as the baby's shoulder and the sound of the baby's heart rate filled the room. They both listened and their eyes met in mutual acknowledgement of the wonder of childbearing. 'There you go,' Sophie said, as she turned off the Doppler. 'One hundred and forty beats a minute and just as perfect as his mother.'

She helped Odette sit up. 'Everything looks great.'

'Thanks, Sophie. I feel better just talking to you.' Odette climbed down and smoothed her clothes. 'How much do I owe you?'

Sophie shook her head. 'I didn't do anything. Free service. Anyone can walk in and get the same.'

'You and Smiley should come over to Xanadu on the weekend and have dinner with my brother and me. Our treat. As a thank-you for this.' She gestured to the examination couch. 'I could come and get you in the chopper. Or Levi could.'

Lord, no. And she thought they were going in a day or two? It was only Monday. She walked her to the door. 'Thanks, Odette, but the weather's still too unsettled for me to fly—I'm a chicken in the air—and I don't know what Smiley's planned. I've only just moved back from Perth.'

'Sure. I'll ring later in the week.' Odette stopped and turned back with a new idea. 'If you're not keen on flying, you could stay overnight and drive back the next day. In fact, that sounds more fun anyway.'

Sophie felt she was being directed by a small determined whirly wind, like the one that was lifting leaves outside her window and the one inside her chest when she thought of staying anywhere near Odette's brother. 'I'll mention it to Smiley.' Not.

Odette pulled a gold compact from her bag, flicked open the mirror and touched up her lipstick. Not something Sophie did regularly out here in the bush and the thought made her smile to herself.

Odette snapped shut the compact. 'What's your brother's real name?'

Sophie had to think for a moment. 'William.'

Odette nodded as if she liked it. 'I think I'll call him William.'

'It's been a while since anybody has.' Now where was this going? Nowhere, she hoped. 'He may not even remember it.'

'Even more reason to,' Odette said cryptically.

* * *

That afternoon, Levi poured his sister a chilled juice and himself a cold beer before he moved to look over the veranda at the gorge below. Then her words sank in. He turned back to her. 'You what?'

'I invited William and Sophie to stay over for a night on the weekend. The midwife and her brother. To have dinner and drive home the next day.'

He'd strangle her. 'Did I mention we didn't want to draw attention until I find out if anyone around here hated our father enough to push him into that river?'

Odette crossed her arms and lent them over her large tummy. 'Hated him more than you?'

Levi shook his head. 'I didn't hate him. I didn't respect him. That's all.'

He fully intended to sign the ownership he'd unexpectedly inherited back over to his sister, another baffling development his estranged father had left for him, when they'd all expected Odette to benefit by the resort automatically.

Odette rolled her eyes. 'Because you've just found out he's had another son to another woman. Humph.' She returned to topic. 'Besides, they wouldn't know anything about Father's accident. Sophie's only just moved back from Perth and William is—' she paused and her mouth curved '—just William. He hasn't a mean bone in his body.'

He flung his hand out towards the view. 'We don't know that. Your new best friends. You've met them, what, once?'

'You've met her too.' Odette sat forward as he frowned.

He'd done his part. He'd avoided meeting anyone. Not likely. 'When?'

'She said she'd met you by the river—' Odette didn't quite poke out her tongue but he knew that look '—this afternoon.' A winning point.

The little honey in the car? The last person he needed to be exposed to, as she seemed lodged like an annoying bindii from the grass in his memory bank. 'Blonde ponytail? Nice, um, features?'

Odette coughed and he couldn't help the curve of his own lips. He really didn't have socialising on his agenda on this trip. He needed to go home; he'd already been away past his expectations, and his theatre list would be a mile long.

His sister would be the death of him. He sighed. Too late now. 'So why can't we fly them in and out? That way they don't have to stay.'

Odette shrugged. 'Sophie doesn't fancy the chopper.'

Chicken, eh? Good. Though she hadn't seemed a shrinking violet. 'Maybe she wouldn't mind so much if the pilot didn't look like she was going to break her waters any moment?'

Odette flapped her hand at him. 'You're too used to your own way. Let me worry about me.'

CHAPTER TWO

Five days later

'I DON'T know how you talked me into this.' Sophie glared at her brother.

Smiley kept his eyes on the road. 'You've been twitchy all week.'

'And you've been moonstruck like a big old cow.'

Smiley turned to look at her briefly but didn't say anything.

It was disappointing. A bit of a spat might have taken her mind off the nerves that were building ridiculously at the thought of meeting the brooding rich man again. She was even avoiding his name in her thoughts. How ridiculous.

Unable to get a rise out of Smiley she turned to watch the scenery flash by. The overhanging escarpment of the Cockburn ranges in the distance ran along the right side of the vehicle and the stumpy gums and dry grass covered the plains to the left before they soared into more ochre-red cliffs that tinged purple as the sun set.

Sophie knew the darkening gorges hid pockets of tangled rainforest and deep cold pools like the dread she could feel at meeting him again.

But the stands of thick and thin trees made her smile. She'd missed the pot bellies of the grey-trunked boabs the most while she'd been in Perth.

'Why don't you like Odette?' Smiley was stewing. Something in his voice warned her not to be flippant.

'Who wouldn't like Odette?' she said carefully. 'She seems lovely. I just don't want you hurt when she flies back to Sydney.'

Smiley frowned at the road ahead and Sophie winced at his displeasure. Now that was something she'd very rarely encountered and she didn't like it. 'I'm sorry, Smiley. I have no right to judge your friends. I think Odette's great. I just can't see her as an outback girl and I can't see you in the city. But it's none of my business.'

'Thank you.' His voice was dry and the two words were a statement. Thanking her for agreeing it was none of her business.

Oops. She really had upset her brother and that was something she'd never consciously do. Since her parents had died she'd become used to bossing Smiley around, giving her opinion, and he'd never seemed to mind.

Obviously she'd crossed the line with Odette. She'd just have to button her lip and trust Smiley's instincts.

It would've been easier if she'd sent him to Xanadu

on his own though. She had the feeling her trepidation for Smiley was tied up in the trepidation she held for herself with Odette's mysterious brother.

Smiley turned off the main dirt road onto the red dust of the track through the scrub. They splashed through several watercourses and wound through the ochre-coloured hills until they turned into the Private Property, No Entry sign that hid the homestead.

'Welcoming,' she mumbled, and Smiley glanced at her.

'You've met the brother?'

'Briefly.' She could be just as taciturn. She didn't expand her explanation and Smiley didn't ask again. Then the homestead came into view.

Xanadu Homestead was a long low building, and she'd been too young to remember visiting in her grandparents' day. Apparently now it had been divided up into luxury suites, if what Sophie had heard was right, perched on the edge of the escarpment above the river that flowed beneath it.

The main building faced into the sunset which glowed deep red as it faded. Nice place to holiday if you had the platinum or even a black credit card, but not when you were eight months pregnant. Why would Odette and her brother come here now?

At least the thought gave her something else to concentrate on as they drew up at the house. She wondered what the other guests would think of outsiders being invited to invade their sanctuary. What month was this?

April. The resort would only just have opened for the season anyway.

Odette swayed onto the main entrance portico in a muslin caftan that must have cost a bomb, and Sophie wondered how she could still be graceful when she was supposed to be awkward in the last month of pregnancy. Sophie glanced at Smiley and judging by his face he'd just seen the Holy Grail.

Sophie sighed and felt for the handle to climb out of the truck when her door moved away from her grasp.

'Welcome to Xanadu.' Levi held out his hand and Sophie wasn't sure if he wanted to shake hers or help her from the vehicle. Where'd he come from? She'd been hoping to see him from a distance and get her face straight.

She resisted the urge to snap her hand back to her side and forced herself to let him take her fingers. Initially cool, the strength in his fingers surprised her, but not as much as the feeling of insidious connection, a frisson of ridiculous warmth that passed between them and echoed the impact of his eyes. There was something she'd deny with her last breath.

No. She hadn't felt a thing. So why rub her hand surreptitiously behind her back? And why did he look down at her with one enigmatic eyebrow raised as if he'd been surprised as well?

Then Odette was dancing around the car like an elegant puppy as she looked adoringly up at Smiley, and Levi left her to shake Smiley's hand.

'It's so good to see you, William.' Odette flashed a smile at Sophie before she looked back at Smiley and captured his hand. Odette tugged his fingers to make him follow her. 'This is my brother, Levi,' she said dismissively. 'Now, come and see the place.'

'William' looked back at Sophie, who managed a tiny smiling shrug that said she'd be fine.

'My sister can be impetuous,' Levi said grimly.

'My brother can't.' She watched Smiley leap up the stairs after Odette. 'Or I didn't think he could.'

Levi lifted one eyebrow sardonically. 'Welcome to Xanadu. I'll send someone for the bags when we get inside.'

Sophie glanced in the back of the truck. 'Actually, we're used to carrying our own.'

He inclined his head. 'But I'd be offended. Please come in.'

The bags weren't worth standing out here with him so she turned resolutely towards the entrance. He went on. 'The resort's not technically opened for the season and we have the run of the place.'

'Well, that's very nice.' But she couldn't help thinking, How the heck did you do that? They must know the owners extremely well or have unlimited funds. Best not go there. 'When does it open?'

He glanced at the sky. 'Depends on the weather and the state of the roads, though apparently next week, if all continues well.'

She slanted a look across at him. 'I guess you and Odette will be gone by then.'

Another enigmatic brow rose. 'Trying to get rid of us?'

They crossed the gravel drive to the stairs and she paused. 'You did say you were passing through. A week ago,' she said calmly.

'I lied.' Straightfaced, no remorse.

Sophie blinked. She'd known he was dangerous. Like sniffing the briny scent before a storm. Her instincts had been right. He was trouble. She started walking again, faster now, but he kept pace. 'People don't tend to do that up here.' Liar like Brad.

His eyes narrowed as if he sensed some history there. 'Necessity can make liars out of us all.'

She could feel her lip curl. 'So some people say.'

He looked across at her and no doubt he could see her distaste. She hoped so. 'Had a bad experience with a man, have you?'

'I think I'll look for my brother.' She turned away but before she could take a step he caught her hand again and she pulled up short to look back at him with raised eyebrows, actually astounded that he would invade her intimate space.

Maybe he didn't know that people from the bush— used to wide-open spaces and few people—didn't do space invasion well. Smiley tended to wave at people rather than shake their hands. Not like those from the city, who were used to people brushing up against them in elevators and on city streets.

He let go. This time she didn't hide that she rubbed her hand.

'I apologise, Sophie.' To give him his due he looked as confused as she felt. 'We seem to have got off on the wrong foot. Twice.' Those deadly lips of his were as devastating in an almost smile as she'd imagined. Damn him.

'Now why do we rub each other the wrong way, do you think?'

No way was Sophie going there. She looked him up and down. Coolly, she hoped. 'I'm not interested in rubbing anyone at all.'

His almost smile, which she decided was forced anyway, departed and he nodded. 'Let's go in, then.' He gestured with his hand for her to precede him, but he didn't touch her. And she didn't thank him for the courtesy because she could feel his eyes on her back uncomfortably the whole way up the steps. And he was still in her space.

Levi watched her attempt to walk sedately ahead of him; they both knew something had happened. He wanted to come up beside her and put his hand on the small of her back—lay claim, in fact—and he crunched his fingers into his palm to stop from reaching out. She'd invaded his head with the tiny bit he'd seen the other day but in full-blown glory she took his breath away.

Her dress was simple and blue but smoothed the slender line of her back and hips as she swayed in front of him and her legs were bare and brown and long enough to dream about. This was crazy. She smoked, just by walking in front of him.

It felt as if a wire from one of the fences dragged him along in her wake, and there was a tautness he could see in her shoulders that said she wasn't comfortable either.

He didn't know what it was. Apart from totally impractical and heinously inconvenient…but then again the travel agent had quoted the Kimberleys as a destination of adventure. Suddenly he was thinking of a side tour of a different sort.

He ushered her, with great restraint and no contact, through to the veranda where they all shared the sunset, or at least her brother and his sister shared it; he and Sophie separately observed. Maybe not even that because he wasn't looking at hills bathed in purple.

He'd always had a thing about women with long necks and hers flowed like an orchid to her throat. He'd bet her skin felt as soft as a petal. He shifted his scrutiny away from temptation and looked higher. He couldn't see her eyes from where he stood but he knew they were blue. Like her dress. High cheekbones, snubby nose that should have just been snubby but turned out deliciously cute, and those lips. He reefed his eyes away and took a long swallow of his beer. Who was he and what had happened to the normal, sane, over-worked man who'd arrived last week?

Shame it wasn't prehistoric times because dragging her off to his cave looked mighty appealing to him at this moment. And no one had appealed for a while. He'd better find something to stay focused on, something apart from how to get her into bed.

'Odette tells me you're a midwife,' he said, and now he could see her eyes. Her pupils were big and dark and he'd read somewhere that was a sign of arousal. He hoped so 'cause he was sure his eyes would be all pupil to his lashes.

She ran her finger around the rim of her glass and even that tiny movement made him swallow. 'And community nurse, and anything else that needs medical attention,' she said.

He almost wished he was sick. 'Sounds diverse. It must be a heavy workload.' He watched her face light up.

'I enjoy it,' she said. 'Love it, in fact. Now it has the added dimension of meeting people like Odette who'd benefit from access to a midwife.'

Passion for her job. Bless her. He used to have that. Now he didn't even want to talk about work. 'Odette said you've just returned from Perth.'

He felt the cold breeze and even her pupils constricted until her eyes were light blue again. She jutted her chin and he regretted the question. Obviously bad choice of conversation and a major setback. Probably a good thing.

'Yes. It's great to be home.' Such a cold voice, so different than when she'd spoken of work.

She put her glass down and turned to his sister. 'The view is wonderful, Odette.' Sophie pretended to be absorbed and tried to fade Levi into the background. She didn't want to think about Perth and the fool she'd made of herself there. Though it served as a reminder not to be foolish here. Just because externally Odette's brother was hard to ignore, internally he'd be the same as Brad. He'd already shown his arrogant, untruthful side. Rich, callous, oblivious to hurting others. And she'd promised she'd never become that vulnerable again.

She just wished he'd stop studying her. She could feel him watching. Could feel the brush of his analytical study as if she were some strange species he hadn't figured out yet and it made her want to think of some witty, slash-cutting thing to make him back off. But of course she couldn't think of something. No doubt tonight in bed it would be there on her tongue.

Well, he could look, but she refused to squirm. He'd be used to city women falling all over him but he'd come to the wrong place for that. Here a woman wanted a man with more to his repertoire than looking good.

'So what do you do, Levi?' Apart from watching me. Not that she was interested.

'I have a business in Sydney.'

City slicker. She'd bet it wasn't a physical job because his hands looked too clean. She wasn't going to comment, even mentally, on his obvious fitness.

He raised his eyebrows. 'You have a very expressive face. By the curl of your lip I'm surprised you think I do anything?'

'Perhaps.' She abandoned the subject. If he didn't want to tell her, then that was fine. The less she knew about him, the better. She turned her shoulder further away from him.

'My sister tells me you don't like helicopters much.'

Politeness meant she had to turn back. No doubt he would see her reluctance and maybe then he'd leave her alone. 'Nothing personal to helicopters, I don't like to fly.'

He shifted his body so she was lined up with him again. 'Shame, then. A pilot's licence would be useful with the distances they have out here.'

Like Kate and her plane. She'd never feel comfortable enough to do that. 'My friend flies. I'll do without.'

He acknowledged her aversion with a flick of his hand. 'It's a different world, immediate, stunning, and even I admit this country is spectacular from the air.'

She felt her hackles rise and she sipped her drink before she answered to damp down her desire to demand he appreciate her home. 'The Kimberleys are spectacular from the ground as well.'

He put his glass down. 'I've offended you again.'

'The bush is not for everyone.' She shrugged, thankfully.

'And you're happy about that?'

It seemed she couldn't cause him offence. 'There are advantages.' Well, at least they were conversing in a fairly normal way, and then a waiter appeared and it was time for dinner.

Levi gestured her ahead of him and Sophie pulled up short at the candlelit veranda; a glass ceiling show-cased the glorious starlit sky above a table that glowed with white linen and silver cutlery. 'Amazing room.'

'Very civilised,' Levi agreed, as if he were still sur-prised by it. Even that offended her, as if they couldn't put on a good show up here in the bush.

She took her seat and, much to Sophie's amazement, dinner proved a delightful affair. They were joined by the resort manager, Steve, a handsome young man—more Odette's age than Levi's—who said and did all the right things and was very anxious to ensure that Odette was safely seated or served, as if she were an invalid. Baby phobia, Sophie guessed, but he left Sophie with a feeling of awkwardness she couldn't explain.

The rapport between Levi and Odette showed gen-uine affection. Reluctantly Sophie admitted she liked that—family was important—so he had some redeem-ing features which she didn't really want to see. And Levi devoted himself to being a wonderful host. Then again, her ex, Brad, had been a great host too.

Odette remained animated and 'William' held his own end of the conversation up for a change. Sophie had to shut her mouth when she would normally have answered for her brother until finally she subsided in awe at his previously hidden ability to socialise. He could have come on his own after all. Great!

Until the talk turned to helicopters and the sugges-tion of a joint expedition the next day. This she couldn't keep silent on. 'I hope you don't expect me to go along. Helicopters fall out of the sky.'

Levi sat back in his chair and smiled at her. 'No, they don't.'

Loosened up by the delightful Margaret River Shiraz, Sophie pointed her finger at him. 'I want to know what happens when the engine stops in a helicopter.'

Her comment came in a lull and stilled the other conversations, and Levi tilted his head at her. 'They glide. Autorotation. Instead of the air being pulled in from the top by the engine, the rotors turn the other way and pull the air in from underneath as you descend. Gives you fairly good forward and downward control. Like a winged aeroplane, just not as far.'

She didn't believe him. 'How far?'

'Enough to get passengers on the ground without hurting them.' He held her gaze, daring her to disbelieve him.

Sounded too simple. 'Then you can take off again?'

He rubbed his chin. 'Maybe not always without hurting the chopper.' He seemed sure of his facts.

Sophie digested that.

'We've two helicopters at Xanadu,' Steve said, 'and never had a problem.' He smiled kindly at her and she almost felt patted like a small dog. Sophie wondered why she had the urge to wipe the smile off his face. Maybe the poor guy had trained himself to be extra accommodating around his VIP guests, but Sophie found his attentions irritating.

She glanced at Levi but she couldn't read anything in his face. He was probably used to people fawning over him.

The conversation moved on and Sophie sat back to observe. She watched mostly Levi, despite her attempts not to be drawn to him. He made no blatant attempt to direct the conversation, he just did. While she didn't like him she had to admit he was smooth. He seemed to know the right thing to bring out the passion in Smiley for the land, and Sophie was surprised by her brother's apparent liking for their host.

Sophie refused to fall for the same thing and she wasn't going to lose. Actually, she wanted to go home or at least get out of this room, away from him.

With the meal cleared away, Sophie drifted towards the end of the veranda where the steps led down to the path around the side of the homestead. The stars winked down at her and the further she moved away from the veranda the brighter the sky lights formed into the constellations and patterns she'd grown up with.

The Southern Cross, the Pot, the Milky Way. A wooden bench under a huge boab looked the perfect place to hide. She sank gratefully down on warm wood in the dimness, and the soft breeze rattled the boab leaves over her head as if to soothe her.

Until Levi strode out onto the veranda with his satellite phone and shattered the magic of the night, along with the calm she'd achieved.

Typical city man. They never stopped. No doubt he couldn't imagine being without a phone at his fingertips, to direct underlings and ensure nobody forgot how important he was, and to order up the next convenience. Or like Brad, to check that his woman was waiting patiently at home, while he dallied somewhere else.

She'd like to see Levi bogged in a bulldust hole with no handy phone. See how resourceful he'd be with nobody but himself to rely on.

Then he saw her, ended the conversation and snapped his phone shut. She leant back into the shadows in a futile move as if he would forget she was there, slightly guilty about her mean thoughts for a man she barely knew, but still bitter by personal experience from the callousness of a man like him.

He paused at the bottom of the steps, and she thought he probably didn't even want to get his shoes dirty out here. Her nose wrinkled.

Levi hesitated at the bottom step, quite sure Sophie didn't want company, and reluctant to force his company on her. 'Coffee is ready if you'd like some.' He glanced at the grass. 'Unless you'd prefer it out here?'

She stood and walked towards him with a swish of her blue dress and he felt the rebuke for ruining her peace. She had attitude all right, he thought, but she carried it well. 'Thank you. Inside will be fine.'

There was no doubt the less she saw of him, the better, and no doubt either that the less he saw of her, the better.

CHAPTER THREE

LEVI stopped as he entered the room for breakfast on the veranda next morning. It seemed he'd interrupted an amusing show.

His sister, with much eye batting and smiles, was trying to convince cowboy William to do the scenic tourist fly in the chopper. Apparently they should fly to the Bungle Bungles, a massive prehistoric range of striped domes at the edge of the Tanami Desert, with a picnic basket, an idea which left a horrified expression on Sophie the orchid's face. Intriguing situation.

He could see a ride in the helicopter was the last thing Sophie wanted to do, make that second last. If he read her expression right when she glanced at him, the last thing she wanted was to stay behind at Xanadu, alone, with him.

Levi could tell. That was amusing too. Sort of. Though he'd never had someone blatantly avoid his company before.

He sat down next to Sophie at breakfast, maybe too

deliberately close, so his thigh touched hers when he turned, and he could actually feel her thrum with awareness. The fresh herby stuff she'd washed her hair with teased his nose and some psycho inside wanted to sniff her head. Now that would go over well as a space invasion.

Even her skin glowed golden in the morning light, like the honey on the crumpet she nibbled at, and reminded him he'd spent more than a few hours in bed last night trying not to remember those lush little hips and lips. He must be having a crisis.

'Good morning, Sophie.'

'Morning.' Her answer was accompanied by a darting look that came and went as she shrank her shoulders to avoid contact.

He had to bite back a smile. Becoming a habit those smiles. Very strange. 'Did you sleep well?'

'Fine, thanks.' Another flick of her eyes and he relented and shifted his chair a few inches away to give her some space. Her delightful shoulders actually sank with relief and he wondered why he was playing with her. He wasn't normally pushy.

'Did you sleep?' It seemed she could talk easier too.

Now how reluctantly had she asked that? He bit his lip. 'No, not really. The symphony of the night seemed especially loud.'

She raised those stern brows of hers. 'Kept awake by nature? Poor you. Well, it is a wilderness park.' She tossed her head. 'Sure beats the heck out of traffic noise.'

Maybe she didn't need sympathy. She could stand up for herself. So they ate their meal in silence as Odette continued to flirt with William.

Levi rubbed his chin as they all stood to leave because, funnily enough, her lack of enthusiasm for the flight made his skin itch.

'Odette?' he said, and his sister turned back.

'Look after Sophie. Remember, she's not comfortable, so no stunts.'

Odette raised her eyebrows at him and saluted. 'Yes, sir.'

Sophie sent him a semi-grateful look over her shoulder as she dragged her feet to follow the other two to the helipad.

Levi frowned to himself as he went the other way. He needed to concentrate on the paperwork he had to get through before they returned to Sydney, but the ridiculously blue Kimberley sky outside the window invited sacrifice. Odette was too pregnant to be pilot. And Sophie looked unhappy.

Unhappy was too mild a word. Sophie didn't know how she'd agreed to this.

Now Steve, the resort manager, had shooed Odette away from pre-flight checks. 'I can't let a pregnant lady do that,' he said with that tilted smile that prickled right up Sophie's nose. There was something about him that reminded her of someone but she couldn't connect the impression.

She'd never had much to do with the people from

Xanadu and apparently he'd been here for a few years
and very close to the late owner. She wished he'd mind
his own business though.

To make matters worse, just before take-off, Levi
appeared and decreed he'd pilot instead of Odette.
Suddenly Sophie could have stayed behind. Talk
about bad luck.

Everyone was looking out for Odette. Which was a
good thing, but Sophie wondered if it was too late to
look out for herself. Now the new seating arrangements
meant she'd be up front next to Levi. This kept getting
better and better. Not.

The front helicopter seat was as bad as she'd imagined. She shrank back into the stiff leather, semi-frozen,
not quite believing she'd agreed to this, when Levi
reached in from the outside to click her belt into place.
His hands pulled the belt firmly across her and snapped
it shut. Talk about space invasion. This whole expedition was crazy and way out of her comfort zone. How
the heck had she found herself next to him in a doorless
chopper with only the seat belt between her and certain
death?

And on that note, surely there should have been
more seat belts or harnesses or something? One belt
didn't seem enough.

Odette and Smiley chatted happily, ensconced in the
rear out of sight and out of earshot. Once they got going,
she thought bitterly, they'd be safe in their own little
world.

Levi climbed in and she squashed herself back against the seat. He pointed to the bulky headphones hooked on the central support in front of her, and indicated she put them on.

'Can you hear me?' His metallic voice made her jump, and she looked across at him and glared. He nodded and she nodded facetiously back. He frowned, then went on. 'It's automatically switched to receive, so for you to be heard by everyone else just press this button to speak.'

He withdrew his attention from her and glanced in the back. 'You guys all buckled up?'

Odette's voice crackled. 'Roger.'

Levi glanced around the deserted helipad and began the pre-flight sequence. 'All clear,' he said to no one in particular and started the rotors.

The next few minutes Sophie missed as her eyes were tightly shut. The distant noise through the headphones grew louder and she felt the shudder from the flimsy craft right through the backs of her knees, then the first sideways swish of movement through the air and then back the other way.

She opened one eye. It was too hard not to look. They swayed a little from side to side as they edged higher and she could see the downdraught from the rotors beating the bushes below.

Then she could see the river at the bottom of the gorge, the roof of the homestead, the tops of the trees, and it was all a little intriguing, though she still pushed herself deep into her seat. She tried to relax her shoulders but the fear she'd fall out kept her rigid in the chair.

They climbed higher, and despite the lack of doors, she was protected from the wind by the bubble of the front windshield, and actually it didn't feel too bad.

She opened the other eye. There was a Perspex floor in front of her feet. What sort of sick person designed a helicopter with a see-through floor? If she'd had eyes in the bottom of her soles she'd be able to look through the Perspex to the ground.

Basically she was standing on a thin edge above certain death. Her eyes closed at the vertigo of that thought, then opened again to risk a glance towards Levi as he concentrated on the dials at the front of the cockpit. What was he looking at? Was everything OK? She studied the instrument panel herself for something familiar. Maybe she'd even find a reassuring needle. Shame the guy wasn't more into smiling but at least he was taking the danger of the situation seriously.

Knots—they were doing eighty knots, and that was faster than miles per hour, so fairly fast. Fuel—there were seventy gallons of fuel; tank was full anyway. Guess that meant if they crashed she'd die in a ball of flame.

She looked away. Maybe don't read the dials. They'd climbed higher while she'd been contemplating the manner of their deaths, and she could look down on the escarpment now.

This was pretty amazing. And when she looked back, carefully, towards the homestead and the serpentine river, it made her appreciate how remote the properties were out here.

She'd flown on jets from Perth to Kununurra but they'd been much higher and she'd never really noticed individual stations, though mostly because she'd chosen the aisle seat and not the window.

'We'll fly up and over the waterfall on the property.' Levi's voice crackled through the headphones. 'Odette likes that and then over to Lake Argyle. We'll pass over a couple of stations William asked to see, then in over the Bungles and back out over the Kimberley diamond mine and home.'

He was telling her this because…? Her stomach sank. She pushed the button to speak. 'Sounds like a long flight. Do we land anywhere?'

His teeth flashed. He couldn't possibly be concentrating enough on his job if he could smile about it, she thought sourly. 'Anywhere you want,' he said.

She resisted saying, *Here*, but not by much, and just nodded and turned away to glance at her watch. They'd be home in a few hours. She hoped.

Actually, the next hour passed fairly quickly. The waterfall looked surreal from above with sparkling drops at the side of the main body of water shimmering on the breeze to the gorge below.

Lake Argyle loomed indigo blue and stretched for ever, apparently seven times the size of Sydney Harbour, so that must be why it seemed to take seven times longer than she expected to cross.

When they flew over the isolation of the two cattle stations, Smiley asked Levi to circle again, so he could point out how they corralled their cattle using the land formations to form a natural bottleneck and arena. These were the stations Smiley had his eye on.

Sophie tried to concentrate on the implications of a station with no contact with the world for at least four months during the wet season, but all she could feel were the g-forces pulling her towards the open doorway. Her whole body seemed to be straining against the seat belt as they circled, and she had this horrible feeling that maybe Levi hadn't fastened her buckle properly and she'd just pop out of it into spiralling space.

Now that was a dilemma. She hadn't checked the belt herself but if she touched it now she might press the eject button.

Come on. Their aircraft was circling thousands of feet above the hard earth and Smiley was going on about the logistical difficulties of cattle to market.

It was no good. 'Can we land soon?' Sophie's voice cut across Smiley's, squeaky with distress, and she felt Levi glance at her.

The helicopter levelled out. 'Bungles in fifteen minutes, you right with that?' Levi's voice was still tinny, but the strange thing was the lack of humour, just genuine understanding and concern in his voice and the reassurance she gained from that. His hand came across and rested on her upper arm as if to transfer calmness. From a man she didn't trust it shouldn't have helped that much. But it did. Like a lifeline.

Funny how she'd never felt that mixture of empathy and support from Brad's touch and she'd been engaged to him.

Inexplicably steadied, she nodded, and allowed herself to sag more into the seat and close her eyes. Think calm thoughts. Take deep breaths. Everything will be fine.

That was when the engine spluttered, coughed and died. Her eyes flew open. Slow motion from that moment on.

Suddenly there was no background noise except the wind and the rotors turning without an engine. She watched in horror as Levi kept his hands glued to the controls, correcting the cabin's inclination to yaw. Levi's voice travelled down the tunnel of her frozen mind. 'Have to land fast.' His voice was much louder without the sound of the engine, then she couldn't hear him at all because he'd switched the radio from the cabin to transmit the distress call. But she could watch his lips move, grimly, as he enunciated their position.

Unwilling to stare frozenly out of the Perspex beneath her feet she kept her eyes on Levi.

Glide. Helicopters can glide like planes but not as far. She remembered him saying that. She believed him. But he did lie. Had he lied then too? Surely not about this?

They weren't falling like a stone at the moment, still going forward, but the altimeter was unwinding like a top, much, much faster than it had wound up. Then she remembered that Odette and Smiley were in the back but she couldn't turn her neck to look. They'd all die. Odette's baby too? No. They had to survive. That thought steadied her. She was the midwife. The only medical person. They'd need her. Odette's baby needed her. She'd better survive in one piece.

She stared at Levi, who looked as if his face was hewn from the same stone as the escarpment they hurtled towards as he wrestled with the controls. No panic, just fierce, implacable determination to win. Thank God he'd decided to be the pilot. Even now he inspired confidence.

Then there was no time for thoughts. Just the sickening rush of the ground towards them, and she tucked her chin onto her chest and hugged her knees, so she must have listened to all those hostesses on flights she'd tried to block out. Thank you, hostesses.

They were coming in too fast.

The impact flung her head back as the helicopter slammed into the ground. Someone screamed and she wasn't sure if it was Odette or herself, then they clipped a boulder and the cabin flipped up and tipped sideways and landed once more with a larger crash and, finally, with agonising slowness, tipped back to settle on its base with a rattle of rocks and debris. They'd stopped. Intact.

That first few seconds of cessation of movement was more frightening than the seconds before, where at least she'd known she was alive. She straightened her aching neck to look at Levi. He didn't move; his long lashes were resting on ashen cheeks, and for a horrific moment she thought he was dead. Then she saw the rise and fall of his chest and the relief made the nausea rise in her throat. She reached across for his hand that lay limply pointed at her and felt for his pulse. It was fast but steady and she heaved a sigh of relief.

A soft moan came from behind her and, gingerly, she turned her head. 'Odette? Smiley? You both all right?'

'I think William's unconscious. What about Levi?'

'His pulse is strong but he's out too. We hit some scrub on their side of the aircraft so I think they bore the brunt of it.' She didn't know whether to ask or not. 'Your baby? Everything all right there?'

'I think so.' Odette's voice cracked. 'We need to get out. Get them out. The fuel!'

Sophie's fingers grappled with her belt clasp. The locking mechanism wouldn't open and those ball-of-flame visions returned to add desperation to her frustration. She rattled the catch.

Levi's hand came across and pushed the release and suddenly she was free. 'It's OK. I'll do it.' Why was he whispering?

He was conscious. Thank God. 'You were knocked out.'

'Hmm,' he said, his voice still weak, and rubbed the

front of his head. Then he blinked and sat up straighter. 'You OK? Out!' He turned his attention to the back seat but Odette was already on the ground and attempting to rouse Smiley.

Sophie scrambled up from her seat and climbed over the scattered wreckage at the front of the craft to help Odette. Smiley groaned but didn't open his eyes and Sophie lifted his lids to peer into his eyes. His pupils contracted with the light and she heaved a sigh of relief. No time for sympathy. 'Wake up, Smiley. Move!'

Smiley's eyelids fluttered and he groaned. 'What happened?'

Levi was out and beside them now too. He swayed ever so slightly and Sophie watched him with narrowed eyes. 'Later, sport,' Levi said. 'Let's get you out of here, though I think if the tank was going to explode it would have done before now.' He shooed both women with his hand. 'Get away, over by those trees, you two. Now.'

Odette turned and hobbled away but Sophie stood her ground. 'Maybe he shouldn't be moved.'

'No choice.' Levi frowned at Smiley. 'Can you move your fingers and toes?'

'My leg hurts.'

'No tingling?' Smiley shook his head, then gri-maced, and tried to pull himself free but recoiled his arm back to his chest with a loud groan.

The hiss of liquid hitting hot metal made them all jump. Levi frowned. 'I'll do the work, just brace your arm.' He heaved Smiley sideways and onto the ground in one huge movement and then dragged him away from the aircraft with Sophie almost glued to his back. The intermittent hiss from behind hastened their steps.

Sophie looked back over her shoulder. 'I'm glad it only just started doing that.'

Levi propped Smiley against a tree. 'I could have lived without it. We'll give it some time to cool down and then see what's happening with the radio, as long as everyone is stable.'

He turned to his sister, who hovered over Smiley. 'What about you, Odette? Your baby?'

'I'm not hurt. He's moving normally. Is William all right?'

'Fine. I'm more worried about you.' He looked at Sophie, who nodded and drew his sister to a fallen tree to sit.

'You need to sit for a while, Odette. We've fallen out of the sky.' She shook her head. Holy dooley. 'We're alive but it's crazily worse than a car accident and babies don't like being in those. You sure you're not contracting?'

Odette stroked her belly. 'It doesn't hurt.'

'OK. But sit. While I check Smiley.'

'His name is William,' Odette said. 'Smiley sounds like a dummy and he's not that.'

Sophie blinked. Good grief. That's all she needed. 'William,' she said but rolled her eyes as she turned away.

CHAPTER FOUR

LEVI glowered at the wreckage of the aircraft and shook his head as they all gathered their breath. 'An engine should never do that.' His jaw clamped tight and she could see the implacable leader who highly resented mechanical failure.

Well, yes. She wasn't too impressed about it herself but even she knew the unexpected was possible.

Nobody else said anything and Sophie asked the question. 'What happened?'

Levi ignored her and turned to his sister. 'You saw nothing out of order in the pre-flight check, Odette?'

His sister grimaced. 'I only started it—Steve finished it.'

Levi's face stilled. 'It's not your fault.' He spoke very quietly, and Sophie frowned as she tried to gather the thread of undertones and make sense of it, but for some reason the hairs on her arms prickled and stood and she lifted her arms across her chest to rub them.

Levi was muttering. 'I can't believe I didn't do my

own pre-flight check as well. You should never do anything last minute when flying. No excuses. First rule of flight.'

He glanced at the sky. 'We're baking in the sun. We need more shade and definitely water. I'll go up the gorge to see if there's a creek or a pool.'

Levi to the rescue? She didn't think so. 'Let me. As soon as I've checked—' she glanced at Odette and corrected herself '—William.'

Levi looked pale; a purple bruise had begun on his temple, and she could see him blaming himself when he'd saved them all. Sophie went on. 'You've been knocked out. You should move to the shade and I'll find the water.' She'd avoided his eyes while she spoke and flicked a glance back to see how he took her suggestion. Not well, judging by the scowl he directed at her.

He straightened, until he loomed over her, but the effect was spoilt when he swayed slightly. 'Who died and elected you captain? I can make my own decisions. Thanks.'

Sophie shrugged. He didn't intimidate her. Grumpy sod. 'It's a small job. As I'm the only medical person and you look like death warmed up, I say you need to rest after your heroics earlier. You're still the captain, just concussed, so that's what you'll do.'

He blinked, didn't quite drop his mouth open, but she knew she'd surprised him. He looked about to say something but didn't and she glanced at Odette and lowered her voice. 'Someone needs to keep an eye on your sister and give me a yell if she complains of any pain too, though I won't be long.'

She looked at her brother. 'But Smiley first.'

Levi hovered while she examined Smiley and it was hard to ignore him. She'd have liked to tell him to sit again but didn't want to push her luck. She doubted anyone had tried to tell him what to do since he was in school. It would do him good. Actually, thinking of him as a scrubby school boy did a lot for her confidence.

She spoke to Smiley. 'How's the head?' She ran her fingers lightly over the swelling under his right eye and then palpated the bulge over his ear. 'You've given it a good whack. Close your eyes for a couple of seconds and then open them.'

He did so and she watched his pupils constrict at the light. They looked equal as much as she could tell.

She checked his ears for discharge but there was none, and it made her think she should do the same for Levi. She looked at him.

'My ears are fine,' he said quickly. 'And I'm sure my pupils are too.'

Sophie shrugged. 'Your choice,' she said, not eager for another clash of wills, and looked back at Smiley.

'So you've dislocated the shoulder again?' A sister's tone.

Smiley grimaced. 'I'd say.'

'We can fix that. We've done it before.' But she really didn't want to think about doing that. 'And the ankle?'

'Pretty sore.' They all looked at it, swollen already, and she ran her hands over it but couldn't feel any blatant deviations of line.

Poor Smiley. 'That's gotta hurt. We'll splint it, get you a walking stick and at least you'll be independent for short walks. You still wear your knife?'

He nodded and patted his hip with his good hand. 'Good,' she said, and looked at him with sympathy for the impending pain. 'You want to do the shoulder now before it swells more?'

Tight-lipped but still brief. 'Quicker the better.'

Sophie looked at Levi. 'Can you help me with this?'

Levi appeared even more dubious. 'You sure you know what you're doing?'

Did he think she did this stuff for fun? 'I've done it for Smiley twice before.' And hated it.

Levi opened his mouth and then closed it again. 'If he's got faith in you, then I'm happy to help. Just tell me what you want me to do.' Deferring to her? Not what he'd said a minute ago but she didn't think it a good time to point that out.

He still looked uncomfortable and she wondered if he was feeling faint again. 'You sure you're OK, Levi?'

'I'm fine.' The terse man was back. He looked at Smiley. 'What about his pain relief.'

She shook her head. 'The sooner I line the bones up again so they'll slide back in, the better. And he's been knocked out anyway. Not a good idea.'

Sophie took a deep breath and hoped everyone

couldn't see how sick this made her. She knelt down beside Smiley and cleared the dirt in front of him of rocks and sticks for him to lie down.

She'd need a piece of material to go around Smiley's chest and under his injured armpit that Levi could pull on while she manipulated Smiley's arm. It needed to be strong like clothing. Probably her blouse would be best. Actually, it could be Levi's shirt. She thought about that and decided she didn't want to see his chest. She had a fair idea of the picture that might lodge in her brain.

'We'll use my shirt.' She turned around before any-one could say anything and slipped it off. Businesslike, as if she wasn't really sitting there in front of them all in her lacy bra, and she refused to think about whether she had little rolls of belly as she bent over. This day just kept getting better and better.

She spread her shirt on the ground to roll the material up in a long sausage and slipped it around Smiley's body and under his armpit until the two ends met back on Levi's side.

'Down you go, Smiley. Shuffle forward so you can stretch out on your back.' Smiley eased down with agonised slowness. She looked at Levi. 'Just kneel down facing him on the uninjured side and hold the ends firmly like handles.'

Levi knelt beside Smiley and concentrated on the task as he gathered the ends. He should be doing this, not her, but it didn't seem the right moment to pull rank on her. It had been a lot of years since he'd done any generalist work like dislocations. He'd bet she'd be wild when she found out.

She was directing them like an annoying but perky little conductor in her bra and shorts and he liked her more than when she'd been sexily annoying in her blue dress. Because she was bending towards Smiley her breasts were falling his way. In a gesture of respect he faded out her cleavage, which was no mean feat, and watched her hands.

She surprised him with her calmness and methodical approach to something he could probably have done but not as confidently as she was. Qualifications meant zip against recent experience, he reassured himself.

Sophie nodded. 'Keep both ends together under his good armpit. When I take his other arm you keep the pressure on his chest so he can't follow me.'

Levi could hear his sister mumbling behind him as she agonised over William's impending discomfort. He wished she'd be quiet.

Sophie must have heard her too. 'He'll be fine, Odette. I know we're all still shell-shocked from the crash but he'll be OK.' Sophie looked his way. 'As long as Levi doesn't tickle him, 'cause it hurts to laugh.'

Levi blinked in surprise at her comment and compressed his lips to bite back the smile. Effective stress relief. She was a tough little cookie, though he'd begun to wonder if she really was as tough as she made out, because he could detect a tiny tremor in her hands every now and then. 'Nurses have a dreadful sense of humour, eh, William?'

Smiley had his eyes shut. 'Hmm.'

But the tension had lessened a little and even Odette got the hint to relax. He watched Sophie's face as she concentrated. Something made him want to reach out and touch her arm, just for support, like he had during the flight when he realized she'd started to panic, but he didn't want to interrupt her thoughts. It was almost as if she was rehearsing the steps.

He was right. She was. Sophie knelt down and after a brief stroke of sympathy she took her brother's elbow and gently bent it so that his fingers pointed to the sky they'd just fallen out of. She didn't even want to think about sky-falling. Bend arm at ninety-degree angle from his body, Sophie recited to herself.

'Keep the pressure on now,' she said quietly to Levi, and began to pull, still gently but firmly, on the bent elbow, away from Smiley's body. Then she rotated the arm on the shoulder joint as if Smiley was trying to throw a baseball.

Sweat beaded on Smiley's forehead as she moved it slowly back and forward until the shoulder slid back into place with a click that made everyone wince.

'OK.' Now Sophie felt like crying or heaving or running away but she couldn't do any of those things. 'We need a sling.'

She looked at Smiley and he gave her a small wink. 'Thanks, Sis.'

'Don't do it again. You know I hate it.' She dropped a kiss on his forehead and Levi was there to help her stand. She hadn't even noticed he'd moved, and secretly she was glad of his support because her legs wobbled.

His hand kept hold of hers and he pulled her gently into his chest for a moment in a purely asexual embrace, though his shirt against her nose meant she could only inhale air laced with Levi. His arms rested around her back, firmly but not cloying, just for that moment so she could rest her head on him and close her eyes and regroup. Strangely, the hug wasn't an invasion of space as much as a recoup of resources and exactly what she needed.

She stepped back and his arms fell. 'Thanks. I hate doing that for him.' She flabbergasted herself with the honesty and he looked just as surprised as she did. Normally she wouldn't let anyone know when she felt overwhelmed. She prided herself on self-sufficiency and she would have thought Levi was the last person she'd want to tell about any weakness on her end. It had to be part of the shock.

She watched his hands flick the dirt from her shirt and smooth it, and he even held it out for her to slip her arms in. She felt strangely cosseted but weepy. Not something she was used to at all. And she wasn't even sure she liked the feeling. 'Well done, Sophie,' he said quietly. She couldn't meet his eyes in case he saw the glitter.

She looked at her shirt in his hands. 'Umm. I need to tear a bit off the bottom to make a sling.'

He shook his head. 'Put it on. Mine's bigger. You don't want to get a sunburnt strip around your waist.'

She took it and turned away to collect herself. A hug was OK but sympathy when she was emotional was such a pain. She sniffed unobtrusively. Men were so good at that. Twisting the knife when you were trying to gain control. She heard the rip of his shirt as he made the sling and she kept her eyes averted. She took a couple of deep breaths and turned back to face the group.

To her surprise Levi had achieved a very creditable sling. 'Distinction in a first-aid course, eh?' she said in a poor attempt of a joke. She saw the look from Odette to Levi and Levi's shake of the head but Sophie was too mentally exhausted to go there.

'Something like that.' He looked at Smiley. 'So how's the shoulder now?'

'Good as new.' They all knew it'd still be painful.

Levi gave him a crooked smile. 'I'll bet.' He glanced at Sophie. 'I can do splints and bandages but we'll do that after you check we have a water supply.'

'Yes, Captain.' She couldn't resist. 'Next time we come into land here I'll try to have a look as we approach.'

'Good idea.' He stood. 'There's a couple of water bottles in the chopper. I'll get them and check the radio if it's all cooled down a bit.' He rubbed his chin.

'Though I think I'll come with you, after I discuss something with Odette.'

Sophie sighed. He was determined, then. His funeral. She had to stop saying that. It was obviously a bad omen.

Levi hadn't been keen for her to hang around the wreck so she wandered slowly towards the gully, pleased to have a moment before he joined her.

The chance to walk away from the crash site was welcome and she dawdled along the gorge, watching the ground for signs of animals. She didn't hear him come up beside her and she jumped when he spoke.

'So you think we'll find water?'

She glanced at him. 'Pretty confident.'

'Fine,' he said, but raised his brow sceptically.

She frowned. 'The wet season's not long finished, and rock pools and depressions in the gorge floor should still hold water.' She should know. She'd walked so many gorges in her lifetime apparently preparing for just such an occasion.

Hopefully, the water wouldn't be too old either, but there'd be enough to keep them until help arrived. Which shouldn't be long if the distress call went through.

As they walked, long grey-green grasses poked out at them, and as they brushed past Sophie inhaled the warm air and everything felt brighter and cleaner—and even more precious for nearly being snatched away.

'I can't believe how close we've came to crashing

badly.' It was very queer how Levi in command had lessened the horror. That they'd all managed to escape fairly unscathed so far—and that even Odette's baby hadn't been fazed by their rough landing—was a miracle assisted by Levi's determination they would survive.

Levi didn't say anything and she wondered if he'd always been this taciturn. He needed to smell the roses. They were alive!

'See how the cliffs beside us soar into the bluest sky. Don't the walls look like red-brick? It reminds you of millions of years in creation and some of the oldest dated rocks in the world, doesn't it?'

'No, Pollyanna. It reminds me we've had to force land in the middle of nowhere with very little to keep us alive.'

She frowned at him. 'Lighten up. The Aboriginal people survived.' Sophie spread her arms. 'You'll see in the overhangs and caves they'll have left their stories for us on the rock. They've been a part of this land for thousands of years. We'll manage a day or two.'

'Spare me from eternal optimism.'

'And me from a grump.'

She was only a hundred metres from the plane when she found the break in the range she was looking for. They looked back before they turned into a narrow gorge off the main escarpment but Odette and Smiley were still sitting on the boulders they'd left them on.

It was cool in the gully, the sun not yet directly overhead to shine onto the narrow strip of valley floor.

'It would be worthwhile moving the others here to get out of the sun,' she commented. 'Especially if we have to wait long for rescue.'

'I'd been just about to suggest that. You beat me to it.'

She slanted an amused glance at him. 'I'm annoying you, then?'

'Not at all.'

Liar, she thought. Tufts of sharp spinifex scratched at her ankles as she scrambled over boulders that had tumbled down from the walls, and Levi followed her. Within only a few minutes she'd come upon the first pool and she raised her brows at him. See!

'OK,' he said. 'It's water. Looks a bit green.'

'It's just starting to algae, but the middle of the pool will be clear and no doubt cold.' He didn't look convinced. 'It's a good time of the year if you have to crash,' she teased him. 'Those tiny fish don't know their pond'll disappear over the next few months.'

'I guess fish prove the water's clean enough to drink.'

'Yep. In fact, the traditional owners use bunches of sharp spinifex to brush the pools and capture the tiny fish in the barbs. Then they burn it and eat the fish. We might try that later.' She crouched at the edge to fill her bottle, peripherally aware of the snake trail to her left. The smooth indent in the fine gravel was a timely reminder to watch for basking reptiles. She had a feeling he wasn't ready to know that yet.

Levi couldn't believe this woman. She talked as if

they were filming for a nature show, not about their survival in one of the most remote places in the world.

She sat back and glanced around as she screwed the lid back on the water bottle, then washed her hands before bathing her face and lower arms. His eyes were drawn to the way she slid the water over the inside of her wrists and then lifted her fingers to allow the trickles to run down her neck and beneath the collar of her blouse.

Hastily he leaned forward and rinsed his own hands. It was cold all right, just what he needed after the heat on the valley floor. Not to mention the other heat.

'So we have water, and a few tiny fish to eat. Our own bush-tucker chef. It could be worse.' He wasn't sure how.

'We're alive.'

He nodded soberly. True. All of them, and that was a miracle. No thanks to the person who'd tampered with the aircraft and the concept still had the power to make him wild enough to want to crush a rock with his bare hands.

She must have noticed his frown because she flicked a tiny drop of water at him. 'Don't suppose you fancy a witchetty grub. Apparently they taste like eggs. I can see a witchetty tree and I could dig the roots up for you.'

He had to smile. Retribution could wait. 'Pass.'

When they returned to the crash site the full extent of their miracle of survival again made itself very plain. Sophie stood for a moment and shook her head and

Levi silently agreed. Pieces of the helicopter were strewn from where they first skidded down past the wreck, and the cabin itself looked more like a drink can that had been beaten by a stick than a mode of travel.

The others had moved a few feet back against the canyon wall out of the sun and sat on boulders that had fallen from the cliffs. 'You'd have to be unlucky, but I'm not sure I'd feel real comfortable waiting for another boulder to fall where they're sitting.'

Levi nodded. 'We'll move to the gorge as soon as I empty the aircraft.'

They separated, he to the aircraft and she to Odette.

CHAPTER FIVE

LEVI spread the first-aid kit and the tool box out on the ground to see what was available, and he looked up as Sophie laughed out loud at something Odette had said. At least someone could laugh about the situation they were in. His eyes were drawn to her when she stood and approached his work area.

Her white shirt was dusty and her disarranged hair looked not unlike the spinifex tufting the bottom of the canyon. Actually, she looked pretty fantastic, considering she'd had her worst nightmare confirmed by a crash landing. He'd been mulling over her behaviour since the crash while he worked and he'd come to the conclusion he'd never met a woman like her.

Her composure when she'd reduced her brother's shoulder still impressed him. She'd done a better job than he would have. It was far too long since he'd done any emergency work apart from eyes and he was glad he hadn't had to practise on Smiley.

His lack of disclosure about his medical background

had become an elephant he could've done without, but it didn't seem the right moment to correct the impression he'd given. Hopefully, when he did, she'd just laugh it off, though it was unlikely, if the first conversation they'd had at Xanadu was anything to go by. The longer he left it, the bigger the elephant grew, but he really didn't have the capacity to take on a discussion of his work.

Still, she looked pretty pleased with herself and it was a bonus to find something to smile about after what he'd just discovered. 'Odette feels better?' Levi said.

'Yep. And Smiley's fine.'

'That's great.' He paused. 'Do you want the good news or the bad news?'

Her smile died and he regretted that, but he wasn't joking. 'Can I have bad and then good to cheer me up?' she asked reluctantly.

'The bad news is the radio's dead.'

'That's really bad.' Her face fell further. 'And the good news?'

'The good news is the aircraft wouldn't have gone up in flames because the fuel tank was on Empty.'

He watched her think about that until finally she said, 'Then what was the hissing?'

She had a logical mind, he'd give her that. 'The oil dripping on the hot engine.'

A tiny line crinkled between her brows. 'But how could the fuel be on Empty? I saw it at Full on the gauge.'

He had an idea but it wasn't a very nice one. 'Must have sprung a leak.'

The crinkle deepened, and actually she looked cute, but it sure wasn't the time to notice that. 'Do fuel tanks do that?'

Never in his lifetime. He sighed. 'Not usually.'

He watched her shake her head—a lot of that head shaking had been going on around here—and he wished he didn't have to explain the rest. He gave her a minute to mull it over and looked at the minimal supplies they had to survive on. Not much there, which was what he'd had a quick word to Odette about before he'd left with Sophie.

'You say the radio's dead. Why is that dead?'

He appreciated how calmly she'd taken his first news. Hysterics would have really done his head in. 'I'd like to know that too.' He saw the beginnings of comprehension as her eyes widened.

'So what are you saying? Didn't you talk to someone as we were landing? I saw your lips move.'

He remembered that moment. It hadn't been pleasant. 'I wish I could offer more reassurance but I can't. I didn't get a response so I gave the position in case they could hear me, even though I couldn't hear them. I don't know if it worked.'

She made a silent *O* with her mouth. Her face was like a book. No subterfuge. No doubt she'd scorn such a thing. She was so different from any woman he'd met and with such a well of strength that was almost scary.

Thank goodness he liked his women sweet and compliant.

By now, Odette and William had left their perch on the boulders to join the others.

'It was a good idea anyway,' Sophie said earnestly, as if sorry he felt bad. She made him smile. That was twice now. Then she said, 'But you've got one of those little GPS tracker things, don't you?'

'ELT. Emergency locator transmitter.' She didn't like what she saw on his face and he watched her transfer her attention to Odette for a more palatable answer.

Odette looked up. 'It seems someone took it out and didn't replace it,' Odette said baldly.

'Someone? Took it out?' Sophie actually squeaked, and suddenly he wanted to put his arm around her, but she backed away as if she knew what he was thinking. How could she know that?

She looked at her brother but all William did was shrug his good shoulder and not comment. Levi admired him for it. There wasn't much to say as the choices were limited. Someone had tried to kill them and nearly succeeded. None of the three of them mentioned the fact the chopper had been tampered with but it simmered there between them, except that Sophie, still focused on the radio not working, didn't get it. No bonus in her knowing.

Sophie sank down on a boulder and, as an afterthought, handed the water bottle again to Odette. She closed her eyes, sighed and visibly relaxed her shoulders. Finally she mumbled, 'Glad I'm not the captain,' opened her eyes and looked straight at him. 'What's the plan? Captain.'

'Now she defers,' he said, but he was inordinately glad of her support. He wasn't quite sure when it was she'd stopped being annoying. 'William says he knows this area from mustering and there's an Aboriginal community a day's walk away if we head north. I'm thinking William and Odette should stay here, and you and I walk out and get help.'

She chewed her lip and glanced around the desolate landscape. 'It's breaking the first rule. Leaving the site. We're not that far from the desert and the sun's a furnace in the sky until five.' She looked at the supplies. 'But there's not a lot to eat out here once we get through the picnic basket.'

'My thoughts exactly.'

She narrowed her eyes. 'If we give them today to send a search party staying put is a good thing.' She looked at his sister and Levi had to keep from shaking his head in disbelief. She seemed so calm about the whole thing. 'How do you feel about that, Odette?' she said. As if it was a mundane cancellation of an appointment.

He watched his sister struggle to match her composure and he wished, fruitlessly, he'd been more firm when she'd been so determined to leave Sydney with him.

Odette brushed the hair off her forehead. 'William

can't walk far and I'm not much better. As long as we have water and a bit of food we'll be fine for a day, I guess.'

Sophie nodded and he thanked God again he'd been stranded with sensible people. He wondered if all of the people who lived out here in the back of beyond were like Sophie and William.

Apart from the fact that maybe someone was trying to kill his sister and him—but that was unproven—the place was growing on him.

'So we leave tomorrow morning early, do you think?' Sophie said.

He almost smiled again. She couldn't help being bossy, though he suspected she'd push herself harder than anyone else. 'Sounds like a plan.'

She nodded and stood. 'What would you like me to do?'

He was right. 'We'll collect wood first for a signal fire, then some for the camp tonight.'

'Sure.' Sophie stopped beside Odette again. 'No pains?' He could almost see the priorities ticking off in her mind.

Odette shook her head but her hand slid protectively over her stomach, as if to ward off the idea. William reached over with his good arm and caught her fingers and held them. Odette squeezed back.

'I'd hate to be the one who's pregnant,' William said.

Levi looked at Sophie. He'd been avoiding that horror. Unfortunately he knew the danger to his sister lay in the sudden deceleration of their landing. Forces that could tear an inelastic placenta off an elastic uterus. He'd seen that in the brief time he'd had in obstetrics, but there was nothing they could do at this moment except watch her.

Sophie crouched down, obviously thinking the same thing because she said, 'So how long since we crashed?'

'I thought it was a forced landing.' Levi pretended to be offended.

'I'm sorry,' she said over her shoulder as she faced Odette. 'How long is it since your incredible brother managed to avert disaster and get us to the ground safely, Odette?' There was humour in the words but none in her voice. She meant every word and he was surprised how they unexpectedly warmed the place that had iced over with the knowledge of foul play.

He'd never thought of himself as needy and he stamped the feeling out.

Odette looked at her watch. 'It feels like minutes but about an hour and a half?'

Sophie crouched and her hand hovered above Odette's uterus. 'May I?' She waited for permission, then rested her hand on the baby bulge. 'I'm thinking the first four hours are the most likely time you'd start contracting if there'd been any problems due to the landing. It's fabulous you haven't gone into labour already. But tell me if you get regular pains.'

Odette shook her head, as if by denying it, it wouldn't happen. 'Don't wish that on me.'

Sophie shook her head vehemently. 'I'm not, believe me. The longer it holds off the less likely your baby has any ill effects from the events.'

Odette chewed her lip as she stroked her belly. 'It's not quite the home birth I'd envisaged.'

Sophie rolled her eyes. 'It's not the day any of us envisaged, except maybe me when we took off.' She smiled ruefully. 'And I apologise if I brought us all bad luck.'

Not the person to blame. 'If it's someone's fault,' Levi said drily, 'it certainly wasn't yours.' He stood. 'I used to be a pretty mean Boy Scout so reckon I could manage a fire in case a plane flies over.'

'Then I'll start collecting wood as soon as we get to the gully.' Sophie looked around. 'So we'll need a campfire and a signal fire?'

Odette wiped her face. 'It's so hot. Hard to imagine we'll need heat.'

'It'll be cold tonight,' Smiley offered and squeezed Odette's hand. Poor Smiley. He'd hate being unable to help. Sophie was glad he was there for Odette. She'd the feeling if he hadn't been Odette would have succumbed to hysterics by now and that wouldn't have been fun. To give her due, she was a city girl and where they'd crashed was as far as she'd get from a city.

Odette scuffed at the dry grass beneath her feet. 'What if we start a bushfire?'

'As long as it blows the other way it's all good,' Smiley said, and spread the map one-handed that Levi had given him from the wreck.

He didn't enlarge so Sophie finished the sentence. 'In the Kimberleys bushfires are a way of life. We try to burn off the whole area every couple of years. Even as far out as here. The Aboriginal people have been burning off for thousands of years. For them it means the scrub stays sparse and they can see the animals they want to hunt. A lot of the trees and shrubs around here don't germinate until they've been through a fire. From our point of view, frequent fires germinate the land and prevent a massive fire that would be impossible to control.'

They packed up their meagre belongings and began walking towards the gully. Odette gazed around at, what was to her, desolate landscape. 'It's so sparse and different from anywhere I've ever been,' Odette said, as if they'd landed on the moon.

'William and I love it.' Sophie thought of Perth for the first time that day, only the second time since she'd seen Levi. Now that was queer. 'Perth's a pretty place— it has the ocean,' she said, trying to be fair but Brad lived there. 'I wouldn't live anywhere else than here though.' She looked at Levi as she spoke, and remembered that his appreciation of her land was confined to flying over it.

He raised his brows. 'Don't look at me like that. The Kimberleys are growing on me. Though you have great rivers and can't swim in them. And apparently it's the same in the ocean up here.'

'Maybe, but we have rock pools and gorges that are

fine. You just have to know where it's safe and where it's not. We're fine here from crocs, but watch the snakes as we walk.'

Levi glanced at his horrified sister and made a strangled sound but Sophie couldn't read anything in his face. Had he just laughed at her?

'I hate snakes.' Odette shuddered.

'If you see one just stop or back off real slowly. They panic too and are just as likely to run the same way as you and you'll think they're chasing you.'

'It won't be really chasing me. OK.' Odette shuddered again.

Levi was watching Sophie and she'd swear he was amused, even though his mouth didn't move. 'So you're a snake lover too?'

Sophie shook her head. 'It's their home too. Someone once told me that a snake has a really short memory, about forty seconds, which always makes me smile when I see one. I imagine them forgetting I'm there.'

After that conversation, when they moved up next to the mouth of the gully, Odette's head swivelled like one of those toy nodding dogs people used to sit on the back window of their cars. She walked with her brother, her hand tightly gripped to his arm.

Smiley leaned heavily on his stick with Sophie on his other side. 'I feel so bloody useless,' he said quietly.

'You're helping Odette which is great. She needs your calm. Will you manage when we go?'

Smiley looked around to ensure the others weren't in earshot. 'As long as she doesn't have the baby.'

Sophie whispered, 'It's just like a calf, Smiley, or a foal.'

He choked back a laugh. 'Great.' They grinned at each other. 'You'll run through a couple of things with me before you leave though?' he said. She nodded. She had to believe Odette wouldn't go into labour in the day they'd be away. It was too frightening a thought. Not that there was anything they could change.

Smiley examined the spot she'd chosen and nodded. 'At least up here I can get my own water.'

'It'll be tricky but you could.'

Levi came up to them with a long branch of dead wood he'd picked up on the way. 'We'll be out of the weather if one of the sudden tropical storms blows up.'

Everyone pitched in and there was a lip of overhang just past the entrance where they'd packed their supplies against the wall.

The afternoon passed as they watched for rescue, without reward, and prepared for the night. Back out in the main canyon they'd erected a signal fire with green leaves on top for smoke as a way to flag down a search plane if one flew over them, but the sky remained blue and clear of aircraft.

Technically they wouldn't be missed at Xanadu until almost nightfall. They'd told Steve they'd be back by late afternoon so they were not technically even missing yet.

Levi began to cut the long grass that Sophie suggested they use for beds for the night along the overhang, while she cleared the ground in front so they could make a fire to keep everyone warm. With the wall behind them the heat would be caught and the flames would keep any animals away.

At four o'clock they sat back and Sophie could see the activity had raised Odette's spirits. 'I'd say we're a clever bunch. We could make it on one of those television survivor shows.'

'Except there's no camera man with a satellite phone.' Odette looked at the depleted picnic basket. 'Who wants to go to the shop for a treat?'

Sophie spread her arms. 'There's plenty to eat around here.'

Levi dropped the last of the sticks for the night fire. 'Spare me from Pollyanna with bush tucker,' Levi said. 'Not witchetty grubs, I hope.'

Sophie refused to be downcast by the lack of enthusiasm. 'Must admit I've never been a fan of the old grub. Though they say ten grubs a day is enough for survival.' Levi didn't look convinced, so Sophie pushed on. 'And I did find a Gubinge tree up one of the gullies. I'll show you where, before dark, in case you want some tomorrow, Odette.' She held up the small greenish-yellow fruit which looked more like a pale pecan nut than a fruit. 'Known also as a Kakadu plum, it's easy to eat.'

Smiley sat quietly amused during her lecture and declined to sample the fruit. She frowned at him for not offering support but forgave him for the discomfort he was still in. No doubt he still felt sick and sore but he wasn't complaining. He never did. Actually, nobody was, so maybe she should revise her opinion a little about some city people.

She directed her attention to Levi and Odette and bit bravely into the skin. The tanginess twisted on her tongue and she fought to keep her face straight as she chewed and swallowed. 'Food for indigenous people for thousands of years and apparently has a hundred times more vitamin C than an orange.' She licked her lips and tried to define the taste. 'The juice crosses between a pear and an apple. There's a zing which I think is from the vitamin C but see what you think.' She tossed one each to Odette and Levi. 'Either way, it's the perfect refreshment if we're right out of grocery shops.'

'Bush tucker.' Levi looked at her from under his brows as if to say, *Are you having us on?* When she nodded encouragingly he bit into the fruit, and then finished it off. 'Not addictive, but not bad.'

Sophie nodded. 'We'll take some with us when we walk out.'

'Awesome.' He rubbed his hands together facetiously. So he did have a sense of humour. Now that was something Brad never had, and why she should think of Brad and Levi in the same minute sent a tiny flicker of fear into her belly which she was determined to ignore.

CHAPTER SIX

JUST before dawn the next morning, when the night birds were settling and the morning budgerigars shared their chatter, Levi and Sophie prepared to leave camp. The gentle breeze lifted the bumps on Sophie's arms and the ground crackled cold and hard beneath her socks. She tucked her chin into her collar as she pulled on her boots.

She glanced across to where Levi wore Smiley's broad Akubra and looked disturbingly like a country man rather than the city slicker she didn't trust. Much more dependable and much more dangerous to her peace of mind.

Sophie could smile at the image of her brother scowling uncomfortably in a baseball cap as he'd handed over his prized possession but not at the image of Levi. What was she doing heading off into the bush with a man she barely knew and didn't even trust?

Then again, there wasn't a lot she could do about it, except be constantly alert for any suspicious behaviour on his part.

Sophie jammed on her own Akubra, and thanked the last fading stars of the night she'd worn sturdy walking shoes, something she needed most places in the Kimberley.

During the night they'd all managed to sleep in snatches after the emotional trauma of the day, and even Odette, apart from the indigestion and backache she normally suffered from, didn't seem any worse for the experiences of the day before.

'Your baby must be one tough little munchkin, Odette,' Sophie said, as she finished her weak tea from the one shared tea bag discovered at the bottom of her bag and boiled over the campfire.

'Tougher than his mother,' Odette said with a wobble in her voice. The young mum's eyes were heavily shadowed and her fingers stroked her belly, as if to reassure herself and her baby that everything would be fine.

Sophie tamped down her own misgivings. Odette and her baby were the greatest worry. 'I think you're holding up amazingly well.' She tipped out the dregs and rinsed the one cup before she slid her bag over her shoulder. 'We'll be as quick as we can. Your baby needs you to be calm. We've done the hard part and survived the landing. You'll have something to tell the grandchildren about in thirty years.'

'If I have grandchildren.'

Sophie frowned. 'You've water and some food and a safe place.' She paused. 'No matter what happens, don't leave this spot,' Sophie reminded her. 'Sighting of the crash site is still the most probable way for rescue, and lost in the bush is the easiest way to die.'

Odette scrubbed her eyes again and the mascara from yesterday was giving her a sad-and-sorry panda look. 'I'm not going anywhere but I wish I'd never left home.'

Sophie felt the loss of the woman who'd touched up her lipstick at the clinic only a few short days ago. 'I know. It's natural to worry about your baby. You're the one with most to fear. But hey, I'd like to think I'd do as well as you are.'

Odette sniffed. 'You wouldn't cry like I do.'

Sophie hugged her and whispered, 'Didn't you see me yesterday after setting William's shoulder? I was a mess.'

Odette scrubbed her eyes with the back of her hand and peered at Sophie, who nodded. 'Really? I didn't see that.'

'Good,' Sophie said and looked around to make sure none of the men had heard. 'But I felt better afterwards.'

'I'll never be as strong as you but thanks for telling me. It helps to know I'm not the only one who can't help it sometimes.'

'I know. And I'm not that strong. Just on the outside.' Sophie glanced at her brother, who was probably giving Levi some pointers as well. 'Look,' she said. 'This isn't going to happen, but if you do go into labour, stay cuddled up to William. He'll look after you. Rest and remember you're designed to do it. Be calm and let it happen. Babies only need to be next to their mother. And remember, first babies take a long time and we'll be back. Don't give up on us.'

Odette shook her head and her eyes filled again with tears. 'You shouldn't go. Levi shouldn't leave me.' She clutched at Sophie's arm. 'Don't leave!'

Sophie drew the younger woman into her arms and hugged her. 'You'll be fine. We'll be back as quick as we can, but we need to walk out before it gets too hot.'

Odette started to cry and Sophie chewed her lip and glanced at Levi. She'd made everything worse.

Levi crossed to his sister and drew her into the circle of his arms. 'Shh, honey. One day away. That's all it'll take. You and William have a day on the land, relax and enjoy the scenery.'

Odette hiccoughed, 'Relax?' Her lip quivered as Levi handed her over to William to comfort. 'Please be careful,' Odette said to her brother.

He nodded. 'We'll be back for you in another chopper.'

'He'll fly back for you,' Sophie said drily. 'I'll be cheering from home.'

Odette's lips tugged in an almost smile. 'Chicken.'

'We won't be long.' Levi sighed. Such a dilemma. He hated to leave Odette, and the thought of her going into labour out here without him made him break into a cold sweat. Please God, don't let that happen. He'd spent his life trying to keep her safe and he'd failed dismally.

But he couldn't send Sophie off on her own, even though he suspected she'd be tougher in the outback than him.

He did have faith in William though—not quite sure how that happened—and they'd be as quick as they could, but there was no use waiting for a rescue that might never happen before they tried to walk out.

They left without looking back and he felt like a deserter as he followed Sophie down a natural trail. Initially he tried to choose the direction but his feet seemed to find the ground more uneven than Sophie did, and eventually he fell in behind her because it was easier going. It felt strange to let another person lead, let alone a woman.

The rocks shifted under his feet as his ankles threatened to twist on the uneven path. It made sense if the whole place was the result of erosion but it made walking fraught for injury.

When he thought about it they'd taken a lot for granted to head off into the hills. He caught up with Sophie and walked beside her. 'I've just had a nasty thought. Actually, we're relying on William's memory of a nomad's camp, from a muster that happened over a year ago?'

She glanced across at him. 'That's what we all decided on.'

He pushed aside a branch that reached across their path. 'What if the camp moved on, which I imagine is likely.'

She raised her eyebrows. 'We can hope the camp moved closer, then, and not further away.'

That was simple, he thought wryly. 'I love the way your mind works.' He bent down and picked up a walking-stick-size branch, tested it and then used it to part the grass in front.

She grinned at him and he found himself grinning back. 'Optimism is the code of the Kimberley.'

Was this woman for real? 'Spare me, Pollyanna. You just made that up.'

'Yep. But you can't change what you can't change.' She glanced around as the first rays of light warned of sunrise. 'More likely a hunter will find us than we'll find them anyway.'

He hadn't thought of that. 'Do they do that? I thought it was all in movies and fiction.'

'The medicine man knows if someone who shouldn't be there is around. I'm just hoping they find us sooner rather than later.'

The growing light allowed them to see the ground in front of them more clearly as the sun crept closer to rising. He'd be interested to see the pace she'd keep up when she could see properly. 'Can we do this? Walk out safely?'

She stopped and looked at him. 'We can be sensible, yes, and cut down the risks, but it's a big land under a bigger sun.' She glanced at the imminent sunrise. 'We should move faster while we can.'

The morning blurred into a fast-paced bushwalk.

Sophie pointed out another Gubinge tree and he began to see others now that he recognised them.

She showed him the low-growing, wide-leafed bush tomatoes, which looked more like brown raisins. 'But you have to eat the ripe ones. The green ones are toxic like green potatoes.'

She picked a few and offered him one. When he didn't look inspired she ate one herself and grimaced. 'They're talking about growing these commercially for a savoury spice. They're pretty pungent but you never know when you'll need them.'

He was over bush tucker. It was pretty hard to be the protective male when she held all the cards. A very novel experience for a man who'd always been the one people came to for help. 'Have you ever been to Sydney?' he said.

She didn't even look at him. 'No.'

'Maybe one day I'll show you my favourite restaurant. The chef is one of the top three in Australia.' He'd actually quite like that.

She looked at him as if he'd offered a space shuttle to the moon. 'You think?'

Apparently it wasn't on her wish list. She had to be good for his conceited soul. He laughed and followed her along another ridge that boarded a treeless plain he hoped they didn't have to cross, but she was heading in that direction. Assuming she knew where she was going.

Almost as if she heard his thoughts she paused. 'If

we keep the sun on our right shoulder we should be heading north. There's a dry creek bed through the middle of the plain and maybe even a few of the pools will have water in them. We'll conserve what we have and try to make it to the next gorge, and I'm expecting more water by midday. Then we'll rest.'

Unobtrusively he pulled his compass from his pocket and checked what she said. She was right! What did he expect? It was pretty different taking orders from a woman and actually not minding it.

Though he hadn't minded his first-grade teacher either. Miss Tee was a honey and the first woman he'd ever fallen in love with. Probably because she liked to take them outside for games when they got bored with English, but he did remember her long, long legs, like Sophie's. Though he conceded Sophie's legs were even better.

She walked with a loose-limbed gait, sure-footedly in her lace-up leather boots and her knee-length shorts that it seemed women wore here. And despite her determination to appear always in command, she couldn't hide her femininity. Her bottom still jiggled.

He realised how few women he'd seen since he'd been here, and they'd all been wearing those knee-length shorts. Maybe that was why she looked so good. Lack of competition. But he didn't think so. He had a feeling she'd look good on a rue in Paris. He caught her glancing at him and it made him smile more.

'What are you smiling at?'

He straightened his face. 'I've only seen four women since I arrived a week ago. And one of them is my sister.'

She flicked her brows up and down. 'Bet that's different to your usual day.' Was that sarcasm?

She had no idea what his life was like. The hours he worked. The impact of having to tell a patient he couldn't save their sight or the sight of their child—the main reason he'd been unable to get here sooner as he'd tried to clear a backlog of people who needed him desperately. How he'd started to think he'd never be able to make a dent in the need out there. 'Yeah, well, it's hard running a playboy mansion.'

She stopped and faced him. 'You run a playboy mansion?'

That actually hurt. Did she really think him that shallow? Nothing like his surgery full of people with visual nightmares. 'It was a joke.'

She brushed his comment away. 'Good. Don't worry. We get women here. When the tourist season properly starts the Gibb River Road really moves. Campers and off-road vehicles everywhere and the resorts fill up. You'll see plenty of ladies then, if you're still here.' She started walking again and he nearly missed her final comment. 'Which you shouldn't be for someone just passing through.'

She'd brought it up again. Wait till she found out about the other, but he didn't have the energy to go into why he didn't want to talk about work. 'Are you ever going to forgive me for a throwaway comment?'

She looked at him innocently. 'Sure. Nothing to forgive. I just don't trust you.'

Be warned, he told himself. To her, he said, 'Nice.'

She ignored his comment and went back to their original conversation. 'The tourist season is only for a few months from April until the humidity comes back again in October-November. Most people leave then because a person sweats like a horse as soon as they step outside.'

He thought about what she said, wondered about the implications on the health resources from the influx of older travellers for such small amounts of health personnel, but if he commented he might end up embroiled in more lies. Better to leave well enough alone, which was a shame, because he'd begun to value her opinion on a lot of things.

They walked on for an hour without talking and surprisingly it was quite companionable. He couldn't remember the last time he'd been with a woman without feeling he had to make the running or listen to a one-way conversation.

He looked to the scenery ahead and there was more of the same to come. 'So tell me about the camp we're heading to.'

She jolted out of her reverie. 'The family tribe we're looking for is semi-nomadic most of the year. They've returned to the old ways and move with the food, so that means berries available, fattest kangaroos, and they rely on guessing the weather.'

He glanced at the bare plains. 'Do they come into town much?'

'The young men muster when needed and that's how Smiley knows about them. I haven't actually met this family but they'd have met other nurses from other towns. I'd like to see if they want the kids immunised and all's well, so it's a bonus.'

He bit back another laugh. A bonus helicopter crash. So pleased he could accommodate her. He'd never understand her.

They walked until the sun was directly overhead and with relief they entered the foothills of the next range and what little shade that offered.

He was determined he wasn't going to ask for a rest, but he'd used most of his water, except for a little he kept in case she needed it. Not that he imagined she'd ask. But enough unusual things had happened to them over the past twenty-four hours; he wasn't guaranteeing they wouldn't have more excitement.

'There looks to be a subtropical pocket ahead, that's promising,' she said, and he could hear the note of weariness in her voice. Strangely, his own tiredness seemed to melt away and he quickened his step. 'Let me lead for a while—I can see where you mean—and you might catch a little shade from my back.'

'I'm fine.'

'I know. You're amazing. Let me do this bit until we stop. Give me your pack.' When she hesitated, he added, 'For goodness sake, let me feel a little useful.'

'Fine.' She stopped and he overtook her, glancing at her face as he passed. Her cheeks were pink with the heat, and she didn't meet his eyes, but she looked tired, then he was past and she fell into step behind him.

Within half an hour they'd moved from the grass of the plains to the spiral Pandanas of the semi-rainforest, and not much further on they found larger boulders and finally a small pool of algoid water.

The creek bed sloped up the gully and Sophie pointed to the narrowing gorge higher up. 'If we climb a little we'll find cleaner water, and it's probably worth the effort. We'll stay here for a couple of hours until the sun is well behind our backs.'

They both needed to rest, which would be hard with the idea of Odette still back at the wreck site, but Sophie was as aware of that as he.

'No problem,' Levi said. 'You said you'd find water. This place is amazing.' He looked around at the narrow strip of tropical foliage which seemed so out of place in the arid areas they'd just trekked through. There was a definite line where wet met dry and the rest of the gorge stretched away from them back to the plain of red dirt and spinifex.

He heaved himself up and around a few larger boulders and the subtle sound of running water gurgled more loudly.

'The flow must have disappeared into an underground creek because there's no flow further down,' she said.

He looked back and all he could see, water wise, was the green pool. She was a cluey little thing.

One last steep-sided boulder, room-size, stood between them and a ring of promising palm trees, but it was too high to step up onto. He wedged himself between the gorge wall and the boulder and crab walked up the gap, and he was quietly pleased he'd mastered the indoor rock climbing he enjoyed in his youth. Crumbly rock grated against his arm as he heaved himself up and it felt good to do something physical apart from walking. When he craned his neck back the sky was decorated with a palm tree on an impossible angle that arched for the sun.

Then he was up. Not easy but worth it. 'This is great,' he called down to her. The rocky pool lay fringed with ferns. Set deep in the gully under the fuzzy roots of an outstretched palm was a big bath-size rock pool catching the water from above.

'The water's clean and deep.'

When he turned to offer his hand, he expected her to shimmy up with his support, but she hesitated and turned her head to search for an alternative route, which was crazy when he could see her shoulders droop with weariness. Stubborn little thing.

He felt another spurt of impatience with her reluctance to touch him. His hand fell as he considered her refusal. There was a limit to independence. He'd thought they'd got over that in the walk. Some of his pleasure in the spot dissipated but he tried to keep his voice reasonable.

'I don't bite.' He held his hand out again. 'There's a nice pool up here. Why skin your knees when I can help you up?'

She brushed the hair from her face and looked at him, as if measuring the danger, and the skidding of her eyes confirmed it was the idea of contact that had her worried. He didn't get it.

'You're right,' she said. Finally she took his hand, and he was surprised at how much that meant that she'd decided to trust him. It was a beginning but he wasn't sure of what.

He lifted her easily, which helped his ego no end, and he acknowledged to himself he was a sad case, until she was balanced on the rock beside him and could see the pool and the tiny waterfall at one end.

'Nice.' A tired smile. 'Thanks,' and she moved from him to the other side of the pool, well away from his zone.

They both looked at the pool, he from his side and she from hers. Tiny fish flickered at the edge of the water and the gurgle of the water over rocks from the waterfall dominated the sounds of the bush.

He crouched down and rinsed his water bottle before he drank deeply, then refilled the one in his bag as well. She did the same and he looked across the small expanse of water at her bent head. He didn't get why she was so quiet. 'Is there something you're worried about or not telling me?'

She jumped. He saw it. 'What?' Her voice faltered

and then strengthened. 'You mean apart from falling out of the sky? Or having to trek in the sun through a desert to get help?' She raised her eyebrows. 'No. Why should I be worried?'

She had a point but the answer was too glib. He guessed her issues weren't for sharing, then. 'Fine.' He should leave her be, stop trying to get her attention. The woman could make him edgy and awkward like a pimply teenager and he didn't like the sensation. He undid his laces and slipped off his boots and socks. Then he pulled his shirt off. When he reached for his shorts she squeaked and he looked across.

Her eyes had widened. 'What are you doing?'

He stopped and looked around for a reason he shouldn't. 'Bathing. I'm hot and bothered and it looks good.' He raised his eyebrows. 'Is there a problem?'

'Only if you take much more off.' She looked away. 'I'm not used to men stripping in front of me.'

No one had ever complained about his body before. He slid his shorts down and stepped out of them. His boxers were black and perfectly discreet. 'I'll keep that in mind,' he said as he balanced precariously on the uneven stones at the edge of the pool. He realised he had his belly sucked in and almost blew it by laughing out loud. She wouldn't be looking anyway.

He'd turned into a peacock but reality was bringing him down. 'These rocks are nasty on bare feet.' In fact, they hurt like hell as he tried to ease into the water without damage to his toes. The rocks shifted and poked him, as if they were intent on unbalancing him.

He'd have to describe the smile she gave him as evil. 'Yes, aren't they?' She sat without making any move to undress.

She had to be as hot as he was. 'You coming in?'

'I'll see if anything bites you first.' Her voice was deadpan and he had no idea if she was serious or not.

Nice. 'What happened to the lady who said I did a good job of landing the chopper?'

Sophie didn't know. All of a sudden she was fighting to keep distance from him and it was getting harder and harder. She wasn't sure when it happened. Just little moments from after the crash when he'd given her that extra bit of support. An embrace, held her shirt.

Or this morning when she knew he'd be as hot as she was, and never complained once so that she had to keep reminding herself that he was from the city and wasn't used to their headlong scramble over the plains and gorges. He probably worked out on some treadmill in a swanky gym for hours like Brad had.

But she thought the big moment had been when he'd suggested she walk behind him to shade her from the sun and offered to carry her bag. The idea was sweet, and thoughtful, useless because the sun had been overhead, but still… Then that was followed by the constant view of sinewy ripples of muscle in his shoulders through his shirt and strong, determined thighs in his jeans as he walked ahead of her. Not fair.

How was a girl supposed to keep her head when he looked so darn strong and confident? She was tired and starting to doubt that she would be able to find the tribe and shouldn't have agreed to leave Odette in case she birthed with just Smiley there.

And just now, when he'd reached down with those big, capable hands, when he was supposed to be city soft and reliant on her, she knew if she let him she'd just sail to the top of the rock with no effort. That was when she'd got scared. When she'd started to realise he was occupying too much of her mind space.

In fact, nearly all of her mind, as she blanked out the horror of the past twenty-four hours and the fear that she'd made some dangerously bad decisions.

That sort of thing would make you think of mortality, with the good things in life she'd like to taste before the end.

But this wasn't the end. This was just a scary interlude and they would get help, and Odette would be fine. Levi and his sister would fly back to Sydney in a few days and everyone in the Kimberleys would forget them. Even Sophie Sullivan. And they would forget her.

Levi's voice broke into her thoughts. 'I said, nothing bit me, are you coming in?'

She wouldn't mind but it was a very small pool. 'It looks cold.'

CHAPTER SEVEN

LEVI floated on his back which gave her too good a view of his chest and shoulders. She swallowed. She'd known it. Levi without his shirt was a bad thing. 'Deliciously cool and I feel one hundred percent better than I did before I got in,' he said lazily.

His hair was plastered to his head and droplets ran down his strong chin and dripped onto his chest, and she couldn't help comparing him to Brad. Poor Brad.

Levi had corded bulk, not just smooth skin, and the ripples and dips of his six-pack made even Smiley look like a kid. Her stomach knotted and she looked away. She'd never seen such a discreetly muscular man in her life and no matter how much she tried to lie to herself she couldn't help but find him powerfully attractive.

If she got in she could float with her face away from him, whereas it would look silly for her to turn her back now, and he'd already seen her bra.

'Turn around, then.' She waited until his water-speckled back teased her again and then hurriedly stripped off her shoes and socks and trousers, and draped her shirt close to the edge where she could get it as soon as she left the water.

She eased herself down on her bottom. She'd been bruised before by the piled rocks getting into pools, and local knowledge suggested sliding in from a low height.

The bottom of the pool would only be waist height if she were to stand but deep enough to hide under, and oh so cool and wonderful after the distance they'd walked in the heat this morning.

The water eddied up her legs and thighs with delicious coolness. Her breath sucked in as the water passed her stomach and breasts, and then came the final shiver as she submerged her shoulders until only her nose and eyes were showing. Not much for him to look at.

She surfaced her mouth again, enough to say, 'I'm in,' and then sank back to nose level.

'You sure you can breathe?' His eyes laughed at her and his mouth curved in that killer smile she'd known would be lethal. Now he had to pull that one out of his arsenal. Darn him.

'What happens if I make a wave?' He crossed his hands and threatened to ripple the water and sink her.

She tried to imagine him as a scrubby toddler, as Odette's teasing brother, as anything but the hunk across from her. She pulled her mouth out of the water. 'Some boys never grow up. Once a bully, always a bully. I bet you were the head of the pack at school. One of those boys who tell everyone else what to do.'

They'd floated quite close now—she on her front using her hands along the bottom in the shallow places to drift around the pool. The brilliant idea of maintaining distance and turning her back had been forgotten as she waited, surprisingly intrigued, for him to answer.

A shadow passed his face. 'Being at the top of the pile is much more comfortable than being on the bottom. But I'm not a bully.'

She sniffed and paddled some more. 'That's what all bullies say.'

He shook his head. 'My father bullied my mother, even into another baby when she wasn't well enough to have one—Odette—until it killed her, and I swore I'd never condone it. Apparently my grandfather, a very rich man who didn't need to be grasping, was not a nice person either, so maybe he got it from there.'

A tantalising glimpse at the life of Levi the child was not something she'd expected and it touched a maternal instinct bone she didn't know she had. And didn't need. Please don't tell me more. She didn't want to know. Really she didn't.

A wild budgerigar, bright green and busy, hopped with his mate and chattered in a tree above their heads and she gazed up at it, trying to form the sentence to change the subject. 'Did he make life hard for you?' Not the words she intended.

'Not me. While I was young and vulnerable I wasn't there enough to be harmed by my father. I had an older brother who bore the brunt in holidays. Kyle was one of life's gentle men who shielded me. He made sure I knew the difference between good and bad behaviour and what was right. I'm eternally grateful to him for that.'

'You said "had"?'

He looked through her. 'He died, when I was thirteen. He had macular degeneration, went blind, then stepped out in front of a truck. My father said Kyle knew the truck was coming. I called him a liar.' He fingered the scar on his chin.

Sophie wanted to reach out and comfort him. 'What do *you* say?'

He focused on her face. 'Never. Kyle hated being blind but he loved us too much to think of leaving us alone.'

She could easily imagine how awful it would be for a young boy losing his big brother, after losing his mother.

'I took over the protector role and made sure Odette was never worried by him.' He rubbed the scar again and she wondered if that was how he got it. No wonder he worried about Odette. He'd feel he had to do for her what Kyle had done for him.

'That's a terrible tragedy for your family to go through.'

He shrugged. 'Even the strongest of us are shaped by events in our childhood.' He shook the droplets of water from his hair as if to shake off the past. 'What about you? There's just you and William?'

She sank back further in the water, loosening her neck as she realised she'd tensed her shoulders while he'd shared his past. 'Just Smiley and me. Our parents died four years ago—truck accident—so I guess we were lucky we weren't children. Smiley's easy to live with and we both have work we love.'

'Smiley. Great name.'

A vision of her brother, tall and serious, with just a twinkle in his eye to let her know he found something she'd said amusing, was the one solid thing in her life. The one person she could trust. But she couldn't quiet that voice that said there were facets in Levi that appealed to her, and not just the external ones, and maybe she could learn to trust him too.

He floated to the edge of the pool and rested his back against a flat rock while he considered her. 'So who let you down and broke your heart?'

Just when she thought she might trust him. 'What makes you think my heart's been broken?'

He shrugged. 'OK. So who let you down?'

She never talked about it. Smiley hadn't asked. Her friend, Kate, had a new baby on the way and was immersed in her new husband. Kate didn't need Sophie's baggage. She'd come back from Perth and buried the lot.

Suddenly it was easy to talk. 'Some guy I worked with.' Was he really interested in this? She glanced across at him and then away. Something in his face told her he hadn't asked her lightly. That he genuinely wanted to understand and she guessed it would help explain why she was the way she was.

The picture of Brad in her mind wasn't quite as sharp as it had been. One good thing. 'He was the head of Obstetrics, in my training hospital actually. Born in Australia but his parents were wealthy immigrants. He never talked about where their money came from. I guess he grew up with different values than I did.'

'In what way?' He asked the question quietly, not demanding. If she didn't want to answer she didn't have to, but maybe she needed to clarify what went wrong in her own mind.

'The way he treated people.' Yep, that was what she'd disliked the most. 'Like they were servants under his feet. He wanted old money joined with his new wealth. I kept telling him I had no money, but he was so impressed that my great-great-grandfather was one of the first settlers in Western Australia. Kept telling people when he introduced me. That I had a history his family didn't have. Had this funny idea that because two generations ago my great-grandfather opened up the Kimberleys it made me almost outback royalty.'

'Princess Sophie,' he teased.

'Yeah, right. Not a lot of call for a crown out here in the heat and the dust.'

He shredded a leaf while he listened. 'So what attracted you to him?'

She looked past Levi into the fronds behind him. 'The usual, I guess. Not that I'd actually fallen for any-

one like him before. He was good-looking, quite powerful, and in the beginning he wanted to do the things
I really enjoyed.' She shrugged. 'He courted me—the
old-fashioned way—and I liked that.' She avoided his
eyes. 'I'm not a person who is easy with casual sex.'

She looked up to see him slap his own hand. 'I'd
never have guessed.' She'd swear he was laughing at
her but it was strangely liberating to say the things she
hadn't said out loud before.

She pulled a face. 'And you're a smart alec.'

He held his hands up. 'I'm sorry. Couldn't resist. So
what happened?'

She couldn't believe she was talking about this. 'He
changed. Oh, he started off doing the things I wanted
to do. Walks, sailing, museums, but really he wanted
great restaurants, opening-night shows, to be seen. To
show me off on his arm. Don't get me wrong, that was
nice too, but when I agreed to marry him it was as if
he lost respect for me. I became his property.' And he
demanded the sex I hadn't felt ready for, but she didn't
say that. 'I had to wear the clothes he bought me. Sign
the prenuptial agreement. He'd check my jewellery
and shoes and handbag and make sure I had it all coordinated. Had to attend the chosen beauty salon once
a week, and he began to talk about me giving up my
job.'

Levi whistled. 'That's a few rules.'

'Tell me about it.'

Then Levi asked, 'Did you ever love him?' She

really didn't know. She'd thought she had, would have sworn it when they became engaged, but she could see now the unease that had grown enormous had always been there from the beginning.

'I must have because I put up with my reservations by thinking he knew better. Then he began to phone me any time day or night on my mobile. Keeping track. Started this campaign of speak when spoken to.'

'That must have been hard.' Levi tried to keep the smile hidden but he could feel his lips twitch.

She frowned and then reluctantly smiled. He guessed she hadn't succeeded. 'My word it was.'

Not a nice man for Sophie. No wonder she jumped half the time. Levi knew those kinds of men. Image was all-important. And the women had to be aware of the rules. Rules that didn't apply to the men.

He asked the hard one. 'And was he faithful?'

'I thought so.' She looked away. 'I was a fool.'

Levi saw the flash of hurt. The fact that she went on said a lot for her strength and honesty and he had a sudden desire to meet and deal with the jerk for her. And comfort Sophie.

'He'd been sleeping with his secretary the whole time. So everyone knew. He'd told more lies than rocks in this pool.' She glanced at the pebble-lined bath they lay in. 'Apparently it'd been going on for years but he'd never offered to marry her.' Sophie shook her head. 'What offended me the most was his girlfriend wasn't good enough to marry—only to sleep with. Creep.'

Maybe Sophie had given him what he deserved anyway. He wouldn't put it past her. 'What did you do?'

'I sold his ring and gave the money to the homeless. I told him and then I came back home. To Smiley. Got on with my life in a place where people say what they mean and don't cheat. And with a chip on my shoulder about wealthy doctors who lie.'

Levi looked away and winced. Well, he was screwed.

She should shut up. What on earth had she told him all that for and made herself vulnerable again? It had been a dismal time. Best to change the subject.

'Home was good. My brother never said a thing. Except "shortest engagement in history." He's so dead-pan most of the time, you never know what's going on in his head, though apparently your sister can read him. I've never seen him as animated as the other night at Xanadu.'

Levi shrugged but there was a tiny frown between his eyes. 'Odette likes him a lot.'

'I don't think you could get two people more dissimilar in upbringing.' Her forehead wrinkled despite the effort not to. So Levi recognised her misgivings and maybe had a few of his own. Good. It would never work.

Levi shook his head. 'Before she met the father of her baby I'd agree with you. That's my greatest regret so far, that I didn't keep her safe from men like him. Tom was a dangerous and malicious clown and no loss to his unborn child, I'm afraid. I think your brother is restoring Odette's faith in chivalrous men.' He grinned. 'And she's pregnant. No harm can be done.'

Chivalrous. Such an old-fashioned word but, in this context, perfect. The description of Smiley. 'Are you chivalrous?' It popped out like froth from the waterfall and subtly the mood in the pool changed.

'Sometimes. Before I became tired and jaded.'

She let his words flow over her to think about later. Suddenly she was thinking about the way his mouth moved and that curve to his lips that she was finally seeing more of. He'd been expressionless most of the time since that first day.

Originally she'd thought him moody but apparently he'd been worry worn. Well, he was pretty focused right now. She could feel the brush of his perusal as he tilted his head and smiled with that devilish curve to his dangerous mouth.

Time to break back to the previous mood, she thought with a little spurt of panic. 'So what made you tired and jaded?'

The smile straightened and disappeared. 'Someone died two years ago. In a way that affected how I thought about my achievements. I've been running on the treadmill since. But I won't bore you with it.'

Boring me might be safer, she thought but she didn't say it. Couldn't make the effort to turn the tide of awareness she'd begun to drift in.

He floated across the pool and closed in on her. His

eyes seemed darker and his lips parted as if he might whisper something—or do something else…

'I must admit I feel more alive than I have in a long time,' he said, and she felt the pricks of gooseflesh along her shoulders and arms.

She tried to move away but her body felt so heavy in the water she barely moved. Sound had receded and even the water temperature faded. 'Might be something to do with the fact we nearly died yesterday.' Now her voice sounded breathy and unsure.

'No doubt.' He sank under the water until not just his strong, brown shoulders were under but his chin as well. Just his angular face showed through, shadowed by the overhanging palms that darkened the planes of his cheeks. 'It's good to be alive.' He pursed his lips and blew a leaf across the water towards her. The leaf spun and twisted and bumped against her chin.

It was just a leaf. She could feel her heart thundering under the water. His gaze locked with hers, and it was as if he blew the air over her skin, but that was ridiculous. She was under the water, for goodness sake.

Yet here she was, with tiny flutters of heated awareness in a cold pond of sudden desire. It shouldn't have been erotic. But it was. A stranger, in a strange place, and strange feelings she hadn't experienced before. Enough to kick in her belly and make her aware of the fullness in her breasts and the beat of her heart.

Then his breath rippled across the water to tickle her face. She moistened her lips to say something inane, but before she could form the words he'd drifted closer until their noses touched with a little bump, like two leaves in a deserted pond, and she shivered.

All the time he stared into her eyes, and she could do little but breathe in and out and stare back and wonder at the dozen different blue rings inside his eyes and those dark, dark lashes drawing her closer.

She knew he was going to kiss her. Should be backing away when, in fact, she was drawn towards him by the primitive magnetism she had no control over.

When his mouth finally touched hers it was incredibly slow and gentle, an open-mouthed brush of his lips that impacted like an earth tremor against hers, and her lids drooped as she breathed in. His mouth slid to her cheek and down her neck, darting electrical tremors along her arms and legs that sent waves of mingled breath and kicks of desire back up into her chest. The sensations expanded in seismic rings of awareness and lust, and suddenly it was closer she needed to be, not further away.

Then he returned, took her mouth and enslaved her with a long draught from a well she hadn't known she had that meshed their souls in this primitive place, a day after they'd nearly died. Somehow, with that potent kiss, he touched the part of her that no one, not even Brad, had ever touched…and she was his. That simple and that complicated.

Immersed in sensation, she sighed as his hands slid from her shoulders down past her waist until he cupped both hips and pulled her toward him. Somehow, her fingers became entangled in his thick hair and luxuriated in the springiness as her breasts were squashed against his chest.

Time passed, moment by glorious moment, and she slipped deeper and deeper under his spell until she realised she was clutching at him as he tried to pull back.

She opened her eyes, focused and, horrified, she jolted herself away and would have moved further if he hadn't put his hand out and stilled her.

'It's OK. It's just a kiss. You're so beautiful,' he said, his voice heavy and deep, and she shuddered another breath in as he lifted a strand of hair off her forehead before he pulled back and floated away. And left her bereft.

The blood pounded in her ears and she watched him, like a rabbit in headlights, mesmerized, as he increased the distance between their bodies. Gradually she began to feel the world again and with it the sounds of the birds overhead and the wind in the leaves and the thunder of her heart.

Levi forced himself away. God, she was beautiful. And luscious and so, so ripe for the taking. And he wanted her. There was no doubt about that, but what the hell was he doing? There was no future in this, just heartbreak for Sophie, and maybe even for him.

It was lucky this pool was cold, which would help, but even then he'd have to stay submerged till he had himself under control. He nearly lost himself—both of them. It would only have taken another minute to pass the point of no return, and she was too innocent and trusting to realise.

He guessed he wasn't chivalrous.

He fisted his hands under the water and forced himself to calm. What had he been thinking? Fool. Of course, he hadn't been thinking—he'd been feeling, indulging in a daydream, or more like an erotic fantasy to play nymphs and satyrs in an oasis. A great way to say thank-you to the woman trying to save them all. But she'd looked so kissable with her satin skin and fine-boned shoulders that it made him ache like he hadn't ached for years. If he were honest, he'd wanted to kiss her since the night she'd come to Xanadu. Do more than kiss, and he'd very nearly had his way. She would have hated him. He would have hated himself.

The silence between them was broken only by the noisy budgerigar and his mate. Levi floated with his back to her while she climbed out, carefully, so as not to hurt her feet.

Sophie's hands shook, were stupidly clumsy as she wiped herself over with her shorts, and her lower limbs still wobbled as she redressed damply. Still in a daze from one kiss? A mouth-tingling caress like nothing she'd ever experienced before.

Sleazebag Brad had been practised, smooth and—now she could see—one dimensional, not like Levi, a city marauder of devastating understatement and finesse.

She shivered, not with cold, but with new knowledge of greater danger. Where was the line between attraction and wanting to be lost in a man's arms and the terrible danger of falling in love? She knew how much pain that could cause.

Her damp shirt stuck to her bra and outlined her nipples and she pulled the material out from her body to air it. It would dry all too quickly when they crossed the next plain but it embarrassed her horribly at this moment. She settled herself facing the gorge they'd climbed and breathed slowly and carefully to regain her composure. She could do that.

Still she couldn't look to the pool at Levi. Her lips thrummed as if she'd just eaten a Kakadu plum. When, in fact, she'd tasted something much better.

The water splashed behind her and a muffled curse forced a reluctant smile. He'd stubbed his toe. Good. Take his mind off kissing her.

She dug in her bag and pulled out the chocolate bar. It bent in her hand, soft and squishy, and she looked at it with a sigh. Hot chocolate was good in winter, and even like this when you hadn't had anything to eat since a tart piece of fruit. Something to take her mind off other parts of her body. The paper ripped in her teeth and the first sweet taste oozed onto her tongue.

She sucked the wrapper as she considered their options. Anything not to think of the pool and what passed between them. They'd cross the plain in the afternoon sun and hopefully find the camp before dark. That was the scary part. If they didn't...

CHAPTER EIGHT

BY TWO they were on their way again and nothing was said of the kiss in the pool. The heat bit into Levi's shoulders through his shirt and the grass crunched drily under their feet. The plain stretched ahead of them in a seemingly endless roll with stunted trees and anthills their only shade.

Levi could feel the difference—the awareness between them had increased, the air vibrated and not just with heat from the sun. He'd caused this. Created her distress. He could regret implementing the kiss but not the kiss itself because there was something about that moment that said it had to be. But his stupid lack of control had caused her discomfort. He needed to find some way to lighten the strain between them. 'So what's with the big anthills?'

She jumped when he spoke. He wished she wouldn't do that. Not for the first time wondered whoever that bloke was he'd like to have a go at him.

'Termite mounds. Not anthills.'

He looked again. Termite mounds, then. Everywhere, from small bumps in the dirt to huge towers taller than a man. Even on the cliff faces when he looked.

More interesting than he expected. 'So tell me about termites.'

She stopped and put her hands on her hips. 'What makes you think I know?'

She had a cute pose. 'You know everything.'

'You are so full of—'

'Ah-ah.' He shook his finger at her and cut her off. 'So you don't know?'

She sighed. 'Termites are blind.' She may pretend to be resigned but he saw the lessening of tension in her and it made him feel good about himself. Strange.

She went on and he smiled at the way she loved to explain things. It was one of those little things he'd grown to recognise and like about her. The passion for her world. He didn't see a lot of passion where he'd come from. Just day-in, day-out twelve-hour days. Certainly he hadn't exhibited any for a while, probably not for a couple of years. Well, not that kind anyway.

'Termites are opaque and the workers can live for thirty years.' She gave him a tentative smile. 'The queen can live eighty years.'

Nice smile. 'That'd be right. Poor man doing all the work.' He gestured to the adult-size tower of dirt. 'So what are these made of?'

She rolled her eyes at him. 'Mounds are made with saliva, spinifex, mud and termite poo, and they grow at a rate of about one foot every ten years.' She pointed to a mound that was broken. 'You can tell when they're abandoned because an active mound that's broken is repaired very quickly.'

He whistled and patted a six-foot mound they were passing. 'There're a lot of years here.'

She paused and looked around with that passion shining from her eyes. 'The story of the Kimberleys—lots of years. This whole area is the product of erosion of a giant mountain range, the Leopold, millions of years ago. That's why the ground's so rocky.'

And why not much grew around here, he guessed. 'So no bushrangers right out here in the past?'

'Not so much bushrangers, not enough people to rob, but there's a story about an escapee who killed a policeman and hid the body inside a termite mound.'

The woman was a mine of scary information. 'Don't tell me. The termites repaired the mound and he was never found.'

'You got it.'

She made him smile. Suddenly, most of the time. Even through this disaster. 'So I'd better not annoy you.'

She showed her teeth. 'Or you'll never be found.'

Sophie had sealed what had happened between them at the pool like the termites sealed their mounds, but she still felt embarrassed that she'd let him kiss her. She didn't have the headspace for the questions that had arisen from that kiss. She was focused now on getting home. Desperately.

She was doubly glad of his environmental interest because she could feel the fear build as the day lengthened. She'd been fairly confident this morning, and still sure they would find the camp at lunch, but this afternoon her water bottle emptied and conversation between them dried up like the sweat on their bodies, and she began to worry about their options.

She must have sighed because he looked across at her and touched her shoulder. 'What's wrong?'

She stopped and unconsciously her hand came over the top of his for comfort. 'It's taking longer than I'd hoped.'

He turned her into his chest and moved so she was out of the sun behind his body—a different type of embrace than the last one she didn't want to think about—and she rested her forehead on him for a moment. His voice rumbled in his chest. 'We'll find them, if not today, then tomorrow. If we don't, we know we can make it back to the others.'

Could they? She thought about how far they'd walked. Yes, they could. She could almost feel the strength transferring from him to her. His confidence boosted hers, probably unjustifiably, not that she wanted him to tell her otherwise. She had enough doubts for both of them.

Her stomach growled. 'I don't know about you but I'm getting hungry,' she mumbled into his shirt.

'Where's a drive-through Gubinge tree when you want one?' He kicked the ground. 'There's always the grubs. Ten fat ones a day, did you say?'

She had to laugh. Or she'd cry. But she did feel better. Then he put her away from him and dug in his pocket. He held up his liquid chocolate bar. 'I was saving this one for you.'

She shook her head vehemently. 'I'm not eating your chocolate.'

'Sure you are.' He pointed to the hills up ahead. 'We'll stop there and fight about it.' Then he patted her hair and took her pack from her back and captured her fingers. 'Let's go.' He pulled her fingers gently, and suddenly the strength came back along with her focus, and she walked beside him with their hands swinging together over the red earth.

She didn't know when it happened but suddenly she did trust him. Was happy to allow him to shoulder some of the burden, something so out of character for her she didn't understand how he'd achieved it. Especially after the kiss. Or was it because of the kiss?

They were close to the last foothills when the Aboriginal elder appeared. His wizened skin crinkled in mahogany folds and his grey hair hung long and straggled. Levi saw him standing beside a termite hill before Sophie did.

He carried a spear for hunting and little else.

Levi stopped suddenly when he saw him but Sophie kept going. 'He wants us to follow him.'

Levi glanced across at her. 'Guess you were right again.'

Sophie sighed with relief. Not before time. They were running out of afternoon. She'd done one thing right, then. 'This was a good one to win.'

The elder took them to a side gully and presented them with another fresh pool to drink and cool themselves. He didn't speak and she watched Levi, with hidden amusement, as he attempted to sign their story but the old man just stared at him.

'I doubt he's learnt English for the little use he'd have for it.' She handed him a stick. 'Maybe if you drew a picture in the sand?'

Levi's sand helicopter left a lot to be desired but a broad grin from the elder seemed as though he'd figured where they'd come from. Levi drew four people and then pointed to himself and Sophie, indicating the other two were still at the helicopter.

The old man nodded, seriously, and pointed to the sun and then an arc in the sky to almost sunset, and gestured they follow him, and that they'd be able to get back to the others after that.

Sophie didn't know if it was her imagination, or just the relief, but the walking was less strenuous, more shaded, and yet seemed as though they covered more ground.

An hour before sunset they came to the camp, a collection of half a dozen lean-tos, with several brown-eyed, brown-skinned toddlers scuffling in the dust.

It was unusually quiet and a quorum of women seemed congregated around a lean-to at the end of the camp. The hair on Sophie's arms stood up. Something was wrong. She glanced at Levi, who raised his brows and shrugged. He could sense it too.

The oldest lady pointed to her. Sophie approached them diffidently, used to not catching the elder's eyes. The lady, probably the grandmother, pointed her finger at Sophie. 'You that nurse, sheila, eh?' She gestured into the lean-to with her head.

Weariness swamped her and Sophie forced her head to lift as she glanced back at Levi. It seemed this day had more in store for her. Lord knew what she'd discover and it seemed she would soon find out.

He took a step to follow her. 'Do you want me to come with you?' But the old lady gestured him away.

Sophie sighed. 'Nice thought but it's not going to happen. I'd say it's secret women's business.' Sophie bent and followed the woman inside, and her heart bumped at the thought of the unknown and what might be expected of her.

The air inside the lean-to was stifling; the place seemed full of aunties and the grandmother. The young girl who lay on the dry grass bed looked more like a frightened rabbit than a woman about to give birth.

'Oh, Lord,' Sophie muttered. The sight of one tiny baby's foot resting between the mother's legs was enough to make Sophie feel like a frightened rabbit too. Footling breech, so the baby's legs would come out long before the head. If it all went well.

'As it should,' she said out loud, to bolster her own conviction.

Of course a Caesarean section would be a nice option to have in the wings in case of complications, Sophie wished fruitlessly, but that wasn't going to happen. All she could think of was the mantra from her training—hands off the breech.

Then she saw the little foot move. So the baby was alive and the day improved enormously.

Now wasn't the time to ask why the girl wasn't near a hospital if she was close to birth time. Far too late for that. Sophie knew that sometimes the fear of being away from their families made the young women hide their pregnancies so they weren't sent away. But Sophie also knew the girl would be in trouble with the elders later.

She knelt down and tried for a smile, then tapped her own chest. 'Sophie.'

The older lady pointed to the girl. 'Pearl.'

'Hello, Pearl,' Sophie said, but Pearl's frightened brown eyes skittered to the gaggle of aunties and refused to return. Sophie gestured for permission to feel the mother's abdomen and the grandmother shooed her on to the task as if to say hurry up.

Pearl's baby seemed smaller than term, which could be a good thing, or maybe it was just because it was breech and a lot of the baby was already in the pelvis. Pearl was fine boned with no extra weight, and Sophie would love to have known how long the labour had been going on.

The next contraction arrived and Pearl screwed her face up and whimpered with the pain. Her baby's little foot descended another centimetre into the world.

At this moment there wasn't much Sophie could do except be there for the end. And pray. She couldn't listen to the baby's heartbeats because she didn't have any form of stethoscope. She didn't have gloves, nor could she even wash her hands, but she couldn't leave Pearl alone either.

Levi's support was denied because culturally Pearl's birthing was women's business and men were banned. Though, if she had a problem when the baby arrived, Sophie knew darn well she'd be yelling for Levi.

Just knowing he was there gave immense reassurance. She'd expect Levi's first-aid skills and common sense would help more than anyone else's.

She guessed that even if she'd some way to contact the Royal Flying Doctor Service the plane wouldn't be here before it was all over. So much for her brief respite from responsibility. There was nothing to be done but settle herself slightly more comfortably on the dusty floor and try to ignore the trickle of perspiration that ran down between her shoulder blades. She licked her lips and tasted the dryness of her mouth. A drink would have been good.

Sophie began to pray for a rapid second stage of labour but there was only so much praying she could do. She glanced around for something else positive to focus on and her gaze rested on a brown shawl she could dry the baby with when it was born. That was a positive thought. When it was born.

The aunties all looked at her as if she should do something and she tried to block out the thoughts that didn't help.

Thoughts about drugs, and oxygen, and paediatricians who may as well be on the moon. Hopefully the baby had grown well and wasn't too premature.

If the young mum had had no antenatal care, then she was probably anaemic to start with which increased her chance of bleeding afterwards, and any blood loss would make her dangerously depleted in red blood cells.

But there wasn't a lot Sophie could do about that either. She could rub the mum's tummy to encourage clamping down of the uterus when the placenta was delivered, and she could put the baby to the breast as soon as possible to release the natural hormones that were there to do the same thing.

Women had been birthing for thousands of years in the camps, she reassured herself, well before twentieth-century medicine had decreed they were safer at the hospitals. Trouble was now the elder women had lost their skills as attendants over the past hundred years.

She needed to think of more positives. At least the

heat would make it unlikely the baby would get cold, which breech babies tended to do as their bodies waited for the heads to be born.

For some reason she thought of Levi's Pollyanna comment and it steadied her because there was nothing wrong with looking on the bright side of things.

Pearl moaned again and this time the baby's ankle came down almost to the knee and suddenly there was a second foot. 'You're doing great, Pearl.' Sophie plastered a happy face on and nodded her head at the frightened girl and her attendants. The least she could do was be supportive, instead of a harbinger of doom.

If the cervix was not fully opened, then Pearl was going to push against it anyway. If she sat up it would be easier for the baby and put even more pressure on the cervix. Sophie looked at the grandmother and gestured that they help Pearl to squat in a supported position.

Gravity would help bring the baby down and hopefully all would happen quickly before the baby's cord became too squashed by the after-coming head.

With Pearl upright her labour did seem to progress more quickly. First the baby's knees and the thighs appeared with just the change of position and then Pearl pushed until a swollen black scrotum appeared and the women broke into voluble noise and exclamations at the evidence of a new male for the family.

The elder woman gestured to Sophie to grab the baby but Sophie shook her head emphatically.

This was where "hands off the breech" was most important. Sophie knew the natural curves of the mother's pelvis shaped the baby into having his chin tucked into his chest and the arms by his side. If they pulled the baby downwards, his head would tip back into a bigger diameter and his arms might drag behind his head to create a complication that should never have happened.

'No touch,' Sophie said and waved her hands in a negative sign. 'Baby knows.'

Little skinny buttocks followed by hips, back and umbilical cord all came through next, and Sophie resisted the urge to feel the cord and check the heart rate of the baby. She'd bet it was slower than her own thumping heart was, but the less she touched, the less spasm the cord would endure.

There certainly wasn't anything else Sophie could do except prevent people pulling on the baby as he descended. She'd just ensure Pearl's baby came out with his back facing Sophie, so his head could lift from his chin-on-chest position to birth, just like a head-first baby did.

Grandmother clutched her hair and moaned, and gestured to Sophie at the paleness of the baby, and Sophie could tell she wanted to help make the baby come quicker. 'Soon,' Sophie soothed. 'All over soon.'

Sophie tried another prayer and slipped her wrist between the baby's legs so that when the chest was through and first one shoulder and then the other was born the baby was hanging all out with only the neck and head to come. Sophie's heart was thumping so loud in her ears she didn't doubt the aunties could hear, but she was strangely calm.

She allowed the weight of the baby to hang a little to ensure the head stayed deflexed until the last moment. Sophie's bent legs ached from squatting in almost under Pearl.

Now. Time to deliver the head. She placed one hand on top of the baby's shoulders and back of the neck and the other underneath on the baby's cheeks so when the head birthed it didn't spring out suddenly. The hardest part.

The baby's head had been rushed through the pelvis. To ease a baby slowly out of the constriction of the birth canal was less risky than a head being forced out quickly into sudden expansion.

'Here he comes,' Sophie muttered. She achingly raised herself from her own squat to lift the baby slowly, holding shoulders and cheeks between her hands as the baby made an arc in front of his mother's belly. His head was born with chin, mouth and nose, then eyes and finally the whole baby was out.

Pearl sagged back onto her heels and then onto her back, and Sophie wiped the still-flaccid baby over with the shawl until his little limbs contracted in reflex and he breathed. She pulled Pearl's T-shirt up and lay her son directly skin to skin across her chest.

At the first touch of his mother's skin he gasped and cried—which by this point was exactly what Sophie felt like doing herself. But there was no time for that.

Grandmother tied the twine where Sophie indicated, and the baby was totally separated from his mother by the lethal-looking knife they cut the cord with, and finally she could back away a little as the aunties crowded in.

Her hands shook and she wiped the sweat from her face with her forearm. Cord and placenta followed shortly and a gush of bright blood seeped and began to form a pool. 'Pearl—' Sophie leant in to catch the young woman's eye '—I need to rub your tummy.'

Sophie nudged the grandmother and showed her how rubbing the now-grapefruit-size uterus in Pearl's belly stopped the flow of blood until the uterus was a hard nub beneath their fingers. The grandmother nodded and brought her gnarled hand in over Sophie's. Sophie wondered if one day another woman would be as lucky if the grandmother remembered this part.

Another aunty put Pearl's baby to her mother's breast and Sophie sat back and drew a deep breath. Baby whimpered and then cried again before he latched and began to suck. They didn't need her any more and she had to get out of here before she fainted from the heat.

CHAPTER NINE

IT SEEMED hours since she'd disappeared. Levi paced himself a worn strip under the tree as he watched the opening of the humpy.

Even hand signals with the children as he attempted to take a health stock of those he could see hadn't passed the time. Eventually he'd found an elder who conversed more easily, immunisation status not something he'd normally have pursued, but Sophie wanted to know. And there was only so much washing and drinking in the creek he could do when all the time he slaked his own thirst he knew she'd be parched. At least he'd soaked a cloth and filled her bottles for when she came out.

But he should have told her earlier about his qualifications, or at least discussed where he could help. The longer she'd spent inside with the women, the deeper his guilt. An uncomfortable feeling he could have done without.

Not that he had a lot of experience with obstetrics,

except for Odette's pregnancy and one small obstetric rotation that had him back-pedalling away from something with too much emotion attached to it, but he hadn't forgotten how helpful it could be to have another medical person to discuss things with.

His own career path had opted for something he could achieve on his own, something technical he could master and something he'd decided on when his brother went blind, and he'd been very successful. Though the past two years had been hard since Darla's death, where he'd driven himself to work outrageous hours—and he'd almost burnt out, he realised now—which must be why it felt so different to smile around Sophie so often.

Then again, perhaps a near-death helicopter crash could enliven one too.

But that didn't help his guilt about Sophie. Apart from his sister, he'd been accountable to no one since his brother died. He'd disliked his father, but that was moot now. Women had been in and out of his life, but none had left him with doubts about his behaviour like this outback dynamo did.

When Sophie finally unbent herself from the humpy Levi felt the air whoosh out of his lungs as his shoulders dropped with relief. Now he could watch her draw a deep breath and gather herself. He remembered she did that a lot and it said volumes for her stamina and inner strength. Another thing he admired about her.

He'd bet the air outside seemed sweet and cooler, especially as it approached sunset. The sound of a very new baby roaring his lungs out followed her. This woman continued to amaze him.

For the briefest moment he thought he recognised something in her eyes when she looked at him that made the stress of waiting worthwhile—and brought back the guilt tenfold.

For Sophie, the sight of Levi made her want to throw herself into his arms for comfort. But she needed to wash and she needed a drink and she needed not to think about all the things that could have gone wrong that hadn't.

'Sophie?' Levi took her arm and sat her down under a tree. 'Sit.' He handed her a water bottle and she took a long drink with her eyes closed. It felt so good to be outside.

'Another amazing job?'

She opened her eyes, glanced around at the plains surrounding them and sighed. 'Footling breech. We were all lucky.' The exhaustion hit her as she sagged back against the knobbly trunk behind her.

Levi gave her a searching look. 'I'll get your other drink.' He handed her some damp cloths. 'Here's something to wash with until you're up to a walk to the creek.'

He'd torn both sleeves off his shirt and soaked them. Brilliant. Amazing. Just what she needed. When he offered them to her she could have hugged him or, for a brief, mad second, run her hands over the bulge of his upper arms that were very nicely displayed without sleeves. There was something about a man in a shirt without sleeves that called to her, not that she'd noticed that fetish before—no doubt it was especially true when that man supplied what she desperately wanted most.

It must have shown in her face because he gave her a lopsided grin. 'I've been to the shop. Maybe you'd like a Kakadu plum?'

The giggle surprised her. Probably hysteria but the release of emotion actually felt good. A little out of control, but good. He was cosseting again and she wallowed in it for a few indulgent seconds while she wiped her hands and, with a clean corner of the damp material, her face. The coolness against her forehead was worth a hundred facials Sleazebag Brad had insisted she have.

In fact, she was growing to appreciate this man more and more, though she wouldn't fall for him. But it was hard. He made her feel crazily alive and special. A safe harbour to come into. Strong arms when she needed them. But she wasn't in love. Not going there! She was very glad he was here with her though.

'There's hope for you yet.' She looked across at him but he only grimaced and her euphoria dimmed. He didn't look as happy as she felt.

Levi looked away and rubbed his neck and, to Sophie, the afternoon suddenly seemed stifling again. 'I'm glad,' he said, 'because there's something else I have to tell you.'

Lightly spoken but determined, and her stomach

sank as she wondered how much bad news a person could take in one day.

'The good news.' She was too weary for bad at this minute. 'Please.'

'From what I gather, our tracker was on his way back when he found us and the Flying Doctor is coming for your girl. We'll be able to use their radio when they land.'

Her shoulders dropped in a heartfelt sigh. Not just good. 'That's great news.' The day would work out. This whole draining adventure would end. She could get home in the not too distant future, shower and have a cup of tea, and maybe she and Levi—and the others of course, she hastened to remind herself—could share that steak she'd kill for. She didn't want to hear the bad news. She glanced around for something to divert him.

Barefoot, dark-eyed children huddled into a little giggling group to one side and darted mischievous glances across to where Sophie and Levi sat. 'Have you been making friends while I've been busy?'

He smiled at the children and pulled a silly face which sent them off into a new fit of giggles. 'So it seems.'

So he was good with kids too. She sucked her breath in and felt the warmth expand in her stomach. He really did have qualities she admired, and of course he was different to that man in her past. She shied away from the comparison, although it did Levi no disservice against Brad. It was far too early to think about the future.

She looked from him to the little brown bodies that had begun to poke and wriggle amongst themselves. These children looked lean, but full of energy. 'I wonder if the kids are up to date with their immunizations?'

'Apparently,' he said a little smugly, and she had to smile. 'I asked. And they look well.'

He'd asked? Why? Because she'd said once she wanted to know? More warm and fuzzies buzzed in her belly and she smiled up at him. 'You've been busy. Anyone I need to look at?'

He hesitated. 'There's an elder here almost blind with cataracts. He'd benefit from surgery.'

Sophie looked around the camp. Lean-tos, red dust, a couple of shady trees and the creek. 'It's hard to encourage elders to leave their home for something they've learnt to live with.'

Levi shook his head. 'He's sightless. The results would be brilliant.'

Sophie nodded. 'I know. But he has to have the money to travel to the doctor.'

'What money?' Levi looked at her. 'The operation is free in public hospitals.'

Sophie shrugged, only giving half her concentration as she began to relax. She watched the children. Sipped more water. Exhaled. The baby was fine. She'd done the right thing. And now the Flying Doctor could take over the care. She could unwind. 'He'd have to leave here, travel, live away from his family. And for these people the thought of an operation is beyond frightening.'

'It's a minor operation.' Levi was like a terrier and his intensity began to intrude on her equilibrium.

Something in the way he persisted made her look away from the children to him. She spoke slowly as the implications sparked a question, and then a creeping disquiet that maybe she'd missed something. Been blind. More blind than an elder with cataracts? And stupid? 'Do you have much experience at diagnosing cataracts?'

His eyes searched hers and she knew. Felt the red dusty world fall away from under her feet. Felt the heat in her cheeks as she flushed with embarrassment and not a little anger.

'I could have,' he said.

Her eyes narrowed as she looked into his face. The same wary expression as the first time she'd met him. The face of a liar. All the boxes slid into place in her mind—the comments, the looks between his sister and himself, his 'first aid.' She tried to keep the hurt out of her voice. 'What sort of business did you say you had?'

'I didn't.' Still he looked at her so she had to break eye contact.

'And…?' She gazed at the children across the camp.

He paused, waited until she met his eyes again. 'I'm an ophthalmologist specialising in microsurgery. I have a very successful practice in Sydney.'

'You're a doctor?' Quietly. 'You said first aid.' Her voice dropped even lower. 'You lied again.'

His voice was low too. 'I didn't lie.'

'You didn't deny.' It hurt; actually, it crushed her that she'd been fooled again. 'Liar by omission.'

'That was the bad news.'

What did he want? A pat on the head? It was bad all right. She'd started to like him. Like him a lot. Please God, not love him. She'd certainly begun to lean on him more than a little. And he was a doctor. A rich doctor. And a liar. Just like Brad. The man who'd stripped her heart, and taken a part of her that had been precious and new and untarnished, and stamped on it.

And she'd ordered Levi around because she'd been the only medical person. Did he understand how hard it had been to wear that responsibility, and now he tells her he's better qualified? Even if he was a surgeon he'd started as a generalist.

He could have put Smiley's shoulder in. The weight of unshed tears made her face feel heavy. Like a big rock tied to her cheeks, pulling her whole face down. She blinked her stupid stinging eyes and gritted her teeth. No way was she wasting water on this creep.

'I'm struggling to think of a reason you wouldn't make this all easier on me. Was this some kind of test to see how much I'd take before I broke?'

He shook his head and reached his hand out. She looked at his fingers as if they were covered in slime. He must have seen it because his hand dropped. 'Look. Sophie. I think you're amazing.' He dragged his hand through his hair. 'You didn't need my help.'

Holy cow. How dare he? She so didn't want to do this now. Or ever. She climbed wearily to her feet and with her eyes fixed past his shoulder she took off down the hill to the creek to gather herself, almost tripping in her haste to get away from him.

The water splashed cold against her fingers and she plunged her hands and forearms in to shock herself out of the stifling blanket of cotton wool she felt smothered in. She'd been so close, had almost fallen in love with exactly the type of man who could crush her—again— and in just a few short days. Didn't she learn from her mistakes?

She washed her face, washed the trickles that weren't creek water and then washed it again. Damn him.

Slowly composure returned, or at least her hands stopped shaking and her tears dried. Her head ached with a dense weariness that seemed to wrap around her bones, and she forced tired feet to carry her back to the camp. But she walked straight past him to the humpy to check the mother and baby.

By the time she emerged she had control again and an impenetrable barrier around her higher than the escarpment they'd nearly flown into. The sound of an aeroplane droned in the distance, and Sophie searched for the sight of it over the hills like she needed it to breathe.

Anything instead of looking at Levi.

The sooner that plane landed, the better. She wasn't even worried about flying out of here.

She had to think of Odette, still out in the scrub, unaware that help was coming, and the possibility of her labour. Once she was safe Sophie could release all responsibility. And she would. Posthaste.

When they made town he could worry about the disaster of the helicopter and she and Smiley could go home. With just a little luck she'd never see him again and she could forget what a fool she'd almost been.

Finally the noise of the plane dominated the sky and the shadow crossed the ground in front of them as the pilot circled to land on the area the men had cleared. Bring it on, Sophie said under her breath.

When the twin-engine aircraft landed, surprisingly smoothly on the rocky soil, the plane held three people—the doctor, Jock McDonald, a Scottish larrikin who raised his eyebrows at the sight of Levi and Sophie; the nurse, who strode purposefully towards them; and the pilot, who waved but stayed to shut the engine down.

'There'll be a story there, I'm noo doubting,' Jock said to Sophie, whom he'd met at the clinic. He waved at Levi. 'I'll talk to you in a wee moment.'

The nurse hailed Sophie and the two women accompanied Jock into the humpy, suddenly critically crowded until the doctor shooed away all except the grandmother, then checked Pearl and scolded her in such a broad accent there wasn't a hope she'd understand what he said. But he smiled and patted her head when he'd finished and again when he'd checked the tiny but vigorous baby over with obvious admiration.

'You're verra lucky. You'll both still come to the hospital so we can keep an eye on you for a day or two,' he said to Pearl and again to the grandmother, 'In case baby goes off his food. He's only a wee thing.'

Then he left the humpy and he raised his eyebrows at Sophie. 'I'd like to hear your side of it. You did well, lassie.'

Sophie didn't feel anything but tired. 'Everything went right. Hands off the breech until the head. Baby fine by a minute after birth. We weren't unlucky but we would have been up the creek if it hadn't panned out as well as it had.'

'Aye. But you weren't. So no use worryin' about the ones that go good like they're supposed to.' He pulled his hand antiseptic from his pocket and offered it to Sophie and she lathered herself. Unimaginable luxury.

Dr Jock inclined his head towards the tree. 'So who's this big fella and how're you two here?'

She shook her head. She didn't want to talk about it. 'He'll fill you in. Have you room for us?'

He looked at the plane. 'Och, no, not for two, but we can contact the Bungles and they'll fly in and get him. We'll have to take the mother and bairn or she'll have no care if either get sick.' He gave her a searching look. 'I'm thinkin' you need to come with us.' Then he crossed to where Levi was talking to the pilot under the tree with a map spread between them.

Fifteen minutes later, Sophie joined Pearl and her

baby in the RFDS plane with Dr Jock, while the nurse rode up front with the pilot.

Levi had been in contact with a helicopter service at the Bungles who were en route to pick him up. Another had flown to the crash site. More red tape would follow at a later date, but for the moment Odette and Smiley were on their way back to the hospital at Kununurra and Sophie could drop the last of her responsibilities.

An hour later she finally stepped out of the plane at the airport in Kununurra too. But it wasn't where she wanted to be. She ached to go home, back to her own space, a place to hide and lick her wounds and take stock of the new disaster she'd brought on herself, but she'd have to wait for the hospital to release her brother.

The nurse from the flight lent her flat keys and spare clothes, and Sophie spent an hour soaking red dust from her legs and her hair in a long bath that should have relaxed her but didn't.

She could hear the sound of helicopters taking off and landing at the airfield across the road and the sound grated across her ears like gravel over her skin. No doubt one of them held *him*. All the time she wished she'd never let her guard down—couldn't believe she'd done it again, fallen for the words and caresses of a smooth-talking liar. But never again.

Levi watched the entrance to the hospital as cars with lights drove up and deposited people. Watched every taxi, truck and bus that pulled up. He watched families walking and couples talking and single women who didn't matter, but nowhere did he see a ponytail in an Akubra hat that quickened his heart.

It was night now but this day never seemed to end. He'd spent an hour at the police station. The aircraft crash investigation team were coming from Perth and until then nothing could be proved, but they were on alert. He wasn't having his sister put at risk again. He'd arranged a light aircraft flight to get them all home, and told the men at Xanadu to put the lights out on the strip, as well as the men at the station township to put another set out, and he'd seen Odette and William. Neither had spotted Sophie but William had heard her on the phone.

She'd been on the ground for two hours now; he'd checked. She should be here soon.

He still didn't know what to say. She hadn't allowed him a word since he'd told her, hadn't looked at him before she left, but the hurt in her eyes had bitten harder than he'd expected. He just hoped she'd cool down and then he could explain before he had to take Odette back to Sydney.

The digital clock in the hospital foyer flashed ten past nine and a taxi pulled up. There she was. Strangely smaller than he remembered, in a pair of long trousers that didn't suit her as much as her shorts. The toss of her head when she saw him gave a pretty accurate picture of what she thought. Not a good omen for explanations.

Fair enough. Maybe he deserved it.

There was too much happening to do anything about it now but later he'd try to explain. It seemed his sister had come through the ordeal unscathed. He wasn't sure Sophie had—and it was his fault.

She lifted her hat off and held it in her hand as if to ward him off. The way she walked past him with her head down made him want to kick himself. He fell in behind her as she headed for the casualty room until he caught up. 'You OK?'

Sophie gritted her teeth. She was fine! Was this guy for real? 'Yes.' She didn't look at him.

'Sophie. Let me explain.'

'I'd prefer you didn't.' She stopped. 'Look. Levi. Dr Whatever-your-name-is.' That was when she realised how deep the perfidy went. 'I don't even know your last name.'

'Pearson.'

The name rang a bell. Pearson? Pearson? But she couldn't place it. She shrugged it off with a tiny shake of her head. Was it really Pearson? Who could tell with this guy?

Levi stared down at her. 'Don't you think you're being a little harsh, considering what we've been through together?'

'I really don't care if you think I'm harsh. I'm tired. I'm over this. I have to see you for the next hour but I don't have to listen. I'd appreciate it if you'd respect that.'

So they sat in the waiting room, not speaking. To start with, Sophie flicked through a magazine but every page of upmarket advertisement she turned to she imagined Levi driving that car. Eating at that restaurant. Dancing with that girl. Wearing that suit.

She threw the magazine down and leaned back in the chair and closed her eyes. She hadn't lost her heart to another city slicker. She hadn't.

Finally, after another torturous half hour, the patients were released. Odette hugged her and Smiley nodded and even put his hand on Sophie's shoulder and squeezed it.

'Thanks, Sis.'

'We were lucky,' she mumbled, and reached up and gave him a kiss. She needed to dwell on the fact that all of them were alive and that it had been pretty close. Maybe that was why she was weepy.

Sophie avoided Levi's attempt to catch her eye and she only then wondered how they were getting home. Not a helicopter, she hoped.

'I've hired a plane to get us back,' he said, as if she'd asked the question.

She risked a glance at him and he was looking at her. 'Thank you,' she mumbled but that was all.

Apparently Smiley would fly on to Xanadu to collect his vehicle and Sophie would be dropped home to sleep. First stop: Jabiru Station Township. Yes, please. Sophie couldn't wait.

The flight was short and when she finally closed her

front door behind her she leaned against it with a sigh. The wood was hard and scratchy from peeling paint and she rubbed her head against it as if to rub some sense into her brain. What had she done?

Sleep proved impossible after the events of the past two days and ridiculously the most disturbing factor was Levi's decision to keep her unaware of his profession. Maybe that was a concept which was totally ridiculous in the scheme of things but she couldn't help it.

She needed to get back to work and forget her adventures, her weakness and the high-flying people at Xanadu.

CHAPTER TEN

WHEN Sophie opened the front door the next morning she glanced across the street and Levi leant on the veranda rail of the clinic as if he owned it.

There he was. Designer jeans and Rolex flashing in the sunlight, and there she was, clutching her throat like a wimp.

She would have pulled back, hidden inside, if he hadn't straightened when he saw her, but it was too late. Too darn late.

Her hand shook as she pulled the door shut behind her and when she crossed the veranda it felt like a creek full of crocodiles were shifting underfoot. What could he possibly want? She hated that it mattered so much it made her tremble.

The dusty road, usually wide in the sunlight, seemed narrow today, and in far too little time she stood beside him. Just a drift of some expensive aftershave letting her know he was still way out of her league. 'How can I help you, Doctor?'

His eyes narrowed and when he spoke his voice was very low. 'Don't call me doctor and don't talk to me as if you don't know me.'

She blinked. Was he trying for best defence is attack? Well, she could do a little attacking of her own.

'I thought you'd be long gone.'

He sighed. 'I can see the thought of that upsets you no end.'

'Hmm.' The deserted street didn't produce any distractions so she had to look at him. 'Perhaps not.' She shrugged. Self-preservation's like that, she thought. 'Nothing personal. How can I help you?'

'I have to stay for the crash investigation team. It looks as if the chopper was definitely tampered with and there's a police investigation. I thought you should know.'

What? Ice trickled down her neck despite the heat. Deliberate sabotage? With a pregnant Odette on board? 'Tampered with? That's horrible. Who'd want to do that?' She'd no idea but it seemed the concept wasn't new to him. How surprising he hadn't shared that with her earlier.

'There's some suspicion on Steve, the resort manager. He's disappeared.'

'Steve?' She shook her head at the crazy notion. 'I don't understand.'

He ran his hand through his hair. 'It's a long story.'

Long stories take time. That meant he'd stay longer and she didn't think she could take that. 'No problem.'

She couldn't help the tiny bitterness that laced her words. She forced herself to hold out her hand and braced for that frisson she felt every time he touched her. 'All the best, then.'

He looked down at her fingers but made no move to take her hand. 'I was hoping we could part as more than friends.'

She shrugged, not without a little relief, and tucked her hand away safely by her side. She didn't want to be his special friend. They came from different worlds. Had different morals. 'I don't think so.' Blowed if she'd hold her hand out again. 'So when do you go?'

'It's taken a day to get the team in from Perth. The preliminary reports will be through late this afternoon and we leave tomorrow. I tried to send Odette back today but she refused to go without me.'

She could understand that. Especially when she'd just found out someone tried to kill her. The idea was almost too far-fetched to believe. 'She's been through a lot. I guess it would make anyone nervous to travel on their own, let alone in her circumstances.' Unconsciously she scrunched her hands inside her short pockets. Already her heart rate was palpable and she could feel the moisture on her skin—and still he hadn't come to the reason he was here.

He paused, waiting for her to ask him something, and when she didn't he went on, as if searching for a topic. So he wasn't comfortable either, she thought. Good.

'At least Odette didn't have her baby in the bush. My biggest fear. She should never have travelled so far in her pregnancy. I can't believe I didn't stop her.'

To be fair, not that she really felt like it, Sophie didn't see that. Odette was pretty much her own woman and well past the age of consent. But it was none of her business. Right?

She couldn't take much more of this. 'Why are you here?'

He stepped forward and she stepped back until her spine was against the unopened door. He cupped his fingers under her chin and gently lifted her head so that he could see straight into her face.

She wanted to shake him off but with the feel of his hand on her she lost all power. His hand was cool and firm against the heat in her skin, and his gaze captured hers as easily as when—was it only a week ago?—she'd first seen him. Despite the need to do so she couldn't look away.

Now, after the time they'd spent together, she knew his irises were rings of blue, his lashes were dark brown, not black. Memories of that time she'd felt his skin against her cheek and his mouth against hers made her shoulders droop with comfort, as if he'd done it again.

Why did he have to touch her?

Those times in Levi's arms were a whole different world—one she wasn't going to get used to—and unfortunately those few touches had been indelible. How much more proof did she need to get out? Imagine if he could read now how much she wanted to be back in his arms.

Step sideways, move away—the litany in her head drowned out his words. But her body didn't obey. Then she tried to concentrate on what he said to block out his eyes and the feel of his hand. 'I'm sorry you've been involved in this, Sophie. I'd like the chance to sit and talk before I go.'

Finally her body responded and she pulled her chin away and walked to the rail with her back to him. She couldn't sit and talk! No way. 'Was there something you wanted to ask about your sister's pregnancy?'

He came to stand beside her. 'It's nothing to do with Odette,' he said with a skyward glance of frustration. 'It's about the way we parted after extreme circumstances and I don't like that I've upset you.'

She'd have to make a good show of it. There'd be no other way to get rid of him. She held up her hands. 'Look. I don't want to talk about it. I'm over it.'

He searched her face. 'I'm not.' His scrutiny seemed almost abrasive to her skin but she blocked it out. He went on. 'What's happened to you in the past is not me. Can't you forgive me for not being more open with you?'

Nope. She was too darn scared it was the tip of the iceberg of deceit she hadn't discovered yet. Too terrified if she trusted him he would break a part of her that would never heal. She shook her head and looked back in time to a hurt that was nothing to this. 'I can't help how the past has shaped me. Men who can't tell the truth seem drawn to me. I've even a family history of being scammed by liars.'

She risked a glance at his face. 'I'm a simple girl, Levi. I say what I mean. I want you to go.'

He rubbed the back of his neck. 'What do you want me to say, Sophie? I'm sorry I misled you but there are things going on here you don't know about, and if I tell you, then you could be in danger.'

She shook her head. Not good enough. 'There's nothing more to say, then.'

He frowned at her. 'You're not giving me a chance.'

'Tough.' She shrugged her shoulders at him but they felt as heavy as if she carried a yoke with two loaded buckets. When he raised his brows at her, as though she was the one being childish, she actually felt like a child. A small one. Who'd discovered the world wasn't magical any more.

He'd tricked her just when she'd started to believe she might have found a man she could trust her heart to.

A man who warmed her when he looked at her and listened when she was off on her tangent, who stretched her mind and made her laugh and had a strong hand she could hold when she needed, and arms that comforted… All gone.

She'd thought she'd seen things in Levi that she hadn't seen in any man she'd been drawn to. But he'd dashed her fledgling hopes when he lied—the one thing she could never forgive—and she didn't have any reserves left. 'Please go.'

His face shut down until he looked like the stranger she'd seen the first day. Aloof, arrogant, then finally dismissive. 'I'm sorry you feel that way.' He turned but before he left he said, 'Where's William?'

Confusion held her answer. Smiley? 'Work. Why?' Would he never go? Her eyes stung and her throat bulged so thick with tears she could barely breathe.

'Something's come out about the family that used to own Xanadu. Do you know what their name was?'

She didn't have the energy to talk about her foolish, gullible grandfather. It was easier to say, 'No. Why?'

'Nothing important.' He took a step towards her and she panicked that she'd throw herself into his arms. She stepped back as though he'd raised his hand and her panic must have shown on her face. That stopped him.

'Goodbye, Sophie.'

He stepped off the veranda into the dust and as he walked away she realised she'd done what she'd blamed him for. She'd lied to him. And not just about her grandfather.

Levi drove back to Xanadu, too fast, which involved concentration on the road but he was grimly thankful about that. He didn't want to think. Didn't want to relive the distress he'd recognised in Sophie's eyes.

In fact, it was probably safer she wasn't seen with

him. Safer for her because he could feel the danger closing in. If the results came back as he expected it upped the ante for Steve. They were all in danger.

Two hours later Smiley burst into the clinic as Sophie sutured a nasty gash from a poorly wielded chainsaw.

The young jackaroo had been lucky he'd only touched his leg on the way through the log and had opened the skin in one thick stripe. Sophie looked up. People burst in often, but never Smiley.

She took one look at his face. 'Odette?'

'She rang me on the satellite phone. Her waters broke, and the contractions are coming every three minutes. She's refusing to move and they're at the Pentecost crossing. Then the phone died.'

That didn't make sense. 'The same spot I saw Levi the first day? Why would they go there?'

Smiley shook his head at the delay. 'It's where her father was taken.'

Her father? Taken? It all came back. Crocodiles. 'Pearson.' Levi telling her his name at Kununurra and it had rung a bell then. She couldn't believe she'd forgotten it. Such was the state Levi had her in. The name of the people her grandfather had lost the family station to. Levi hadn't been a guest; he'd been the owner. Hence, the question about her family.

Liar. No wonder they could use the choppers, drive the vehicles, do whatever they wished. Levi had lied again. She yanked the final suture through and the unfortunate young cowboy yelped in protest. Sophie bit her lip and looked at the jackaroo. 'Oops, sorry.' She tied off, snipped the ends of the suture and put a see-through dressing over the top in minimal time. 'Keep it dry. Come back in a week and I'll take the stitches out.'

The young bloke glanced at her once as if to say, *I'll take 'em out myself*, then scurried out of the room. Sophie sighed. She'd never have done that before Levi had disrupted her life.

'Xanadu.' She looked at her brother. 'They own it.' So many lies. Smiley didn't look surprised. More unpalatable truth. 'You knew?' That hurt more than anything else.

Impatiently he answered, 'Odette asked me not to say because she wasn't even supposed to tell me.'

'For goodness sake, why not?' Now these people were infecting Smiley with their subterfuge.

Smiley shook his head. 'Come on.' He gestured to the room as if to ask what do you need. 'It's not important and I really don't care. Let's go.'

Smiley drove as if driving the Dakar Rally—a man who never drove fast—and they made the crossing in an hour. A Kimberley record that Sophie never wanted to break. Her teeth rattled in her head and the dust stung her eyes but she didn't say anything. Smiley's words repeated in her head. 'It's not important and I really don't care.'

So why did she care so much when she'd been led

astray by Levi? Why did it matter in the big scheme of things? Had she overreacted? Been precious about semantics? She didn't even want to think what she could have risked if Levi really wanted to see her again.

Smiley was right. Now wasn't the time. It didn't matter. She needed to put any emotion over Levi's deceit aside and think about Odette.

She squeezed the emergency delivery pack on her lap and ran over a few scenarios. At least when she'd felt Odette's uterus the baby had palped head first and not breech, and she had medical backup in Levi, she thought bitterly.

Why wouldn't Levi just pick his sister up and move her? Surely he didn't agree with her having a baby out in the wilderness? She'd never understand these people.

When they arrived she saw why they were still there.

Levi's vehicle sat low to the ground, four flat tyres, a very reasonable excuse not to leave. The local police vehicle had pulled up next to them and the two officers were talking on the two-way.

Smiley pulled up in a shower of gravel and threw himself out of the car towards Odette, who sat with her back against a boab in her trousers and bra, and burst into tears when she saw him. Sophie blinked. That was different.

Levi sat next to her with his arm around her until Smiley took his place.

Sophie glanced back at the river, which wasn't far enough away from them, and scanned the bank. Two large saltwater crocodiles sat patiently at the edge in the shade and watched them with unblinking yellow eyes. Yikes.

Antipathy forgotten she glanced at Odette, who was lost in Smiley's arms, and turned to Levi. Her brows creased. 'You OK?'

'Will be,' he said grimly. 'Satellite phone went flat after we'd got through to the police and William.'

She frowned. He didn't look right. 'Are you hurt?'

'Stray bullet nicked me. It's nothing.' He lifted his arm from his chest and showed a wad of heavily blood-stained material tied around his left arm; she guessed it was Odette's shirt.

'Let me see.'

'Sort Odette first.' He was still giving orders. Typical.

Sophie scanned his sister quickly. She didn't sound like a woman in the final throes of labour. 'You OK, Odette?'

Odette spoke from Smiley's arms. 'I am now.'

She turned back to Levi. 'Right, now show me.'

He glared at her and held up his arm. 'We don't have time for this. He could shoot again.'

Sophie busied herself undoing the material. 'I'm assuming we're on the right side of the tree for safety.' She inclined her head towards the river. 'And that's not all who's here. The police will protect us from him but not from the couple of salties who fancy a piece of you too.'

He raised his brows at her. 'It must be your fate in life to warn me about crocodiles.'

'And yours to keep me in the dark. But we'll talk about that later.'

Gingerly he held his injured arm as she eased the wad away from the skin below his shoulder to expose a neat in hole and a less-neat out hole. The bullet had passed through in a jagged tunnel without causing major damage. Blood oozed as soon as she took the pressure away and hastily she put the wad back. He was right. It wouldn't kill him. Levi's indrawn breath made her wince. 'Sorry.'

'It's nothing. I'll heal. Get Odette away from here.'

The man was mad. 'I imagine the police will get us all away from here.'

Short sharp shake of his head and she felt her own impatience rise.

'I'm not going anywhere until I find him,' he growled.

She gestured to his shoulder. 'Not like that surely.'

'Steve, or someone, shot at us while Odette was saying goodbye. Here. Shot the tyres on the car. Tried to kill my sister. He's still out there, though the police think he's gone.' His eyes burned into hers and she shivered a little at the implacable decision to go after the shooter.

His voice lowered but was no less definite. 'I'm staying until we get him. Now, please do what I ask and take Odette. If you stay here he'll try to kill you too.'

She glanced at Smiley, who was attempting to disentangle Odette and calm her at the same time. He looked up at Sophie. 'Let's get 'em out of here.'

The bullet hit the tree beside them a millisecond before the shot rang out.

Smiley scooped Odette like she was a feather and dived around the back of the tree. Levi grabbed Sophie and pushed her behind the tree onto the ground and flattened himself on top of her. The breath whooshed from her lungs and a bunch of dead boab leaves crackled under her. The gunman had moved. She didn't want Levi to protect her with his body. Did he want to get shot again?

She sucked in another laboured breath. He was darned heavy but she doubted he'd listen to her right at this moment. Thankfully, when no further shots rang out, he eased himself off, but kept his body between her and the direction the bullet had come from.

'You all right?' he said, and she nodded. The fact that he'd cared enough to protect her made her eyes sting. Though maybe he'd have done it for any woman and she shouldn't read anything into his actions.

The hardest part was trying not to remember the feel of his strong chest against her or the male scent that reminded her of other times she'd been in his arms.

As they crouched and dusted themselves off Sophie could see a fresh splash of blood in the dirt beside her. Levi had dislodged the makeshift bandage and his wound oozed sluggishly again. 'Come here,' she said, and resettled the wadding as she frowned at him.

His eyes caught hers. 'Thank you.'

She couldn't help the heat that rode in her cheeks. 'Any time.'

He raised his brows. 'I might take you up on that.'

'This guy means business,' Smiley commented grimly when the four of them were crouched behind the thankfully wide trunk of the fat boab. The police had dived behind their own car and one of them fired back.

Levi grimaced. 'I'm so sorry you two are involved in Steve's plans.'

She looked from one man to the other. 'Involved in what plan? Now what don't I know?' Sophie demanded.

Levi sighed. 'You know the helicopter was definitely sabotaged, but I'm now convinced my father was pushed into the river here five months ago. Whoever did that is shooting at us now and I think it's my half-brother, Steve.'

She did not believe this. 'Steve's your half-brother?' This was outback Australia, not some gangland setting. Who were these people?

Levi saw her confusion. 'Because of Xanadu. It seems that my new-found half-sibling expected to inherit Xanadu, and he wants it.' He paused. 'In case we all die here…' He pulled her in close with his good arm and dropped a kiss on her lips. 'I think you are the most amazing woman I've ever met.'

He'd kissed her. In the middle of a gunfight. And by the look on his face he'd enjoyed it. Yep. He was mad. 'You must be delirious. We're being *shot at*!'

'That's why it seemed a good idea to tell you now.' He stroked her cheek. 'And I'm not lying.'

The sound of a vehicle revving and then driving

away had Smiley peer around the tree. 'Could have been someone else parked and they got scared,' Smiley said.

Levi hit the tree with the side of his fist and then winced as the vibration ran through his body to his injured arm. 'Or could be our man.'

The police car started and the officers drove off in pursuit. 'It seems the coppers agree,' Smiley said.

'Damn. Wish I'd seen the car.' Levi growled, 'Let's get the girls out of here and back to Xanadu.'

Smiley nodded, grimly, and went for the truck to reverse it back to Odette.

Sophie slid down the tree next to Odette to see how she fared. 'You OK, honey?'

The girl's head was down and she held her stomach. 'I think the baby's coming.'

She whimpered and then a tiny strangled moan had Sophie peer at her with a frown. 'We might just sit for a minute,' Sophie said to no one in particular, and rested her hand on Odette's arm. 'What's happening?'

Odette turned agonised eyes to Sophie and whispered, 'I need to go to the bathroom.'

Sophie looked at Levi. 'I think she's pushing.'

CHAPTER ELEVEN

'No. Not here.' Levi cast his eyes skywards but all he could see were the sparse leaves of the boab above him. He could handle the idea of being shot at but not the birth of Odette's baby.

He needed her safe, with doctors, and theatres, and sterile surroundings. He couldn't lose Odette like his mother. His worst nightmare. He'd failed in every aspect of keeping his sister safe. He'd involved her in a helicopter crash, a shooting and now this. He wanted her out of here and surely she could stand.

'Please stand, Odette.'

'You can't prioritise this.' Now Sophie was shaking her head at him. 'She's pushing. It's coming.'

Prioritise? He wanted his sister in a nice safe hospital. Preferably a Sydney one. How had it come to this? 'Come on, Odette. You have to get up.'

Odette looked up at him and he could see the fear behind her tremulous smile. 'Sorry. Can't do.'

He looked at Sophie and despite the sympathy he

saw in her eyes she shook her head. She was right. Again.

The truck backed up to them and Smiley jumped out. 'Let's go.'

Levi looked helplessly down at both women, distanced from him by their silent communication. 'Sophie says Odette's having the baby.'

'She can't have it here.' Smiley cast a quick glance to the river. 'The crocs will have the lot of us if we don't get out.'

'Then make sure they don't,' Sophie said with a touch of asperity. 'She'll move as soon as the baby's born.'

'Tell the men to go away,' Odette whispered.

Sophie obliged. 'We're busy.' Smiley blinked, then nodded and drifted away to keep watch between them and the river. Levi looked down at this woman who'd come into their lives and continued to cope with one disaster after another. Thank God she was here. What would they do without her? What would he do without her?

When had everything changed? When had Sophie become more important than the guilt he lived with when he couldn't help everyone? More important than finding his father's killer. More important to protect than himself. Was she his unforeseen destiny?

Sophie and Odette leaned with their backs against the tree. 'You concentrate on listening to your body and I'll worry about everything else. Just breathe it out,' she said quietly and looked up at him. 'I need the kit out of the truck and the rugs I brought, please.' At least it seemed he could be of use.

He did as requested and then returned with what she'd asked. 'Where do you want it?'

'Spread around us and the thin rug over Odette. And pass me the pack and the towel. Thanks.' She helped Odette adjust her clothing under the rug, then undid the delivery pack and laid the cord clamps aside. She drew up the Syntocinon for after the birth, washed her hands with antiseptic, then pulled on the gloves. 'A little primitive but this tree has great facilities compared to the camp the other day.'

Levi strangled back an inappropriate laugh. He supposed it did and he watched her lean back against the tree next to his sister and wait. Her capable hands were clasped loosely on her lap. As if just another April day in the Kimberleys. How was he ever going to go back to Sydney and leave her? Except for the minor fact she wouldn't have him.

Odette looked up once, an arrested expression on her face as she stared at Sophie. 'William said you told him birthing a baby was like having a foal or a calf.'

Sophie brushed the hair off Odette's forehead with her finger and smiled. She had a great smile, Levi thought as he pretended not to listen.

'He's a bad boy for repeating that. I said that because he was scared for you. But you're doing so well it might be true.'

Levi saw the tears well as Odette sniffed. 'I want to go home. I can't believe it's happening here.' His fault.

'After meeting you two?' Sophie rolled her eyes and she glanced at him quickly before looking back at Odette. 'I can.'

Odette's laugh was cut short by the next pain and Levi winced as it dragged a low groan from her as the baby moved down.

Levi twisted his hands; he felt so damn powerless to do anything for either of them.

'Beautiful,' said Sophie in that quiet, almost hypnotic voice he'd never be able to match in the circumstances. 'Slow breaths. Not long now.'

She looked up and frowned when she saw him watching her. He stretched his lips into a strained smile but she must have seen his tension. 'Take a few breaths too, Levi. It's OK.'

He was always in trouble with this woman. 'Can I get you anything, Sophie?'

'Sip of water, for Odette, thanks. There's a bottle in the truck. And maybe check on Smiley.' In other words, his marching orders. OK. Maybe he would be better out of the way until it was all over.

'Call him William!' Odette mumbled through gritted teeth, as she finished the pain and breathed out.

Levi handed her the water and drifted away and Sophie watched him go. He appeared unflappable considering the day he'd had and that his sister was doing what he'd dreaded all along. Sophie couldn't guarantee everything would be fine; she could just assume it would, and deal with the variations as they came.

And Levi would be there for support if she needed him. She had enormous faith in him and she didn't quite know where it had grown from. He'd become a good person to have around. She could've become used to that.

Odette gripped her hand and Sophie refocused where she should have been all along.

Odette panted and bit her lip. 'I don't think I want to do this.'

Sophie closed her fingers around Odette's shoulder in support. 'I know. Let it happen. Just push your tummy out as you breathe in, and let it fall as you breathe out, and the baby will move down.'

Odette breathed and finally Sophie could see the first signs of descent. 'I can see some dark hair now, Odette, so he's not bald.'

Odette's eyes stared into hers as she searched Sophie's face. 'The contraction's gone and it's burning.'

'As it should,' Sophie said quietly. 'Everything needs to stretch and the head sitting there is the best way to do that.'

'I am so not doing this again,' Odette ground out as she panted the pain away. Then her voice changed. 'Can I touch him?'

Sophie smiled—she loved this bit—and took her hand to guide it down to the baby's head. 'Of course.'

Odette stretched tentatively until she realised there

was a hard little scalp right under her fingers and her hand jumped away. 'Oh, my Lord. This is so not right.'

'Afraid it is.' Sophie smiled. 'The next pain will move baby out more, just remember to push slowly with your breath. You don't want your baby to come out too fast.'

'I don't?' She whistled her breath in between her teeth. 'You've got to be kidding.' Odette closed her eyes and breathed, and by fractions the baby descended.

Sophie stroked Odette's hair out of her eyes. 'You are amazing, you know that?'

The next contraction built and the amount of the baby's head grew slowly as Odette breathed him out. Wrinkled forehead, eyes and nose, and finally mouth and chin, until the whole head rotated to face his mother's leg. Sophie dried the little face and hair gently as they waited for the next contraction.

'He's blinking,' she told Odette.

Odette panted. 'But his body's not out.'

'He's awake, that's for sure.' And as Odette pushed for the last time, the baby eased into Sophie's hands. She ran the towel over him as he opened his eyes wider—a dark, dark blue—and he blinked as he looked around.

'It really is a boy? I have my son?' Then, 'He's not crying,' Odette said as Sophie slid him up his mother's body skin to skin until he lay across Odette's breasts. She covered them both with the rug and tucked the edges in.

'He doesn't have to, he's breathing. He's pink and happy to be on you. And yes, he's definitely a boy.'

Sophie gave the injection, clamped and cut the cord and waited for the third stage to complete. When it was over she checked Odette's uterus through her soft belly skin, and found it rocklike beneath her fingers. Everything had done as it should. She pulled the rug back again and checked Odette's pulse.

'It's over.' Odette smiled up at her. 'I've done it.' Her smile seemed to light up ten feet around them. She glanced down at her son. 'I can't tell you how having you here helped me do that.'

'My privilege.' They sat there quietly for a minute or two. Just breathing and allowing the peace of the bush to steal over them. To appreciate the wonder of childbirth in such a primitive setting. The baby squirmed and Odette laughed and stroked his head and she glanced at Sophie. Their eyes met and they both smiled.

'Can you ask Levi and William to come see him now, please?' The softness in those powerful new mother's eyes made it hard for Sophie to swallow and her eyes stung. This was why she loved this job.

'Sure.' Sophie tucked a little escaping hand back under the blankets around Odette's new son and stripped off her gloves. 'Congratulations. You were amazing.'

'Thank you, Sophie. I just let you worry about everything else.' She stroked the downy head as her son wrinkled his forehead and blinked up at her. 'He's so gorgeous.'

Sophie stroked his tiny hand that escaped again and nodded. She signalled Levi over and watched the men fuss over mother and baby. Her face ached with a broad goofy smile that faded with just a tinge of melancholy for what might have been. She walked towards the river to keep watch.

A few minutes later Levi stood and crossed the grass to her side and she moved back to a safer distance. He smiled ruefully, and then stepped forward and deliberately eased in closer to invade her space. 'You are getting a hug whether you like it or not.'

'Oh.' She didn't know what to say to that, and in the end she didn't have to say anything as Levi lifted his good arm and drew her against his chest. She sighed against him. She was glad he insisted, she thought as she sighed again.

'Thank you, Sophie,' he said quietly, and they stood there, with the sound of the river gurgling behind them and the raucous laugh of a kookaburra punctuating their isolation.

His arm was warm and heavy around her shoulders and the amount of comfort she gained was disproportionate to the gesture. She leant her head more heavily against the good side of his body for a few precious seconds and allowed her facial bones to savour the hardness of his chest against her cheek, the feel of his shirt against her skin and to hear his heart beat, like a rhythmic drum that beat out a cadence of support.

She'd never really been a girl to lean on people. Hadn't really learnt how until now. There was something magic about the way Levi could remove weariness from her like a blanket lifting from her shoulders. He could energise her with a look, let alone the circle of his arms. Shame she'd refused to listen to him when she'd had the chance.

Her nose wrinkled. She could smell his blood. She focused on the damp patch a few inches from her nose and it was as if a beam of stark white light had been switched on in her brain. Her stupid brain that hadn't seen it all before while she'd been distracted by Odette's need. How could she have missed it? Like a splash of cold water from the river, the concept of Levi's death stared at her, shocking and far too real. It had been that close.

He could have died. Been dead right now. The reality squeezed her chest and her throat closed over. She'd been the greatest fool. Imagine if the bullet had been a few inches closer to his heart. For the first time she realised how narrow her escape…to losing the man she suddenly couldn't doubt she loved. Why had it taken her so long to realise?

She loved him. The tears prickled then, and stung, and burned at the thought of Levi in mortal danger. She'd been obsessing about his perceived faults to protect her own realisation. Of course she loved him. What had she been thinking?

'So here we are again,' he said into her hair, and the vibration, more poignant for his mortality, felt so much more precious than her own pride. If he'd been dead she'd have missed this. Any of this. All of this. Oblivious to her epiphany he went on musingly. 'I thought I'd seen the last of you.'

Thank God he hadn't. She closed her eyes and two fat tears ran down her cheeks. She swallowed and tried to level her voice. 'Fate conspires apparently.'

'Hmm,' he rumbled beneath her. 'Unfortunately, fate wasn't the only one conspiring. I'm sorry you and William were involved in this mess.'

Then she remembered she'd lied to him too and she hadn't told him. Suddenly it was so hard to start. Funny that. After all her bluster about being kept in the dark and offence at the misconceptions he'd practised, she'd done the same.

'Congratulations on your nephew,' she said weakly as she pulled away. She turned to surreptitiously wipe her cheeks.

'Lucky baby to have a new beginning,' he went on drily, and she could feel his eyes follow her as she widened the distance.

New beginnings. Could she do that? 'What would you do with a new beginning if you had one?' She took her eyes off the bank in front of them to look back at his face. Maybe they could laugh about the irony.

She didn't see the grey crocodile move a foot closer to where they stood on the gravel. The whole world had condensed down to Levi—the fact that she wanted to run back to his arms and didn't know if she could go through life denying that she'd had the chance and blew it. Now she'd stopped lying to herself.

Motionless, the huge crocodile watched her with unblinking yellow eyes and even Levi didn't see the danger until the reptile moved again.

Levi must have sensed or seen the sweep of the jagged tail out of the corner of his eye as the crocodile moved because he caught Sophie's hand and pulled her back into his arms and back towards the truck. 'Let's go. The crocs are getting hungry.' She'd forgotten the danger again. When she'd promised herself she never would. Far too close for comfort.

Levi pulled her to him. 'My turn to warn you.'

His hand was tight around her wrist, painfully so, as he shuffled them both backed towards the tree and Sophie glanced back. 'Too close,' she said as she shuddered.

'Time to go, William,' he called over his shoulder, and all Sophie could think about was the way her dog had died and the fact that she'd forgotten her own rules. She was the one who was supposed to know the dangers. When she leant up against the truck her legs trembled and threatened to collapse. They both could have been killed. She shuddered again and he gathered her up and put her on the seat.

They both looked back and the crocodile had stopped in the spot they'd been standing. His thick reptilian tail swayed back and forth in frustration. His mate left the water and came to stand beside him.

Smiley whistled as he gathered the belongings and helped Odette move with her baby to the truck. 'We need to relocate those fellows,' Smiley said. 'Before they wipe your whole family out.'

'And yours,' said Levi grimly.

Smiley shook his head. 'Never seen 'em so nasty. It's not normal.'

'Spare me from feeling sorry for the crocodile.' Levi stared at the water. 'Though I wonder if that was planned too? Steve could have been feeding them. Knowing Odette wanted to put a plaque up here.'

'If they don't catch him we'll never know.'

It was a subdued party that returned to Xanadu. Smiley drove, and the others crammed like sardines, with Odette's baby, into the front. Sophie sat on Levi and his arms held her as if he'd never let her go. Considering the day, Sophie was more than happy with that.

Levi drew her into the resort building with his arm still protectively pulling her against him. Every now and then her mind recapped the morning, dwelling on Levi's close escape. 'I need to see to your wound before we go.'

He frowned. 'It's nothing. We'll get Odette settled first and get you a stiff drink.' He signalled to one of the indoor staff.

She was over the crocodile. It was the shooting that knocked her. Levi could have died. 'Fine. But I'm not leaving until I've had a good look.'

He glanced at her as he waited to be put through to the police. 'Think about yourself for a change.' She watched him organise Odette, call the police—where he learned Steve had been placed in custody—then break the news to the staff of Steve's involvement.

She should be dressing his wound, not watching him direct the world. 'Can't you do this later?'

He smiled down at her, and the way even that brief lift of his lips affected her heart was enough to warn her how bad it would be when he'd gone. 'What will you do when you don't have me to boss around?' he said.

Not what she wanted to dwell on. 'Be lonely, I guess.' She said it more to herself than to him and she didn't see his arrested expression. 'I'll find some first-aid gear.' She began to move off and he caught her hand. Like he had that night they first came here, only this time her hand seemed to tangle in his as her fingers clasped his back.

'Wait. Sophie.' He looked around and ushered her, not resisting for once, through the door and out onto the veranda and down the steps to the rustic bench under the massive boab.

He stared into her face and this time there was nowhere to hide. 'What did you mean? "Be lonely"?'

Could she do it? Throw it all away or be brave? The fear was there. The risk of pain greater than anything she'd experienced, but today's close shaves had taught her a valuable lesson. She had to take that risk. 'I'll be lonely without you.' She looked back at him. That strong jaw, that mouth—the man who'd stormed into her heart when she'd been kicking and screaming the whole way, and he'd achieved it so easily in such a short time. 'I must have become used to having you around. In a week.' She laughed mirthlessly at her foolishness.

It was too late to deny a recognition on a different level and that something in him called to her the way no other person did. She saw the trappings of wealth she'd said she despised and the bender of truth when she'd promised she'd never listen to another lie. But she'd also seen the man who completed her. Who instinctively knew when she needed support and gave unstintingly.

No one had ever understood her before. That was the crux. Levi got her. Knew where she was coming from almost before she did. 'Why is that?'

'Why is what?' he said, and she realised she must have asked out loud.

'Why do you seem to understand me when others don't?'

His voice softened. 'If you tried, you could understand me too.' When she looked into his eyes she saw him clearly, as if through a fresh pane of glass, unmarked by what had come in the past.

His caring, readiness to learn new things, listen to her point of view. His willingness to be there when the burden became too much, his hand there to pull her up and his arms to comfort. Maybe she did understand him in ways she'd never wanted to understand others. And finally, with tiny tentative steps, she allowed herself to glimpse what life with Levi could be like. If she allowed herself to trust him.

Was it that easy? 'Maybe I understand you a little.'

He slipped his good arm around her. 'Two people, from opposite ends of a huge country, meet and share extraordinary events. We've both changed, shared things—perhaps it's meant to be.'

She shook her head. It was all so confusing. 'How can it be meant when you live somewhere I could never live?'

He smiled. 'And vice versa.'

Hopeless case. She'd known it. 'See.'

'We will. In time.' He hugged her and stood to help her up. 'Come on. You need to rest after all this excitement. It's been a big day.' He touched her cheek. 'But we're not finished with this subject.'

Then she remembered. If she was going to be brave she may as well finish it. 'And there's something I have to tell you.'

He stopped. 'Really?' He searched her face, frowned and then slowly he smiled. 'Do I detect a hint of guilt?'

She blushed and he laughed. His eyes opened wide with amusement. 'Oh. I hope so. From Miss Trustworthy herself?' She didn't say anything and he pulled her back down on the seat.

She tried to stand again but he kept hold of her hand and she subsided. 'I'm not rushing this,' he said. 'This is priceless. Do go on.'

She ducked her chin, suddenly shy, then resolutely raised it. 'You know when you asked if I knew the original family from Xanadu?'

'Hmm.'

Why did it feel as if he were watching her face more than listening to her words. 'Pay attention. I'm feeling bad here.'

He squeezed her shoulders. 'Good. You look very cute when you're guilty.'

'I told you I didn't know—' she drew a deep breath '—but I do. I lied. It was my grandfather. Oh, and Smiley's grandfather. Our father's father.'

He laughed. 'You lied to me?'

She looked away. 'It was such a long story—I didn't want to talk about it then.' How dare he laugh at her.

'You lied.'

She glared. 'Not as many times as you did but there is a certain irony.'

'Brilliantly so.' He tilted his head and he wasn't smiling. 'But I don't think I can talk to you any more. I'm too hurt that you deceived me.'

She frowned, frozen for a moment in time that she'd offended him deeply, then realised he'd teased her. She glared at him. 'So under all that moody exterior you're a comedian?'

'Moody? Never. Work worn.' He kissed her. 'And you have to admit, you not telling the truth is hilariously funny.'

She glared at him again but he'd moved on musingly. 'So Sullivan was his name. Your grandfather? You and Smiley are the true owners of Xanadu?'

In another life. 'No.'

He tilted his head as he worked it out. 'But my grandfather cheated at cards and documented it. Was, in fact, very proud of scamming your grandfather out of his birthright.'

Her foolish grandfather had lost it though. 'Nice genes you have, Dr Pearson.'

He winked at her. 'I'm working on that.'

What was that supposed to mean? 'Anyway, whatever he wrote, it's not legal.'

'Another thing we'll discuss later.'

There was that money issue. She wished she could get over it. 'Are you very well off?'

He didn't smile but she could see the flicker of amusement at her prejudice. 'Afraid so. Stinking rich. Grandfather tripled the family coffers in his day and I've made some pretty useful investments too.'

'Oh.' He seemed so different to Brad. 'You still work hard to help others though. When financially you don't need to do anything?'

'I need to for me. I'm not proud of my father or grandfather. Never a thought to benefit their fellow man. When my brother died I vowed I'd make him proud of me. Do some good.'

She savoured the way he looked down at her. As if she'd lightened his day just by being there. No one had looked at her like that since her parents had died. 'You seem so different from when you came.'

'Am I? Then you've made me so. I've been beating myself up for the past two years and had forgotten how to smile. A certain determined young midwife has made me realise there is more to life than regretting what can't be changed.'

'What couldn't be changed?' She needed to know. Needed to see what had formed this man she'd grown to love. To try, if she could, to help him. 'What hurt you? Tell me.'

'The loss of one of my patients. I blamed myself.'

'She died in an operation?'

'No, Miss Impatient. She didn't die in an operation. None of my patients have died in their operations.'

'Sorr-ry.' He wrinkled his brow at her and she realised she'd been distracted by his rebuke. But he was still smiling at her. Then his smile departed and she could see the sadness.

'The day we confirmed there was nothing I could do to restore her sight she stepped in front of a truck.'

Sophie drew a sharp breath. Of course that would affect him. 'Like your brother. That was probably an accident too, you know,' she said earnestly. She saw the pain he still held and she squeezed his hand and her heart lifted when he squeezed back. She was glad to offer even that tiny comfort.

'It was no accident.' He went on. 'It hit home and I blamed myself.' He shrugged. 'Maybe there'd been something I could have tried. Should I have encouraged more strongly her hope for the future of technology?' He shook his head over a tragedy that could never be rectified. 'It's too late for her but I've doubled my workload. Tried to help more people until even my colleagues were telling me to take a break.'

She understood the concept of never doing enough. Had run herself ragged since returning to the Kimberleys but for a different reason. 'You can't help the whole world.'

'When my father died suddenly, things in his will puzzled me. I'd thought he hated me, but I regretted I'd never tried to sway him towards a more fulfilling life. Grown up enough to talk to him, perhaps?'

Sophie squeezed the hand holding hers. 'People die unexpectedly and we regret what we didn't say. We all do.'

'I know I do,' he said, and gave her a thank-you-for-understanding smile, and she felt her heart expand with his pain.

One thing she didn't understand. 'But your father died five months ago. Why so long before you came here?'

He shrugged. 'I had to clear the backlog of cases I'd promised. And wait for the wet season to finish.' His gaze brushed over her and the glow in his eyes when he did so made her blush. 'I wish I'd come earlier.'

Imagine that. She'd have been in Perth and missed knowing him. Even if he broke her heart now she could never regret that she met him. Had grown from knowing him in ways she'd never believe. 'Then lucky you didn't because I wouldn't have been here.'

He smiled down at her. 'Fate.'

'Serendipitous.' She snuggled under his arm, reluctant for this camaraderie to end. She'd learnt so much that helped her understand.

'Sophie.' He spoke into her hair.

She sighed. Soaking the moment in, in case it was the last time. 'What?'

'Look at me.'

He lifted his arm and she sat back and turned to face him. Her eyes met his and what she saw in them made the breath jam in her throat.

He lifted her hand and kissed her wrist. 'I see in you all the good things I wanted to find in myself. Things I find precious and uplifting and make me want to be a better man.'

She shook her head. She hadn't done anything.

Then he took both her hands in his and squeezed her fingers. 'I've come to know you—and love you.' Her breath caught in her throat but he went on. 'I can't imagine going home without you. I can't imagine anywhere without you.'

She searched his face, not believing his words, but unable to stop the sudden gallop in her chest. He couldn't love her.

She looked again and this time became a little less unconvinced as she saw the confirmation in his eyes. 'What are you saying?'

He smiled down at her. Like he really did love her? She hugged that impossible thought tightly as hope began to build. 'Will you marry me? Be my partner for life?' He lifted her hand to his mouth and kissed her palm, then folded her fingers over his salute. 'Can you love me back?'

She reached up and stroked his face. Those strong lines of cheek and jaw with the first regrowth of dark whiskers bristly beneath her fingers. How had she found him? Been so fortunate? Her eyes stung and she chewed her lip, suddenly too frightened to say the words out loud. She took a deep breath and then she did.

'I already love you. Too much. Apparently since the waterhole on our trek. The moment you reached down to lift me. And then you kissed me and nothing was the same again.' She remembered the instant. 'I was so frightened you'd hurt me again I wasn't game to let the feeling out. And now you've exposed me.' Her eyes filled with happy tears. 'So, yes, please. I'll be your wife.'

Levi looked down at her. 'So you'll keep me on the straight and narrow?' He gestured to the gorge below them. 'Even away from your beloved Kimberleys?'

She shrugged. Suddenly home wasn't home if Levi wasn't there. 'We can visit.'

Levi barely dared to believe he wasn't going to lose her. Sophie's beautiful face turned up at him, so sincere and open and honest and shining with love. How had he been this blessed? His throat tightened and he pulled her close and held her against his heart as the world receded. His Sophie. His heart. His love. The other stuff they'd work out.

CHAPTER TWELVE

Sophie gazed around at the guests at their wedding, an unlikely mix of smiling faces, as the setting sun dusted the rugged ranges in the distance a glowing and loving lilac. Loving like the vows she and Levi had exchanged above the stunning gorge at Xanadu and glowing like the look in her new husband's eyes.

She smiled at her friends—the sun-frocked women, and their sun-browned men in best Akubras and polished boots—and Levi's friends in the sprinkling of suits and designer dresses, and the way the two groups melded with much gaiety under the leafless branches of the giant boab.

A tree that had grown more bulbous over the thousand years it had stood under a blue Kimberley sky and watched each turn of fortune this grand old homestead had seen since it had been built by her great-grandfather and lost for two generations. Now her and Levi's children, and maybe Smiley and Odette's children, would visit, and one day those growing children would learn to love their heritage.

The cries of sulphur-crested cockatoos filled the late-afternoon air and she lifted her head to allow the noise to soak into her memory as she inhaled the delicate aroma of the frangipani called Kimberley Gold in her bouquet. The heady scent enveloped the wedding party better than any designer fragrance yet to be fashioned by man.

She'd be fine in the city. Beside her stood Levi, her husband, so tall and straight and gazing down at her with such a look of pride and love in his dark blue eyes the tears pricked behind the mascara that Odette had insisted she wear, and she had to force her fingers not to rub her eyes.

He must have seen the glitter she tried to hide because his thumb gently rubbed her palm in comfort. Already he knew what she was thinking, and magically the tears receded as his fingers entwined through hers. He looked down at the impressive pink Kimberley diamond ring they'd chosen from the mine and she tutted as she followed his gaze. 'You have too much money.'

He smiled. 'Would you like me to give it all away?' The words were spoken lightly but the look in his eyes assured her he was deadly serious, and her heart thumped at the lengths this man would go to make her happy.

She blinked back more tears, refusing to weep even tears of joy on her wedding day. 'I could help you.' She smiled up at him. 'There's lots of things I'd like to improve around here.' *Even if I'm not here to see them*, she thought, with barely any regret.

He hugged her to him. 'I can see I've taken on an expensive wife.' She felt his arm around her, so strong and sure of their love, and the truth was there to see. This was home. In Levi's arms. Not Xanadu, not busy Sydney, or wherever his work took him—-anywhere was home as long as she had Levi by her side.

The small plane—Levi had declined the helicopter with a smiling glance at his new wife—flew out the next morning, and with his hand in hers Sophie watched the brown earth pass beneath her with no regrets. The timeless mountains and steep-sided gorges would be there for ever. Xanadu would stand watch over the land until she returned.

Now she could look to the future and new adventures with the man she trusted with all her heart.

That night in Sydney they dined at an exclusive restaurant overlooking Sydney Harbour and Sophie could see why Levi loved it.

'This used to be my favourite place to eat,' Levi said as he gazed around at the panoramic harbour views and then back at his wife. Then he looked down at his plate and somehow she knew he was thinking of their bush-tucker walk through the hot bush. 'You've broadened my palate.'

'Do they serve grubs here?' she teased, and stretched her hand out across the fine white tablecloth to his. A frisson of magic passed between them and curved her lips in that persistent secret smile she'd had since last night. How could she not have known what had awaited her in Levi's arms? Yet what could have prepared her for the experience Levi had created as he'd shown her the meaning of giving and taking in all that love had to offer. Still her skin tingled and quivered as even a fleeting touch like this brought back memories and sensations she'd never imagined, and their rings glinted as their fingers entwined.

His eyes smouldered and she felt her belly kick. 'You're blushing, my wife,' he teased.

Sophie fanned herself. 'Must be the food.'

'Strange, how the food is the last thing I'm thinking of. For you I would even eat a witchetty grub.'

Thank goodness this restaurant was discreet but she needed to change the subject before her wicked husband said something even more outrageous. Sophie poked at the delicacies he'd ordered for her. 'I won't ask you if you don't make me eat that oyster.'

He laughed and took the morsel from her plate. 'I've something better for you.' She frowned as he reached into the pocket of his suit and withdrew a long white envelope.

Thick and embossed, he placed it in her hand with such an air of expectation she frowned.

'To my darling wife with love.' For a fleeting moment the weight of the paper sent an echo of mistrust and dread left from her dealings with Brad, but she banished it easily with her unswerving knowledge of Levi's love. Now what had he thought up?

She frowned down at the envelope and then back at him. 'What's this?' She weighed it in her hand and the thickness of paper folded had her intrigued.

'Open it.'

She tried, but it was sealed and stubborn, and Levi smiled as he handed her a knife to slit the edge. She glanced across at him. Whatever it was, he was enjoying this. Finally the envelope opened and she eased the thick wad of paper out and unfolded it.

It couldn't be! Her eyes widened as she moistened suddenly dry lips.

'A million acres?' She looked at him again and his blue eyes danced with amusement and love. 'You can't give me a million acres for a wedding present.'

He sat back to enjoy the view more. 'Why not?'

'It's too much.' She looked up at him. Not sure how he'd take the next thought. 'I'd want to give Smiley half.'

He grinned. Well pleased with himself. 'I thought you'd say that, but he's agreed to be bought out.'

She frowned. 'Xanadu needs managing. We're living in Sydney.'

He raised his brows. 'Perhaps we should only live in Sydney six months of the year.'

He was enjoying this. Stringing her along. But she couldn't help the excitement that grew with each tumbled thought. 'And where will we be the rest of the time?'

'Guess.' He lifted her hand and ran his fingers along

the soft skin before he gently, and so reverently that her face flamed, kissed her wrist. 'Let's spend that money you said I should give away.'

'By buying out Smiley?'

He shook his head and kissed her again and she watched the gooseflesh rise on her arms. She wished he wouldn't do that now because concentration was hard and she wanted to understand.

'By buying an outback eye clinic. The Sophie Pearson Mobile Eye Clinic, in fact.' He smiled. 'You'll be pleased to know it's made quite a dent in our wealth.'

She shook her head, overwhelmed by his vision, but he hadn't finished. 'I thought, if you agree, we'd travel north and visit out-flung camps and missions during the dry, from May till October, and work together.'

She saw the passion in his eyes. The chance to do good work. She felt the tears well at her own fortune in finding a man she could be so proud of.

She tilted her head and she'd bet there was the same excitement shining from her own eyes that she could see in his. 'Of course, we'll need a base to work from and Xanadu fits the bill perfectly.'

She struggled to hold back her tears as she tried to take in the vision he'd created. 'Funny that.'

'And should you become otherwise engaged—' he glanced wickedly down at her narrow waist '—I can hire an assistant while you wait at home with our family, at Xanadu.'

He'd done this for her. 'You've thought of everything.'

His eyes darkened and she blushed right down to her toes and in all the places he'd discovered last night. 'And if we have children they will grow to love both homes.'

The warmth he created just by looking at her expanded until she could feel herself glow. 'You really have thought of everything.'

'I just follow the rule.' He leaned across and kissed her lips. 'Always tell the truth. And the truth is, I will love my darling wife for ever and ever.'

"If someone tells me I can't do something, it only makes me want to do it twice as much," April said.

Ryan helped her steady her vintage Schwinn. "Very rebellious of you," he said. "Very tough."

She squinted upward, trying to gauge if he was making fun of her "toughness." In the sunlight, it was hard to tell. But she could tell one thing, all right . . . that wonderfully sure and steady voice of his definitely *sounded* sincere.

"Tough? Some people might think so," April said, semi-defensively. She straddled her bike, and busied herself with slinging her purse over her shoulder and across her chest, where it would be secure during her ride.

"Hmmm," Ryan murmured, unrevealingly.

He stepped nearer, and for some reason, all her senses went on red alert. Cautiously tightening her grasp on her handlebars, she glanced up at him.

He was watching her with a rapt expression, almost as though he really *had* never met anyone like her . . . and was thoroughly fascinated by the experience.

"The thing is," Ryan said, "that you don't strike me as the tough type, exactly."

"I don't?"

"No. You strike me more as the feisty on the outside, sweet on the inside, make-your-move-before-she-gets-away type."

Carefully, he leaned closer. April caught her breath, her heart suddenly skipping along double-time. Their lips met. Once. Twice. And a thrill sizzled down her spine . . .

Books by Lisa Plumley

MAKING OVER MIKE

FALLING FOR APRIL

Published by Zebra Books

FALLING
FOR APRIL

Lisa Plumley

ZEBRA BOOKS
KENSINGTON PUBLISHING CORP.

http://www.kensingtonbooks.com

To my three favorite people:
John, Kyle, and Ian
for loving, listening, and
laughing in all the right places.
Thanks.

Chapter One

Standing in the vestibule of San Diego's Oceanside Presbyterian church, Ryan Forrester awaited his cue to walk down the aisle. The organist was tuning up, and according to the clipboard-wielding wedding planner he'd hired, they'd be ready for him soon.

At the thought of what was to come, a fresh attack of nerves struck him. To overcome it, Ryan adjusted the cuffs of his perfectly tailored, custom Armani tuxedo and concentrated on his surroundings. His very tasteful, very well-coordinated, very ... flowery surroundings.

He glanced at the mounds of blossoms—orchids, roses, gawky sunflowers—crowding the vestibule, a testament to his fiancée's last-minute indecision. They made it a veritable allergy commercial set in here, their mingled scents overpoweringly sweet. Striding to the window, Ryan opened it to admit the seaside breeze.

The salty tang that swept inside felt weirdly liberating.

He rolled his shoulders, listening to the hum of voices beyond the closed door of the room. Rows of family and friends had gathered there, waiting for the wedding to begin. Just over three hundred of them had been invited—and even that had been a mere drop in the bucket of his socialite mother's socialite social circle.

After all, as Mimi Forrester had so often reminded her son during the past whirlwind month, the wedding of a Forrester—even the *rushed* wedding of a Forrester— was big news in San Diego. It wouldn't do to do it halfway.

"The organ music stopped," Jackson Hart said. "Sounds like your trap must be nearly set."

With a wolfish grin that suited his shaggy post-prep-school looks, Ryan's groomsman glanced up from the game of solitaire he'd been playing atop a box of hymnals. He unscrewed his pocket flask, slugged back some of the mixed martini he kept inside, and wiped his mouth on the sleeve of his black tuxedo jacket.

"You ready?" he asked.

Ryan nodded, ignoring the flash of unease that whipped through him as he did. Wedding jitters. Every groom probably experienced them. More than likely, they were nothing to worry about. And in any case, he wasn't a worrying kind of man.

"I was born ready," he told Jackson.

And he had been. Nearly. As the last in a long line of successful and celebrated Forresters, Ryan had been born with the proverbial silver spoon in his mouth. In the thirty-two privileged years since then, he'd removed it mostly in honor of throwing parties, attending parties, and, on one nerve-shattering day, proposing marriage— really just another big party, right? Which was what had brought him here, to—

A flash of white outside the window caught his eye. *Wedding dresses were white,* he thought instantly. So were wedding dresses worn by runaway brides. Could it be . . . ?

Nah. Frowning over his suddenly overdeveloped imagination—after all, why would his bride run out on him?—Ryan buffed clean the face of his Rolex and squared his shoulders.

"Sucker," Jackson muttered, returning to his game.

"Nice talk, for a groomsman." Ryan glanced out the window again, at the grassy bluff the church was settled on. In the distance, the Pacific Ocean sparkled in the late-April sunlight. He squinted, unable to resist searching amid the twisted Torrey pines for another flash of white. *"That's* why you're not best man. You'd jinx the whole damned thing."

Jackson grunted. "You'll find out. Just like the rest of us trust-fund fellas. You get fleeced once, and you're careful forever. Believe me. Women can't be trusted. Particularly around guys like us."

Ryan didn't want to believe that. "Some women can be trusted," he said. "Like the woman I'm marrying."

He smiled as the old-fashioned horse-drawn carriage he'd hired to drive him and his bride to the reception came into view outside, festooned with ribbons and bows and still more flowers. The horses' clop-clopping hooves were a steady counterpoint to the organ music that began playing again outside the vestibule. This time, the song carried a note of expectancy. Hearing it, Ryan felt a new rush of optimism.

"You know, all I've ever wanted," he said, "is a woman who will always smile when I walk into the room. Not one of those phony smiles, either, but a really big—"

"Try flashing your wallet. That ought to do the trick."

Jackson grinned. Ryan ignored him.

"A really big, really genuine smile," he went on semi-wistfully, suddenly needing to be understood. Especially on this important day. "A woman who will remember exactly what I like for breakfast every day—"

"Her. Rrrruff!"

Ryan took away his friend's martini flask and set it beside an arrangement of peonies, safely out of reach until after the ceremony. Walking back to the window, he continued, "—and who will drop whatever she's doing, no matter what it is, when I want to kiss her."

"Now you're talking!"

"Look, I'm not asking for the moon, here. I want what everybody wants," Ryan finished with a shrug. "True love."

"Awww, stop!" Making a sappy face, Jackson clutched his chest. The ace of hearts and several more playing cards poked from beneath his spread fingers. "You're breaking me up, here. I think I'm going to cry."

Ryan grinned. "Save it for the wedding, hankie-boy. There won't be a dry eye in the house."

"Hmmm. Maybe not. Not if you've *really* found what you're looking for."

Jackson went back to his cards, frowning in pretend concentration. In reality, he pretty much saved his attention for good times, beautiful women, and fast cars. He and Ryan had always been alike in that way—or at least, they had been, until Ryan's rushed engagement two months ago.

"And especially not"—Jackson laid out an ace of clubs, and gave a pretend sniffle—"if you don't give me my martini back."

"Har, har."

Feeling the time draw near, Ryan checked his tux in the mirror. Ran a hand through his freshly cut, straight blond hair. Mentally reviewed the painstakingly detailed and shockingly expensive nuptial arrangements he'd made. And hoped like hell it would all be worth it in the end.

Jackson was wrong. True love wasn't dead. And Ryan

wouldn't be fleeced. He wouldn't be taken advantage of by a gold-digging socialite wannabe, the way so many of his friends and acquaintances had been. Especially not with every last person he knew there to witness it.

The vestibule door opened, and the wedding planner called out a greeting. At the sound, Ryan turned away from the window . . . and saw a sudden look of absolute horror pass over his groomsman's face. What the hell?

"Looks like you forgot one thing on that lovey-dovey wish list of yours," Jackson said slowly, staring out the open window. He nodded toward it, just over Ryan's shoulder. "Clueing in your bride-to-be."

"Huh?"

"Look for yourself. Ah, man. I'm sorry."

Dread trickled into the spaces that had been so filled with optimism moments before. At Jackson's finger-whirling-in-the-air prompting, Ryan turned.

Glimpsing movement in the churchyard, he walked closer to the window. It felt as though he were moving in slow motion. Sea breeze ruffled his immaculate groom-worthy suit, and blew a hank of hair into his eyes. Brushing it impatiently away, he squinted outside.

And then he saw it.

Or, more accurately, saw *them*. His fiancée, with her long white wedding dress hiked up in one perfectly manicured hand. One of his groomsmen—a hotshot lawyer from his father's firm, who'd recently struck gold writing legal thrillers on the side, à la Grisham, and, according to Mimi, simply *had* to be included in the wedding party to ensure appropriate coverage in the society papers. And with them, a gray-haired man whom Ryan only vaguely recognized.

The wedding planner used her clipboard to wedge her way beside him. She pressed her fingers to the glass above their heads.

"They've kidnapped my minister!" she cried.

Ah-ha, Ryan thought numbly. So that's who that was.

As he watched, the trio alighted the carriage, helped in the task by the driver Ryan had paid for—and had tipped in advance, in case his marital happiness had made him overlook such ordinary concerns as good service bonuses.

Sucker, rolled through his mind.

He shoved the window higher. It thunked against the frame, the glass within shuddering beneath the impact. Driven by some force he didn't understand, Ryan propped his hands on the ledge and stuck his head outside.

He shouted his fiancée's name.

She looked up, the wind making her veil flutter around her face and blonde hair in a merry fashion. She recognized him, and had the audacity to smile.

Ryan felt sucker-punched. He opened his mouth but couldn't seem to make anything emerge, aside from a strangled repetition of her name.

Her name, the initials of which had been painstakingly and expensively embroidered along with his own on everything from silver soupspoons to three-hundred-thread-count sheet sets to custom Crane stationery . . . all things Ryan had imagined would last them for the rest of their happy lives together.

As the fake Grisham looked on lovingly, his runaway bride glanced down, fiddling with something. Her engagement ring, Ryan saw when she'd wrenched it loose. The showy, two-carat square-cut diamond that embellished it sparkled gaily in her hand. Was she planning to hurl it back to him, or . . . ?

She dropped it into her tiny white satin bag, and snapped shut the fastening with evident satisfaction. Then she grabbed something else from near her feet, and hurled it from the carriage.

Beside him, the wedding planner shrieked. "Her shoes!" she wailed as the things landed on the grass beside the carriage. "How *dare* she? I crawled on my hands and knees through dozens of designer showrooms to find those Jimmy Choo shoes for her!"

Sympathetically, Ryan patted the wedding planner on the shoulder of her tailored blush-pink suit. Within seconds, he felt slightly less compassionate, though— the woman's screech had brought guests running from within the church proper, and his friends and family crowded up beside and behind him, craning their necks to get a view of what was happening.

Outside, his ex-fiancée didn't notice. Or didn't care. Instead, she snuggled up to her new catch—*sucker,* rolled again through Ryan's mind—said something to the driver, and waved good-bye.

The last thing Ryan saw of her was her bridal veil, which she snatched hastily from her head as though she couldn't wait to be free of it. *Free of him.* Four feet of handmade Brussels lace sailed through the air, tumbled in the ocean breeze . . . and landed atop his white BMW roadster, parked outside the church.

So that was that, then.

"Baaaa," Jackson bleated to no one in particular. "Fleeced."

April Finnegan was doomed.

She wasn't sure how it had happened, or how long it would last. Or even if there was a cure at all. But from the minute she'd opened her door to find her outrageously cheerful, good-for-nothing older brother standing on the doorstep of her sunny Saguaro Vista, Arizona, apartment—only hours after she'd been deserted by her just-married former roommate—April *had* been sure it was true.

Doomed, doomed, doomed. She was doomed like a shoe shopper with unlimited store credit, like a chocoholic in a room full of Cadbury Easter bunnies. Like a woman with prickly unshaven legs, cozying up to a hunk after a great, great date. And since bad things always came in threes—and April had experienced only the first two so far—she was waiting with *un*bated breath for the big *numero tres* to drop on her at any instant.

Oh, she'd survive Mickey Finnegan's untimely couch-crashing, April figured. For at least as long as it lasted, until he took off for parts unknown again like the flighty Finnegan he was. She certainly had before.

And it wasn't so much her ex-roommate Paige's leaving that bothered her, as the fact that now she was stuck with twice the rent, one hundred percent less camaraderie, and a lonely, nearsighted cat to console. But still . . . for a person who prided herself on unpredictability—and April did—there was nevertheless such a thing as *too* much uncertainty.

What, she wondered, would the big, fat, other-shoe-dropping-type disaster *be*? And when would it strike?

To distract herself from the question, she retreated to her usual retreat.

Work.

Because where other people found their salvation in bibles, bottles, network television, and other things that required a minimum of thinking and a maximum of letting outside forces decide things *for* them, April found hers in butter, flour, sugar, and eggs, and a recipe complicated enough to demand the best performance from her *and* all her ingredients. For the one thing April excelled at—aside from making friends, hitting a wicked grounder, and scouring the flea market for bargains—

was baking. It was her job, her calling. With any luck, it would also be her means *out* of the shiftless Finnegan trap she'd been born into.

So at dawn on the morning after the day of the *doomed* revelation, she dove headfirst into measuring, stirring, and shaping. Alone in the expansive professional kitchen of Ambrosia, small-town Saguaro Vista's most exclusive—and only—gourmet catering company and bakery, April stacked profiteroles on petit fours, muffins on macaroons. She sprinkled streusel and cut out cookies. And by the time she was dusted in flour from her long auburn curls to the tips of her vintage shoes, she was three quarters of the way to feeling like herself again.

With a sigh of satisfaction, she boosted herself onto the just-cleaned worktable and sat with her bare legs dangling. All around her, the stainless steel ovens threw off heat, the heavy-duty upright mixers hulked at the ready, and the marble pastry counter gleamed in the early morning sunlight. From this vantage point, April felt like a gawky nine-year-old, all elbows and knees and sweet-tooth smiles. And she liked it. It was sure as hell preferable to feeling doomed.

Mission accomplished.

She lifted her mug of mint tea and fished out the tea bag, setting it aside to save for her second cup, as was her habit. She swigged. The zingy scent of peppermint reached her moments before she tasted the tea, and she swallowed with a sensualist's appreciation of both.

"Oh, wow!" Jamie Barrett said beside her, her mouth filled with a bite of *pain au chocolat*—chocolate-filled croissant.

Her friend had arrived between the orange poppy seed scones and the miniature carrot cakes, and had been sampling ever since. Already dressed in the black pants and white shirt she'd wear during her shift at the beauty salon next door, Jamie chewed and swallowed with a blissful expression.

"I swear," she said, using her nimble hairstylist's fingers to tear off another bite, "you just keep getting better and better. This is incredible!"

April grinned. "Almost orgasmic, isn't it?"

Jamie coughed, slapping herself on the chest. *"What?"*

"You heard me." April's grin widened. Maybe she couldn't control her upbringing, her past, her wayward brother, her roommate's desertion due to "true love," *or* the dreaded third-disaster-to-come, but she could still get a rise out of her longtime pal. "Almost orgasmic. Really delicious."

"Oh, baby, baby," Jamie deadpanned, blowing a kiss to the croissant. "Don't stop!"

Laughing, April slid from the worktable and removed the roomy bib-style apron that covered her vintage fifties-style, yellow shirtwaist dress and the silver link belt she'd slung loosely at her hips. Then she went to wash up at the sink. There, she noticed a dollop of carrot cake batter on her comfy black and white saddle shoes, and wet a paper towel to clean it.

"At the rate my luck's running," she said as she bent over and began scrubbing, "those croissants are as close to 'yes, baby, don't stop!' as I'm going to get for a while. Unfortunately for me, pastries don't offer up good pillow talk afterward."

She paused, still bent over her shoe to adjust the cuff on her bobby socks. "I mean, what would that be like, anyway? Oooh, baby," April mimicked. "I loved the way you took off my *wrapper*. I crumbled at your touch?"

Jamie laughed. "Glaze me. Frost me. Roll me in sugar," she suggested. "I'm all yours!"

"*S'il vous plaît*, come on," April pleaded, gesturing with one outflung hand as she spoke in her best bawdy-pastry voice—a French-inspired baritone she imagined might suit a chocolate-filled croissant. "Your hip circumference be damned! We must be togezer again, cherie. Soon!"

"See, now?" asked a familiar masculine voice behind her. "If you'd let someone make an honest woman of you, you wouldn't have to worry about things like dirty-talking desserts."

Straightening, April flipped her low-slung ponytail over her shoulder and grinned up at her boss, Mark Wright, who'd just entered the kitchen carrying a box of supplies and a clipboard. He was wearing a slightly disapproving—if good-natured—expression, and as he set down his box, she noticed his neatly pressed khakis, button-down shirt, and ever-present necktie, too.

Although he was only a few years older than her and Jamie, his "Leave It To Beaver" outlook on life needed serious work. *Really*, she thought. *Who said* make an honest woman of you *anymore?*

Still, she liked Mark. And so long as he hadn't progressed to wearing cardigan sweaters and smoking a pipe in Golden Age of TV sitcom–husband style, she figured he was reformable.

"You're right," April agreed. She wadded up the wet paper towel and scored three points tossing it into the farthest wastebasket. "Then I'd trade up to a whole new batch of worries. Is he really the one for me? Am I really the one for him? Are we really the ones for each other, or are we kidding ourselves?" She made a face. "Who can tell with this stuff, anyway? I say, no, thanks."

"It's not all that tough," Jamie disagreed. "People find true love every day, you know."

"Hmmph. You're just indoctrinated to think so."

April eyed the ever-present stack of bridal magazines at Jamie's elbow, and raised her eyebrows meaningfully. "In the non-glossy, non-monthly, non-one-thousand-and-one-hot-honeymoon-spots world, true love is hard to find."

"I don't buy it," Mark said, shaking his head. The gesture made his neatly combed Ken-doll hair shine in the halogen lighting. "I sell tenth, twenty-fifth, even fiftieth anniversary party cakes every week. People are still finding true love, still getting married, and still living happily ever after. It could happen to you, too."

April snorted. "Look, I hate to be the cynic in this pie-in-the-sky crowd, but I can't even find a man who will call before Thursday for a Friday night date, much less one who's able to mention the 'M' word without breaking out in hives. Sorry, you two, but chivalry is dead, romance is dead, and I'm afraid true love is dead, too. People are just too selfish these days."

"Selfish?" Mark said, looking affronted.

"Dead?" Jamie cried, looking wounded.

"Just one girl's opinion," April told them, holding up her palms. "Don't shoot the messenger." She shrugged, then went to the box of supplies Mark had carried in and flipped open the cardboard flaps on top. In addition to baking for Ambrosia, she'd been lobbying Mark for a self-created position as community relations manager, and was trying to involve herself in all aspects of the company in preparation for it.

Any day now, April was sure, Mark would cave. She would get the community relations position—and the job security that was bound to follow, soon after. *Then* she'd have a shot at living happily ever after . . . and it would be a happily ever after she could really get behind, too. One earned through hard work, not serendipity. One found through ingenuity and creativity, not via blind faith and hoping. Because what April Finnegan believed in—aside from doing all she could to escape her flighty Finnegan destiny—was making the absolute most of what she'd been given.

Including the hot pink, impossibly curvy glasses she'd just uncovered beneath the packing material.

Carefully lifting one from its foam peanut nest, April held it toward Mark. She raised her eyebrow.

"Special-ordered from Phoenix for the Shaeffer-Nieman wedding," he explained. "They want to serve frozen luv-o-ritas at the reception."

"Ah. That explains it."

As the person who was in charge of catering the bride's upcoming bachelorette party, April was more than familiar with the engaged couple—and their "unique" ideas. She looked at the profiled likenesses of the soon-to-be Shaeffer-Niemans etched in turquoise on the hot pink glass. Multicolored hearts bounced from their images, trimmed somehow in glitter.

"These," she announced sadly, "are in incredibly poor taste."

"Poor taste?" Jamie scoffed. "This, from the woman whose favorite chair was salvaged from the not-a-chance pile at an estate sale in Scottsdale?"

"Hey." April raised her chin. "I can't help it if they didn't see that vintage barcolounger's value. All it needed was a little stuffing and a good cleaning."

"And a ritualized burning," Jamie muttered.

"Har, har," April said, making a face.

"Is this the same woman," Mark asked, taking the glass from her and grimacing slightly as he replaced it in the box, "whose headboard is an old wagon wheel from the side of the road someplace?"

"Someplace *historically significant*," April informed them. Sheesh. Was there something *wrong* with being frugal? "Besides, I had permission from the historical site, and it looked great once I'd finished painting it."

"Once you'd finished—" Jamie stopped abruptly and gawked at Mark. "How'd *you* wind up in her bedroom looking at her headboard, anyway?"

He blushed. Actually blushed. "Ahh—"

April leaped into the fray. "It was that night of hot, steamy, passionate passion we shared, wasn't it, Mark?" she asked, grinning, glad to be out from under the gun herself. She winked and put her arm around his shoulders, urging his self-consciously inflexible body closer.

"When was that?" she asked chummily, looking up at him. "Last Tuesday? Or was it Wednesday? I'm not sure, because I had fettuccine Alfredo at Morenci's one of those nights, and I'm positive I wouldn't have subjected my wild secret lover to a garlic extravaganza. So—"

"I saw it when I helped her move in with Paige," Mark interrupted, ducking away from her arm and shielding himself with his clipboard. He gave both her and Jamie an exasperated look. "It was all perfectly innocent. The headboard wasn't even attached to the bed at the time."

"Kinky," Jamie said.

"It wasn't kinky! It was *relocating.*"

"Awww," April pouted. "Call it what you like, dreamboat. But you're ruining my reputation, here." She tweaked his cheek affectionately. "If you keep that up, I might never find that so-called true love you two keep yammering on about."

As if she was going to, anyway.

Suddenly, Jamie and Mark exchanged a look. A very meaningful, very mysterious, very lightbulb-over-the-head look. A look that made April nervous—the same way a checkbook in her infamously spendthrift, check-bouncing mother's hands made her nervous. In fact, if she hadn't known better, she'd have thought her best friend and her boss were about to hatch a scheme that would make her very, very sorry.

But all they did was share that look. And then turn to her.

"If you found it, how would you know it was true love? Or if it wasn't?" Jamie asked. "Just for argument's sake, of course."

"Uh, well, uh . . ." Noticing Mark's intent—and suspicious—interest, April was stuck for an answer at first. Not because she had the hots for Mark, despite her teasing earlier, but because she was suddenly afraid that Mark—when he was wearing that expression, at least—would settle for nothing less than the absolute truth. The very idea scared her.

So she prevaricated. "I guess I would just know. I guess."

"Mmmm-hmmmm."

"I would!"

"Right."

"Okay." Driven to a slightly more thorough answer by their combined doggedness, April relented. "I guess . . . I would know it wasn't true love if he didn't take me seriously."

"Good, good." Jamie made flapping motions with her hands, urging her onward. She glanced at Mark. "What else?"

"Well, he'd have to get along with Calypso," April went on, mentioning her non-pedigree, slightly neurotic, red and white tabby cat—which was probably sleeping, right this minute, atop her shiftless brother Mickey's feet. "Otherwise, if he couldn't even nurture a cat, I'd be too scared to have kids with him. Someday, that is."

Mark brightened. "Kids? That's encouraging."

April let that pass. "And he'd have to have a sense of humor about things, you know? Like if I came home all floury from baking, he wouldn't freak out and whip out the Dustbuster."

"Like Reggie," she and Jamie said in unison.

Like all of April's former boyfriends—and Jamie's, too—Reggie had been discussed, ad nauseam, over many too many bottles of Bud. Ladies' Night at the Saguaro Vista bowling alley kept them supplied with both feminine solidarity and two-for-one drinks.

They laughed. Feeling introspective now, April went on, "And he'd have to want to pursue me, too. To woo me." The old-fashioned word was utterly unlike her, but it fit, somehow. "I mean, a bouquet of flowers isn't totally out of the question, once in a while."

Jamie nodded, frowning thoughtfully.

So did Mark. Equally thoughtfully.

Shrugging off their combined ... thoughtfulness, April let her imagination take flight. She was picking up steam now.

"He'd hold my hand when we walked," she said. "Whisper endearments in my ear in a crowded room. He'd take me in his arms and kiss me, even in the middle of a rainstorm." She'd always thought rain was romantic. "And he'd—"

"Rainstorm?" Jamie asked. Her hands flew to her carefully coiffed, close-cropped dark hair. "No way."

"Uh-uh," Mark echoed, shaking his head. His gaze slipped to his brown suede loafers. "No way."

April looked at them both, surprised. She threw up her hands. "See? Even you two die-hard romantics aren't buying this. I should've known this 'true love' thing was doomed. Real life just doesn't make room for romance."

But somehow, she realized now, she wished it did. Having pulled out her ideas of a wonderfully romantic hunk-turned-soul mate, April found she was reluctant to tuck them away again. Wistfully, she looked toward the Shaeffer-Nieman wedding glasses, and stroked the protruding rim of the one Mark had begun putting away. Was it possible?

Nah, she decided. The day true love entered her life was the day the Finnegan clan paid their bills on time, bounced not a single check, kept steady jobs, and had simultaneously functioning cars to drive. In short, it was a day that would never come.

"You might be surprised someday," Mark said, shaking his head as he picked up his box and headed for his office.

"You just never know," Jamie agreed, hefting her bridal magazines for the trek to the salon next door. "Keep your mind open, April."

"Oh, I will," April said cheerfully, following her friend to the front of the bakery with a tray of scones for the glass display case. "I will."

The door swooshed shut behind Jamie, leaving April alone.

"I will," she said to the silence. She leaned an elbow on the countertop and propped her chin in her hand. "I'll keep my mind open . . . and my heart untouched."

Because even if she found someone to love, he'd have quite a hurdle to jump in accepting the bunch of misfit Finnegans who were her family . . . who were what *she'd* likely turn out to be, in the end. After all, biology was destiny, wasn't it? She'd heard that someplace. And although she struggled mightily against it, April figured it could catch up with her at any moment. Just like *that.*

Just like the *numero tres* disaster, too. Because just as she turned away from the counter to fetch more baked goods, April heard a bellow come from the direction of Mark's office. It was followed swiftly by a crash, a swear word, and a loud, no-nonsense summons from her boss.

If this was Mark's reaction to seeing what she thought he was seeing . . . well, it looked like the other shoe had finally dropped.

Chapter Two

The headquarters of Forrester's Department Stores, Inc., located in a sleek downtown San Diego high-rise, shared many things with its business-minded neighbors. Early-eighties architecture. Dozens of bustling employees hurrying from floor to floor. A general air of purpose.

Fort Knox–style security.

It was this last which, unexpectedly, put a crimp in Ryan Forrester's newfound desire to put the "family" back into the family business. Because no sooner had he approached the inner sanctum of the top floor of Forrester's offices, than he found himself surrounded by burly types in security uniforms.

"Excuse me, sir," one of the guards said, grabbing his arm. "Visitors aren't allowed in this area."

They hustled Ryan back into the elevator, crowding him shoulder to shoulder like a linebacker-and-executive sandwich. He couldn't move an inch without coming up against their immovable blue-polyester-covered force.

Since he wasn't exactly a tiny guy—at six foot one, Ryan figured he passed for decently burly himself—this was fairly impressive.

Still . . . "I'm not a visitor!" he protested.

This was technically true, seeing as how Ryan hadn't actually visited the family business in years. Not since the requisite post-collegiate visit to see his official Vice President in Charge of Somethingorother corner office, which he'd pronounced "very nice" and had promptly forgotten about in favor of more interesting things, like travel, women, parties, women, and travel.

"I'm a vice president!" he added.

"Sure, buddy." Another of the Rambo-types pushed the lobby button on the elevator, and they began their descent downward. "Vice president in charge of what?"

"Uh . . ." Damn it! Why hadn't he paid closer attention to his official title? He could almost picture the brass nameplate on the door, engraved . . . engraved with . . . oh, hell. He'd been in the throes of a champagne-induced hangover at the time, Ryan recalled suddenly, and now his memories of that day were a little, uh, blurry.

Thinking he'd just call his board-member father and ask, Ryan reached into the pocket of the lightweight jacket he'd tossed on over his casual knit shirt, khaki pants, and loafers.

"He's armed!" yelled one of the security goons.

Moments later, Ryan was smashed up against the elevator wall, rapidly developing grid marks on his cheek. One security guy frisked him. The other elbowed the elevator's stop button, jamming them between floors. The third wedged his forearm into Ryan's upper back— in case he "made a break for it," Ryan presumed— while he radioed for possible backup.

All this, Ryan thought, just because he'd decided to cure his jilted-guy's broken heart by immersing himself in the hundred-year-old family department store business. What next?

After a brief scuffle, the frisky security guy stepped back. He held up something in his meaty fist. "All clear. It's just a phone."

All three of them sagged. Visibly. Giving Ryan the unmistakable impression that this job wasn't, well, ultimately fulfilling for them. Collaring him was probably the most excitement they'd had all week—which might explain the eager way they'd pounced on him as he'd approached the Forrester's offices.

Thick-necked guard number three resignedly pushed the elevator button again, taking Ryan farther and farther from his goal for the day. As they descended, the guards glared at him, scowling, with jointly accusing looks.

"Hey, sorry to disappoint you guys." Ryan retrieved his cell phone, and knew he should resist the urge to say what came next. Predictably, he couldn't. "That crazy 'Q.'" Giving a mock chuckle, he shook his head. "He *told* me everyone would mistake this for an ordinary phone, but I didn't believe him."

He leaned forward and confided in a low voice, "We top-secret, international spy types tend to have problems with that. Trust issues, I guess."

Ryan twirled the phone in his hand, gunfighter style, and grinned as it came to a stop in his palm. He pushed a button, and the antenna snapped up.

The security guys leaped to attention. At the same time, the elevator surged to a stop, its doors sliding open with a cheery *ding*.

Thirty seconds later, Ryan landed butt-first on the downtown San Diego sidewalk. The security goons brushed off their hands, adjusted their walkie-talkie belts, and swaggered away into the building.

Ryan winced, resisting the urge to rub away the pain in his posterior. Evidently, security guys couldn't take a joke. Especially one delivered double-o-seven style.

Jackson sauntered up, carrying a racetrack betting form and gnawing a pencil thoughtfully. He looked down at his friend.

"Hey," he said. "Good thing your wallet broke your fall."

"Very funny." Ryan got to his feet. On the street beyond them, he saw that Jackson had parked Ryan's Beemer illegally. It was, at this very minute, earning itself a ticket. "Let's just say this day isn't working out as I'd planned."

"We can still make brunch at the OceanView," Jackson suggested, naming a popular resort in nearby La Jolla. "They serve a wicked mimosa. And Buffy and Tabitha will be there."

"No." Feeling a renewed determination, Ryan gazed up at the building he'd just left. "This didn't work out, but I'm not quitting. I mean, sure. They didn't recognize me. An innocent mistake, given that I haven't set foot in my 'office' in years. But I'm going to make this work."

"Sure, you are. Look, just make a charitable donation or something, and let's go."

Ryan shook his head. This was the final straw. The outer limit. The breaking point. The . . . hell, the end of the end of the line.

He figured himself for a pretty tough guy. Resilient. Smart. Fun to be around, even. But it had been a difficult few weeks, and he had finally had just about enough.

Sure, watching his fickle fiancée ride into the sunset with the Grisham clone hadn't been easy. Truthfully, it had knocked him for a loop. But in the two weeks that had passed since then, Ryan had realized a few things.

First, he couldn't grieve for long over a woman who clearly did not love him, and obviously never had. Second, he'd passed the point where things had to change in his life. Being thrown out of his erstwhile office today had brought that fact painfully to life for him.

Being dumped twice in the same month could do that to a guy, he guessed.

Ryan strode to his roadster. Jackson trailed behind, muttering something about the odds on an upcoming horse race.

"I've spent the last thirty-two years of my life in pursuit of a good time," Ryan said, snatching the ticket from his windshield and tucking it into his glove compartment. "It's time I shake things up a little."

"Shake things up?" Jackson checked his watch. "Girls-A-Go-Go opens at noon."

Ryan shook his head and pulled into traffic, headed for his father's office. He'd have to earn some credibility, he knew. But he was up for it. Now that he was free of wedding planning, what else did he have to do?

"That's not what I mean," he said. "No A-Go-Go."

"No A-Go-Go?" Jackson looked disappointed.

"No. I mean, it's time I got involved in the family business. Made something of myself."

"Uh-oh." Jackson shot him a warning glance, edged with something that looked an awful lot like . . . sympathy? "Listen, buddy. We all went through this. I'll tell you right now, it's not worth it."

"What's not worth it?"

"The self-improvement routine. I did it when Monica and I got divorced. Brewster did it when his showgirl pulled that bogus paternity suit of hers. Corrington did it when his second wife took him for the house, the cars, *and* the vacation cottage in the Islands. You think it will help, but it won't."

"That's not what this is about."

"Sure. You say that now, but—"

"It's not!"

"—but when you're all done with this be-a-business-man routine, you'll wait for whatshername to be bowled over by the changes and come back to you," Jackson insisted. He'd actually put down his racing form, he was so serious. "And she won't. And you'll be crushed."

"I won't be crushed," Ryan said. He tightened his grip on the steering wheel and gazed determinedly into the distance, wishing he felt more certain. Did his new-found industriousness owe itself partly to the impulse Jackson was talking about? "And anyway, I'm over her. I don't want her back. In fact, a woman—any woman—is the *last* thing I need in my life right now."

Jackson made a disbelieving sound. "Even one who does the smiling thing, and remembers breakfast, and lets you kiss her at the drop of a hat?"

His dream woman. He remembered rhapsodizing about her ideal qualities—so sappily and so naively—on the brink of the wedding that wasn't, and regretted it soundly. It wasn't that he was bitter. It was simply, Ryan believed, that he was now a little wiser.

"Even a woman who does all that," he told Jackson, nodding.

After all . . . what were the odds he'd run into the woman of his dreams anytime soon? Especially if he was working his ass off, trying to make his mark in the family company?

Things were going to work out fine, Ryan assured himself as he pulled into the parking garage at his father's law firm and got out of the car. Just fine. In fact, he felt better already.

At that moment, Jackson leaned over. He squinted.

"Hey," he asked, "are those grid marks on your face?"

Just fine.

* * *

"Whoa! Where are you off to so early?"

At the sound of her brother's sleepy voice, April stopped in her tracks and glanced toward the sofa. There, Mickey raised himself on one skinny elbow and blinked at her.

"Work," she said.

"Oh. Work." Looking vaguely confused, Mickey frowned. He rubbed at the pillow crease on his cheek. Tugged at a hank of his strawberry-blond bedhead, and cleared his throat. Then something seemed to occur to him.

"You got fired, Ape," he said.

She pursed her lips over the hated nickname, but couldn't work up too much of a temper. Mickey looked almost ... concerned about her, and although he couldn't keep a job to save his life and didn't quite know the meaning of the word "responsibility," her brother was entirely kindhearted on the inside. He always meant well. So April gave him the benefit of the doubt, and elected *not* to bean him over the head with her four-pound handbag.

"Yes, I got fired. Two weeks ago," she agreed. The memory was still painful, and she preferred not to dwell on it. This was merely a temporary setback, she assured herself. Nothing more.

She couldn't *allow* it to be more. Her entire sense of self depended on it.

Mickey shifted, then groped at the sheets slipping away from his naked chest. "I know you're not familiar with the process. But getting fired means you don't have to go to work. Ever. Again."

"Thanks for the tip, genius."

Grinning, he snagged his cigarettes from amid the Pepsi cans, video rental boxes, and day-old Cheetos littering the ottoman-style coffee table, and prepared to light up. Before he could, April snatched both the cigarette and the crumpled pack away and thunked them out of reach at the far end of the table. Beneath the want ads, where Mickey would never think to look later. Her brother's crestfallen expression let her know he'd just remembered her no-smoking policy.

"Remember Granny Finnegan," she said quietly.

He looked away, as though fascinated by her small apartment's meager furnishings. The stereo had gone with her former roommate, as had the second bedroom's furniture, the sole armchair, and all the rugs.

The thriving plants were hers, though, as were the funkily painted dining table and chairs, the barcolounger, and the refurbished sofa Mickey slept on. A moment passed, during which they both remembered Granny. Then Calypso jumped with feline grace onto Mickey's blanket and rubbed up against his arm, and the mood was broken.

Absentmindedly, he pet the cat. Then he glanced up at April, taking in her pegged, orange plaid skirt, ruffled yellow blouse, and lace-up knee-high boots.

"You look nice," he said. "What's the occasion?"

"I told you." Sometimes it was awfully hard to resist rude, forehead-smacking gestures around Mickey. "Work!"

"But Ape . . . you got fir—"

"I'm meeting with Mark this morning." *The same way I have every morning, for the past fourteen days.* April Finnegan was nothing if not doggedly persistent. "I'm going to suggest that he let me prove myself in the community relations manager position. For free."

"Free?" Mickey wrinkled his forehead. "Why would you do that?"

"If Mark sees what I can accomplish, on a trial basis," April explained, pleased with the idea she'd come up with sometime between the late-night hair-in-a-can infomercial and the tossing and turning that had come after, "he'll agree to give me the job permanently. Sure, he's a little peeved at me right now, but I know I can convince him."

And if she couldn't . . . well, that disastrous possibility just didn't bear thinking about. Mark was reasonable. *And* he was a sucker for a bargain. What was a better bargain than free? The only mystery here was why April hadn't thought of this idea before now.

"Huh." Thoughtfully, Mickey nodded. Then he dragged Calypso onto his chest, nuzzled the cat with his chin, and lay them both down onto the sofa cushions. He dragged up a blanket over his head. "Good luck, then," he mumbled from beneath it.

"Thanks," April said, hoping she wouldn't need luck. She headed for the door again, keeping her new mantra steadfastly in mind.

Things were going to work out fine, she told herself. *Just fine.*

Rubbing his tired eyes, Mark Wright looked up from the stack of Ambrosia invoices he'd been checking. It was only a little after nine o'clock in the morning, and already he felt as though he'd been at the bakery all day.

More than likely, he figured, that impression came from being solely responsible, shakily indebted, and now, regrettably, shorthanded. *Damn that April.* As usual, she'd gone and pushed him too far.

With the fate of his business resting squarely on his shoulders, Mark didn't have the luxury of indulging his employees when they stepped out of line . . . no matter how fond he was of them. And he *was* fond of April. More than fond, in fact.

Not that she knew it, of course.

Brightening, he contemplated the silver lining inherent in his situation: with April no longer his employee, he could consider dating her. Or at least, finally asking her out for dinner and a movie, without tongues wagging in small-town Saguaro Vista.

Because the one thing Mark couldn't tolerate was notoriety. Scandal of any kind made him nervous, which was why he'd hidden his attraction to April for this long already. But now . . . now, new options were opening up.

"Hiya!" April said.

He jumped in surprise, scattering his pencils and knocking over the adding machine. Straightening them both, Mark looked up to see April waiting in his office doorway, wearing a bizarre combination of vivid clothes that should have looked weird, but did not. And a smile. It seemed a little tentative, but it was definitely a smile.

At the sight of her, something inside Mark softened. April was his friend, at least. Perhaps he owed her a chance to . . .

No. He suddenly noticed what she was eating, and all bets were off.

"I can't *believe* you're eating one of those," he said.

She took it from her mouth and gazed at it. Her cheeks colored guiltily. With a mumbled apology—and a "Well, we can't use them for anything else now, anyway, can we?" —April whipped it behind her back.

That thing was, after all, what had started all the trouble in the first place.

Even though Mark couldn't see *it* at the moment, he remembered it clearly. Remembered *rows* of it clearly, in fact, waiting on his desk two weeks ago. He'd taken one look, suffered a near apoplexy at the thought of what people in town—customers!—would say when they saw April's newest creation, and yelled for her to come in. She'd come in, had seen what he'd seen, and then . . .

"What, *exactly*, are these?" Mark had asked her.

"Chocolate Adonises," she'd replied blithely, picking up one six-inch semisweet figure to show him a three-sixty view. "For the Shaeffer-Nieman bachelorette party. Vicki didn't think it could be done, but I—"

"You! You!" He couldn't say more, so horrified was he by the sight of the three dozen chocolate figures arrayed in their clear plastic, confectionery molds.

"—but I did it," she finished proudly.

"These things" —he waved toward the one she held so innocently— "are nude chocolate men. Anatomically correct, nude chocolate men. Anatomically correct!"

"I know." April rolled her eyes. "Vicki's special request. And if you don't think it was a job tracking down the molds for *these* suckers, well . . . let me tell you—"

"Arrgh!"

She looked puzzled. "They're only on your desk because I needed the space. If they offend you, if you want me to let them finish hardening elsewhere—"

Mark felt himself blush—actually blush!—at that.

"—I'd be happy to move them."

"That's not the problem," he gritted through clenched teeth.

"What, then? Is it the teeny tommy that's the trouble?" April peered at the chocolate Adonis in her hand. "I guess I could paint on a little bittersweet loincloth to cover it, but it would be tricky to do it without messing up the—"

Mark still didn't know what had come over him. But at that moment, he'd had it. He'd absolutely had it.

"No!" he'd shouted. "No loincloth. No indecent chocolates. And no—"

"I guess this means I ought to take the extras out of the display cases out front?" April had asked, edging away.

"And no job! For you!"

At that, she'd gone pale. Mark had been too fed up, too filled with visions of straitlaced customers deserting him once they got a load of his bakery's newest, raciest confection, to stop what he'd already begun.

"You're fired, April!" he'd yelled. "I should have let you go after that incident with your mother's bounced checks—"

"I made good on them, Mark! You know I did."

"—and I *really* should have let you go after the time your uncle Finnegan smuggled out that batch of green bagels beneath his shirt on Saint Patrick's Day."

"I—I—Uncle Bobby is just—"

"But, no! I liked you, and so I kept you on." He'd shook his head. "But this. This endangers my bakery's reputation. This" —Mark had waved one of the chocolates furiously— "*this* is the final straw."

And that, as they say, had been that.

April had packed up her whisks and apron, Mark had asked another of his bakers to substitute respectable petit fours for the chocolate Adonises, and life had gone on as usual. Sort of. Except for the daily visits April made to him . . . and the weakening effect those visits were having on his resolve.

"I should have known better than to hire a Finnegan in the first place," Mark muttered now, half to himself, as April strode into his office and took a seat in his extra chair. "I just should have known better."

She looked up, pinning him with a hurtful gaze. "I'm not like that, Mark. You know I'm not."

He raked his hand through his hair, feeling himself soften toward her still further. "April, I—"

Mark didn't know if he'd meant to apologize, or if

he'd meant to reiterate his "you're fired" stance. Either way, April beat him to the punch. She leaned forward in her chair, intent and solemn, and laid her hand on his arm.

"Since the day I was born," April said quietly, "people in this town have been expecting me to become another shiftless Finnegan screw-up. I swear to you, I'm not like that. Please, give me a chance to prove it."

He looked away, knowing that if he gazed into her pretty face and sweet green eyes any longer, he'd give in.

"Please," she said again, as she had every morning for the past fourteen days. Her voice broke with earnestness. "Give me another chance."

"April . . ."

"That community relations position I pitched to you?" she hurried to say. "I'll do it for free. On a trial basis, for two weeks. If you're not satisfied with all the new business I bring the bakery by that time, if you're not happy with the bakery's improved community awareness, then I'll leave you alone. I'll quit pestering you. But if you *are* happy with my work—and I think you will be—then you give me the job for good."

Intrigued by this new proposal, Mark dared to glance back at her. That was his first mistake. April looked so vulnerable, so determined, so *desperate,* that the last of his resistance crumbled. Which was his second mistake.

"With a twenty-percent pay raise from my old job," she added hastily.

He raised his eyebrows. "Always have to push, don't you?"

"I wouldn't be me, if I didn't." April grinned, and squeezed his arm. He was already a goner, and she must have known it. "Besides, I'll need the extra money to make up for this month's lost pay. Do we have a deal, then?"

Looking around his office—and decidedly *away* from the non-loincloth-covered chocolate hunk she'd been noshing when she'd come in and had set aside at the edge of his desk—Mark hesitated. Giving April another chance was probably a mistake. A mistake of colossal proportions. But with the woman he secretly admired gazing at him so hopefully, he didn't have the heartlessness to say no.

"This is the *only* last chance you get," he told her sternly, pointing his index finger. "Understand me? If you blow it—if you don't increase business and improve the bakery's visibility in Saguaro Vista—then there'll be no going back."

Despite his deliberate strictness, April squealed with delight. She leaped from her chair, hurried to his side of the desk, and enveloped him in a happy hug.

"Oh, Mark!" she cried. "You won't regret this. I swear you won't. I promise."

He hoped he wouldn't regret taking her back, Mark thought as he returned her embrace. Because on so many levels, he *could* come to regret this. Very deeply . . . and soon. But for now? For now, he'd take his chances. And hope for the best.

After all, she was only one woman. One woman, set loose in town to wreak whatever havoc her highly original mind could come up with. How bad could it be?

Oh, no, Mark realized as April released him and stepped backward, glowing with gratitude and anticipation. *This was April Finnegan. It could be very, very bad, indeed.*

Chapter Three

He was doomed, Ryan decided.

Doomed, doomed, doomed. Doomed like a starving man facing down eight o'clock without dinner reservations. Like a bleary-eyed caffeine-craver whose favorite *barrista* had deserted the coffeehouse. Like a partygoer forced to buy celebratory clothes off the rack. Off the rack! Because when he ended the long drive from San Diego to Saguaro Vista, Arizona, nothing was as he'd expected.

Everything he was accustomed to was missing. Highrises, professional landscaping, steady traffic, little things like, oh, say, *modern conveniences* were nowhere to be found.

In their places, low-slung adobe buildings whipped past, shabbily picturesque in shades of brown and cream. Feathery-leaved mesquite trees studded the sidewalks, providing shade for the people meandering past. Old-fashioned parking meters edged the main street, glinting in the early May afternoon sunlight and monitoring the older-model cars parallel-parked beside them.

Ryan drove farther, passing the occasional dusty car or battered pickup truck. Feeling vaguely out of his depth, he gripped his roadster's steering wheel more tightly as he surveyed the rest of downtown. All four blocks of it.

A theater marquee to his left advertised a movie six months old. A bowling alley caught his eye, its gigantic ball-and-pins sign badly in need of paint. A lone stoplight loomed ahead, swinging in the breeze on a wire strung between a pair of two-story buildings.

One of those buildings was the original Forrester's Department Store, Ryan knew. It had been built by the Forrester brothers—one of them his great-great-great grandfather—in the late 1880s, originally intended to provide supplies for miners and early settlers to the Arizona Territory.

The building itself, Ryan saw now as he neared it, was an ancient-looking adobe box studded with windows in the front and an awning to the side, adorned with the recognizably ornate *Forrester's* logo.

It was his heritage, he realized. And he'd never even seen it, until now. He'd have liked to have shared the moment with someone—unfortunately, his cell phone and PalmPilot had lost their connections hours ago on I-17, and showed no signs of coming back to life now. He was stranded.

Stranded, in Podunkville.

There was no turning back now, though. Ryan had set his course, and he was sticking with it. No matter what.

He'd just resolved to cheerfully meet his fate—and to start right away on the project he'd pitched to the Forrester's board—when a flash of multicolored light caught his eye in his roadster's rearview mirror. Ryan glanced back.

Just as he'd thought. A police car. Pulling him over.

Well, there were worse ways to embark on a new venture. A speeding ticket wasn't necessarily a bad omen . . . was it?

He sure as hell hoped not. Because it looked like he was about to get one.

Charlie's Pizzeria Funhouse was one of Saguaro Vista's most popular restaurants. There wasn't a child in town between the ages of two and twelve who hadn't had at least one birthday party inside its candy-striped, pizza sauce–splattered walls. For that reason, April was convinced Charlie's could be an important bakery account. Supplying the pizzeria with birthday cakes alone would be unbelievably lucrative. Until now, the owner, Bernie, had resisted Mark's casual inquiries . . . but April was prepared to take things one step further.

Which explained why she was dressing in a furry chipmunk outfit even now, waiting for a chance to speak with Bernie about Ambrosia.

She tucked one yellow Capri-clad leg into the bottom half of the jumpsuit-style suit, determined to have her say. When she'd first visited Bernie, in her new capacity as Ambrosia community relations manager, he'd blown her off. He was too busy looking for a replacement "Chipmunk Charlie" to wave in customers from the street and hand out balloons to the kids to talk to her, he'd said. Never one to be outmaneuvered, April had volunteered to act as Chipmunk Charlie for as long as it took to make her pitch . . . and now, here she was.

Zipping up the suit, April grabbed the headpiece by one ear and bundled it beneath her arm. Bernie was nowhere in sight. With a shrug, she went to look for him.

It would take more than a fuzzy tail and painted-on whiskers to discourage *her,* April vowed. When she'd finished with him, Bernie wouldn't know what hit him.

And he'd give her the bakery account she wanted, too.

Bringing his roadster to a stop in a parallel parking space in front of his destination, Ryan got out and was immediately confronted with a dilemma. The parking meter.

He patted his pockets, looking for change. Nada. And the old-fashioned device didn't have a slot to swipe his credit card through, either. He'd checked.

Well, he decided with a shrug, what were the chances they patrolled meters closely here, anyway? It wasn't as though parking was particularly scarce or the streets especially crowded here in Podunk, after all. The meters looked antiquated; they were probably a formality, more than anything else. That decided, he peered through his sunglasses and sized up the place before him.

Charlie's Pizzeria Funhouse. The first stop in the Forrester's Department Stores community outreach effort he'd planned. The outside looked like an amusement park ride, with bright painted-on stripes and a gigantic clown head for embellishment. The entrance was through the clown's smiling mouth.

Tacky, but probably fun if you were a nine-year-old. Maybe. Ryan wasn't entirely sure. He'd been in boarding school when he was nine, and Northam's Academy had obviously missed its quota of smiling clown heads. Probably, he mused as he watched Saguaro Vista residents coming and going inside Charlie's, that deprivation had done its part to send him on his lifelong search for a perpetual good time.

He'd damn well found it, too, Ryan thought with a grin.

At least until lately.

He located the owner, Bernie, inside making pizzas. Ryan saw him glance up through the kitchen pass-through when the counter girl relayed his request to meet with the management. Bernie wiped his wide hands on a kitchen towel, finished a conversation he'd been having with his chipmunk restaurant mascot— Ryan did a double-take and saw that it was, indeed, a faux, furry brown chipmunk beside the man—and then held up a palm in greeting to Ryan.

Ryan nodded in response, steeling himself against the urge to make sure the suit and tie he'd changed into were still in order. He hadn't been this nervous since . . . well, since he'd stood in a custom-made tuxedo and waited for his wedding plans to fall apart a little more than two weeks ago. Blowing out a deep breath, he waited for Bernie to make his way to the other side of the counter.

"Somebody die?" Bernie asked, immediately after shaking Ryan's hand.

"No. I'm—"

"Somebody suing me? Auditing me? Selling me insurance?" Bernie persisted. He eyed Ryan's suit. "Nobody wears stuff like that 'round here. Not unless somebody has kicked off, is on their way to court, or is looking to make a fast buck. Which one fits you?"

Ryan could have sworn he heard the chipmunk stifle a guffaw behind the counter in front of him. He saw the pizzeria mascot exchange a few words with the counter girl, then make a swivel-hipped Elvis-style motion. Momentarily distracted, Ryan blinked in surprise.

"Huh?" Bernie asked. "Which one fits you?"

Ryan redirected his attention. "None of the above," he said, putting on a reassuring smile. As he introduced himself, he indicated a nearby booth, and waited for Bernie to take a seat opposite him. "But I *am* here with a proposition for you. Something that will be good for Charlie's Pizzeria Funhouse—"

"Just call it Charlie's," Bernie interrupted with a wave.

"—good for your customers, and good for the community, too."

Bernie looked intrigued. Ryan breathed a sigh of relief. He'd practiced his pitch for miles between the California state line and Saguaro Vista, and it looked as though it might actually succeed.

"Okay," Bernie said, sitting back. "I'm listening."

"Good. Here's what I'm suggesting . . ."

With an intensity and enthusiasm he hadn't known he possessed, Ryan launched into the rest of his pitch.

At the heart of it was his idea to strike alliances with neighborhood businesses, forming partnerships between them and Forrester's Department Stores' flagship store. The plan had come to him only hours after being tossed on his butt outside the San Diego offices, and less than a day after having examined stockholders' reports and other data provided by his father.

"Traditional midsize department stores are hurting," Ryan had told Andrew Forrester and the board of directors when he'd finished. "They're being squeezed out by 'big box' superstores, even in their longtime market— small town U.S.A. I have a way to fight back. And that's what I intend to do."

And now, here he was. Fighting back. Fighting for the future of the company he'd neglected for so long. And fighting for himself . . . and the man he wanted to be. It had been too long in coming, Ryan knew. He needed to work fast, to make up for lost time.

"So if you'll purchase all-new employee uniforms," Ryan told Bernie now, "custom-designed by Forrester's, of course—maybe with a small Forrester's logo beneath yours—our flagship store here in Saguaro Vista will reciprocate in kind. A Charlie's Pizzeria Funhouse promotional display in the housewares department. Free pizza coupons with every purchase. Whatever you want.

"Forrester's wants to help build the community," he said earnestly, coming to a close. "And we're open to coming up with ideas that will suit you and your store."

Hey, Ryan thought to himself as he finished his pitch. *Not bad for a guy who spent Marketing 101 at Stanford trying to score a date with the cute blonde in the back row. Not bad at all.* Maybe all the socializing he'd done over the years had had a greater purpose, all along.

"I dunno," Bernie said, scratching his balding head. "I don't have a whole lot of budge in my budget, if you catch my drift. And I just committed to a partnership with a bakery here in town. For birthday cakes."

Bernie's attention shifted to the counter, where the chipmunk still stood with a handful of balloons. Ryan would have sworn Bernie's gaze met—*meaningfully*—with the chipmunk's. Which was ridiculous, of course. Whoever was in that costume, they couldn't possibly be relevant to the discussion at hand. Could they?

"We get a lot of birthday parties in here. It's a core business," Bernie explained, bringing his attention back to Ryan. "Brings in most of the town, at one time or another. 'Til now, my sister's been makin' the cakes, with some of them, whatcha call 'em, Betty Crocker mixes."

Ryan nodded, as though he'd been using Betty Crocker mixes himself for years. In truth, most of his meals came from restaurants. They were presented in tantalizing descriptions, preceded by aperitifs, and delivered by solicitous uniformed wait staff. Afterward, someone whisked away the plates to . . . to take care of them. No muss, no fuss, no such thing as a declining balance on his platinum card.

Thinking back, Ryan couldn't remember the last time he'd tasted *anything* homemade, much less a just-add-water birthday cake. He didn't think he was missing anything. But he listened attentively as Bernie continued.

"The chocolate ones are pretty good," he was saying. "But the spice cakes—" Suddenly, Bernie cleared his throat and shook his head regretfully. "Anyhow, no can do, Mr. Forrester. I'm sorry, but I don't have the money to invest in bakery birthday cakes *and* new uniforms, all at the same time. That's an interestin' idea you got there, but I'm gonna have to pass."

He stood, ending their conversation with a few more words and a handshake. Ryan pushed back his disappointment long enough to assure Bernie that his offer remained open, then said his good-byes.

At the counter, the chipmunk gave away the last balloon to a chubby-cheeked toddler standing in line to pick up an order. Watching the growing numbers of people waiting gave Ryan an idea. There was more than one way to make a memorable first impression, after all. And Ryan Forrester didn't go down without a fight. Not anymore.

He edged his way to the front and spoke with the counter girl. She gawked at him, openmouthed, then nodded her understanding when she glimpsed the cash Ryan pulled surreptitiously from his inside suit pocket.

"For the next hour," the counter girl announced, "every pizza is paid for by Forrester's Department Stores! Courtesy of Mr. Forrester here, himself! Come on up and place your orders, folks."

Cheers and whoops went up. Smiling, Ryan accepted the thanks that came his way from the crowd . . . along with the nod of approval from Bernie, back behind the counter.

Score! Ryan thought. He barely resisted a celebratory fist-pump.

"Hmmmph," said a voice nearby, interrupting his proud, new-man-of-business moment.

He turned. The chipmunk stood a few feet away, paw on hip, watching him. Ryan tilted his head in puzzlement. The posture suggested undisguised scorn, although what mascot-aggravating thing he'd done, Ryan couldn't say.

"Free pizza?" he offered.

"Hmmmph," said the chipmunk again, and then it flounced away.

Yes, *flounced*. Because, Ryan saw as it raised both paws to remove its headpiece as it left, the chipmunk was a woman. He caught a glimpse of tumbling red hair, flashing green eyes, and a speculative, over-the-shoulder expression . . . and then she was gone, through an employees-only back door.

Why he felt disappointed at that fact, Ryan couldn't say.

Ridiculous.

So . . . there was a new guy in town, April mused. A new, blond, suit-wearing, fancy-talking, gorgeous-enough-to-peel-paint—or was that panties?—guy. Here. In Saguaro Vista.

Amazing.

And she'd thought nothing ever happened in this town, aside from the annual chili cook-off and gold miner's days.

He was obviously lost. On the lam. Stricken with society amnesia. *Something.* Maybe, April speculated, he'd been abducted by aliens, dressed in a spiffy suit, and dropped back off again—minus a working sense of how to get back to his usual cocktails-and-country-club life.

Nevertheless, as April stepped onto the sidewalk outside Charlie's a few minutes after her meeting with Bernie, her mind was filled with images of the mystery man. Something about him—Mr. Moneybags, not Bernie— piqued her interest . . . and a few other things, too. Definitely. She was definitely piqued. Piqued in ways she hadn't felt since . . . since she couldn't remember, actually.

In true movie-cliché style, she hadn't been able to take her eyes from him. Sure, his face was just a face— however gorgeous and arrestingly masculine. And his body was just a body—however gorgeous and expensively attired. But his voice had wound its way inside her somehow, all deep and certain and *smart*-sounding; and his hands had captured her interest, all strong and neat and deftly square-fingered as he talked; and his gaze, when he'd glanced at her chipmunk-suited self as though seeing the woman beneath . . . well, his gaze had been so perceptive and blue and *different* than what she was used to, that April had been positively thrilled, all the way to her chipmunk paws.

Giddily intrigued, she'd begun plotting pickup lines, straight out of *Cosmo*. Suddenly, an approach like "Didn't I see you on the cover of *Hunks Monthly* recently?" had seemed perfectly viable. So had a variety of other cheesy, yet effective, openings.

But then he'd whipped out his wallet. He'd all but bought his way into Bernie's budgetary affections. And her dreamboat fantasy had lost its sizzle.

How *could* he try to bollix up her bakery deal with Bernie that way? How *dare* Ryan Forrester walk into *her* town, with his easy smiles and big-city ways, and wave around a wad of cash, as though—as though—as though that would solve anything?

Of course, it *had* gotten Bernie's attention . . . but that still didn't make it right, damn it. And April intended to let Mr. Moneybags Big City Department Store Forrester know it. If she didn't, who knew how his actions might affect her Ambrosia community relations plans?

She'd overheard enough of Big Spender's pitch to Bernie to know that his ideas would probably be making their way all over town. With her employment prospects hanging in the balance, April had to do something. So she tracked down Mister Big's car—not tough, since the luxe convertible stuck out like a diamond in a gravel pit among the dented Chevys, bumper-stickered used Hyundais, and camper-embellished trucks parked along the street—found herself a good waiting spot, and exercised her skimpy patience.

When her quarry finally emerged from Charlie's Pizzeria, April was tapping her sandaled toe and picking polyester fur from her Wonder Woman T-shirt. Fake chipmunk fur, she'd discovered, was like Velcro. She'd be finding it in her hair for a month. But at least she'd wrangled the bakery deal with Bernie. That was worth a celebration in itself.

Maybe her new job, and her second chance with Mark, would work out after all.

The sound of jangling keys snapped April from her reverie. She glanced up, smoothing Wonder Woman's star-spangled outfit across her chest as she did, and was walloped with two contradictory self-revelations at once. First, that her life would have been completely different if puberty had lent her a tremendous set of man-magnet ta-tas instead of non-attention-getting A cups. Second, that she couldn't help smiling at the man approaching her, even though it undoubtedly made her look like a total loon.

At the sight of him, giddiness bubbled up inside her all over again. Confused, April tried to tamp it down, but nothing worked. She felt drawn to grin—grin *hugely*—at Ryan Forrester's approach, and so she did.

He missed a step, glancing behind him as though looking for the intended recipient of her megawatt smile. Seeing no one else, he smiled back. *This must be what they do in Podunkville,* that smile of his seemed to say. *Grin like goons.* For a money-flashing buttinsky, she thought, at least he was a good sport.

"Hiya," she said, putting out her hand. "April Finnegan."

He murmured an introduction as he slid his hand, steady and large, into hers. His touch made her insides flip-flop in an embarrassingly girly girl way, and April ended the contact quickly.

"Nice set of wheels you've got here," she remarked. *Geez, up close he was even dishier-looking,* she couldn't help but realize. *Hard-edged jaw, pampered close shave, assertive nose, witty eyes.* Feeling unfamiliarly flustered, April slapped her palm jovially onto the white convertible she was leaning against—mostly sitting on, really. "What's it going to be when it grows up?"

Surprise flashed over his features, followed closely by humor. *This guy wouldn't break out the Dustbuster over some harmless flour and sugar,* April thought immediately. *No way.* Ryan Forrester suddenly looked way too easygoing for that. And that surprised her, too.

"It's going to be sorry to see you go," he said, putting both hands in his suit pants pockets. He tilted his head. His gaze honed in on her backside, which rested against the hood. "I think my car likes you. Look. One of the windshield wipers is waving."

"It's pointing out this." April twisted, whisked the traffic ticket from beneath the opposite wiper, and handed it to him. "I put a couple of quarters in the meter for you, but you can't stay long. Wanda patrols this area pretty fiercely."

He took the ticket and gave it a shake of his head. Looking as though he'd somehow expected it, Ryan folded it and tucked it into his suit pocket.

"So do I, as it happens," April went on. Visions of not proving herself to Mark, not making her rent, not being able to keep herself in Lean Cuisine, or electricity, or bargain-hunting flea market sprees, goaded her still further. She crossed her arms and tried to look tough. "I happened to overhear part of your conversation with Bernie, and I think you should know—I'm the birthday cake supplier he was talking about."

He squinted. "Somehow, I imagined Bernie's sister would be . . . more . . . less . . ."

"Less?" She raised a brow, wishing suddenly and stupidly that she'd plucked it for the occasion.

"Less . . . gorgeous. I mean, ripping open boxes of Betty Crocker mixes all day probably doesn't do much for—"

"I'm not Bernie's sister." She was, however, absurdly flattered that he found her gorgeous. "I'm the community relations representative for Ambrosia, a bakery in town. We just contracted with Charlie's Pizzeria for birthday cakes."

His abashed grin was more charming than a thousand devil-may-care smiles would have been.

"I'm sorry," Ryan said. "I should have known. It's just that you look different when you're not . . . a chipmunk."

April waved her hand. "Being Chipmunk Charlie was a one-time-only thing," she explained. "I was helping out Bernie, so he could listen to my pitch."

"Smart," Ryan said. *And gorgeous,* his expression added, all over again. "I should be taking lessons from you, while I'm here."

"Lessons? Don't be silly. All you do is put one leg in your chipmunk suit at a time, then zip. It's easy."

He laughed. "Business lessons. I'm launching some community initiatives for Forrester's Department Store."

"So I heard."

She noticed a dimple, just beyond the corner of his mouth. It should have lent him a boyish look, but somehow, it made Ryan Forrester look surprisingly roguish. Roguishly appealing. Okay, just plain appealing. *For a business-stealing wannabe,* the still-rational part of her reminded. *Stay focused!*

"Does that mean," April asked, careful to keep her voice casual as she lifted her gaze to his, "you're planning to stay here in Saguaro Vista, then?"

"Just until my work for the department store is done."

Given his attempted poaching of her business contacts, April figured she should have been worried. But she was too confident for that. Besides, her brain was busily fixed on the *he's staying, wahoo!* station. Everything else was static.

She nodded, temporarily unable to speak thanks to the zing of anticipation inside her. It was a tangible force, awakening April all over . . . and making her completely forget what she'd set out to accomplish.

Ryan must have felt something, too, because his gaze locked with hers, and another semi-smile edged its way onto his mouth. They stayed that way for a moment, April leaning against his car but feeling drawn toward him, Ryan standing casually but appearing drawn toward her. If they'd been in a movie, meaningful ballad-y type music would have swelled up at that moment, but since this was real life, the only soundtrack was the sudden clearing of throats and shuffling of feet as they both regained their senses and pretended that downtown Saguaro Vista was the most fascinating sight they'd ever seen.

April's attention zeroed in on a cardboard box blown

against the side of the Charlie's Pizzeria building. *Yikes,* she realized. If she wasn't careful, she'd be scouting places like that for her and Calypso—and probably Mickey—to live in. She had to get back to business.

"Well, then," she told Ryan, keeping her voice brisk. "You'll be needing a guide. Someone to show you around town, introduce you, get you acquainted with the way we do things around here. And I know just the person."

His attention swerved back to her. Instantly, that tell-tale giddiness whirled up inside her, but this time April was ready. She wasn't going to let some mushy gushy crush deter her from the course she'd set. Ryan Forrester was just a hunky, handsome, out-of-his-depth big-city guy playing at bringing business to the small town. He wasn't a threat to her job-saving, Ambrosia community relations plans. Or to her.

Right?

Right. Not so long as she kept her eyes on him. And that's exactly what she intended to do.

"Only if it's you," he said, "who's guiding me."

Wowsers. The heat in his voice left April battling an urge to fan herself with her hand. Getting a grip on herself, she smiled.

"Oh, you bet it's me," she told him. "Come on."

Chapter Four

The next morning, Ryan eased himself into a duct tape–patched vinyl restaurant booth opposite April Finnegan, his Saguaro Vista guardian angel, and focused his attention on not wincing as he straightened into a sitting position. His body felt battered and broken, bruised and bloodied—or at least, incredibly achy—after having been contorted atop what passed for a mattress at the Saguaro Vista Motor Court Inn all night.

" 'Morning," April said over the cup cradled in both hands, all bright and cheery. "Sleep well?"

He murmured a noncommittal reply and looked for their server. He needed coffee—a double cappuccino with a twist ought to do it—and he needed it fast.

Clearly, he was going to have to fire his travel agent, Ryan decided. Or at least have a serious word or two with the woman. True, his "hotel room" was housed in its own *casita*, as she'd promised. And it did possess the requisite amenities. In a sense. If you could call a lumpy, thousand-year-old bed, mysteriously groaning faucet, faux wood bureau, and wall-to-wall orange shag carpeting *requisite amenities*. Ryan called them atrocities. And he still couldn't believe he'd actually slept among them.

"You should have let me pick you up this morning," he told April, to take his mind from his hotel fiasco. Usually women were impressed with his car. Despite everything, Ryan wanted to impress April, too. "I would have been happy to do it."

"Nah. No need." She gave a nonchalant wave, and light winked from the array of costume-jewelry rings on her fingers. "I get where I need to go just fine. Thanks, though."

She squeezed his hand in an appreciative gesture. Then April nodded toward the window beside their booth. Through its smeared plate glass, he spotted a bicycle parked and chained to some kind of utility pipe beside the diner. The bike had curvy lines, retro styling, wide handlebars, and bright yellow paint that somehow suited someone as patently cheerful as April. And yet . . .

"You rode a bike here?" he asked.

The only bikes that women of his acquaintance were familiar with were those in spinning class, at the country club gym. They wouldn't have been caught dead using something so hair-mussing, perspiration-provoking, and physically exerting as a bicycle for actual transportation. After all . . . you couldn't valet-park a Schwinn while you shoe-shopped at Nordstrom's, now could you?

April gave him a funny look. "Rode it? All over town. Sure. That's what's with the jammin' footwear." Grinning, she thrust one shapely bare leg into the diner's aisle and raised it so he could see the cuffed sock and flat-heeled hiking boot on her foot. Then she shrugged. "Why not?"

"Don't you have a car?"

She tucked her leg beneath her again, calling Ryan's attention to the flowered, gauzy miniskirt she had on. April Finnegan had some terrific legs, he decided, some of the sleep-deprived crankiness exiting his brain. And the rest of her—he took in her laced-up white shirt, glittery disco-style scarf, and attention-getting lip-glossed lips—was pretty terrific, too.

"Yes, I have a car," she replied, pushing a Downtown Grill menu across the table toward him. It got stuck in a maple syrup drip, and she had to peel it up to make the last few inches. "Pete Wykowski is holding it hostage down at the shop right now. Another hundred bucks, and it's mine to keep again, though. I'm making payments."

Payments? On a hundred-dollar bill? Ryan couldn't grasp it. He probably spent more than that on a round of drinks at his club. He *had* more than that in his wallet right now. For the first time, he pondered the economic realities between his life and April's.

"Say"— suddenly, she set down her cup, and he noticed the squeezed, used tea bag on the saucer beside it— "did you want something to eat before we get going? Because our waitress just passed by."

"Yes, I'm starving. Thanks." Ryan flagged down their waitress, who came to their table with an excess of green eye shadow and a motherly expression. She chatted for a few minutes with April, then turned to Ryan.

"You got a question about the menu, hon?" she asked, eying the closed, blue vinyl-bound menu at his elbow.

"No, thank you. Just a simple order," he said. Just his *usual* order. "Two eggs, lightly poached, rye toast, and bacon, please. With a side of hollandaise sauce. A glass of orange juice. And chocolate milk. Large."

He handed over the coffee-stained menu. The waitress only stared at him.

"Oh, are you out of chocolate milk?" Ryan asked.

She shook her head. Slowly.

"No rye toast? Sourdough would be fine."

"Uhhh." The waitress glanced at April. "Is he for real?"

"Big as life." Grinning, April gave Ryan a wink, and another hand-squeeze. "He'll have the Papa's Special. Scrambled easy. Whole wheat."

The waitress nodded and turned away. Ryan remembered one more thing.

"Oh, and a double cappuccino too, please. No foam, with a twist. Extra hot."

Raising her eyebrows, the waitress looked at April.

"Pot of regular too, please," she translated.

With a bemused expression, April refused Ryan's offer to order something for herself besides tea. She'd already paid for it, too, he realized, noticing the handwritten, green guest check and coins near the napkin dispenser. He wouldn't even be able to buy her breakfast.

Which, for Ryan, only meant he'd have to be doubly vigilant about lunch. Lunch was definitely his treat.

April watched their server leave, then picked up her discarded tea bag and reused it to make another cup with her diminutive pot of hot water. The weak scent of peppermint wafted across the table to Ryan, competing with the breakfast-y restaurant aromas of bacon, sausage, and maple syrup.

"Poached eggs?" she asked, giving him a sassy look as she sipped. "Hollandaise sauce? You don't get out much, do you?"

"I get out plenty. In the city."

"What city?"

"San Diego. Born and raised." *And socialized*, Ryan thought. How did people survive in places like this? Last night he'd asked for a decaf mocha at the coffee shop adjoined to the Motor Court Inn, and the server had brought him a Styrofoam cup and a *packet* of something. Apparently, this was just-add-water headquarters. "How about you?"

"Saguaro Vista. All my life."

She looked inexplicably pained by that fact, so Ryan asked, "You don't like it here?"

"I love it here. Most of the time. I really do."

She looked around the crowded diner, and as she did, a weight seemed to press upon her. It was as though the hubbub surrounding them—the clatter of plates, the hiss of food on the grill, the jumble of conversations—all combined to weigh her down. To mute her glow, just a little bit. She sighed.

"It's just that . . . well, people in small towns have long memories."

With that cryptic comment, April fell silent. Ryan took that moment to study her, noticing the way her glossy red hair curled around her shoulders, the way her nose crinkled when she took a sip of tea, the way her attention skittered from person to person in the packed diner. Something about April Finnegan captivated him. *Had* captivated him, ever since he'd seen her whip off her chipmunk head and look over her shoulder at him.

More than likely, it was April's sheer *unusualness* that interested him, Ryan decided. She couldn't have been more *un*like the women he'd known all his life.

As though sensing his evaluation, she put down her cup and gave him a once-over too, starting at the top of his head and roving lower to his buttoned-up shirt, tie, and pants. Her speculative expression gave him a sudden urge to bolt from the diner, before things could spiral any farther beyond his expectations.

"You're a quick study," April said, nodding toward him. "No suit coat today. Good idea. But so long as you look like that, people will still think you're selling something."

"I *am* selling something." In a sense, he was.

"Not looking like a stiff, you're not."

She rose suddenly, stirring up a whoosh of fresh air as she came to his side of the table. Ryan braced himself for the inevitable gust of perfume to follow, which experience had taught him wouldn't be long in coming. Most women he knew were walking five-alarm olfactory assaults—and paid handsomely for the privilege. You couldn't miss them. Even if you wished you could.

But April didn't smell like perfume, Ryan noticed at once. As she nudged her hip against him and crowded her way into his side of the booth, only lingering traces of soap and shampoo reached him. Clean. Pure. Bright. He liked it. He liked her. He liked the way she was putting her hands on his shoulders, and scrutinizing him still further.

Boy, was he in trouble.

Her flashy disco scarf whisked over him, a soft collision of glitter and tailoring ... a microcosm of the differences between them. That scarf was cheap. Tacky. Undoubtedly unfashionable. And yet, looking at its fringed ends whispering back and forth over his Hugo Boss–clad lap, Ryan had a nearly irresistible urge to grab it—*grab her*—and tug. To pull April closer, to sample the diversity he saw. To walk on the wild side.

"Geez, your shirt is like cashmere or something," she said, a delighted expression on her face as she stroked her fingers over it. "Not that I've ever felt real cashmere, I guess, but wow. Really, really nice. Those department stores of yours must do very well."

"Uh, yeah." Her fingers smoothed a wrinkle near his collarbone, igniting pleasurable sensations beneath his shirt. The subtle curve of her breast pressed lightly against his upper arm, making rational thought difficult. "I mean, no. I don't own Forrester's. I'm just a vice president."

In businesslike fashion, she unbuttoned his top shirt button. Loosened his tie. Examined the effect critically, then lowered the knot another fraction. Their faces were only inches apart, hers looking downward in concentration. All at once, Ryan had an insane urge to tilt her face upward, to skim his lips along her cheek, to find out if she tasted as fresh as she seemed.

"Vice president in charge of what?" she asked offhandedly.

His mind went blank. Damn it! He had to start carrying a business card, or something.

April glanced up. She quirked an eyebrow.

"In charge of this community outreach effort, here in Saguaro Vista," Ryan said. He felt the loss of her as she scooted back to her side of the table, mission accomplished. "For one thing."

Briefly, and because she obviously wasn't going to touch him anymore, *damn it,* he outlined the threat mass merchandizing, big box retailers posed to traditional, privately owned department stores like Forrester's. His coffee arrived and, fortified by several gulps of the strong brew, he went on to describe his plans to revitalize interest in local Forrester's stores by making partnerships and becoming involved in the community.

"It's a whole new way of doing business," he continued explaining. "Neighborhood-based retailing. And this is the test market. If I can make my plan work here, the board should agree to broaden it. Eventually, it should go nationwide."

"So . . ." April traced her finger around the rim of her cup, then looked up. "You want to make sure business at Forrester's keeps booming. That's why you're here."

"I'm not sure I'd call two hundred and eighty-nine stores in fifty states 'booming,' exactly. Not in a world of three-thousand-unit discount store chains and ever-increasing Internet retailing." Ryan's breakfast arrived, and he unrolled the cutlery from his dinky paper napkin with anticipation. "But sure. 'Booming business' about covers it."

Her gaze sharpened. "How many 'alliances' do you hope to forge here in town?" she asked.

"As many as possible. The sky's the limit."

She went suddenly still. Then inexplicably poker-faced. "Optimistic of you," she said quietly.

He felt April watching as he forked up some wobbly, non-poached eggs and tried them. While he chewed, she laid her hand on his forearm gently, as though preparing him for bad news.

"Listen, don't take this the wrong way. But I have to say," she leaned forward to confide, "you don't strike me as the optimistic type, exactly."

"I don't?"

"No. You strike me more as the get in, get rich, get out quick type."

Her head tilted from side to side. Her hands waved as she spoke, lively and expressive, taking some of the *ouch* from her blunt assessment. April communicated as much with her body—her touch—as she did with words, Ryan had noticed. She was unusual in that way, too. Especially when compared with his air-kissing, "I'll call you" circle of friends.

"Take your clothes, for instance," she went on, nodding toward him. "They're designed to impress, and they do. They do! But here in Saguaro Vista, things work a little differently than you're used to. You might not get the results you expect."

Ryan thought of the pink-stuccoed, ramshackle *casita* he'd been assigned at the Motor Court Inn, and figured she had a point. His travel agent had described the place as "charmingly Southwestern," with an "authentic flavor." But the only thing authentic about it was the feeling of relief Ryan got when he stepped out of its dingy purple and orange confines into the sunshine beyond.

"Then again," he said, raising his chin stubbornly, "I just might."

A man didn't admit weakness. And he didn't quake beneath greasy-spoon predictions of failure, either. He was a Forrester! Ryan reminded himself. Retailing was in his blood. Probably. So was success—he had the flourishing trust fund to prove that much. And what was that old saying . . . biology is destiny? Well, Ryan believed it.

For better or worse.

April lifted her hand to gesture toward his plate. "You might? The way you did with breakfast? That wasn't what you expected, either."

"I can handle it," he insisted.

She murmured noncommittally.

Her obvious skepticism stung. Okay. So maybe his party-going, good-time bachelor self didn't have much experience with the world of business, Ryan thought, but he did have determination to spare. And a working knowledge of human nature. And, if push came to shove, enough money to smooth his way into Saguaro Vista—the same way he'd smoothed over Bernie's refusal to buy new uniforms for Charlie's Pizzeria yesterday. He could do this. And he would.

He *would*.

And if he couldn't? If he proved unequal to the task?

Well, Ryan would rather give up his vacation home in Aspen, buff his Beemer with sandpaper, *do his own laundry* than admit he was scared he couldn't pull this off. So he focused his attention on pouring a fresh cup of scalding, tar-flavored, so-called coffee, and tried to look nonchalant.

"And if it doesn't work," he said, shrugging, "oh, well. I'll be off to something else."

"Interesting viewpoint." Settling back into her side of the cracked booth, April regarded him thoughtfully. "I can honestly say, I've never met anyone like you."

"That goes double for me." He grinned over her surprised expression, then raised his drippy chocolate milk glass to her teacup for a toast. "Here's to a most unlikely alliance."

"Cheers."

They clinked and drank, April watching him with an unreadable expression as she did. "We'd better get started," she announced, and moments later, they were off.

Whew, April thought several hours later, as she parked her bike near her next stop and chained it to a spindly mesquite. *Ryan Forrester had some kind of stamina.*

She'd figured him for a lightweight, a trust-fund fella who'd buckle after the first few "no"s from local businesses. After all, he'd obviously dodged her question about what kind of vice president he was at Forrester's. Almost as though he wasn't quite sure exactly which title he'd been bestowed with. And he'd come right out and admitted his community relations work in Saguaro Vista was only an experiment.

With an apparent lack of commitment like that, who'd have guessed Ryan would have doggedly approached Main Street businesses all morning, one after another?

Of course, they'd all turned him down. So far. Thank God. Betty at the bowling alley had refused Ryan's offer to display Forrester's Department Store artwork and knickknacks, explaining that the space had just been allocated to Ambrosia for a cookie counter.

The manager at the fairgrounds had regretfully

informed him that no, Forrester's couldn't buy the last available advertising space on the painted wooden rodeo ring fence—Ambrosia had purchased it two days earlier. The Saguaro Vista *Territorial* had explained to Ryan that no, he couldn't have the sought-after front-page newspaper advertising space he wanted. Ambrosia had reserved it, via April, for every day next week, to spread the news about a new pastry-naming contest she was sponsoring at the bakery.

In his defense, April had to admit that Ryan had accepted his defeats manfully. At first. And then he'd found a way to whip out his wallet at every business they'd visited, buying his way into every owner's fiscal good graces.

Free games for every bowler at the Pins 'N' Strike.

Complimentary Forrester's baseball caps for all the overly suntanned fairgrounds employees.

A five-hundred-dollar donation to the *Territorial* editor's favorite charity.

Now, walking to meet Ryan outside the two-story red-brick Saguaro Vista high school building, April had to wonder what would be next. Gold-plated desks for the students? State-of-the-art audio-visual equipment for the teachers? Season tickets to see the Phoenix Suns for the administration?

She didn't doubt Ryan could do it. Compared with the resources at his disposal, the paltry three batches of triple-chocolate supernutty cookies she'd used to soften up the administration for her Ambrosia scoreboard-sponsorship deal were small change. It was a good thing she'd hatched her plan to stick close to him. Otherwise, she'd have fatally underestimated what she was up against.

Keeping her new job—proving she wasn't another jobless, ambitionless Finnegan—meant everything to April. Succeeding in his venture meant almost nothing to Ryan. Especially if his words in the diner could be believed.

And if it doesn't work, oh, well. I'll be off to something else.

She believed him, too. Otherwise, April would have felt much too guilty to accompany Ryan on yet another sure-to-fail business meeting with the high school faculty.

Forty-five minutes later though, watching Ryan shake hands with the principal and then Coach Jason Haffy, she was wobbly with the beginnings of uncertainty.

They said good-byes all around, then Ryan and April left the school, crossing the football field on their way back to the parking lot. Behind them, the scoreboard she'd worked so hard to advertise on loomed overhead. At her side, Ryan put his hands in his pockets and lifted his face to the sun. Its glow cast his features in a flattering light, making him look sculpted and confident. A life-size Adonis—no chocolate loincloth necessary.

"I think that went well, don't you?" he asked.

His was a massive understatement. Kind of like saying Shaquille O'Neal was "on the tall side," and Arizona summers were "warm." Ryan fairly crackled with a conqueror's energy. His straight shoulders, self-assured gestures, and buoyant swagger made it obvious he was pleased with himself. Tickled pink, if appearances could be believed.

A person would almost think he'd never struck such a deal before. Which was silly. Wasn't it? He sure *looked* every inch the experienced, successful businessman.

"I was beginning to think I'd hit dead ends all over town," he went on. "You've canvassed this place pretty thoroughly."

His admiring glance lifted her spirits a little. This was only one small setback, April assured herself. One minor glitch. She could afford to be generous.

"Well, I did my best. But you have an awfully persua-

sive way about you." *And bottomless resources, too.* "There's
really no reason we can't share the scoreboard advertising space, the way you suggested to the principal and
Coach Haffy."

The words were hard to get out. *There's every reason!*
her survival instincts screamed. *You're butting into my
territory!* But at least this way Ryan wouldn't be forced
to return to San Diego in utter defeat, April rationalized.
She liked him. She didn't want that for him. And so
she did her best to steady her panicky feelings, and
looked back at him squarely.

"Congratulations on your deal," she said firmly.
"That was a masterful presentation you gave."

He smiled, looking boyishly pleased. "Thanks."

They strode a few steps farther, the field's grass damp-
ening their shoes. April twisted the toe of her hiking
boot on a clump of turf at the fifty yard line, and Ryan
took her arm to steady her. He didn't let go. Their
shoulders and hips rubbed lightly and companionably
together, every few steps, as they continued onward.

"You know what the Forrester's board of directors
called my plan to come here?" he asked suddenly.

April shook her head, dragging away an errant curl
that had glued itself to her passionfruit lip gloss. She
liked the protective feel of Ryan's hand on her arm . . .
the gentlemanly way he led her past threatening cleat
holes and a discarded Budweiser bottle. He was different
than the men she'd known. Different, and intriguing.

Even if he *was* a wannabe sponsorship-stealer.

"No, what did they call it?" she asked.

"Idiot Savant Retailing." Ryan kicked at a dirt clump,
his rich leather oxfords and expensively tailored clothes
incongruously out of place on the football field. He
ducked his head, then looked into the middle distance

as he went on talking. "I, uh, haven't had much interest in the family business until recently. Most of the board is rightfully skeptical of my abilities."

"I don't know," April argued. "Sometimes it takes a fresh eye to see the best solution to a problem."

He looked surprised. "That's what *I* said!"

"Sometimes people underestimate . . . someone, and think they're capable of less than they are."

"I know!" Ryan grinned, as though he found their newly discovered harmonious views unbelievably terrific.

April bit her lip. "Sometimes people think the way you've been"— *the way your family's been, for four generations*— "is the way you'll always be. That nothing can ever change."

"Passionately said." He cast her a curious look. "Something you have personal experience with?"

She shrugged, and slipped from his hold as they reached the blacktop parking lot. "I just think each new day is its own experience, that's all. Each new opportunity is there for the taking. I—that is, *people*," she corrected hastily, "shouldn't be limited by what someone else thinks."

"I agree."

Despite her attempts to seem as though this meant no more to her than a source for small talk, April felt herself speaking more and more from the heart. She stooped to unlock her bike, and went on talking.

"Limits are for wimps. I'll fight against knee-jerk judgments every step of the way," she said, stowing her lock with decisive movements. "And you'd better believe something else about me, too. If someone tells me I can't do something, it only makes me want to do it twice as much."

Ryan helped steady her vintage Schwinn. "Very rebellious of you," he said. "Very tough."

She squinted upward, trying to gauge if he was making fun of her "toughness." In the sunlight, it was hard to tell. But she could tell one thing, all right . . . that wonderfully sure and steady voice of his definitely *sounded* sincere.

"Tough? Some people might think so," April said, semi-defensively. She straddled her bike, and busied herself with slinging her purse over her shoulder and across her chest, where it would be secure during her ride.

"Hmmm," Ryan murmured, unrevealingly.

He stepped nearer, and for some reason, all her senses went on red alert. Cautiously tightening her grasp on her handlebars, she glanced up at him.

He was watching her with a rapt expression, almost as though he really *had* never met anyone like her . . . and was thoroughly fascinated by the experience. His attention slipped to her lips, and his hand raised to gently finger the curling ends of her hair. His chest rose on a deep, indrawn breath.

"The thing is," Ryan said, "that you don't strike me as the tough type, exactly."

"I don't?"

"No. You strike me more as the feisty on the outside, sweet on the inside, make-your-move-before-she-gets-away type."

He slipped his hand to her jaw, his thumb stroking slowly over the sensitive skin near her earlobe. Carefully, he leaned closer. April caught her breath, her heart suddenly skipping along double-time.

She registered the warmth of his touch, the significance of his step forward, the almost tangible pull between them. When she would have expected him to assume too much, Ryan hesitated, and caught her eye.

When she would have expected him to pretend this meant nothing, he gazed at her with a seriousness that meant everything. Infinite possibilities lived in the moments between his unspoken invitation and her reply, and April dizzily savored every one.

He left her plenty of time. Time to refuse, time to jump up and down with delight, time to grab him and make *her* move, if she chose to. She appreciated that about him. Ryan Forrester was a man—a man who'd made his desires known. A man who would accept no less than equal strength. Equal giving. Equal taking.

Hey, she could respect that, April told herself. So she raised her hands to his necktie, gave a tug, and encouraged his move with one of her own.

Their lips met, once. Twice. A thrill sizzled down her spine, and made her fingers curl on the heavy silk beneath her hands. Barely moving, April glanced upward, saw the pleasured curve of Ryan's smile. It made her smile, too. With a movement as necessary as sugar on cereal, she kissed him again . . . and found herself quickly losing control. Of their joining. Of their closeness. Of her admittedly loosely held caution.

Ryan commanded their kiss. Leisurely and expertly, dizzyingly and compellingly, he swept his mouth along hers, tasted her lower lip, teased her until she couldn't help but open to him. Heat filled her as their kiss grew more intimate.

It should have felt strange, such intimacy between people who'd known each other only days. But here, now, with Ryan, it didn't. Instead, it felt right, and wonderful. It felt as though she'd waited years to experience the synchronicity of this man, this moment, this closeness.

Losing herself to it, April wrapped her arms around his shoulders and stepped even closer, not caring when her unattended bicycle bumped against her hip and a car drove past in the parking lot and her whole world shifted in the space between one breath and the next. An inexplicable sweetness turned her heart to a thumping, vulnerable, *aching* presence inside her, and what had begun as a simple exploration . . . almost a dare . . . quickly became something much more meaningful.

Moments tumbled past, time during which the spring breeze pushed them together, and lifted April's hair to whirl around them both with soft silent swirls. Their clothes caressed, custom-made wool carousing with thrift-store poly-cotton. Their bodies leaned and touched, completing the inevitable momentum begun at their first meeting. No embrace could have been more embraceable; no beginning, more irresistible.

Slowly, they drew apart.

Reluctantly, April opened her eyes.

"Wow." Ryan cradled her cheek, tweaked her ear playfully between this thumb and forefinger, and smiled. "Wow."

He looked as stunned as she felt. And stunned didn't describe the half of it. Taking a step backward, April wrenched her bike sideways, away from her hip, and gripped the handlebars again. She wasn't quite sure where to do. What to go. How to be.

All in a muddle, she searched for a way to hide the fact that he'd rattled her. In the end, she summoned up what she hoped looked like a sassy grin and hoped for the best.

"Nice moves, moneybags," she said. "Let's hit the road."

If anything, Ryan's expression turned even more taken aback. But he didn't argue, or question any further, and for that, April was grateful.

After all, who knew what she'd tell him. Especially since she'd just realized a truth both scary and certain. Her biggest, toughest, most resourceful business competitor had just morphed into something unexpected and far more dangerous ... her craziest, sexiest, most tempting crush in years.

Chapter Five

Humming to herself, Jamie Barrett shook open a purple vinyl cape with the *HairRazors* logo printed on one corner, and smoothed it over her next client's shoulders. This was the first time she'd had her next door business neighbor Mark Wright in her chair. And to be perfectly honest, her fingers trembled as she fastened the protective cape beneath his jaw.

Her humming took on new momentum as she launched into the melody of a tune from her favorite underground band. Jamie always hummed when she was nervous—had done it since she was a kid in pigtails, and hadn't been able to stop since. Hypnosis, behavior modification tapes, rubberband-snapping aversion therapy, positive affirmations taped to her hairstylist's mirror—none of them had worked. At this point, she was more or less resigned to it . . . but she wasn't resigned to Mark not noticing her. And she didn't think she ever would be.

Trying to remain professional, she sifted her hands

through his fine blond hair. Maybe a messier, seventies-revisited, layered 'do, Jamie deliberated. Like the one she'd seen in the April *Weddings Today* "grooms" column. Or a classic buzz cut, with a few styling products for edge—and the need for frequent trims. *Frequent trims.* Yeah, that was it. A side bonus! Besides, anything that got rid of Mark's too-tidy Ken-doll look would be welcome.

Her hands-on style musings sent a few hanks over his forehead, and he looked up at her from beneath them.

Be still, my heart.

"So, what do you hear about this new guy in town?" he asked. "I'll bet you get all the gossip, here at the salon all day."

Jamie stilled her hands. "I should have *known* you weren't in here for a cut! In all the years we've known each other, you've never let me near your head with a pair of shears."

"Protective instincts."

"Cowardly impulses. You're afraid to look different."

She crossed her arms over her chest. In a routine as familiar to both of them as April's croissants in the morning, Mark gave back as good as he got.

"Oh, I'd look different if *you* cut my hair, all right," he said. "Different as in bizarre. I'm not one of those dye-your-hair-purple, pierce-your-tongue, wear-black-leather types you artsy women are so fond of."

He had no idea what "types" she was fond of. Or if she was even an "artsy" woman, as he assumed. Stifling her disappointment that Mark hadn't actually come to see *her* for once in her eternal-sidekick life, Jamie scoffed. "Purple hair and piercings are *so* turn-of-the-millennium. Fashion marches on. But then, you might not be aware of that, seeing as how you're still stuck in 1992. Those corduroy pants went out with the macarena."

"Oh, yeah? At least I'm not the kook who brought nonmeat hot dogs to the Fourth of July cookout last year. I hear the whole park smelled like grilled Alpo."

"Oh, really?" Jamie blindly grabbed for a comb. "Well, if you ever went *out* for any *fun*, Mister Workorama, you'd *know exactly* what they smelled like!"

They glared at each other in the mirror. In the background, salon business went on as usual. A blow-dryer whirred, shears could be heard snipping in the hands of another stylist, and the receptionist whisked the broom over the floor. Jamie never took her eyes from Mark. He never shifted his gaze from her. *Showdown at the Shears-R-Us Corral.*

As usual, she caved first. The edge of her mouth quirked. Then a twitch at the corner of Mark's eye betrayed him. Jamie drew a breath, stifling a laugh. Mark made a face, and she couldn't hold it in any longer.

At their combined guffaws, the stylist at the next chair shook her head. "You two do this often?"

"Just often enough," Jamie said.

"To stay in practice," Mark finished.

"Come on, then," she told him with a hand to his caped shoulder. "Now that that's over with, let's get started. You game?"

"Oh, all right. Twist my arm."

And to her amazement, he cooperatively headed for the shampoo station. A few minutes later, freshly Redken-ed and dripping, he walked from the sinks back to her stylist's chair. He settled in and let her get started.

"So, what *do* you hear about this Forrester guy?" Mark asked. "I hear he's been all over town the past few days, throwing around money like it was toothpaste at a dental convention."

Jamie quit snipping. "Your mind runs along weirdly traditional lines, doesn't it?"

"Just tell me what you know."

"Okay." She breathed out, and surrendered to the inevitable. "Yes, Ryan Forrester is in town, trying to form alliances with local businesses. Yes, he was in here, hitting up Monica for hairstyling services at some prom-and-bridal fashion show he's planning at the department store. Yes, she referred him to me for an answer. Yes, he's just as good-looking, charming, and well-spoken as they say. And *yes*, April has been spending a lot of time with him."

Mark gave her a sham-innocent look from beneath his half-styled hair. "What? Who says I wanted—"

"Of *course* that's what you wanted to know! And before you ask, no, I didn't give him an answer about the stylist gig yet, and no, I don't know what's going on between him and April."

All Jamie knew was what April had confided in her. Which hadn't been much . . . and had been mostly revelatory for the glowing look on her face when she'd revealed it. *Something* was going on between Jamie's long-time friend and the new hottie in town, but it didn't take a genius to figure out it was still in the fledgling, easily taken-off-track stages of new romance.

It also didn't take a genius to figure out that Mark didn't really want to know any of that. For as long as Jamie could remember, Mark had secretly had the hots for April, and Jamie had pretended not to know because she secretly had the hots for Mark. Neither of them had dared reveal any of it to anyone. She and Mark tended to leave the whole unspoken subject . . . well, mostly unspoken.

"But you'll be seeing him again, right?" Mark asked. He frowned at his reflection and smoothed his hair with his hand.

She gently slapped it away. "Don't touch the work in progress, buster. And yes, I'll be seeing him again to give him my answer about the fashion show, I guess.

But I don't see—" Jamie broke off as a determined gleam came into Mark's eyes.

"Oh, no," she said, shaking her head. "I'm not going to do it. Whatever put that devious look on your face, I want no part of it."

"What?" His overly innocent expression returned. "All I'm suggesting is, you're single, the new guy's single . . . if sparks were to fly between you two—"

"Sparks?" Jamie snorted. Although she did find Mark's old-fashioned turn of phrase sort of . . . cute. Against all odds, she liked the comforting steadiness of him. "Not hardly."

"Oh."

His mouth turned downward, making her wish she dared to kiss it into happiness again. Instead, Jamie concentrated on cutting his hair, her mind busily turning over the possibilities inherent in Mark's suggestion.

She didn't want to hook up with Ryan Forrester. Especially not for the purpose of detaching him from her best friend's side. Gorgeous and wealthy as he was, Ryan just didn't turn her crank. Not the same way Mark's earnest, dependable, ready-to-settle-down-ness did. But if, somehow, Jamie *helped* along Ryan's romance with April . . . gee, that would leave Mark available to finally notice *her*, wouldn't it? And then everybody would be happy.

Her mind made up, Jamie reached for the styling gel, ignoring Mark's wide-eyed, uneasy glance at the squeeze tube.

"Oh, all right," she said. "Twist my arm, why dontcha? I'll see what I can do."

Standing outside the adobe building that housed the Saguaro Vista recreation department, Ryan angled the pay phone receiver between his chin and shoulder and listened to Jackson rattle on about showgirls, blackjack, and the overall glitzy wonders of Las Vegas. In the background, slot machines jangled. The woman who was with Jackson squealed occasionally. And a steady buzz of background noise hummed over the connection.

Compared with the quiet surrounding Ryan—where the loudest sounds were the leaves rustling on a nearby mesquite and a lone Buick passing by on the blacktop road—the whole effect was . . . well, pretty surreal.

"No way!" Jackson was saying. "If you think I'm ditching Lola here in Vegas, just to bring you a Winnebago in the middle of nowhere—"

"I didn't say to ditch her," Ryan said. "Bring her along."

"Ha! You'd fit right in in Podunkville, U.S.A., wouldn't you, honey?" Jackson asked Lola. Sounds of smooching were heard. "Yeah, I thought so. A perfect match. Kinda like pâté on a Ding Dong."

Ryan made a face and held the phone away from his ear. When he returned it, Jackson and his latest conquest were still cooing baby talk to each other.

"Look, I'll pay for everything," Ryan said, raising his voice to be heard over the cooing "cuddlekins," and "sugarpies," and casino chaos. "Just pick out a nice Winnebago or something" —*one with a decent mattress, and a lower polyester-to-purple-and-orange ratio than the* casita *from hell*— "and drive it down here to Saguaro Vista. You can catch a flight back to Vegas from Phoenix. It's only an hour or so from here."

"I dunno, Ryan . . ."

"I'd rather not order one sight unseen over the phone," Ryan explained, thinking of the Winnebago ad he'd seen on his room's twelve-inch black-and-white TV last night, which had given him this whole idea.

"And I'm not sure whom I'd trust to deliver the thing here, if I did," he went on. "But I've got to do something about the accommodations situation. Hotels in Saguaro Vista aren't all they're cracked up to be. Are you sure you and Lola aren't up for a road trip?''

"Are you sure *you* aren't ready to bail out of there?" Jackson countered. "I can't believe you've stuck with this 'work' thing for so long, as it is. You haven't demonstrated this kind of dedication since eighth grade, when Jenny Arbuckle offered to teach you how to—"

"All right, never mind," Ryan said, interrupting his friend in mid-ribaldry. "I'll come up with something else. Thanks anyway."

"Hey, no problem. And anytime you're ready to return to the real world, buddy, you just give a whistle. We'll come reconnaissance you out of Palookaville anytime you want. Or at least send you a plane ticket."

"There's no airport in Palookaville."

"No airport? Jeez, do they have electricity, at least?"

Ryan thought about the fake gold lamps that illuminated the velvet Elvis painting over his Motor Court Inn bed, the fluorescent lights that illuminated the lack of shoppers at the flagship Forrester's store, and the old-fashioned outlets in his *casita,* none of which accommodated the three-pronged plug on his brand-new, "I mean business" notebook computer.

"Unfortunately, yes," he answered. "Sort of."

"Like I said" —coins could be heard pouring into a metal slot machine receptacle. Lola squealed more loudly— "be smart. Get out while you still can."

Shaking his head slightly, Ryan tightened his grip on the pay phone. If he'd been able to secure service for his cell phone, he would have been able to pace, too. Unfortunately, Saguaro Vista was too remote for anything but analog access, something his state-of-the-art phone was too advanced to support.

"I'm not leaving yet," he said. There was still work to be done. And there were still worthwhile experiences to be had. Catching a glimpse of a yellow Schwinn from the corner of his eye, Ryan was reminded of an important one of them. "In some ways, Saguaro Vista has its . . . appeal."

And ninety-nine percent of that appeal was wound up in one quirky, leggy, touchy-feely woman. The same woman who was headed his way, right this minute. With a quick good-bye to Jackson, Ryan turned to greet April, and couldn't help but be bowled over by the amazing smile she gave him as she spotted him.

That smile did things to him. Mushy, knock-him-over-with-a-feather, *seriously* tantalizing things. It filled him with an unexpected sense of happiness. It made him step closer, to be nearer to April sooner. It reminded Ryan of the kiss he'd shared with her yesterday . . . and made him yearn for more of the same, right now.

"Nice office you've got there," she said, nodding toward the dilapidated pay phone and the semi-shredded phone book dangling from a chain at its base. "Maybe after your car grows up, it can give some pointers to your work space. Before you know it, you might even have yourself a desk."

Her hug of greeting took all the sting from her teasing. It was a light embrace, and brief, but it was enough for Ryan to register the lithe shape of her, the fresh scent of her, the va-va-voom girliness of her. He blinked, and worked up a comeback.

"Hey, before you know it, you might even have a car of your own to grow," he said, grinning. "Speaking of which—"

He slipped his wallet from the pocket of his khakis, feeling concurrently pleased with himself for having finally nailed the casual-clothes look and for having arrived at one way he could repay April for introducing him to Saguaro Vista during the past two days. Still talking, he counted through the bills.

"—I've been meaning to help you out with that. You did me a favor, showing me around town the way you did. Here. This ought to cover it."

He held out some money, roughly equivalent to April's car repair bill, plus a generous—*very generous*—tip.

She stared at it. Very slowly, she straightened her spine.

"What's that?"

"Ransom money for your car."

His joke fell flat. "No, thanks."

"A gift from a friend, then," he tried.

"Look, I'm not for sale, okay?" Her voice sounded strange, flat and faraway. "I'm not for sale, and neither is this town."

What the—? Confused, Ryan waggled the money. Its color matched her Army surplus–looking wide-legged pants, he noticed. Not that that had encouraged her to accept it. And what was he doing paying any attention to April's bizarre outfits, anyway? If she chose to wear canvas pants with spiky pink high heels, a sheer white blouse over a lace tank top, and a baseball cap, was it any of his business? Even if she looked inexplicably sexy in the whole mess?

Hell, no. Just like her obvious problems with accepting common courtesy weren't any of his business.

"Just take the money," he said, feeling frustrated at being stymied when he was trying to be helpful. "You need it and I've got it. Plenty of it."

"Rub it in my face, why don't you?"

"Oh, now we're in third grade again, huh?"

"If the shoe fits, Mr. Big."

They glared at each other, suddenly wary. Ryan didn't get it. He'd morphed from being delighted at seeing her to being confused as hell. It figured. He'd finally met a woman who could temporarily take his mind off his recent romantic foibles, and she turned out to be even more inexplicable than the debutante types he was used to.

All at once, a revelation struck him.

"Is this about the kiss yesterday?" he asked.

Her eyes widened. She gasped. "No!"

"Because if it is—"

"It's not!"

"—you should probably know I never meant for that to happen." With a jerky movement, Ryan refolded his money and put it away. For now. "I just—you were— and so we—well, it just happened."

"And it was great!"

"So if you can't handle it, I—*what?*"

"It was great." Sighing, April turned her face skyward, seeming to remember it. As though their tense moment had never happened, she relaxed. "Just don't try to pay me for it, okay?"

"I wasn't!"

"Good. Now, let's get a move on. We've got businesses to haggle with."

Their first stop turned out to be their first mistake. April got an early hint at that fact when she parked her bike outside Saguaro Vista's lone public-access television station and saw Ryan waiting for her on the concrete front steps . . . with a brightly colored gift bag on his lap. With it, and with his plaid shirt, khaki pants, and brand-new hiking boots, he looked like a designer lumberjack going to a kids' birthday party.

But he looked pretty terrific, too.

"What's that?" she asked, nodding toward the bag. "Did you gift-wrap your payoff in the hopes I would accept it this time?"

His face fell. Instantly, she wished she'd never said a

word. So Ryan Forrester could buy and sell the whole town—and her new job prospects, along with it. Did that mean she had to be rude to him? Rude to the best kisser she'd ever encountered, the smartest man who'd ever taken her seriously, the most hopelessly fashion-challenged fella who'd ever struggled out of Forrester's "outdoorsman's" section with a prefab "rustic look?"

Nah. It didn't.

"Sorry," she said. "Let's just go inside."

They both had appointments to meet with the hostess of the local TV talk show, Veronica Velasquez. April's had been arranged last week—five days' delay was the least she'd been able to wrangle out of the prissy receptionist. Ryan's had mysteriously been agreed to yesterday, on a moment's notice, and was scheduled immediately after April's.

Five minutes after their arrival, Veronica herself swept into the lobby to greet them. Dressed in a flowing emerald-green ensemble with enough gold jewelry to sink a barge, the talk show hostess smiled with pleasure at their arrival and shook hands with them both.

After introductions had been made, April presented her super secret weapon. It had never failed her yet. And given Ryan's semi-success yesterday, she figured desperate measures were called for.

"Here," she said, fishing around in her handbag for the Ambrosia box of two homemade apricot-almond muffins she'd baked that morning. "This is for you."

"Here," Ryan said at the same time, brandishing his showy gift bag. "This is for you."

"My goodness!" Veronica flattened both hands on her chest and gazed at their joint offerings. "Aren't you both *sweet?*"

April glared at Ryan's bag. Undoubtedly, it contained something expensive, exclusive, and out of her league. Damn it! Sticking close to his side to keep tabs on him obviously wasn't enough. She'd have to resort to something fiercer.

"What we are is competitors," she told Veronica in careful, confident tones. "*Friendly* competitors, for sponsorships here in Saguaro Vista. And, we hope, for invitations to appear on your program. It looks as though Mr. Forrester and I" —she gestured with her box toward Ryan's bag, indicating their, let's face it, joint bribes— "both had the same idea at the same time."

"Now isn't that funny?" Veronica said.

A bemused expression crossed her face. April waggled her box, trying to produce an enticing waft of apricot-almond-scented air. And then, for the first time ever, her baking expertise failed her. Failed her!

Veronica completely ignored April's offering and reached instead for Ryan's gaudy "pick me, I'm expensive" bag. "I've heard about you, Mr. Forrester," she all but purred, "from some people in town. I wonder what *this* could be?"

Ryan smiled. "Call it an introductory bonus," he said.

And at that moment, something inside April snapped.

Only one thing was clear when it came to her and Ryan Forrester: this town wasn't big enough for the both of them. And starting right now, April intended to do something about it.

"Um, Veronica? Can you excuse us for a minute, please?" she asked.

At the hostess' murmured assent—she was busy plucking tissue paper from the gift bag like a demented reverse-gift-wrap girl—April plastered a wide fake smile on her face and grabbed Ryan's Paul Bunyon–wannabe sleeve. Trembling with nerves and frustration and the effects of having gulped three too many cups of peppermint tea while maniacally baking this morning, she kept going until she and Ryan reached someplace quiet and private.

The door swished closed behind them. April manhandled a heavy chrome wastepaper basket into position next to it, to ensure it would stay that way.

Ryan cleared his throat. "Look, I hate to be a stickler, but this is the ladies' room."

"So what?" Striding purposefully to the other end of the rectangular pink-tiled room, April barely avoided growling the words. She ducked her head for a quick occupancy sweep. Good. All the stalls were empty. Leaving her alone with Mister Hot-shot Gift Bag Man. "You got a problem with that?"

"Depends on what you plan to do in here."

He raised his eyebrows hopefully. Teasingly. Lasciviously.

She laughed. "Are you dense? I didn't drag you in here for a getting-to-know-you quickie."

Ryan looked disappointed. He rallied quickly, and grinned instead. "In that case . . . would you consider a suggestion?"

"Ha!" Against all reason, she found his teasing endearing. He didn't back down. April had to give him credit for that. But still. . . . "What I would consider is *you,* leaving town!"

"Leaving town? Because of" —he gestured toward the door, beyond which Veronica Velasquez was probably ooing and aahing over his latest big bucks incentive, even now— "because of *that?*"

Folding her arms, April faced him down. He was a smart man. He'd figure it out.

He did. "Look, other people don't have your problem with accepting gifts. They actually *like* them."

"And you like feeling like Mister Big when you hand out the goodies."

Ryan scoffed. She'd struck a nerve, though, she could tell. He buffed the face of his bazillion-karat-gold watch on the sleeve of his lumberjack shirt, and didn't look up.

In desperate times, desperate women took aggressive measures, April told herself, beginning to pace. She had to protect her fledgling job, and she had to do it now—before Ryan wooed away any of her other prospective Ambrosia sponsorship providers. In Saguaro Vista, most of the small Main Street merchants were just like Bernie at the pizzeria. They had limited budgets and not a lot of negotiating room. Most of them, April knew, could not afford to make alliances with both Forrester's Department Store and her bakery.

It was either Ryan, or her. They couldn't both win.

And April intended to win.

He'd already gotten her dander up by trying to buy *her* this morning, the same way he'd bought the rest of the town's affections. *Ransom money for your car.* Ha! It wasn't exactly a big leap from there to here.

Ryan frowned. "Mister Big?"

"Yes, Mister Big," April repeated, stopping in mid-stride just a few inches away from him. "As a matter of fact, I'll bet you couldn't go a *week* without pulling out that overstuffed wallet of yours to get what you want."

At her challenge, he raised his head. "Oh, yeah?"

"Yeah!"

"You're wrong."

"Prove it," she dared, an idea beginning to take shape.

"I will!" Ryan met her gaze head-on. There was a pause. "How?"

Caught up in the heat of the moment, April didn't stop to think too deeply. "How? Here's how. Don't buy anything, don't charge anything, don't whip out any cash to make people see things your way. For one whole week."

"A week? Piece of cake." Ryan's chin jutted at a stubborn angle. "I could do two. Easy."

This time, it was April's turn to scoff. Sure, he was cute. But he was obviously deluded. "Two weeks? Ha! You'll crumble the first time you get a craving for one of those designer breakfasts you like. You'll be busing in a chef from Scottsdale, rounding up caterers and hollandaise-sauce makers—"

"And if I don't?"

The solution to her dilemma presented itself, just like that.

"If you don't, if by some chance you survive, cashfree" —April sauntered nearer and straightened the collar of his soft plaid shirt. She focused on the rustic stripes and checks, determined to keep her bravado going— "then the remaining town sponsorships will be yours to take. Uncontested."

Holding her breath, she waited for him to buckle. And for her bluff to pay off. After all, a guy like Ryan couldn't seriously believe he was capable of—

"Uncontested?" Ryan asked. A beat passed. "You're on."

"But if you *don't* make it," April felt compelled to warn, speaking quickly, "if you fall back on your bigcity, rich-guy ways" —which he would, of course— "*I* win. All the marbles. You back off, and leave the rest of Saguaro Vista to me."

It was everything she wanted, wrapped up in a tidy package. She didn't doubt she could convince Mark that her new community relations coordinator job was a success. All she needed was a clear shot at it. *Without* big-deal super-kisser Ryan Forrester getting in her way, and mixing her up.

Ryan tilted his head, as though considering the flip side of their impromptu wager. At his gesture, April suddenly realized the magnitude of what she was proposing. She felt a little wobbly. What if he could do it? What if she lost everything?

To Ryan, this whole thing was a lark. To her, it was the difference between Ramen noodles three times a day and food that was actually edible. Between listening to her beloved music CDs and selling them at the swap meet to raise water bill money. Between scoring a promotion and earning her own flighty Finnegan spot on the unemployment line—the same spot everyone in town expected her to occupy, sooner or later.

Subtly, April's fingers tightened on the button placket of Ryan's shirt. *Whoop, whoop!* went her internal bad-idea sensors. *Bail out! Quick!*

But it was already too late. And besides, April Finnegan didn't bail out. She didn't bail out, back down, bounce checks, or pay anything more than seventy-five percent off. And she didn't, *really didn't*, like being pushed around on her own turf.

"Don't you think you should meet some kind of challenge, too?" Ryan asked, all of a sudden.

"It's challenge enough just being near you without mentally divesting you of those awful faux lumberjack duds," April shot back. "Consider us even."

He smiled. Seductively. "If you wanted to see me naked, all you had to do was ask."

"Fat chance." Geez, she actually sounded as though she meant that. Amazing. "I don't sleep with the enemy."

"No? Bummer. If you'd told me that," Ryan said slowly, "I wouldn't have taken the bet."

His voice rumbled sexily on that last, and the bedroom-worthy look he gave her from those baby blues of his made April feel tingly all over. *This was dangerous,* the last vestiges of her common sense warned. The last thing she needed was a fling that would distract her from securing her reputation—once and for all, damn it!—as a *steady, serious, dependable* Finnegan.

So right then and there, she made a decision. No matter how tempting Ryan might look, he had to be off-limits to her. Period. Like budgeting to her mother, résumé-writing to Mickey, and spontaneity to Mark. From here on out, Ryan was one big, intriguing, cute-booty-possessing No Trespassing Zone.

It was only sensible.

And there was always a chance she could be sensible, too.

Okay. An outside chance, sure. But it was there.

"Too late. The deal's done," April said, to seal their bet. They shook hands. "Get ready to lose, Mr. Bigshot."

Ryan's smile widened. "Get ready yourself, Red. I never lose."

Chapter Six

By the time happy hour arrived that afternoon, Ryan had embarked on his new cash-free, credit-free, April-endorsed lifestyle. Hers was a challenge he'd instantly risen to meet. After all, what guy backed down from a dare?

No guy, that's who. Not if he had any self-respect. And especially not if he was Ryan Forrester, the same guy who'd won his country club's charity golf tournament three years running, and who'd scooped up the pot in his monthly poker games so often the chips just naturally gravitated toward his side of the table these days. He'd sooner have given up his summer share in the Hamptons than refuse to play April's game.

And he'd sooner play April's game than admit the truth: he was afraid she was right. What if, Ryan thought as he examined his wallet, he really *couldn't* survive without the Forrester fortune to smooth his way?

All his life, he'd relied on money and family connections to get what he wanted. He hadn't thought about it, because money and family connections defined his life. Those privileges had been his in the same way blond hair, a knack with parties, and point guard–style height had been his. They'd simply been *there*. And he'd taken advantage of them. But now, facing a privilege-free two weeks with no resources except himself, Ryan felt the smallest quiver of worry.

Refusing to dwell on it, he opened the drawer of the bedside table at his *casita* and dropped his wallet inside. It landed beside the bible and the quarter-inch-thick Saguaro Vista yellow pages. He shut the drawer. Walked away.

And just like that, Ryan felt naked.

He looked at the drawer. It grew larger in his imagination, pulsing like some macabre identity-eating furniture monster in a B movie. Steeling his will, he looked away.

An instant later, he could have sworn his wallet called to him. Its voice was authoritative, commanding and reassuring at the same time. Evidently, he'd been carrying the billfold version of James Earl Jones in his pocket all these years.

This bet is ridiculous, it said. *You need a Winnebago.*

Ryan closed his eyes and gave his head a quick shake.

And a decent meal. And a working cell phone.

This was nuts. Finally, he understood what his constantly dieting sister Tabitha meant when she said the Triple Chocolate Decadence Cake called her name at midnight. He went to the marble-laminate sink for a glass of water to clear his head.

A nice merlot would be good.

The plastic hotel cup bent in his hand. He glanced back at the bedside table. Had the drawer actually slid open a little?

And about this drawer, his wallet went on, becoming

more insistent now. *I really deserve better. I'm made of Italian leather. Hand stitched! Don't you think—*

"Enough!" Ryan yelled. Cripes, he'd only tried to get by on his own merits for an hour and thirty-five minutes, and already he was losing his mind.

"What's enough?" asked a voice from outside his *casita* door. "I haven't even knocked yet."

April. Digging his hands through his hair, Ryan strode to the flimsy wooden door. On the way, he briefly considered aiming a well-placed karate kick at the drawer containing fifty percent of his current worries, but didn't. After all, it wasn't his wallet's fault he'd become platinum card codependent.

He opened the door. April stood on the threshold, beaming at him the way she always did.

"Hiya," she said. "Can I come in?"

Before he could answer, she ducked under his arm and entered the room, looking around curiously.

"I've decided it's no use," she announced, only her backside visible as she peered at the furniture and stroked the orange chenille bedspread. She dumped her handbag atop it. "I have the world's worst verbal hangover, and nothing else is going to cure it. Nothing but the hair of the dog that bit me, that is."

"Huh?"

"Nice Elvis." April nodded toward the velvet King. "My mom has the one where he's holding the roses."

"April—"

"Where was I? Oh, yeah—the hair of the dog. I figure you might be feeling like I'm feeling right now, so I decided to come over. You might have guessed by now I'm not the 'stew alone' type."

She sat on the bed, and bounced up and down. The motion made her wild red hair toss around her head, and sent the edges of her unbuttoned transparent shirt fluttering wide to reveal her lacy top beneath. Apparently oblivious to his "bed's" lumpy horribleness, April nodded with satisfaction and got up to investigate the rest of his *casita*.

He decided to backtrack. "Verbal hangover?"

"Mmmm-hmmm. You know, that woozy feeling you get when you know you've probably blurted out something stupid, but you're not quite sure *how* stupid, because you can't remember exactly what you said, but you think it was pretty dumb?" She paused near the Massage-o-Matic control panel on the bed, and looked at him over her shoulder. "Got a quarter?"

For you, anything, Ryan thought instantly. Stupidly. Because they'd only met a few days ago, after all, and April Finnegan was really too ... unusual to be taken seriously, wasn't she? But despite that fact, he found himself taking her very seriously, indeed.

"No," he said, pantomiming pulling out his empty pockets as he put on a mournful expression. "I'm dead broke."

She rolled her eyes. "No, you're n—"

He raised an eyebrow.

"—yes, yes, you are. That's right."

"You're trying to trick me into losing our bet," Ryan said, grinning. "It won't work."

"It might work." April wore a siren's smile as she rested her forearm atop the Massage-o-Matic's control panel and languorously leaned against it. "You wanted to give me a quarter. You know you did."

He had. But only because the idea of joining April atop the quivering Massage-o-Matic mattress held an illicit, *non*–country club–type appeal. It was as though she brought out some untapped *wildness* in him. And if there was one thing Ryan knew for sure, it was that his life until now had definitely not prepared him for wildness. For *her*.

"Look, did you come here to harass me?" Ryan asked.

"Because if you did, I think we need to apply some guidelines to this wager of ours."

"Harass you? Of course not." She straightened, perpetually in motion. "I told you, I needed some of the hair of the dog that bit me. That's you."

"Ooookay."

She bent down to peer at the miniature plastic coffeemaker perched atop the vanity beside his razor and toothpaste. Scooping up one of the shrink-wrapped premeasured "gourmet" coffee packets, April gave an exclamation of delight. She rifled through the other varieties, then examined the powdered, flavored creamers.

"Nice amenities," she murmured, nodding. "In-room coffee *and* a blow-dryer. It figures you'd wind up in the nicest place in town."

Nicest place in town? His worst fears were realized. In Saguaro Vista, it didn't get any better than this. And he'd agreed to blow an extra week here, meeting the conditions of April's spur of the moment bet.

He had to take control of this situation. Ignoring the vulnerable feeling being without his wallet gave him, Ryan went to April and turned her around to face him.

"I hope you're ready to give it up," she said blithely as he did, "because they won't let you stay here for free, you know. Hey!" She gawked at the TV. "Do you have *cable?*"

"Yes. No. I don't know." Feeling confused, he returned to a subject he did have answers to. His *casita*. "I had a reservation. I only planned to be here a week, so my room's paid up through tomorrow night."

What would he do the next night, without cash? Yikes.

"Mmmm. I'll bet you get HBO."

She gazed longingly at the TV, as though she could make "Sex and the City" magically appear through sheer willpower alone. Then, as though only that moment realizing how closely they stood together, April blinked up at him.

"You're awfully good-looking," she said. "Did you know that?"

"Have you been drinking?"

"I told you. Verbal hangover. You know, woozy—"

"Woozy feeling, saying something stupid, hair of the dog. Got it."

"Geez, you really listen." Her eyes widened, and that sunburst smile of hers shined on him all over again. "You know, I feel much better now. Thanks."

She hugged him, then wriggled gently from their embrace. Ryan was left with a confused impression of delicate arms, slender torso, and happiness slipping inexorably from his grasp.

"You're leaving?" he asked.

April paused in the midst of picking up her handbag. She frowned slightly. "Sure."

"But what about your hangover?"

She waved a hand carelessly. "Cured. You're not being weird around me, so I don't have to be weird around you. Whatever I said while making our bet, it apparently wasn't embarrassing enough for *you* to be embarrassed for *me*."

"What?"

With a patient expression, April came to him and took his hand. She led him to the bed and sat him down beside her.

"You're a nice guy," she explained. "I can tell that about you. It's probably one of the things I like about you, in fact."

"A nice guy?" Why didn't she just shoot him and get it over with? Being called a "nice guy" was the next best thing to having a "good personality." He couldn't *believe* this. In all his thirty-odd years of life, no one had *ever* accused Ryan Forrester of being A Nice Guy.

"Sure. And because you're a nice guy—"

There it was *again*!

"—you would be embarrassed on my behalf if I did something really ridiculous. Get it? So now I know I don't have anything to worry ab—"

"Wait." With a move as spontaneous as accepting her wager had been—and probably as foolhardy—Ryan leaned in. Cupped her jaw in his hand. And kissed her.

She tasted sweeter than the finest chocolates, richer than the lifestyle he'd temporarily abandoned. With barely a rumble of warning, he angled his head and took what she so wonderfully offered. Kissing April was like stepping into sunshine, Ryan discovered for the second time. Hot. Pleasurable. Dangerous in large quantities.

When their kiss ended a few minutes later, they were sprawled atop the gaudy chenille, April surrendered beneath his outstretched body with her fingers entwined with his. She blinked the way she had a few minutes earlier, and Ryan noticed the surprise in her expression with—he had to admit—a healthy amount of masculine pride.

How's that for Mr. Nice Guy? he thought.

"Wow," she said.

"Yeah," he replied.

"That tough-guy, take-what-you-want routine suits you remarkably well. I like it."

"Routine? *Routine?*" He shook his head, still enjoying the feel of her beneath him. "That was all me, baby."

April burst into laughter.

"I'm bad to the bone."

Her body shook with suppressed guffaws.

"I'm" —Ryan searched for something suitably macho-sounding— "the hair of the dog that bit you."

She gasped, and said something unintelligible.

"Am I tickling you?" he asked.

"No. No." The words emerged between breaths. April seemed to gather her self-control, then a smile cracked her composure. "Rrruuuuff!" she yelped, then nipped him on the neck.

All of a sudden, Ryan was laughing, too. He hugged her close, not caring who heard as they rolled across the bed together, tickling and making dog sounds. Somehow, in the midst of this kooky moment, he felt alive . . . alive, and free, and closer to April than he ever had to anyone. He didn't need a wallet for this. Didn't need a bar tab, impossible-to-get dinner reservations, ski tickets, or a limited-edition car. All he needed was April, and the warmth that being near her filled him with.

"Ahhh, you're amazing," he said, rolling them both to a stop. He tweaked her nose and kissed her, and felt a huge reserve of untapped sappiness welling up inside him. "Absolutely amazing."

Suddenly, April stiffened. "What am I *doing*?"

Her hands clutched at his shoulders, and she gave a mighty push. Ryan rolled away, confused, and watched as she sprang to her feet.

"Doing?" he asked. "Well, you could call it cheering up a temporarily destitute man. Or, if that doesn't work for you, getting to know the competition."

His mention of their rivalry for town sponsorships seemed to send her into getting-away mode even faster.

"I can't do this," she said, fussing with her handbag again. "I'm sorry. I'm responsible and sensible, and you're—"

"*You're* sensible?"

"—you're just a rich playboy type, passing through town on the way to your next big thing. Shindig. Debutante. Yacht. Whatever."

"*Sensible?*"

April straightened, and looked him square in the eye.

"People like you don't take anything seriously. You're not *real*, not the way Saguaro Vista—for all its faults— is. Not the way I am."

"You're . . . real?" Still sitting on the bed, which felt lumpy again now that April wasn't sharing it with him, Ryan frowned. Something about her words dug into him, touched a raw spot he didn't want to acknowledge. What did she mean, he wasn't "real?" "You're the most amazingly *un*real woman I've ever met! Nobody I know is even remotely like—"

"No." She held up her palm. "Let's not do this, okay? Bottom line is, I don't need my life messed up anymore than it already is. Thanks, but no thanks."

"But—"

"I shouldn't have come here. Damn it!" She framed an imaginary sign with her arms. "No trespassing!"

"Huh?"

She slapped her forehead with the heel of her hand, shaking her head. Then, with a regretful gesture, April bent forward and slid her hands along the sides of his face. Her handbag thumped into his knee, and her energy surrounded him. Ryan was still wondering what the heck had gone wrong when she pressed a small kiss to his cheek.

"I'm sorry. See you around."

"No." He caught her wrist when she would have turned away. "We have to stick together," Ryan said.

Her gaze, suddenly solemn, pierced his wallet-less self.

"Why?" she asked.

Because I need you, he thought, insanely.

"Because otherwise you'll never know who won the bet," he said instead, sensibly. "I could be blowing money all over town, and you'd never know it."

April narrowed her eyes. "I'd know it."

"Maybe." He shrugged, as though it didn't matter to him one way or the other. Didn't matter to him enormously whether or not she bought into this whole "sticking together" thing. "Maybe not."

Holding his breath, Ryan waited for her to buckle. And for his bluff to pay off. After all, a woman like April couldn't seriously believe he was capable of—

"What do you mean, stick together?" she asked cautiously.

Although he was still befuddled—the combination of a verbal hangover, a mind-blowing kiss, searing closeness, and an existential debate on the nature of reality, all in the space of fifteen minutes—could do that to a guy, Ryan figured, he managed to come up with a reasonable explanation. One that might make her stay.

"I mean we'll have to spend most of our time together," he said, unanticipated relief pouring through him. "*Close* together. Day . . . and night. Otherwise we won't know for sure who won the bet."

She lifted her chin, seeming to reason out something within herself. She tilted her head back and forth, inaudibly weighing the pros and cons. Then she sighed.

"You're right," April said. "This is too important to risk."

He felt as though he'd won the battle, as though he were about to enjoy the victor's spoils. Smiling, Ryan stood up to pull her into his arms again.

And then the other shoe dropped.

"You'll just have to come with me to my family's weekly Wednesday barbecue tonight," April announced, and then she took him by the hand again and hustled him into the great unknown.

"Pssst, Mickey. Over here," April said.

Her brother lumbered to the far corner of their mother's concrete patio slab, dodging gold-painted cherub statuary and the assortment of wind chimes dangling from the ramada's edge.

"Ape? What are you doing behind the bougain-villea?"

Frowning over the nickname, April peered around the closest edge of the vine-bedecked trellis. There wasn't much room back here, but it was cool and dark and it felt safe. "Hiding."

"Hiding?" Mickey scratched his head, making his shaggy hair stand on end. "You're not the hiding type. What's the matter?"

"I think I'm going crazy. Has anybody guessed yet?"

His frown deepened. "Yeah. Six years ago. When you graduated the U of A and actually came back here to live, we all knew you were whacked."

"Har, har."

Her college years were a sensitive subject with April, paid for as they had been with a combination of academic scholarships and Granny Finnegan's savings. The concept of a "brainy Finnegan" had completely discom-bobulated her teachers—all of whom had taught Mickey in previous years, and some of whom had taught one or both of her parents. They hadn't known quite what to make of April. But the one thing they hadn't been able to make of her, the one thing no one had been willing to admit, was that she might wind up successful.

Proving those naysayers wrong would have been reason enough for her to come back to Saguaro Vista after college. But there'd been other reasons, too.

"Very funny, Mickey. I'm serious, here. Something's wrong. I don't feel like myself."

"Maybe a bougainvillea thorn is poking you."

"Do I look okay?"

He peered closer, giving her a blast of Nacho Cheese Dorito breath. "Well . . ."

"Or different, I mean," she clarified.

In the distance, conversations carried from the yard and inside the house, and nearby the wind chimes tinkled. A smoky breeze wafted from the grill, sending the aromas of hot dogs and hamburgers toward her. A housefly buzzed at her head, as pesky as the weird unsettledness inside her.

She'd acted like an idiot in Ryan's hotel room. April knew it. But somehow, she hadn't been able to get a hold of herself. Whenever he was around, she lost all semblance of cool. She was an eighth-grade geek all over again, giggling around the cutest boy on the bus. Any minute now a monstrous zit would pop up on her nose and finish her off, for sure.

"Mickey?" she pleaded, feeling more desperate now. "Ape?"

Short attention span theater. "Do I look all right? Normal? Because I'm worried. I'm feeling really—"

"Normal? Not hiding behind a bush, you don't look normal."

She stuck her head out farther and rotated it for inspection. She had survived arriving at her mother's house, had endured the requisite introductions between Ryan and her family with reasonable aplomb, and had even managed to leave her "date" alone with her scheming cousin Darla without freaking out. But now . . .

"Well, your face *is* kinda smushed-looking," Mickey conceded, examining her thoughtfully. "And your cheeks are, like, Bozo the Clown red."

"That's my blush, genius."

"But other than that, you only look a little crazy."

"A *little?*"

"About like usual."

"Very helpful." She was *definitely* channeling eighth-grade geek. And clearly, this was getting her nowhere. Fighting her way from behind the vine's glossy leaves and brilliant fuchsia bracts, April decided it was time to bite the bullet. Show some backbone. Face the music. Whatever. She emerged into the open, just as Ryan shot outside from between the open patio doors.

His trendoid lumberjack clothes flapped in the breeze. Pale-faced, he dodged a pair of molded plastic deck chairs and Fiona Finnegan's refurbished crystal gazing ball. When he reached the grass, he surveyed his surroundings, spotted April and Mickey in the patio corner, and headed straight for them with an expression of profound relief.

"Hide me," he said. "Your cousin is—"

At that moment, Darla came out of the house, vividly eye-catching in a tight yellow T-shirt and matching mini-skirt. "Oh, Ryan!" she called, tottering on three-inch platforms. "You forgot your belt, sweetie!"

She held up a long strip of leather, looking toward the yard as though her target might be sandwiched between the swing set, the ToughShed, and the small clump of Finnegans talking there. In unison, April and Mickey gawked at Ryan's waist.

"Oh, no," April said.

"Dude, is that belt really yours?" At the sight of Ryan's belt-less khaki pant loops, Mickey looked ready to high-five him.

"Yes," Ryan said to Mickey. "And no, oh, no," he said to April. "I'm trying to escape, remember? Darla offered to give me a tour of the house, and the next thing I knew—"

"Ambushed in the laundry room with Darla whipping your clothes off?" Mickey asked.

"How did you know?"

April hmmphed.

"She's got this thing about christening every room of the house," Mickey explained. "We all know about it. So far she's made most of them, but my mom would freak if anybody did the wild thing on her Maytag. She's still paying it off on her Sears bill."

Ryan looked confused. "Fiona doesn't want anyone to get lucky on top of her washing machine? Or she doesn't want anyone to get lucky on top of her washing machine until it's paid for?"

They both looked at him. "It's fifty-nine dollars a month!"

He raised his eyebrows. Apparently, he couldn't formulate a reply, though. It was just as well. Darla had zeroed in on him, and was headed toward the patio.

At the sight of her, Ryan stepped backward. More than likely, he'd never been mauled by the likes of a bottle blonde with cast-off Candies and a take-no-prisoners seduction technique before, April reasoned. And against her better judgment—Darla *was* holding his belt, which, after all, was more than *she'd* achieved so far—she decided to come to his rescue.

She maneuvered herself in front of Ryan and grabbed both of his forearms, wrapping them around her middle. Then she leaned her head against his shoulder, raised one arm to cradle the back of his neck, and did her best to ignore the dangerously arousing effect this whole rescue thing was having on her libido.

April had just achieved a cozy pseudo-coupleness when Darla sidestepped a group of playing nieces and nephews and reached them. Her gaze dropped to Ryan's arms, then she took in the way Ryan played his part by nibbling the side of April's neck.

"Geez, April. Sorry." She handed over the belt. "I didn't know you two were—*you know*. He's yours?"

Ryan stiffened behind her, probably taking offense at being talked about like a stud on a stick. April snuggled against him to take the edge off, and smiled at her cousin. "Yes," she said. "He's mine."

She meant it superficially, to save Ryan. But once the

words were out there, April couldn't shake the feeling they would dig in deeper, somehow. A part of her *wanted* a man like Ryan, wanted the romantic hunk-turned–soul mate of her dreams—the man she'd described to Jamie and Mark on that long-ago day at the bakery. And the more time she spent pointlessly indulging her crush on Ryan, she realized, the less likely it was she would find him.

Dream man, where are you?

"Sorry, Darla." She snuggled closer into Ryan's arms and surreptitiously passed him his belt, pretending not to hear Mickey's guffaws. "I'm afraid you'll just have to go Maytag somebody else."

"Great," Darla muttered. "First live one in a month, and he's taken."

"Hey, it could be worse," Mickey piped up. "You could have nobody to share the news with." He examined his Budweiser can. "I'll bet my mom would love to hear about Ape's new boyfriend."

"What? Aunt Fiona doesn't know about" —Darla waggled a scarlet Press-On nail between April and Ryan— "these two yet?"

"Nope."

Darla, obviously interested, raised her penciled-on brows. She gave April and Ryan a speculative look.

Oh, no. April stiffened. She couldn't do a thing to avert the coming disaster, either. Behind her, Ryan shifted, more than likely restoring his belted sense of manly modesty.

"Ape?" he whispered in her ear. "Cute."

Those weren't exactly the whispered endearments she'd hoped for from her dream man, but the "crowded room" part almost fit. There were barbecue-loving Finnegans all around. Interesting.

"Well, nice to meetcha, anyway," Darla trilled, waving. She gave Ryan one last up-and-down look, then swiveled on her platforms. "I've got some chatting to do with my aunt. Byeee."

This couldn't be happening.

"Thanks a lot, Mickey," April said when she'd gone, punching his arm.

"Ouch! What'd I do?"

"You know perfectly well what you did."

"Huh-huh." He swilled some Bud. "Good luck."

Ryan stepped from behind April, wearing a quizzical— and grateful-not-to-be-Maytagged—expression. "Good luck with what?" he asked.

"You'll see."

Thirty seconds later, a scream came from inside of the house. Then Fiona Finnegan appeared in the patio doorway, marched to April and Ryan, and dragged them both inside with her.

Chapter Seven

Ryan had been inside kitchens before. For instance, he and his friends had once occupied a special dining table in the "chef's" area of the Chez Henri kitchen, watching the culinary experts at work preparing Chilean sea bass and coconut-caramel flan. He'd also spent many happy hours as a child sneaking cookies from the Forresters' personal pastry chef.

On his last birthday, the socialite he'd been dating had invited him into her penthouse kitchen for cake and ice cream ... à la Buffy. And, of course, his own luxury town house near the Pacific Coast possessed a kitchen. He remembered letting the decorator loose in there with granite samples and appliance catalogs.

But Ryan had never been inside a kitchen the likes of the Finnegans' crammed, colorful kitchen. And he'd never been around anyone—*ever*—who was anything like April's mother, Fiona.

Before he'd known what was happening, she'd grabbed him and April by the shirtsleeves and dragged them both from the patio with unnatural petite-but-round strength. Then she'd dumped them into the cool dimness of her ranch-style kitchen.

At first, Ryan had thought hers was just an especially gung-ho invitation to dine. But then Fiona had hiked up the waistband of her flowered Capri pants, brushed off the front of her puffy-painted T-shirt, and let them have it.

Ten minutes later, she was still at it.

"If I thought this relationship was right for you, April," she was saying, her short red hair spiking around her head as she worked at the countertop, "then I would get right behind it. You know I would. Hand me that colander, would you, doll? But I'm just not—it's right there."

Belatedly, Ryan realized Fiona was talking to him. He looked around for a likely seeming kitchen utensil, and handed it over.

"That's a can opener."

With a shake of her head, Fiona reached around him and extracted a round perforated-metal bowl from a nearby cupboard. She slapped it onto her work space beside her pan of boiled potatoes, cutting board, and lethal-looking knife, then went on talking.

"But you're a different kind of girl," she said. "Not like the society types this one" —she jerked her chin toward Ryan— "is probably used to dating. Plus, I dunno. He looks sort of . . . ineffectual to me. His hiking boots are suede, for Pete's sake!"

Maligned boots aside, Ryan felt compelled to defend himself. "I'm *very* effectual."

Fiona looked at the colander and raised her eyebrows.

"Outside the kitchen," he clarified.

"Mmm-hmmm. Well, hot moves between the sheets aren't everything." She directed her attention to an amused-looking April, who wordlessly handed over the bowl of hard-boiled eggs she'd been peeling and slicing. "Believe me, April's father and I had plenty of woo-woo going on. Was he hung! But—"

"Mom!"

"—but then he ran off with that checkout girl from the Safeway, like he was selling shares in the schlong-of-the-month club instead of used and rare books." Fiona frowned, and began ladling mayonnaise into the hubcap-size bowl in front of her. "Left him a wife and two poor, heartbroken little kids behind, too."

"I was twenty-two, Mom," April said, sounding as though she'd repeated the statement many times. "And Dad only moved down the street. We still see him all the time."

She glanced at Ryan. "All the time," she assured him in a whisper, as though she wanted to make sure he knew she'd survived the desertion okay.

"I know," Fiona muttered. "The *nerve* of him! He could've at least had the decency to move to another state."

Ryan cleared his throat. "You know, a good prenup could have made sure he resided someplace—"

April waved frantically from behind her mother's back. She pantomimed dragging a knife across her throat. He shut up.

"What's that, doll?"

"Uhhh." Considering all he'd been through so far this afternoon—the verbal hangover, the kiss, the reality debate, the struggle to persuade April to accept a ride over here in his roadster, *and* seduction by spin cycle—Ryan figured he rallied pretty quickly. He pointed to a nearby dish. "That looks delicious. What is it?"

Fiona looked from him to April, then back again. "Lime Jell-O mold."

"Mmmm. Never had it."

Drawing a deep breath, Fiona looked at him quizzically. Then she returned to her previous topic. "Like I was saying, April, what you need is a steady, dependable, responsible guy. Like that nice Mr. Wright you work with, for instance. He owns his own business, has all his hair and teeth—"

"Mom, he's only thirty-three. Teeth, at least, are standard at that age."

"—he visits his mother once a week, and he's an upstanding citizen, too."

"I'm an upstanding citizen!" Ryan said, beginning to feel aggravatingly overlooked.

The hair and teeth, he figured, were gimmes. And he attended his mother's various fund-raising soirees at least once a month.

Fiona jabbed her spoon at him. "Wanda told me about those traffic tickets of yours," she said as though that explained everything, then went on ladling mayonnaise.

Evidently, mayo was the soup du jour. Or something. He hoped it wasn't supposed to be the entrée. It was tough to tell, here in just-add-water Podunkville.

"Mom, I don't want Mark," April said, bustling around the kitchen with admirable purpose.

She seemed to know exactly where to go, what to do, and how to do it. Ryan would've bet she knew *exactly* what a colander was. *And* what it was for. Around her, various Finnegans ducked in and out of the kitchen, retrieving Budweisers and Pepsis and helping with different meal-preparation tasks. They looked wise to the colander issue, too. He began to feel out of his depth.

"We're friends, that's all," April went on. "Besides, Ryan's not so bad." She stopped beside him and gave him a sunny grin. "He's actually very nice."

Nice. Grrrr.

"Really, I'm a corporate raider," he said.

Fiona pursed her lips. Maybe he'd gone overboard with the anti-nice-guy macho occupation.

". . . raider*like* vice president for Forrester's Department Stores," he amended.

"Hmmm. Start in on that fruit salad, would you, doll? Everything's right there. Just use the colander"—she slapped the can opener into his hand with a smirk—"to open those cans of fruit, then put everything in that bowl."

Ryan stared at the canned peaches and pineapple, the tub of Cool Whip, the bottle of cocktail-garnish cherries, and the miniature marshmallows. He mentally rolled up his sleeves.

If it was the last thing he did, he decided, he'd get on Fiona Finnegan's good side. Provided she had one.

"Vice president of what?" she asked idly.

April groaned.

Ryan paused. He'd opened the cans in record time, he noticed. Evidently, years of upper-crust sports like rugby and lacrosse had prepared him for more than life as a walking, talking, Abercrombie and Fitch ad.

"Community relations," he answered truthfully. He'd lobbied successfully for a new vice-presidential title change during his last conference call with the Forrester's board.

April's sidelong "I'm impressed" glance made him proud. He may have only secured half a high school billboard for all his efforts in town—so far—but he knew he'd come out ahead in the end. He wanted her to believe it, too.

"Sounds wishy-washy," Fiona said. "Your parents must be *so* proud of you."

"Mom." April shot her a warning glance. Something passed between the two women, something silent but serious.

Fiona shrugged. "Sorry. I can get a little sarcastic."

"You don't say?"

At Ryan's rejoinder, she chuckled. "So can you, I see."

"Just trying to get along," he said, flexing his biceps as he ripped the plastic safety seal from the Cool Whip. "My parents taught me to let no good comeback go unsaid. Also to tip the valet with twenties, to always call any woman under the age of ninety 'miss,' and to never, ever, let anyone look at your portfolio unless they were a certified financial consultant."

"Cozy," April observed.

He tipped his head, still working on his masterpiece first-ever fruit salad. "Not every family is cozy. Some are . . . polite."

It grew quiet in the kitchen. Even the muffled schlump-schlump of mayonnaise piling into Fiona's bowl stopped. Intent on applying just the right amount of whipped topping to his salad, Ryan didn't look up. He assumed everyone else had finished their preparations first, and was waiting for him.

"But hey," he said, "I had four nannies, Northam's Academy followed by Stanford, a whole slew of sports coaches, lessons of every kind, and lots of other things to fill the gaps. All right." Carefully, Ryan raised the bowl of fruit salad toward the women. "What do you think?"

"Oh!" April sniffed, then turned away. "I think you should have put the marshmallows in," she said in a strangely croaky voice.

Frowning slightly, he looked toward her mother. "Fiona?"

"I think you need a hug!" she wailed.

Moments later, Ryan found himself engulfed in a surprisingly warm, surprisingly pleasant, maternal hug. The mingled fragrances of mayonnaise, boiled eggs, and drugstore perfume whirled around him, and two sturdy arms embraced him. Sniffling slightly, Fiona patted him on the back.

"Ooof! But I—"

"You poor, poor boy," she said, shaking her head against his shoulder. "You poor, poor boy."

He couldn't remember the last time his own mother had hugged him. Or his father. Typically, he and his parents exchanged kisses on the cheek during their regular—provided any of them were in the same city at the same time—brunches, and progressed to kisses on *both* cheeks at Christmastime. Being hugged by April's mother was like having thirty-two years of sloppy, affectionate parenting crowbarred into him, all at once.

Awkwardly, Ryan patted her, too, holding out the fruit salad safely in his other hand. He still wasn't sure exactly what had brought all this on. But if it put a stop to the can opener–colander jokes, he was all for it.

They separated, and Fiona wiped her eyes. Then she peered at his fruit salad. "Definitely marshmallows," she said.

And somehow, just like that, Ryan knew he'd been accepted into the family.

Much to April's amazement, they made it all the way through the hot dogs, Lipton onion burgers, potato salad, and Jell-O mold, and had started on Ryan's fruit salad, before the inquisition began.

"So, Ryan," Uncle Bobby said, getting things rolling with a grin, "what exactly are you doing here in Saguaro Vista? I hear you're making the rounds of local businesses."

All the interested Finnegans at Fiona's two gold-painted backyard picnic tables quieted down to listen.

"I am." Ryan looked up from his plate, abandoning his forkful of marshmallows with what looked like a relieved expression. "I'm here to launch a community relations initiative for Forrester's Department Store."

He explained a little about his theory, going into big box retailing, declining profit margins, community profiles, and other details in a way that made April want to rest her chin on her hand and just *listen*. Watching him gave her a funny little happy-proud feeling, very much like the feelings she'd gotten during her toddler nieces' and nephews' early attempts at walking. Despite the fact that she and Ryan were technically competitors, a part of her wanted him to do well.

He finished explaining, and Uncle Bobby nodded.

"People around town make you sound like Santa Claus, though," he said, eying Ryan's watch. "What's the story there? And is that a real Rolex?"

Ryan frowned, and seized on the second of Uncle Bobby's questions first. "Real? What makes you think it isn't real?"

"Sometimes they're fakes, that's all."

"*This* one is real." He buffed the gold band and shiny watch face with his sleeve. "Do you want to try it on?"

He unfastened the band and slipped off his watch, offering it for a try-on. Uncle Bobby leaned forward eagerly.

With a yelp, April intercepted. She half rose, levered her upper body across the tabletop full of ketchup and mustard and potato chip bags, and seized Ryan's watch. Everyone stared.

"Uhhh . . ." Frozen in mid-grab, April searched for an excuse for her actions. Visions of her uncle blithely walking out of Ambrosia last Saint Patrick's Day swirled through her head. His flapping shirttails and bulging instant "potbelly" had been a dead giveaway as to his green bagel–smuggling proclivities. Now, the covetous look he gave Ryan's watch as it dangled from her grasp warned of similar Rolex-wrangling inclinations.

No one knew about the bagel incident, except April and Mark. And Uncle Bobby, of course. For the sake of a peaceful weekly Wednesday barbecue, April wanted to keep it that way. So she settled for scolding. "Uncle Bobby, you know you're allergic to gold! Do you want to break out in a rash?"

Or be forced to break out of jail? asked the stern look she gave him as she sat down again.

He shrugged, and surrendered. But April knew she'd have to be wary. A trusting type like Ryan would be easy pickings.

Nicking things was a sport to Uncle Bobby. His hobby, really. And he'd gotten much more ... *active* in the year since Aunt Betty died. He only did it to challenge himself, and he never kept anything for long—the goods always wound up, mysteriously, in the victim's possession a few days later. But the last thing April wanted to do was try and explain short-term familial kleptomania to Ryan, and so she kept mum.

She handed over the Rolex to Ryan, impressed by its heft and fineness, in spite of herself. For the first time, she considered all the posh things he must have left behind by coming here.

"Anyway, what's with the goodies all over town?" Uncle Bobby asked again, a little more subdued now.

"They were just friendly incentives," Ryan answered. He speared a chunk of pineapple on his plastic fork with a decisive gesture, sending his paper plate skidding out of its gold spray-painted wicker holder. "Promotional bonuses, to encourage businesspeople to ally with Forrester's."

April reached over and snapped his wayward plate back into place. Sheesh, a person would think he'd never encountered paper plates, wicker holders, and plastic picnic forks before. And the way he'd left aside half of the mayonnaise from his potato salad—that was the good part, wasn't it?

Ryan's gaze lifted. Caught with hers. He smiled his thanks, and her heart flip-flopped. He was awfully appealing. Too bad she'd had to relegate him to cute-booty-possessing No Trespassing Zone status.

"I won't be using incentives anymore, though," he announced when he'd finished his pineapple. He propped his forearms on the table's edge and steepled his fingers. "In fact, I've decided to go completely cash- and credit-free from now on, while I'm here in Saguaro Vista."

At his announcement, several Finnegans slumped in their places. Muttered "awwws," were heard.

"Yes," April agreed loudly, ashamed of her family's obvious incentive-getting hopefulness. "Ryan and I have a little bet going, to see how long a trust-fund fella like him can survive without his wallet."

"Without your wallet?" Fiona gawked at him, then looked suspiciously at her daughter. "That hardly seems fair, April. How's the man supposed to survive?"

"Wit. Cunning. Barter." Ryan stood and began gathering up plates, cups, and forks for the trash. Hands full, he grinned. "Blackmail, if necessary."

Across the table, Darla gasped.

April rolled her eyes at her cousin, knowing damn well her Maytagging secret was safe with Ryan. No matter how much he teased.

"Hell, that won't work," Uncle Bobby announced. He pulled out a toothpick and went to work on his molars. "Try thievery," he advised. "But only steal from the rich."

"I *am* the rich."

Mumbled "oh"s were heard around the table. "Well, now, that *is* a problem," said her mother's ditzy ex-sister-in-law, Vickie. "What will you do?"

Ryan shrugged. "I'll get by. If I win, I get the rights to all the remaining town sponsorships. Only a few have made their final decisions so far, and I'll be approaching the rest this week. April and I agreed that we'd ask all the businesses to listen to our pitches, but postpone their sponsorship choices until next Friday." He gestured to the items he held. "Where do I put all this?"

Darla tottered to her feet, her Candies sinking into the grassy turf. "*I'll* help you, sweetie!"

She sashayed alongside him to retrieve an empty trash bag, intent, April figured, on making sure he wouldn't reveal her house-christening secret to Fiona. When they emerged from inside a few minutes later, Ryan looked unnerved. And Darla looked pouty. She schlumped to the picnic table and rattled it when she sat down.

April grinned up at Ryan. "Your shirt's misbuttoned."

He looked down, temporarily abandoned his clean-up chores—which had surprised the heck out of her in the first place—and repaired his rumpled shirt. All the while April watched him, and felt a surge of optimistic good cheer swoosh through her.

None of her dates had ever withstood Darla. To a man, they'd crumbled at her first squealed, "Oooh, you look strong!" and had wound up, sooner or later, helping her break in the den, or the coat closet, or the guest bedroom. But Ryan . . . well, Ryan was obviously different.

He'd actually ditched Darla. *Twice.* The realization made April feel positively gleeful.

"But April, I thought that was *your* new job for Ambrosia," Aunt Vickie asked, puckering her mouth as she applied a fresh coat of apricot lipstick in her compact mirror. "Improving the bakery's publicity in town, I mean. Are you and Ryan competing with each other?"

"Yes, but—"

"Oh, no, dear. Men don't like competitive women."

She leaned backward to speak privately with her niece behind Fiona, and scrunched up her face in an I-know-this-is-distasteful-but-necessary fashion. "You'll have to lose. But don't be too obvious about it," she suggested, in a falsetto voice about as subtle as her advice.

"Lose?" Fiona sputtered, overhearing. "I say, nail 'em to the wall. If men can dish it out, they ought to be able to take it."

"Yes," Darla purred. "They should."

April groaned. Ryan listened. And suppressed a grin.

Was it possible he was amused by her crazed family? That he was actually *enjoying* spending time with them?

Nah. After all, he generally tended to make sense.

"Doesn't matter who wins," Uncle Bobby offered, speaking around his toothpick as he helped himself to more fruit salad. "Everything's temporary anyway. 'Cept the Diamondbacks' losing streak."

Everyone at the table launched into a debate about baseball. Amid it all, April found herself sneaking glances at Ryan, watching for the moment when he reached Finnegan overload. Curiously enough, it never came.

How much had he had to drink, anyway? she wondered. She hadn't seen anything stronger than a Pepsi in his hand all evening, but what other explanation could there be? A fancy society type like him couldn't possibly relate to any of this.

Suddenly, Mickey piped up from the other table. "I still think Ape should win," he announced, and everyone quieted down again.

His loyalty touched her. "Thanks, Mick."

"I don't," Fiona disagreed.

"Mom!"

"Well, you have an unfair advantage," her mother explained, only a little defensively. "You've lived here all your life, and you have friends all over town. Naturally, everyone will choose to cosponsor the whatchamacallit with Ambrosia." A mischievous glint came into her eyes. "And that *nice* Mark Wright."

"They might," Ryan agreed. "I'm willing to take that chance."

"Me, too!" April said. "Look, taking Ryan's wallet out of the running simply levels the playing field between us. That's all."

He nodded, agreeing with her. Impulsively, she reached across the table and squeezed his fingers in hers, inciting an immediate *woo-woo* sensation in her middle. *Whoops. Got carried away, there,* she thought. Reluctantly, she withdrew.

"But April," her mother persisted, "everyone knows you. Knows the Finnegans. I still think that gives you an unfair advantage."

"Believe me, Mom," April replied, speaking more loudly to be heard over the Budweiser-spraying fight just breaking out between Mickey, Uncle Bobby, and one of her cousins, "being part of this family is a real mixed blessing." She ducked a frothy spray. "I don't think Ryan has anything to worry about."

Clouds scudded across the darkened sky. A balmy breeze swept April's hair away from her face, and Ryan's convertible smoothly and expensively ate up pavement between Fiona's house—which they'd left, bearing leftovers, twenty minutes ago—and her apartment. The modest outlines of her stuccoed duplex came into view.

"That's it, right over there on the left," April said.

He squinted. "Cute."

For some reason, his observation bothered her. "Cheap," she countered, the leather seats beneath her hands suddenly feeling twice as luxurious. "Cheap, clean, and available on a temporary basis. Just like me."

In the awkward silence that followed, Ryan brought the roadster to a stop in the only unoccupied parking space—the space where her VW Rabbit would have been, if April had had enough savings to cover both a month's worth of lost wages *and* her car's ransom.

She and Ryan shared a love of convertibles, although he didn't know it. Hers wasn't this deluxe, but the wind whooshed through her hair in exactly the same exhilarating way when she was in it. April told herself that was all that mattered.

He cut the engine. Looked at her. "You're not like that."

"What, cheap? Clean? Or available?"

Her falsely chipper tone didn't fool him. *"Sarcastic,"* he said quietly, and leaned over to regard her seriously. "You're not cynical, or brittle," he murmured, tucking her hair behind her ear with a tender gesture. "Not like some people I know."

He kissed her, softly, the touch of his lips a promise that he spoke truly. And when he pulled away again afterward, April didn't want to open her eyes and let the taste of magic he'd given her dissipate. She felt awash in longing. Drunk with it. Although Ryan's kiss had been brief—almost casual in its ease—it had stirred her, all the same. Exactly the way all his kisses did.

Or would, if she didn't put a stop to them.

She looked at him. "I've got to go. Thanks for the ride."

He blinked, one hand on the steering wheel. "You're welcome. But—"

"See you around." She got out and shoved the car door, which closed with an expensively subdued thunk. Concentrating on not seeing the disappointed expression on Ryan's face, April dug in her handbag for her apartment keys. "Good luck on the bet. And on the sponsorships."

"May the best person win." He got out of the car. "I'll walk you to your door."

Her door. Where date-type kisses good night happened. She didn't possibly have the resolve to withstand temptation like that.

"No! No, that's okay."

"Then I'll pick you up tomorrow," Ryan offered, standing on the opposite side of the convertible. She felt his gaze on her, curious and intelligent. "We can grab some breakfast, and I'll take you to get your bike."

She'd left her Schwinn chained to the bike rack outside the Saguaro Vista Motor Court Inn, after agreeing to accept Ryan's ride to her mother's house.

"Don't worry about it," April said. She had to get away before she started acting crazy again. It wasn't like her to lose control over a man. "I can catch a ride back to the motel with Jamie."

"I'd be happy to do it."

Suddenly, he was there. Warm. Tall. Nice-smelling, even. His broad, flannel-covered chest and wide shoulders filled her vision. Ryan tipped up her chin.

The gesture felt like a prelude to a kiss. *Another kiss.* A kiss that would rattle loose her good sense, incite several more *dream man* fantasies, and generally make a hash of April's intentions *not* to let her attraction to Ryan interfere with her new-job ambition.

Well, she had to stand firm.

Determined to end this night on her terms, she levered upward in the moonlight and briskly kissed him on the cheek. His day's-worth of soft stubble caught her by surprise, and April touched her fingers to her mouth as she lowered again. It occurred to her that she'd been with Ryan during the time it had taken that masculine shadow to darken his jaw. Somehow the realization seemed oddly intimate.

"G'night," she murmured, and walked to her front door without looking back.

She didn't know if Ryan followed her, or even if he watched her. She only knew that her willpower dissolved more with every moment she and Ryan spent together. If she didn't get away soon, she would invite him in.

And *then* how would she let him go?

Inside, April dropped her handbag and her leftovers, and sank to the floor. After a few minutes, she heard the finely tuned rumble of the roadster's engine start, then the crunch of gravel as Ryan drove down the drive. Through her apartment window, the car's headlights briefly illuminated the room. And then he was gone.

Picking up Calypso, April cradled the cat against her chest and gently rubbed her face against her downy marmalade-colored fur. Inexplicable tears welled in her eyes. With a sniff, she turned the cat to face her.

"There'll be other guys, right Calypso?" she asked in a croaky whisper. "Other guys who *aren't* off-limits."

But despite the tabby's yowling agreement, April wasn't so sure. It didn't matter how many other guys were out there, and in that moment she knew it. She only wanted one.

Ryan.

Driving away, Ryan flexed his fingers on his roadster's steering wheel and watched the darkened scenery pass by. Given the ridiculously low speed limits posted in Saguaro Vista, he had plenty of time to enjoy it . . . but his mind wasn't on the small stuccoed houses, convenience store, mobile home park, and "downtown" that slid past. All he could think about was April.

April, and why she'd run away from him tonight.

Was it because of their bet? Because of their competition for sponsorships? Because, God forbid, she thought he was too *nice?*

Whatever the reason, Ryan vowed as he turned the corner leading to the Saguaro Vista Motor Court Inn, he meant to get to the bottom of it. And then he meant to get around it.

Plainly enough, April Finnegan intrigued him. Thoughts of her chased through his days, and imaginings about her brightened his nights. His mother's friends would have said he was "smitten," and Ryan figured that pretty well summed it up. He *was* smitten, smitten and tempted and ready to—

Oh, hell. Reality struck him upside the head with all the delicacy of a piled-on quarterback sack. It didn't matter how interested he was in April—because he didn't have any possible way of getting *her* interested in *him.* His dating years had been a parade of happening restaurants, hard-to-get theater tickets, exotic locales, and extravagant gestures. They'd worked, he'd wooed, and everything had been good. After all, not many women could resist those little blue Tiffany boxes.

But now . . . *hell!* Ryan slapped his hand on the steering wheel and scowled into the night. He couldn't use any of that to win over April. All he had was . . . him.

Would it be enough? Momentary panic gripped him, but Ryan valiantly shoved it back. It would have to be enough. Period.

Parking his Beemer, he slid from behind the wheel and walked to his *casita,* his footsteps loud in the lonely stillness. He went inside and shut the door, and lay down on the bed, face up.

The King stared down at him, resplendent in velvet.

The drawer of the bedside table seemed to pulse weakly.

His wallet mumbled a low-pitched recrimination.

Groaning, Ryan grabbed a pillow and hauled it over

his head. From beneath its leaden protection, he began to brainstorm ideas to impress April using his inner resources alone.

Fifteen minutes later, he had nada. He'd contemplated serenading: too Ricky Martin; smiling: too obvious; and sending a mash note: too "Dear Playboy." What was he going to do?

Get help, Ryan realized with a jolt. That's what he was going to do. The only question now was . . . from whom?

Chapter Eight

"You have *got* to be kidding me." Mark Wright looked up from the bakery display case, setting the last tray of lemon bars inside with a clatter. He stared at Jamie. "That Forrester guy went to the Finnegan's weekly Wednesday barbecue?"

Jamie nodded, and sympathetically patted his forearm. At her touch, something strange and exciting sizzled through Mark—that is, if things could be said to "sizzle" through him at all. Ordinarily, he wouldn't have allowed it. But now . . .

Their combined gazes dropped to her fingers. She snatched them away.

"Yes," she said, using her hand instead to track her progress as she scanned the Ambrosia display case—probably for her now-requisite chocolate croissant. "April told me all about it this morning, when I took her to pick up her bike at the Motor Court Inn."

"Her bike? She left her bike behind? And—and what? Drove with Forrester in that flashy, unsafe car of his?"

It upset him that she'd been seeing so much of that guy. "You know, I've seen the consumer crash test ratings on those imported sports cars. They're not necessarily favorable. Not favorable at all. Especially the convertibles."

Feeling overwrought, he shoved his hands through his hair. They got embedded in the multiple styling products Jamie had insisted he use on his new haircut, and he had to backtrack to release them. Why had he allowed her to change his hair, anyway? It wasn't as though it was *Jamie* he wanted to impress.

At least, Mark didn't think so.

"I'm sure Ryan's car is perfectly safe," Jamie said, still scanning the display cases . . . just as though a friend of theirs *weren't* at risk every time she sat her cute curvy backside in Mr. Hotshot's leather seats. "Where are the—"

"Right here." Using a square of parchment paper, Mark retrieved a chocolate croissant. He slid it across the top of the case to Jamie, feeling himself relax a bit at her smile of thanks. "Doesn't it worry you, just a little?" he asked.

The parchment paper crinkled. "Doesn't what worry me?" She swallowed her first bite, and gave an enthusiastic *mmmmm.* "Wow, this is *orgasmic.*"

Mark boggled. Had she just said what he thought she said? And had the temperature just gone up in here, or what?

Jamie glanced up, the suggestion of a smile curving her lips. "Doesn't what worry me?" she asked again.

"April. And Forrester," Mark made himself say, trying desperately to stay orgasmic—er, *orderly,* and on track. "I thought you wanted him for yourself."

"No." She swiped away a smudge of chocolate from the corner of her lip and licked it from her finger. "*You* wanted him for me. I'm still on the fence about the idea."

She took another bite of croissant, her expression dissolving into radiant bliss. Two finger-licks and one "mmmm" later, Mark found his libido sitting up for a closer look.

This is Jamie, he reminded himself sternly. *Settle down.* After all, he was interested in April, not artsy, unconventional, dye-your-hair-purple-and-dance-the-conga Jamie. But if she, say, *kissed* as enthusiastically as she ate a *pain au chocolat* . . .

"But you agreed to get to know him better," he pointed out, forcing himself back to the problem at hand. "The day you did this to my hair."

" 'Did this' to your hair?" Eyes narrowed, she reached for a napkin from the dispenser and wiped her now-empty fingers. "What do you mean, 'did this' to your hair? I'll have you know it looks fabulous. Very classic. Very *Gorgeous Grooms.*"

Mark glanced at the stack of wedding magazines jutting from her bag, resting on the Ambrosia floor. He meant to say something appropriately dismissive, but then he took a second look at the happy wedding couple on the cover of the top issue.

"Is that the new banded-collar tuxedo?" he asked.

Jamie followed his glance, and nodded. "The latest thing. Why, have you rented one like it?"

"Rented? Who rents? I own two, one black tie and one white tie. You never know when you'll need something for a special occasion."

"I know!" Taking a step closer, Jamie gazed at him, semi-starry-eyed. "It's better to be safe than sorry, I always say."

"*You* always say that?"

"Mmm-hmm."

With a sigh, she rested her forearm along the top of

the display case and propped her chin on it. They looked at each other for a silent, thoughtful moment. Mark felt himself weakening, felt himself wanting to say something more. Something to encourage this unexpected new bond between them. He searched his mind for something suitable . . . and said, "You're still going to get to know Forrester better, right?"

Her face fell. Mark wanted to kick himself. Evidently, his brain was more single-minded than even he realized.

"I guess so," Jamie said, reluctantly. She stooped to pick up her bag, laden with those dreamy, impractical magazines of hers. "But I don't—"

The bakery door opened. Its bell chimed.

She paused, and turned to see . . . Ryan Forrester. Obviously, Mark realized—feeling somewhat encouraged—the man's appearance here was A Sign. Fate was on his side.

Forrester and Jamie greeted each other, exchanging a few minutes of chitchat while Mark went to the kitchen for trays of glazed donuts. By the time he'd emerged with the fourth one, Jamie and Mr. Hotshot were laughing over some joke. Although that should have been a positive harbinger for his plan to pair the two of them off—leaving April free for *him*—Mark found himself feeling strangely irritated as he watched them. He lingered behind the cash register, trying not to glower.

"Oh, Mark!" Several eons later, Jamie noticed him again. She touched Forrester on the shoulder and turned him toward the bakery counter. "I don't think you two have met. Mark Wright, meet Ryan Forrester."

They shook hands. Peevishly, Mark squeezed as hard as he could, but his strong-man gesture didn't seem to affect Forrester at all. Damn it.

"We haven't officially met," Forrester said, "but I've

heard a lot about you. April talks about you all the time. She's dedicated to this bakery, you know. And now that I'm here"—his expansive gesture, as confident as the rest of his demeanor, encompassed Ambrosia's sparkling picture windows, clean white walls, chrome-and-glass fixtures, and trio of café tables— "I can see why."

Smiling, he scanned the display cases and reached into his pocket, as though preparing to buy a scone or a muffin. At the last instant, though, a strange expression crossed his face. He withdrew his hand.

Curiously, Mark raised his eyebrows. Surely Mr. Moneybags could afford a dollar-fifty blueberry muffin. Maybe, he decided with less than one-hundred-percent conviction, Forrester was working on whittling his physique into something less action hero-ish and more male model-ish. All the better to seduce April with. Damn it.

"Thanks," Mark said, trying not to think about his own ordinary, two-chocolate-chip-cookies-a-day physique. After all, a man didn't have to be perfect in order to be perfect for the woman he was sweet on. "The place has been in my family for three generations. I'm pretty proud of it."

And pretty terrified of running it into the ground, if business doesn't improve. Quickly, he shoved that nagging worry from his mind and reminded himself that, technically, this friendly seeming man was his competition for April.

He frowned. Cleared his throat. "So, what can I do for you?"

Forrester glanced at Jamie, as though he'd detected the almost brusque tone in Mark's voice. She shrugged.

"Well . . ." Looking suddenly uncomfortable, Forrester examined his flashy gold watch. Then he met Mark's gaze. "I need some advice. And if Fiona Finnegan is to be believed, you're exactly the man to give it."

Interested, Jamie leaned forward. "You don't say?"

Her gaze flicked from Mark to Forrester, then back again.

Mark gave her a "keep your wisecracks to yourself" frown. "Glad to help," he told Mr. Unsafe Convertible, "if I can."

Relief swept over Forrester's features. Against his better judgment, Mark found himself liking the man. Damn it. Anyone who had the guts to stride in here, totally unexpectedly, and ask for help deserved to be listened to, at least. And possibly given a chance, at the most.

"Good," Forrester said. "It's about April . . ."

And simple as that, Mark became his rival's confidant . . . and, much to his surprise, his reluctant advisor.

"I can't believe you got us into this," April told Jamie, shaking her head as she reached for her lip gloss. She lifted Calypso from the bathroom vanity, nuzzled her with her chin, and set the cat down on the tiled floor. "A double date? Are you nuts?"

"No, just out of practice. They asked, I panicked, I answered. Besides, Mark wanted me to."

"Huh? I thought Mark was supposed to be *my* date."

Which was weird, when it came right down to it, April thought. Dating Mark would be like French-kissing her H&R Block tax advisor—*very* surreal, and potentially hazardous to her financial health. But as Jamie had explained to her earlier, it was really less of a date and more of a group get-together anyway. And after all, if she seriously wanted to—sensibly—avoid romantic entanglements with Ryan, what better way could there be than to fix him up with Jamie?

Jamie was friendly, cute, and didn't have any Finnegan-style kleptomania, nymphomania, check-bouncing skeletons in her closet that might scare away Ryan . . . unlike *some* people April could name. Ryan was single, successful, and would look like a real live wedding cake topper if outfitted in a tuxedo. Given Jamie's wedaholic tendencies, they might be ideal for each other.

The plan made perfect sense on paper. Of course, "making sense" didn't go very far in quashing the queasy feeling thinking of Ryan with another woman—*any* woman—gave her. But those were the breaks, right? She had to stand tough. Otherwise, April would never prove herself a *non*-flighty Finnegan. And that was what she wanted, most of all.

"I mean, uh," Jamie said, "it's been so long since I went on an actual date, I forgot what the procedure is."

Standing beside April, she hurriedly picked up eyeliner pencils and blush, shadow and lipstick. She examined each pencil, compact, and tube, and found a way to dab a little of each on her face as she talked. On anyone else, the result would have been a little too Tammy Faye Bakker, at best. But on Jamie's pert features, and sparingly applied, the mishmash of colors looked good.

Ryan would probably love it. *Sob.*

"The procedure is usually *not* to book dates on your friend's Little League night," April reminded her, thinking of the plans she'd already made to attend her nine-year-old cousin's weekly softball game. "And to avoid making bizarre "Blind Date"–style fix-ups between your best friend and her boss."

"Oh, get over it," Jamie said, rolling her eyes. "For starters, I already knew about Rainey's softball schedule, and Mark and Ryan said they don't mind going to the game."

"As a double date."

"Yes."

"Oookay."

In April's mind, a date included fun, romantic activities. Picnicking in a sunny spot. Paddleboating on the Saguaro Vista municipal park pond. Dining in candlelight, followed by a mushy, laugh-out-loud romantic comedy at the local movie one-i-plex. It did *not* typically include cheering on twelve sweaty junior softballers—many in pigtails and glitter nail polish. But she was willing to keep an open mind.

"And for another thing," Jamie continued, "you might think it's 'bizarre' to date Mark, but some other people might disagree with you."

April guffawed. "Like who?"

Jamie lifted her chin, and didn't say. "They might also think someone like you *needs* someone like Mark." She reached down to realign Calypso, helping the cat get properly situated for the shower curtain swatting game she'd gotten involved in. Unfortunately, April's cat was . . . well, a little neurotic. Calypso ducked every time the curtain swung her way.

"Someone like Mark," Jamie repeated, "who's steady, responsible, and dependable. A man like him might be good for you." After one last pat for the cat, she straightened. "I mean, did you ever think about that?"

April shook her head. "I'm going to be steady, responsible, and dependable all by myself. *For* myself. I don't need a man to somehow endow me with those qualities."

Jamie looked skeptical. April shrugged. They'd been best friends for too long to argue over something like this. In some ways, Jamie was remarkably—*frighteningly*—traditional. The two of them didn't quite see eye to eye on matters of the heart . . . and quite possibly never would. At least not until April became a lifetime subscriber of the wedding-magazine-of-the-month club.

"I don't need a man in order to become steady and responsible, etcetera," April went on. "And as soon as I nail all the remaining sponsorships in town and put Ambrosia in the spotlight, I'll prove it, too."

"What about Ryan? It's possible he'll get some of the sponsorships, you know."

"Not without the unfair advantage of his wealth working for him," April said, going on to sketch out the details of her wager with Ryan. "If we're on equal footing, I think I can compete."

"Ah-ha! No wonder he didn't buy that blueberry muffin."

"Huh?"

"Nothing." Jamie fluffed her short 'do, blew a kiss to the mirror, and held her crossed fingers in the air. "Here's hoping you get all the business you need. And here's hoping we *both* have a fun night out. Let's go."

Following Jamie out of the bathroom—and into what was sure to be the weirdest three hours of her life—April crossed her fingers, too. A little luck couldn't hurt. Especially when it came to this—her paired with Mark, Jamie paired with Ryan, Little League paired with high society . . . determination paired with heartache.

Sigh. If only Ryan were a little more resistible.

Suddenly, two of those mismatched pairings she'd thought of came back to haunt her. Hurrying to get her things and catch up with Jamie—who'd already grabbed her purse and car keys—April couldn't help but make one last-ditch stab at crisis prevention. No matter how nuts it was.

"Hey," she asked Jamie, "did you know Ryan has six toes on his left foot?"

Her friend stopped. Looked over her shoulder. "No. Really? Is that true?"

Heck no. "Would it make you avoid dating him, if it was?"

Jamie shrugged, and gave April a curious look.

That just wasn't good enough. So by the time they'd gotten in the car, April had thought of another one. "Did you know that Ryan's favorite flavor of ice cream"—she made a face over the very *blandness* of his choice— "is vanilla?"

"I like vanilla."

Arrgh! Feeling an increasing urge to kick herself over her spur of the moment, numbskull decision to play along with this "fix up Jamie and Ryan" plan, April scoured her brain for something—anything—that might make Jamie see him in a less than perfect light. As they pulled into the parking lot of the municipal field where the Little League games were played, and where they'd agreed to meet Mark and Ryan, she came up with the ultimate Jamie-style anti-Ryan dissuader.

"I understand," April said casually, "that when Ryan decides to get married, he plans to elope to Las Vegas. To one of those roadside chapels, where Elvis marries you and the rings are two for ninety-nine dollars."

Jamie, who'd been inexplicably humming the whole way, went pale. April pushed her point home.

"He says big weddings are a waste of time, money, and energy," she said as she opened the passenger-side door of Jamie's Escort and got out. " 'Keep it small,' that's his motto. 'Small and plain.' "

Jamie got out too, looking shaken. She lifted her chin.

"I think those Vegas chapels are charming," she said.

And that's when April knew something was *definitely* up.

Ryan began to have misgivings about his plans for the night fairly early on. They hit him first as he watched

Mark steer his used Volvo into a faraway, dent-preventing spot on the outskirts of the municipal park's lot. They multiplied when his newfound advisor pulled a padded porta-seat, economy-size bottle of sunscreen, and recycled stadium cup from his backseat.

Ryan's usual dating accoutrements were a wad of cash, an arrangement of hothouse flowers, and big plans for a night on the town. Looking at everything Mark had brought, though, something told Ryan he was on unfamiliar ground. This double date might not go off *quite* as planned.

"Refills are fifty cents off if you bring your own cup," Mark explained when he saw Ryan looking at his armload of supplies. "Those bleachers are hard. And you can never be too careful about the sun."

Ryan glanced out the passenger-side window. In the distance—the far, far distance, thanks to Mark's ultra-cautious parking job—the setting sun cast its last rays over the green ball field. In this lighting, only Dracula was at risk of sunburn.

"Right," he said. "Careful is good. I guess."

Which was fairly ironic coming from him, Ryan thought, given that in the past, his idea of "careful" had been ordering an extra bottle of single-malt scotch for poker night. Or asking his travel agent to book accommodations in Aruba *before* catching a last-minute flight. Or phoning his financial advisor more than twice a year to check the status of his trust fund.

But this was the "new him," Ryan reminded himself as he and Mark got out of the car and began the trek to the ball field. The "him" that relied solely on his own personal magnetism, wit, and charm to impress the woman he cared about.

Mentioning that very woman in an oddly Kreskin-like way, Mark said, "April needs a man who's got a sense of caution, after all. She's impulsive. Scattered. And that family of hers—whoa! I can't begin to tell you—''

"She didn't seem impulsive when she systematically approached all the same top-selling Main Street businesses I researched before coming here," Ryan interrupted quietly. "And she didn't seem scattered when she leveled the playing field between us with that wager of hers. That was smart. Really smart." He shook his head, unwillingly impressed with her audaciousness. "She'll be a tough competitor."

Mark, familiar with Ryan and April's ... unconventional bet, thanks to the conversation he'd had with Ryan earlier—and obviously unconvinced by Ryan's defense of April—only shrugged.

"She'll have to be tough," he said. "Look, there's Jamie."

Grinning, he picked up the pace, his porta-seat slapping against his side. Ryan lengthened his stride, too.

"And April," Ryan said. He waved to her, unable to hold back a grin of his own at the sight of her. They'd parted on uneasy terms last night, but he was determined to make it up to her today. "Hi!" he called out.

Mark nudged him. "Remember, play it cool," he said with a sideways glance. "I've known April a long time, and she'll want you more if she thinks you're unattainable."

Ryan's earlier misgivings flooded back to him. Sure, he'd been the one to seek out Mark's advice. After all, any man whom Fiona Finnegan raved about as being perfect for her daughter had to know *something* about the best way to impress April. But now, faced with an evening of watching April pair off with Mark—for the sake of that "unattainable" air Ryan supposedly needed—he wasn't so sure. Somehow, despite Mark's assurances, this date-switch plan didn't *feel* quite right.

Besides, did he really want to take guidance from a

man who iced petit fours for a living, and persisted in calling his favorite PBS miniseries "edgy, groundbreaking entertainment?"

Stop it, he ordered himself. *You're out of your element, here. It makes sense to get help from the natives.*

Resistant but resigned, Ryan strode closer to the ball field. The powerful multitiered lights switched on as he and Mark approached, illuminating the many people streaming toward the bleachers surrounding the baseball diamond. He didn't spot anyone besides Mark toting a gallon bottle of sunscreen, but he did see many others carrying porta-seats and pennants, mini coolers and reusable stadium cups.

Mark had been right about the correct accessories to bring to a Saguaro Vista Little League game, Ryan reminded himself. He could be right about playing hard to get with April, too.

They dodged a cadre of uniformed kiddie players, all of them giggling and carrying equipment. Their powder-pink jerseys incited in Ryan an immediate wish that he'd thought to lobby for Forrester's sponsorship of a Little League team. He neared April, and saw her watching the players with an equally speculative gleam in her eye.

"I thought of it first," he told her by way of greeting. "So hands off."

She turned. At the sight of him, her smile beamed more brightly than the sequins sewn to her handbag and the rhinestone flower decorating her T-shirt. Even in a T-shirt, jeans, and sneakers, April looked amazing.

Suddenly, she seemed to remember the purpose of the evening. She looked for Mark and said hello, the wattage on her smile dimming. Then she returned her attention to Ryan.

"There are lots of Little League teams," she said in

answer to his earlier comment. "Ambrosia can sponsor one if we want to."

"Which one is the championship team?" Ryan asked.

"Not Rainey's," April said. At his doubtlessly confused expression, she added, "My youngest cousin. I come here every week to watch her play. Despite her team's record—which isn't the greatest—I wouldn't miss it."

A mother passed by, overhearing April's remark. She raised her fist with a grin. *"Go, Puffys!"* they both yelled.

"Every week?" Mark asked, looking uncomfortable.

"Puffys?" Ryan asked, feeling charmed.

"Yes, every week. And yes, Puffys. Short for Powerpuff Girls. Rainey and her friends were big fans when it came time to name her team. The Puffy *boys* on the team weren't exactly thrilled. They voted for Head-Crushing Super Ninjas."

She and a passing parent exchanged a mischievous grin. "But they were outnumbered."

"I see," Ryan said, as though that explained anything. Like him, his younger relatives all went to private schools. He had no idea how much exposure to popular culture they'd had. Seeing the happiness on the powder-pink players' faces, though, he suddenly hoped they had plenty. "Shall we go in? I arranged box seating for us."

"Box seating?" Mark raised his eyebrows. "Isn't that expensive?"

"And impossible?" Jamie added. "I didn't know they had box seating at the Saguaro Vista ball field."

"According to the head coach they do. I slipped him fifty bucks to clue me in."

"Hey!" April said.

"Kidding. I asked around, that's all. Eventually, someone gave me the inside word." Mustering up an enthusiastic expression so as not to hurt Jamie's feelings—it wasn't her fault she wasn't April, after all—Ryan put his hands to both women's backs and guided them toward the nearest entrance. "Nothing but the best for you two. Come on."

Chapter Nine

"Interesting version of box seating," Jamie said a little while later. She looked up and around at the players' dugout surrounding their seats. "You say this is deluxe?"

"Typically, box seating is," Ryan said, having realized his "inside information" provider had obviously misunderstood what he was asking for. Instead of the great view and cushy seats he'd expected, he'd received seats . . . in an actual box. The wooden walls and rooftop of the dugout were decidedly boxlike. "But then, so far in Saguaro Vista, nothing is typical."

Neither were the reactions to his seating arrangements, as the four of them had sat down in Jamie-Ryan-April-Mark order.

Upon seeing their places, Jamie had teased, April had plunked happily onto the wooden bench with her things, and Mark had worried about stray pitches. In Ryan's case, he'd been surprised at the seating, but unconcerned. At this point, he was beginning to doubt there was *anything* deluxe about Podunkville.

Except April, of course. She had an odd sort of luxury about her, a sense of abundance just waiting to be shared. As they'd found their "box seats," she'd greeted at least a dozen people, and had chatted personally with them all. She'd waved to possibly a dozen more. And several of the Little League players had jumped up and down with excitement when they'd seen Rainey's biggest fan hit the dugout.

Now, as the double-daters watched the players exchange warm-up throws on the field, April slid closer to Ryan's spot on the bench. She fingered the short sleeve of his shirt, and gave him an impish grin.

"So," she asked, "is this the latest in the Corporate Raider Goes to Mayberry collection?"

"Har, har." Ryan glanced down at his Nike T-shirt, matching nylon track pants, and sneakers. He adjusted the backward-bill of his baseball cap. "And here I thought I was so smart for stocking up on non-suits at Forrester's earlier this week."

"You were." Her amused glance swept upward, with something very close to affection. "It's just that your idea of 'casual' is a little ... prefab." April waggled some navy nylon pinched from the leg of his pants. "Where's the *you* in all this?"

"Are you going to tell me I'm not 'real' again?"

"No. But I'm still curious about the hidden Ryan Forrester. You know, the guy behind the wallet."

In his imagination, his *casita* drawer's unwilling occupant awakened. *Pulse, pulse. I'm Italian leather!*

"Probing for weaknesses?" Ryan asked. "You won't find any." *I hope.* "I'm going to win our bet fair and square. As for you, I suggest you try losing gracefully."

She rolled her eyes. "Ha! Fat chance, buster."

He grinned, feeling the unusual camaraderie they

shared spark up all over again. April grinned back, making him wonder if she sensed those harmonious, feel-good feelings, too. He hoped, all of a sudden, that she did.

Despite his teasing, Ryan realized as he looked at her cheerful expression, he wanted April to do well. After their wager was finished and he'd locked up the remaining town sponsorships, she had to live here in Saguaro Vista. He didn't. He wanted to let her down as easily as possible.

To further the process, Ryan said, "I was just telling Mark on the way here what a tough opponent you're going to be."

"You were?"

He nodded. "Against all reason, I've been impressed with your strategy on behalf of Ambrosia."

"You have been?" She sat a little straighter, momentarily diverted from the Little League game. "Really?"

"Of course." She was surprised by this? "You might think you're hiding it pretty well behind rhinestones and bicycling and way too many sequins"—grinning, he touched her sparkly handbag— "but you're a formidable woman, April. I take you, and your competition for sponsorships, very seriously."

She wrinkled her forehead, as though perplexed by this turn of events. "You—"

Closing her eyes, she shook her head. The gesture, so patently April, confused him. Did no one here *ever* take her seriously, that she was so befuddled he had?

"You take me seriously?" she asked.

Ryan hesitated. On the field beyond them, players assumed their positions, short beacons of blue versus powder pink against the lighted, scrubby green field. The players remaining in the dugout surged to their feet. The crowd clapped and hooted encouragement in the bleachers behind them.

If he were smart—if he were a real shark-style, corporate raider–type competitor—he would take back what he'd said. He'd exploit her quirkiness and her small-town naïveté. He'd play on her weaknesses, ruthlessly take advantage of whatever loopholes existed in their bet. He'd come out on top, with his place in the family business irrefutably secured. He'd . . . he'd hate himself in the morning.

"Yes," Ryan said, gazing at her honestly. "I do."

She looked amazed. Amazed, and grateful. Blinking, April looked out onto the ball field. She drew in a deep breath. Let it out, and glanced at him again, quickly. That glance held all the disbelief of a woman pinching herself awake from a dream.

"Thank you," she said.

Moved, Ryan reached to take her hand. At the same moment, Mark yelled, "Jamie! Look out!"

Ryan looked up. A fat Day-Glo Little League softball zoomed toward the dugout, headed straight for them. Startled from her bridal magazine, Jamie glanced upward, saw the ball, and froze.

Seconds later, it thunked into Ryan's fist. He hefted it, then tossed it back to the strong-armed junior pitcher who'd accidentally thrown it their way.

"Thanks, mister," she called, trotting back to the mound with her twin blonde braids flying.

"Thank God!" Mark said. "Jamie, are you all right?"

She nodded, one hand on her chest, and murmured her thanks to Ryan. April said something admiring about Ryan's catch. Mark only glared at him, as though the wayward ball was proof Ryan hadn't been paying his official "date" enough attention.

And sure enough, Ryan knew, he hadn't. He also hadn't been playing very hard to get with April, despite his best intentions. Ready to regroup, he gave April a regretful half-smile and turned to Jamie.

She was already on her way toward Mark. In surprise, Ryan watched her juggle her things as she sat down on the opposite end of the dugout bench, next to April's "date."

"You'd better stay here with me beside the wall," he was saying, scooting over to make room. *"Where it's safe."*

"Sorry, Jamie," Ryan said. "I didn't mean—"

"It's okay." Jamie flopped five and a half inches of glossy magazine onto her lap and found her page again. When she looked up from the gowns and place cards and monogrammed tea towels, she looked—strangely enough—absolutely delighted with the turn of events. "I don't mind sitting over here."

"If you're sure . . ."

"Oh"—she cast a pleased-as-punch look at an oblivious Mark—"I am."

"It's, uh, fine with me," Mark said distractedly.

Mark continued to watch the game, alert—if Ryan didn't miss his guess—for another rogue ball as he rubbed SPF one thousand on his forearms. Without taking his gaze from the field, he offered the sunscreen to Jamie, who accepted it with a comment about "never being too careful in the sun," and squirted out some.

Beside Ryan, April watched her friends, a thoughtful look on her face. Then came the thump of bat hitting ball, and she leaped to her feet with both arms held high.

"Yay, Pokey!" she shouted, making air-circles with her fist and forearm. "Woo, woo, woo! Go, go, go!"

The excitement of the moment gripped Ryan, too. He forgot this was a Little League game, not a pennant race. He forgot the players were bubble gum–smacking fourth graders and pink ninja-wannabes, not major league stars. All that mattered was the girl April called Pokey, and her skittish progress from base to base.

"Go home!" he yelled, on his feet now, as well. He motioned toward home plate with both arms. "Home, Pokey! You can make it!"

The girl hesitated a few feet past third. She glanced toward the outfield, where four blue-uniformed opponent players chased the ball. She bit her lip.

The crowd went wild. "Go, *go!*" yelled at least half of them. "You can make it!"

With a desperate burst of effort, Pokey gangled her way toward home plate. Her face was a mask of determination as her pom-pommed sneakers churned through the dust. Ryan and April yelled some more, carried away by the moment. So did the benched Puffy players, waving from the dugout.

The girl slid across home. The whole place erupted into pandemonium. Parents whooped and hollered from the sidelines. The benched Puffys jumped up and down and high-fived each other. Ryan would have sworn he saw the team mother abandon her juice-and-snack station and turn several impromptu cartwheels along the first base line. And then April broke from beside him, and ran toward home plate.

The game fell apart completely. April joined the clump of Puffys hugging each other behind the opposing team's bewildered catcher, jumping up and down right along with the kids. He saw her bouncy red hair gleaming in the lights, saw the jubilant smile on her face as she eased her way into the circle of players and hugged Pokey personally.

The madness didn't last long. In the name of fairness, the volunteer umpires ended the celebration and got the game going again, and everyone returned to their places—looking a great deal happier than they had a few minutes earlier. April came back to the "box seating," and sat down next to Ryan with an unstoppable grin.

"I'm shaking, that was so exciting," she said, sounding breathless. She held out her hands for him to see. "That was the Puffys' first run, all season!"

"You're kidding."

"Nope. They're one for fifteen."

"One? If that was the first run, how'd they—"

"Six of the Tigers came down with the flu at once, and had to forfeit."

"Ahh." Ryan watched the game, back in progress. "Is Pokey your cousin? I thought you said her name was Rainey."

April shook her head. "Pokey is Caitlyn Crozier. All of the players have nicknames. Rainey is . . . well, you'll see."

And then, about four minutes later, Ryan did.

For the first time that night, Rainey came to bat. Already prepared for her young cousin's turn, April grabbed the appropriate supplies from her pile and leaned against the front edge of the dugout. She got ready.

"You brought a *banner*?" Ryan asked, gawking.

"Sure," April said, adjusting the corner of the painted canvas where it had begun to curl back into its roll. "What else? I want Rainey to know I'm on her side."

She spread both arms wide, displaying the banner at its full width. With any luck, the lights would show it off even better here than they usually did from her seat in the stands.

"Yay! Yahoo!" she yelled. "You can do it! Home run!"

Rainey, wearing a batting helmet and track pants to coordinate with her pink Puffys uniform shirt, glanced toward the dugout. She tripped.

"That's okay!" April yelled. "Go get 'em!"

Rainey gave a beleaguered sigh. Even from this distance, the motion was detectable, as was the half-hopeful, half-embarrassed look on her little face.

"You can do it!" April yelled.

Hefting the bat, Rainey swung it downward like a major league player, knocking the dust from her sneakers. She moved to the other side, and accidentally walloped her ankle.

With a sympathetic frown, Ryan watched her hop on one foot until the sting went away. "I hope she's all right."

"She's fine." April waved her banner in encouragement.

Two pitches later, Rainey got a hit. Amid the roar of the crowd, she ran full-tilt toward first base ... and collided with the first baseman.

Ryan winced as the two players separated. "Ouch. Is her nickname 'Bruiser'?"

April shook her head. "Nah. And he should know better than to stand on the bag like that." She cupped her hands near her mouth. "Yay! Good hit!"

They watched the next batter approach the plate. Beside them, Jamie and Mark bent their heads over a *Martha Stewart Weddings* "backyard brides" feature, ooohing and aaahing over rose-bedecked garden trellises and football field–size expanses of green grass. April glanced at them, momentarily distracted by their sudden rapport. Again, she wondered about it. Were Jamie and Mark attracted to each other?

A rumble from the crowd pulled her from her thoughts. April snapped her attention back to the game.

"Rainey just stole second!" Ryan said.

"That's my girl! Gooooo, Speedy!" Yelling encouragement, April held her banner high. She whooped, swiveling her hips. She began a dugout-style "wave," beginning with the benched players and sweeping sideways to a reluctant Mark and Jamie, who bobbed a few inches from their seats.

At all the commotion, Rainey glanced at them. Hurriedly, April started another wave. Rainey groaned, and covered her eyes.

"I can't believe it," Ryan said. He stood, eagerly keeping an eye on the game, and grabbed a corner of the banner to help hold it up. "A few minutes ago, Rainey was an emergency-room visit waiting to happen. Now, Speedy's queen of the ball field."

"I know." Charmed by the way he'd gotten involved in the game, April relinquished the left side of her banner. "The klutz routine is just a decoy. It works, too. Every time."

"I'll say. Woo! Go, go, go!" Ryan cheered as Rainey took third base. Looking astonished, he edged closer to April. "Another steal! She wouldn't by any chance be related to your Uncle Bobby, would she?"

April raised her eyebrows. "Har, har." She couldn't believe he'd recognized Uncle Bobby's . . . uh, hobby. "I thought you were oblivious to that, given the way you were handing over your watch for the picking."

"Only temporarily. I'm not stupid, you know. Despite the Idiot Savant Retailing thing."

Making a commiserating face, April used her free hand to grasp his. She squeezed, liking the feel of their fingers so effortlessly entwined. "The Forrester's board members were wrong to say that."

"I'll *prove* them wrong."

"That's right!" She nodded for emphasis, not ready to concede her victory in their wager, but unwilling to leave Ryan feeling downhearted about his chances. "If not now, then later. With some other brilliant Forrester's strategy. You're bound to succeed, especially given your knack with people. They like you.''

"Like me? Probably because I'm the man throwing the party. Paying for the ski trip. Handing out the goodies. What's not to like?''

He raised his shoulders in a shrug that was doubtless meant to seem careless . . . but which only struck April as lonely. Did Ryan really believe what was most appealing about him was his bank account?

"Nothing," she said firmly. "I like plenty of things about you. Your height, for instance, which makes me feel positively petite by comparison—always a plus in this size-zero-starlet world. And your smile, for seconds, which"—*which makes me go all gooey and girly and hopeful for things I don't dare wish for*— "which coordinates very nicely with your, um, teeth.''

Teeth? Cripes. Next she'd be telling him she admired his nose hairs, or something equally bizarre.

Unable to resist, April sneaked a surreptitious glance. *Whew.* This was a man who wouldn't need a rotary nose hair trimmer ever—or at least not until those well-coordinated teeth made way for dentures and a daily swig of Geritol.

She flashed on an image of Ryan as an old man, gray and proud and grinning at his grandkids. A weird sentimental streak welled up inside her. The days they'd spent canvassing Saguaro Vista together must have gotten to her, because all at once, April wanted to be the sneaker-wearing, hair-dyeing, rock-and-roll granny beside him, companionably cussing out "kids these days" and scoring senior citizen discounts. She wanted . . .

Yikes! Jolted by her thoughts, April shook her head and picked up where she'd left off.

"My teeth?'' Ryan asked, displaying them in a grin.

"As likable as the rest of you. So there," April assured him rapidly. "Now let's watch the game."

Obviously amused, he turned toward the ball field again, where another batter was doing his best to advance Rainey to home plate. April waggled her banner, hoping for a big hit to send Rainey/Speedy home.

Suddenly, Ryan was there. *Right there.* His shoulder touched hers, their sides brushed together, and his presence swept intoxicatingly over her. He put his lips to her ear.

"I think you're likable, too," he murmured.

She jumped at the sound of his voice, at its deep timbre and provocatively slow cadence. Her banner wobbled uncontrollably, making Jamie and Mark glance up from the next wedding magazine they'd chosen. With an easy smile for them, Ryan rubbed April's hand soothingly with his thumb.

"Very likable," he went on. "In fact, from the minute I saw you smile at me, I knew I was smitten with your . . . teeth. We might as well face it. Our chompers are meant to be together."

April snorted. Those weren't exactly sweet nothings— but she found herself liking them, all the same. *Sense of humor? Check,* tallied her inner dream-man meter. *Taking her seriously? Check. Holding hands? Check.* All that remained was for Ryan to get along with Calypso and kiss her in the rain. Then—

Whoa. All at once, April realized exactly how well Ryan meshed with her hunk-turned–soul mate ideal. This could get *really* dangerous.

"But more than that," his breath whispered across her skin, making her shiver, "I knew I had to meet you. To talk to you. To find out if you really were as fascinating as you looked. And now—"

Her, fascinating? Trying to maintain her composure in the face of all this unaccustomed appreciation, April shrugged. "If I am, it's all my dentist's fault," she said, flashing her "chompers." "You know, there's more to good dental hygiene than daily brushing and flossing, which don't necessarily—"

"Let's get out of here. Together," Ryan said, his voice urgent. "Let's ditch our double datees and go someplace . . . alone."

Oh, how she wanted to! But she was trying to be sensible. Sensible, for some reason she . . . couldn't quite remember, with the muscular wall of Ryan's chest behind her and the security of his hand holding hers.

Valiantly, April tried to hold her ground. Geez, but this responsible, reliable, dependable stuff was tough! Maybe her flighty Finnegan genes made it especially challenging for her.

"Well, technically I'm Mark's date," she said. "It wouldn't be fair to him to leave him in the lurch."

"I don't think he'll mind. He just spent the last two minutes rubbing sunscreen on Jamie's shoulders." Ryan nuzzled April's ear, the faint beginnings of his five o'clock shadow soft against her jaw. "And the sun set a half hour ago."

She smiled, feeling a familiar heat—which had nothing to do with the sun, or lack of it—uncurl inside her. "Well . . . okay, then. We'll go someplace alone right after the game. After all, a little talking couldn't hurt, right?"

"Mmmm-hmmm. *Talking.*"

As if chitchat was what either of them had on their minds, April thought hazily. A part of her warned that being alone with Ryan could only lead to trouble . . . but the rest of her enthusiastically applauded the plan. That "rest" of her also excelled at rationalization, it seemed. *What harm could come from a little fling?* it asked. *How distracting could one man possibly be?*

With that decided, April returned her attention to

the game—at least as best she could, while semi-snuggled with Ryan behind three feet of painted canvas, with semi-sweet-nothings being whispered into her ear.

Two outs and a full count, with the latest Puffy batter prepared for another swing. Rainey was still stranded on third base. April tensed. The bat and ball connected. Rainey ran across home plate to the cheers of the crowd.

Two runs. Almost as unbelievable, April decided happily, as finding herself in the arms of Mister Big.

Eight and a half innings later, April and Ryan were still holding hands behind her banner. With their free hands, they held the banner and cheered, and discovered a joint affection for Little League softball. In the end, the Puffys actually won, two to zero, Jamie and Mark had worked their way through several more wedaholic monthlies, and April was feeling remarkably cheerful as she returned to the dugout "box seating" after having congratulated all the Puffy players on their win—and having commiserated with all the opposing players on their defeat.

"Hey, Ryan," Jamie was saying as April began gathering her things for her private just-talking getaway with Ryan, "this guy looks just like you! Check it out."

She nodded toward the open magazine between her and Mark. Glancing toward it, Ryan's face changed. Wearing an odd expression, he leaned nearer.

"Nah. Looks like my secret double strikes again," he said. "You know how they say everyone has a twin, somewhere in the world. Looks like mine has a thing for Armani tuxes."

He straightened, studiously nonchalant, and caught April's eye. "We should probably get going. You know, our plans."

"You didn't even look," Mark protested. He pushed the magazine closer.

Curious, April gazed downward. "It *does* look like you."

"It *is* you!" Jamie said. She looked from the picture to Ryan, and back to the picture again. She jabbed her fingertip at its caption, and read: "One of the San Diego Forresters, Ryan Forrester and his fiancée—"

Ryan held up his hand. "All right. Yes, it's me."

They all gasped. Just as April was about to ask about his hidden double life as a male wedding magazine model, he spoke again.

"My former fiancée lined up the photo shoot with the magazine a couple of months ago. She was a real publicity hound. I'd forgotten all about it."

April boggled. Jamie and Mark stared. *"Your fiancée?"* they asked in unison.

Feeling as though she'd gone inexplicably numb, April lowered onto the dugout bench with a thud. "You're engaged?"

"*Was* engaged." Looking beleaguered, Ryan grabbed the backward bill of his cap and turned it around to shade his face. "I'm not engaged anymore."

"But this says a" —frowning, Jamie spun the magazine around on Mark's lap and squinted at the two-page feature— "a late April wedding at San Diego's Oceanside Presbyterian Church, followed by a gala reception at—"

"The wedding never happened." Brusquely, Ryan held out his hand to April. "Ready?"

Ready? How could she possibly be *ready* when she'd just discovered the man she'd mentally shopped for retirement condos with had—of all things—a fiancée? Still staring at him, April slowly shook her head.

"But what happened?" Jamie interrupted, looking perplexed. "Did the chapel in Vegas run out of two-for-ninety-nine-dollars wedding rings? Did the wedding Elvis come down with a cold? What?"

Ryan blinked. "Huh?"

Remembering her Jamie-style anti-Ryan diversionary tactics earlier, April bolted upward. "Nothing like that," she said, stepping closer to Ryan. She pushed her banner and giant foam "Number One" hand into his arms, in preparation for leaving with him. "Things just . . . didn't work out."

But why? April wished she knew.

Jamie nodded knowingly. "Just goes to show you, eloping is always a mistake. You should have stuck with the Oceanside Presbyterian plan this article mentions. A wedding deserves the proper ceremony, and dignity."

"And handwritten vows," Mark added, "read by the bride and groom."

"Handwritten vows?" Jamie looked delighted. "That's what I want, too!"

They both grinned like loons. Mark swayed a little toward Jamie. Jamie leaned closer to Mark.

"I was jilted," Ryan said.

Everyone stopped moving. April glimpsed the stiff set to Ryan's shoulders, the downward turn of his mouth . . . and despite everything, had to fight an urge to comfort him.

"My fiancée kidnapped the minister," he said, not looking at them, "and ran off with a groomsman a few minutes before the wedding. She ditched her Jimmy Choos, destroyed the wedding planner's morale, and left me and my parents holding a hundred-thousand-dollar wedding bill. She also absconded with my romantic-getaway carriage ride. Do you know how hard it is to book a decent carriage ride on two months' notice?"

Dumbfounded, they all shook their heads.

"Damn hard."

"Two months," Mark observed. "Short engagement."

"Just enough time for my former fiancée to frisk me for my platinum card," Ryan agreed. "Assess my financial worth. And seclude me from my friends and family with promises of the future I thought we both wanted."

"Except you didn't both want it, after all." Catching her lower lip between her teeth—as though to keep from crying—Jamie touched Ryan's forearm. "Oh, that's so sad. *So* sad."

"Sorry," Mark mumbled.

"Wow, rugged," April said in a falsely cheery voice. She grabbed Ryan's arm. "Let's talk about this later."

The three of them gawped at her. Okay, so maybe she sounded a little insensitive, April allowed. But the last thing she wanted was for Ryan to explain all this now . . . and for her two closest friends to see her hopes shatter, right there beside the porta-seats and the discarded baseball bats.

"It's all right." Ryan resisted her tug. "I don't mind talking about it. I consider all of you my friends now."

"Awwww," Jamie and Mark said in unison.

The two of them stared at each other, and smiled goofily.

Friends, April thought as she crossed her arms over her chest and waited. *Hmmph.* Friends didn't keep huge, heartbreaking-style secrets from each other, especially when said friends were . . . romantically inclined.

Adjusting the banner and other things April had given him, Ryan didn't look up as he explained. "April's right. Things didn't work out between me and my former fiancée. Aside from the jilting thing—"

"Ouch," Jamie and Mark said, wincing.

"—there were other things, signs I should have spotted earlier. Her insistence on a whirlwind wedding, for one. Her issues with money, for another."

Issues with money? Dread swooshed into April's middle

and settled with a leaden thump. *She* had, it could be said, "issues with money." Her family usually didn't have it, couldn't keep it when they did, and could always be counted on to squander it in the most idiotic ways possible. She, personally, would be running out of it soon, if her new community relations position with Ambrosia didn't pan out.

But Ryan couldn't possibly understand any of that, could he? No. Not as someone who'd never eagle-eyed the gas gauge on his VW Rabbit while coasting the last half mile to the gas station on payday. Not as someone who'd never held his breath while waiting for a credit approval to come through, and who'd never toted a fistful of coupons and a calculator to the grocery store to stay within his weekly food budget.

No, Ryan would never understand her "issues with money," and April couldn't imagine he ever would. If he knew about her shiftless Finnegan-ness, Ryan would think less of her. He might even feel sorry for her. And that was something April, proud to the core, simply couldn't bear.

Clearly, she had to hide the truth about herself. Until Ryan left town, she would have to keep up a brave front, and conceal her impending financial failure . . . and she would have to be ruthless, *ruthless* about winning their bet.

"Issues with money?" she asked, trying to sound carefree.

"Yes." Ryan pulled a wry face, seeming a little relieved now that everything was out in the open. "As in, she wanted to marry into as much of it as possible, as quickly as possible, for one thing. Obviously, my former fiancée decided the Grisham clone was a better bet than I was."

"Grisham clone?" Jamie asked.

"Long story." Edging closer to April, Ryan smiled down at her, his features a little weary and a lot appealing. Still. How did he keep *doing* that? "The important thing is, I got out alive. With my sanity intact, and my heart only a little bit broken."

A little bit broken. April wanted to sob, both for herself and for Ryan. Why had fate tossed her this man now, when being with him looked so impossible . . . and so tantalizing?

He put his arm around her shoulders. Woodenly, she let herself be tugged next to him.

"And," Ryan went on, "that heartbreak thing is looking like less and less of a problem all the time, I have to say."

His smile beamed down at her. A quick glance sideways revealed that Jamie and Mark were smiling at her, too, in a suspiciously misty-eyed way. What was the matter with these people? Couldn't they see that April was nothing more than Ryan's rebound fling, destined to be cast aside when he got his life together again?

April could see it. And it hurt like hell. Dashed hopes often worked out that way, she guessed.

Well, being a rebound woman just wasn't good enough for her. It couldn't be. It was better she'd discovered all this now, April told herself, while there was still a chance she could get over him . . . given, oh, say, a millennia or so.

Stoically, she ducked from beneath Ryan's hold and started gathering her things from his arms. He jerked them back.

"What's the matter?" he asked. "I thought we were—"

"Not anymore," April said. "Sorry."

And then, after gathering her things and without looking back, she made her escape. Off to call a taxi, off to bawl her eyes out with an armload of Calypso for comfort and a pint of Phish Food by her side. Off, before disappointment drove her to something she'd *really* regret . . . like begging Ryan to forget his ex-fiancée, and fall for *her*, instead.

Permanently.

Chapter Ten

"This is really nice of you," Ryan told Mark later that evening. "Thanks."

"You're welcome." Mark handed over an armload of blankets topped with a pillow, all in tasteful shades of beige. "The sofa bed isn't the most comfortable, but it beats the street."

Ryan gave an uneasy laugh as he piled the bedding into his arms. He might have ended up *on* the street, literally, if Mark hadn't been home at his apartment over the Ambrosia bakery. Following April's abrupt and confusing retreat from the Little League game, Ryan had returned to the Saguaro Vista Motor Court Inn . . . only to find a padlock on his *casita* door and a matching steely glint in the manager's eyes.

"Your credit's no good," the man had explained. "Got the notice this afternoon. Something about a stolen platinum card."

He'd nodded toward the luggage the inn's maid had packed for Ryan. He'd looked at Ryan suspiciously, as though debating whether or not he should call out the sheriff—or whatever they did in the event of a Podunk criminal invasion. Then the manager had edged sideways toward the phone.

Preferring not to take his chances with the law—especially given the increasing number of parking tickets Wanda had issued him over the past few days—Ryan had set out for Ambrosia, and made his plea to Mark.

He was still amazed the man had invited him to stay with him for a few days. After all, Ryan had pretty much blown every piece of advice Mark had issued today . . . and he hadn't exactly been a supporter of his business, either. Ryan still couldn't believe he hadn't been able to buy so much as a blueberry muffin this morning. *A blueberry muffin!*

It might not have been that bad. For someone else. For Ryan, a person accustomed to buying whatever he wanted, whenever he wanted it, no questions asked about the price, coming to grips with the fact that he was temporarily without resources was difficult.

At first it had been voluntary. Ryan had been comforted—more than he'd known—by the fact that he could have abandoned his wager with April at any time. He could have liberated his wallet from its bedside-drawer penitentiary, and gotten on with life as he was accustomed to it. But now . . . this was a whole new ball game. He had no resources, no usable credit, and a mere three hundred–odd dollars cash at his disposal—and his bet with April made even *that* untouchable.

"That's too bad about your ex-fiancée stealing your credit cards," Mark said now, stacking beige sofa cushions in an orderly fashion on a nearby beige armchair. "I didn't know women like that existed, outside of movies. She's a real femme fatal, isn't she?"

"Looks that way." Unwillingly, Ryan remembered Jackson's advice on the day of the wedding that wasn't.

You'll find out. Just like the rest of us trust-fund fellas. You get fleeced once, and you're careful forever. Believe me. Women can't be trusted. Particularly around guys like us.

Well, Ryan didn't believe it. He hadn't then, and he didn't now. If anything, he believed it even less . . . and April was the reason. She'd restored his faith in basic decency. She'd kick-started his downtrodden heart, too. That was why her abrupt departure tonight was doubly confusing—and why Ryan intended to get to the bottom of it. Soon.

But that would have to wait. For now. Turning his mind to other things, Ryan told Mark, "Let me know how much the phone call to my lawyer was, when you get the bill."

He was referring to the long-distance phone conversation he'd had a few minutes ago, during which he'd discovered his former fiancée's continued misdeeds. Evidently, she'd added herself as a signatory to all of his credit cards. Once the first big-ticket charge came through—from the Caribbean, their erstwhile honeymoon spot—his advisors had sent up the alarm.

"I'll send you a check," he went on. "Once my accountants straighten everything out, that is."

"No problem." Mark waved a hand, and finished unfolding the sofa bed's mattress and frame with a grunt. "Don't put yourself out on my account. Whenever you can manage it would be fine."

Humbled by Mark's generosity, Ryan nodded. Most of his friends would have had their accountants immediately devise a promissory note for repayment—if they'd agreed to help at all. Sadly enough, Ryan could count on one hand the number of people he felt even remotely sure would have come through for him. Jackson. A couple of his good friends from college. His parents and sister, if he could have tracked them down.

Not that he was going to. No, siree. He was going to

handle this the manly way, with his inherent skills—as soon as he uncovered what they were—and without feeling sorry for himself. To that end, Ryan thought over his situation with April while he awkwardly made up his beige-on-beige bed. By the time he'd finished his first-ever housekeeping task, he'd devised a new plan.

"Hey, Mark," he asked. "Do you know anyone who owns a pickup truck?"

His host raised his eyebrows. "A pickup? Sure. It's practically the official vehicle of Saguaro Vista."

"Perfect." Ryan sat down, wallet-less and credit-less but still possessing a little ingenuity, and grinned as he plotted the next step in his *wow April* campaign. He could hardly wait to get started.

Determined to do the best job she could on behalf of Ambrosia, April got up early on Friday morning and began visiting Main Street retailers the minute the first stores opened their doors. With only a week remaining in her bet with Ryan, she needed to make her pitch to as many businesses as possible.

By the time eleven o'clock rolled around, she was windblown from riding her bike across town, slightly hoarse from presenting her pro-Ambrosia rationale over and over, and just a little bit discouraged. From talking with the merchants, April hadn't been able to tell if they were leaning toward forming sponsor partnerships with the bakery or with Forrester's. So much was riding on this. She wished she were more sure that she'd done a good job.

She wished she'd seen Ryan, while she'd been at it.

Her unreasoning heart still pined for him, despite everything April had learned last night. Even knowing the truth—that at best she'd be a rebound rendez-vous—with "money issues"—hadn't been enough to crush her hopefulness. She'd found herself watching for Ryan as she'd pedaled to the auto parts shop to offer a mini bakery concession for waiting customers, and as she'd biked her way to the park to pitch a bakery cart at the next Fourth of July municipal celebration. For better or worse, though—probably better—she'd struck out. Ryan had been nowhere in sight.

All the same, standing outside now beneath the Hair-Razors awning with a twice-brewed takeout cup of mint tea and Jamie by her side, April couldn't help talking about him.

"I still don't get what the problem is," Jamie said when April had finished explaining her cute-booty-possessing No Trespassing Zone policy with regard to Ryan. "You like him, right? He likes you. He's not engaged anymore. You're not a gold-digging demon fiancée with 'money issues.' "

April winced.

"So why not go for the gusto?"

"He's on the rebound."

"He seems over her to me."

"He's filthy rich."

"Unless he rolls around in his money like Scrooge McDuck," Jamie rebutted, "which would be fairly kinky and off-putting, I don't see the problem."

"You wouldn't. You're not a Finnegan."

"Oh, brother. *That* again?"

"Yes, that again," April said. "You know what my family is like. You know what everybody says about them. You know everyone thinks it's just a matter of time before I show my true colors and slide all the way into shiftless Finneganville, too."

Jamie rolled her eyes. "Who cares what everybody thinks? True love is more important."

"Spoken like a true wedaholic. What's next in the

wannabe-bride manifesto? Thou shalt tattoo thy butt with monogrammed bride and groom initials?"

"Hey!"

Instantly, April regretted her words. "I'm sorry," she said, giving Jamie a quick hug. "That was out of line. I'm just a little overwrought."

"A little?"

"And this situation with Ryan isn't as simple as it seems."

"Sure, it is." Casually, Jamie swigged her Pepsi. "Tell Ryan how you feel about him. Take a chance."

"Take a chance?" April shook her head, and tossed her empty paper tea cup into the bin. "If he finds out the truth about me, he'll think I'm a loser. I couldn't stand it."

Jamie smiled. It was the same "I know something you don't know" smile she'd worn when they were twelve, and April had been scared to get her ears pierced. "You're not a loser."

"Well, *I* don't think so! But Ryan is . . . different."

"I guess so." Sighing, Jamie twirled her finger around her soda can tab. "Different," she said dreamily. "Like Mark."

"*So* not like Mark."

Jamie blinked, and gave an awkward laugh. April raised her eyebrows.

Someone honked a car horn. They saw Wanda passing by on parking meter patrol, and waved. Afterward, Jamie glanced at her watch.

"You're, uh, not interested in Mark, then?" she asked without looking up. "Are you?"

Was that a hopeful note she'd detected in Jamie's voice? April wondered. Thoughtfully, she remembered the closeness between her pal and her boss at the Little League game last night, and decided she wholeheartedly approved.

Hey, even though April couldn't be lucky in love, that didn't mean the rest of the world had to suffer, too.

"No," she said, stifling a grin. "I'm not interested in Mark."

Something else occurred to her. Ducking her head, she asked, "Are you, um, interested in Ryan? After the date last night, and all?"

Jamie shook her head. She was actually blushing, April noticed. Remarkable. She'd have sworn Jamie had given up girlish things like blushing after she'd had her navel pierced and her ankle tattooed. Twice.

"Because you and Mark," April went on, "really seemed to hit it off last night."

She waggled her eyebrows encouragingly, hoping for more details. All her life, she and Jamie had shared their romantic ups and downs. But this time—

"We were talking about you and Ryan," Jamie said primly, examining her Pepsi can. She looked up, her expression suddenly fierce. "Do it, April. If you think you can be happy with Ryan, don't wait! I'm telling you . . . sometimes if you wait too long, your chance is gone."

April didn't understand the urgency in Jamie's voice. She looked at her friend with concern.

"Hey, is something wrong? Do you want to talk, or—"

"Just believe me." She checked her watch again. "Look, my break's over. I've gotta run. But remember this: fortune favors the bold. It does not favor those who tiptoe into the party and stand by the spinach dip all night."

"Huh?"

"Just believe me." Jamie gave her a wan smile and another quick hug. "If Ryan is the one you want, don't wait. Take a chance now."

"Now?" Perplexed by all this talk of spinach dip and fate, April frowned. "But I don't—"

"Yes, right *now*." Jamie looked over April's shoulder, and her eyes widened. "Look. Here comes your chance."

Jamie turned her around. Even more confused, April heard the chug-chug of an old engine, smelled exhaust, glimpsed a beat-up pickup truck rolling down the street in fits and starts. Weirdly enough, the vehicle's radio antenna, truck bed–cover loops, and bumpers were all decorated with enormous red bows. Wisps of hay flew randomly from the bed, swirling in the tires' updraft before settling onto the street in the truck's wake.

At the wheel was . . . *Ryan?*

"Go get 'em, tiger," Jamie said. "Rrrrr!"

And the next thing April knew, she was alone on the sidewalk with her jaw dropping open . . . and the man she was unreasonably crazy about was headed her way, a bouquet of yellow daisies in his hand.

Pausing inside at the HairRazors window, Jamie watched as Ryan alighted from the crookedly parked pickup truck. Squeezing her empty Pepsi can in her fist, Jamie cradled it against her heart as he approached April. He handed her a bouquet of yellow daisies. April hesitated, and Jamie held her breath.

April took the flowers.

"Yes," Jamie whispered. She leaned her forehead against the window glass, still watching. "Go for it, April."

Don't wait too long, she thought. *Like I did.*

Last night, things had gone so wonderfully at the Little League game. Fate had tossed her a curveball— literally—and had allowed Jamie an excuse to cozy up to Mark. They'd bonded over her wedding magazines, had ooohed and aaahhed over all the same things, had shared a moderately strong disinterest in baseball. Mark had revealed his hopes for handwritten wedding vows, for Pete's sake! Jamie had thought she'd been home free.

And then she'd made her move. After April had zoomed away in her taxi, Ryan had volunteered to fetch Mark's car "from outer Siberia." He'd left with the keys, looking downhearted. And when Mark had offered to walk Jamie to her car, she'd known the moment had arrived to make her big revelation.

She could still picture the shock on Mark's face. The disbelief. Possibly, the horror. Who knew? All Jamie understood for certain was that she'd finally found the courage to confess her long-standing romantic feelings for him . . . and Mark had turned away.

He'd muttered something about "timing." He'd stammered something more about "friendship." He'd even come out with some stupid excuse about purple hair and dancing the conga—whatever the hell *that* meant. In the end, he'd left her at her Escort with a handshake and a bowled-over look, and that had been that.

She'd wanted to sob. She'd wanted to scream. She'd wanted, in fact—Jamie had decided at that very minute—to dye *Mark's* hair purple and dance the conga all over his big fat head.

Instead, she'd chosen to pass on the lesson she'd learned. It was too late for her now. But maybe she could still save April from a similar heartbreak.

Watching from the window again, Jamie saw that Ryan had opened the pickup truck's passenger side door. Standing in front of it now, at the edge of the curb, he held out his hand to April. The hopefulness—the bravery—in his expression made Jamie's heart ache, despite everything. *Do it, April,* she urged silently. *Take a chance. Now!*

April bit her lip. Glanced over her shoulder at the

scattered people walking to shops and driving past. Looked at Ryan again.

She lowered her head, her hair sliding forward to shield her face. She lowered the daisies, their jaunty yellow faces nearly brushing the sidewalk.

All at once, Jamie knew. *April was going to say no.*

Her posture foretold it. Her hesitation. The gentle shake of her head.

Jamie tossed her empty soda can toward a nearby trash bin and lurched against the window, splaying her fingers on its cool surface. April *had* to go with Ryan. She just *had* to.

Ryan wiggled his fingers, saying something Jamie couldn't hear. April's head came up. She took a tentative step forward, raised her daisies so their faces captured the sunlight. An instant later, she took Ryan's hand.

"Yes!" Jamie yelled.

Her manager came over, along with a client in hair color foil and a HairRazors cape. The three of them watched through the window as Ryan guided April into the pickup truck.

"Are those ribbons all over that truck?" asked the client.

"Yes." Jamie felt like laughing aloud. "They are. And those are pink helium balloons tied to the bumper, too."

"Fool man," the woman muttered. "You can't woo a woman with a sissy pickup."

"What's he *wearing*?" asked her manager.

"I think it's one of those Armani suits," Jamie said. "With sneakers. And a yellow smiley-face necktie."

"Atrocious," said the client.

"She don't seem to mind," observed Jamie's manager.

Jamie was too busy watching to reply. The pickup truck's engine roared to life, belching blue smoke and shuddering like a giant wet cat. Truly, April *didn't* seem to mind. And Jamie was glad for it.

The truck lurched away from the curb, April visible through the windshield as she scooted closer to Ryan and smelled her flowers. He smiled at her. She grinned back at him. All three HairRazors spectators sighed.

"Awwww. Ain't that sweet?" asked the client.

It looked as though April and Ryan were on their way, Jamie told herself, taking a satisfied step back from the window. They'd decided to take a chance, to grab for true love and hang on until they found out if it fit. It just went to show that sometimes things really did work out.

A squeal screeched through Main Street, followed by a thud. The truck came to a standstill ten feet from the intersection, surrounded by blue smoke.

Okay, so maybe things didn't work out perfectly, Jamie amended with a shrug. Not the first time, at least. But they just might work out eventually. Despite everything, she felt more sure of it now than ever.

Mark was in the midst of ringing up a customer's chocolate éclair order when he heard the screech coming from Main Street. He and his customer, his former eighth grade English teacher, hurried to the bakery's window and looked outside.

"Awww, heck. Take the éclairs, Mrs. Coughlin," he said as he flipped over Ambrosia's closed sign. "They're on the house."

"Oh, thank you!"

He followed her out and headed for the street, toward the stalled pickup truck he'd seen. Ryan hadn't confided his whole plan to Mark over beers last night—but his pickup truck request had been a leading clue . . . and seeing a daisy-carrying April in the passenger side of his brother Mack's truck now, the overall gist fell into place for Mark fairly quickly.

He should have known he was helping his rival seduce his woman. *Damn it.*

Waving his arms to clear the foul-smelling smoke, Mark made his way to the pickup. The bows and balloons bobbed into view. He shook his head. If he knew his sister-in-law Kim, she was the one responsible for the "romantic" doodads. She always had had a soft spot for matchmaking ... matchmaking newcomers to town— 'fresh meat,' she jokingly called them—in particular.

In the haze, he accidentally jostled someone. Mark moved to steady them, then glanced sideways to apologize.

"Jamie!"

"Mark."

She looked slightly unreal amid the smoke, like a vivid lady genie, or a colorful gypsy fortune-teller with ultra-styled spiky hair and deep purple clothes. Memories of all the things she'd said last night rushed back to him. He felt himself pull away.

If she noticed his abrupt withdrawal, Jamie didn't say so. Instead, she began to hum. She looked around at the truck, and the cars stopped on the street beside it, and the people moving nearer to help, and just ... hummed.

"Look, about last night," he said after a few seconds.

"Look, about last night," she said at the same time.

They both stopped in surprise. Mark recalled the unusual way they'd echoed each other's thoughts all during the baseball game yesterday, and reminded himself, again, that a simple thing like that didn't mean he and Jamie were right for each other. Because they weren't. As simple as that.

If anything, Jamie was an even worse choice for him than April would be—if he could ever get her to look his way. While Jamie came from a slightly more stable family of Barretts, she *looked* twice as unusual. And she had a long history of being, if not the most original woman in town, definitely one of the top five. If he dated Jamie—impossible as the thought was—people would talk. They would gossip, and spread rumors, and probably doubt his seriousness and ability to run the bakery, too.

Plus, she'd actually approved of, *and eaten,* one or more of the much-maligned chocolate Adonises. He'd seen her nibbling upward toward one's semisweet loin-cloth-free zone, and had begun to fantasize about—

No. No, Mark couldn't afford to indulge any . . . passing interest in Jamie, he told himself. No matter that her nearness tripled his pulse rate and made him imagine steamy, sexy things, the likes of which he'd never once imagined about April. No matter the way Jamie's smile and wave as she left Ambrosia every morning with her chocolate croissant brightened his outlook for the whole day. He. Just. Couldn't. Possibly—

His inner struggle jolted to a stop as Jamie went on talking.

"I hope you don't feel funny about what I said last night," she told him. "I don't want things to become awkward between us. I just had to get it out there." She shrugged. "It's not like you're the first inappropriate man I've ever fallen for—"

Inappropriate?

"—and you probably won't be the last. So don't sweat it."

Inappropriate? Not the last . . . ?

Jamie gave him a pat on the shoulder. *A pat on the shoulder!* Then she moved forward to talk to April through the pickup's window, humming again as she sidestepped Pete Wykowski, who shouldered his way past carrying his mechanic's toolbox. Wykowski disappeared beneath the truck's raised hood. More smoke and clunking sounds ensued, drowning out Jamie's humming.

Whaaaa . . . ? Mark wondered, watching her. He scratched his head, unable to figure out exactly what had happened. All he knew was that one minute he'd been sort of . . . congratulating himself on not having snapped at the bait of Jamie's day-old declaration of secret love, and the next minute he'd found himself dismissed. Like a day-old baguette.

Feeling appropriately past his prime, Mark took one more look at the pickup, the smattering of people . . . the conga-dancing woman he'd *thought* he was better off without. All at once, his enthusiasm for helping Ryan and April on their way—admittedly shaky at best—waned completely. He put his hands in his pockets and walked back to the bakery, shoulders down and mind blank—save one troubling thought.

He may have made, Mark decided as he flipped over the closed sign and went back to work, last night and just now, too, a very, very, *very* big mistake.

Damn it.

Chapter Eleven

Getting his loaner pickup truck running again required more time than Ryan expected—and also more, well, *things* than he expected, too. Chief among them were one new hose, several forays into Pete Wykowski's toolbox, a promise to loan Pete his choice of Ryan's suits for his—Pete's, not Ryan's—upcoming bowling league championship dinner in exchange for his usual mechanic's fee, and a round of applause from scattered Saguaro Vista-ites. Finally, though, he and April made it up the bumpy dirt road to their destination—a scenic spot overlooking the Willayump River.

There, he jerked the pickup to a stop and set the brake. He cut the ignition. The engine kept churning. Ryan frowned, and switched the key back and forth.

"It'll wind down eventually," April said, cheery on the seat beside him as she gripped her daisies. "My dad used to have a truck that did the same thing. It's a quirk."

A quirk? It was broken, that's what it was. He was

accustomed to things that worked, and worked efficiently. Ryan waggled the key again.

More whirring. A halfhearted "chug." A wheeze. Silence finally fell, unbroken except for the ping of the engine cooling. He experienced a rush of nostalgia for his prime, limited-edition, non-wheezing roadster, traded temporarily to Mack Wright for the use of his pickup truck.

But this pickup truck, damn it, was *real*. Maybe even *real* enough for April, Ryan reminded himself. And that was the whole point, wasn't it?

"Ahhh." Not bothered by their vehicle's mammoth inadequacies, April stretched out both arms. One arm along the back of the vinyl seat, one all the way out the rolled-down window. Her daisies, at the end of the latter hand, fluttered in the gentle breeze. "Isn't this nice?"

She glanced through the windshield at the gently curved bank before them, with its stooped-over lacy-leaved trees, tall sunburned grass, and scattered boulders. Their surfaces were gritty and sand-colored, like the floor of Ryan's country club sauna following a volleyball game.

After another exhalation of pleasure, April gave him an impish look. "Much better than a lunch break spent at the local greasy spoon. I begin to be glad you persuaded me to come here with you."

"Persuaded you? You didn't take that much persuading," Ryan bluffed. *Only enough to nearly cause me heart failure, right there on Main Street.* He mustered a smile, which felt difficult due to how important this outing had become to him. "But I'm glad, too."

They smiled at each other. Goofily, and in an oddly sexy way. Their instant togetherness made his heart thump faster . . . and made it difficult to believe that, only an hour or so ago, Ryan had found himself seriously doubting both the wisdom of his just-Ryan seduction plan *and* April's likely willingness to buy into it.

He'd pulled up in this damned geriatric pickup, billowing hay like truck dandruff and trailing froufrou bows and balloons, and had wanted to drive right on by when he'd glimpsed April's shocked expression. Then, when he'd found the guts to creak open the door and emerge with the flowers he'd bartered his baseball cap for, Ryan had discovered a whole new level of uncertainty.

Sure, April had accepted the daisies. She'd even seemed satisfactorily and girlishly pleased with the bouquet. But then, when he'd suggested his getaway picnic plan, she'd also all but dusted the sidewalk with them as she'd drooped, visibly, before his eyes. He'd been certain, in that heart-stopping moment, that April was going to refuse him.

Forever.

She'd gotten so far as shaking her head no when desperation had made Ryan act.

"I need you," he'd said.

April's head had come up. Warily.

He'd glanced around at the curious people looking their way as they passed by. He'd held out his hand a little higher.

"Humor me," Ryan had said. "Don't turn me down. At least not in front of all these people."

Even remembering it now, his heart twisted. It had then, too. He hadn't planned for the situation to so closely parallel his wedding-that-wasn't jilt trip, but when it had begun to . . . well, Ryan hadn't been able to stand it.

But in the end, it had worked. April had agreed to come with him, and here they were.

Hey, all's well that ends well, he told himself now, shoving those earlier doubts from his mind. Next, all he had to do was make up for the fiancée debacle at the Little League game yesterday, produce a fabulous romantic afternoon with zero cash, and knock April's socks off. Piece of cake, right?

First things first. That was what his dad had always advised, when showing Ryan how to polish his junior golf clubs, demand the laundry press a stiffer pleat into his prep-school uniform pants, and suppress all evidence of fear. He drew in a deep breath, and cleared his throat.

"About yesterday," Ryan began. He twisted the inexplicably fuzzy steering wheel cover back and forth, as though the motion could somehow wring out these difficult-to-say words. "I didn't mean to mislead you. I just . . . saw that magazine spread, and panicked."

So much for Dad's Credo number three.

"I didn't want to tell you about the wedding. Or the mess it turned out to be. I came here partly to forget it."

April looked straight ahead. "Have you forgotten it?"

Have you forgotten her? asked the look in her eyes, when she turned at his awkward silence and confronted him.

"Because if I'm nothing but your rebound woman," April went on determinedly, "you can just rubber-band off someone else."

"Rubber-band?"

"Bounce back. That's what a rebound woman helps you do."

"Ahhh." Thoughtfully, Ryan leaned his head against the back of the seat. The muzzle of the shotgun holstered there in the window rack nearly jabbed his eye out. *"Ahhh!"*

Suppressing a smile, April scooted the shotgun closer to her side of the pickup. "Mack likes deer hunting," she explained.

He had visions of Bambi. "Uh-huh."

"Do you hunt?"

She raised her eyebrows expectantly.

As if. "Only martinis," Ryan said. "Believe me, it can be a real trick to track down a bartender at a busy club."

At his joke, her expression brightened. He was encouraged.

A silent moment stretched between them.

"Look," Ryan made himself say. "About my former fiancée—"

"No, you don't have to tell me." April waved her free hand. She drew her daisies inside the truck, and lowered her face to them. "It's none of my business."

"It's *especially* your business."

Her gaze lifted. Swerved to join with his. "Mine? Why?"

Her honest question made his heart lurch. He struggled to explain, when revealing his feelings had never come easily to him. *Suppress. Deny. Be polite to the point of pointlessness.* That was the Forrester Family credo.

"Because I want you," he said.

"Oh, *that.*" April exhaled. "We're both adults. If we want to take things to the next level, if we want to begin a sexual relationship, well . . . we can consider that."

The studiously nonchalant expression on her face fooled him not a bit. She was not the kind of woman to "take things to the next level" on a casual basis, and Ryan knew it.

Evidently, he was also not the kind of man to explain things properly. Ryan knew that, too. Now.

"That's not what I mean," he said.

"Oh."

She sagged a bit, looking away. Ryan braved closer contact with the looming shotgun and edged nearer.

"I mean, of course I mean *that!* But I also mean . . . I want *you.* To be with you. To talk with you. To find out what makes you laugh and cry, what makes you mad and what makes you think. I want to know you. I want—"

At his hesitation, April lifted her face to his. "Yes?"

"—I want to take a chance. Let's take a chance."

There. He'd said it. Now, with everything he wanted out in the open, all Ryan could do was wait. And hope he'd explained things a little better this time. And take off his suit jacket, because it was hot enough to make him sweat in here.

Okay, so maybe it wasn't the temperature making him sweat, Ryan allowed. But he couldn't stand just sitting there doing nothing, waiting for April to laugh, or point, or point *and* laugh. He stripped to his shirtsleeves, loosened his shirt and tie, and tucked his suit jacket atop the pickup's seat, feeling uncomfortably exposed.

She plucked a yellow daisy from her bouquet, and brushed it against her cheek. Then without a word, April leaned nearer. His heartbeat kicked up a notch, just the way it always did when she came close to him. Just the way, probably, it always would.

Gently, she touched the same petals to his cheek. Her gaze met his. She twirled the flower, making it tickle his skin.

She smiled.

"If I weren't a Finnegan, I'd probably have enough discipline to resist you," April said, seeming inexplicably resigned—but not entirely displeased. "I'd probably even have enough fortitude to look to the future and see that this can go nowhere, and ask you to drive me back to town right now."

Ryan frowned. Was this an elaborate no? A wishy-washy yes? A maybe? Obviously, he needed more practice time spent with April, to understand her better.

"But since I *am* a Finnegan, all hope of common sense is out the window."

The daisy stem broke, and April glanced down at it

To start your membership, simply complete and return the Free Book Certificate. You'll receive your Introductory Shipment of FREE Zebra Contemporary Romances. Then, each month as long as your account is in good standing, you will receive the 3 newest Zebra Contemporary Romances. Each shipment will be yours to examine for 10 days. If you decide to keep the books, you'll pay the preferred book club member price of $15.95 – a savings of over 20% off the cover price! (plus $1.50 to offset the cost of shipping and handling.) If you want us to stop sending books, just say the word… it's that simple.

If the Free Book Certificate is missing, call 1-800-770-1963 to place your order.
Be sure to visit our website at www.kensingtonbooks.com.

BOOK CERTIFICATE

Yes! Please send me FREE Zebra Contemporary romance novels. I understand I am under no obligation to purchase any books, as explained on this card.

Name _____

Address _____ Apt._____

City _____ State _____ Zip _____

Telephone (____) _____

Signature _____
(If under 18, parent or guardian must sign)

Offer limited to one per household and not valid to current subscribers.
All orders subject to approval. Terms, offer, and price subject to change. Offer valid only in the U.S.

CN032A

Thank You!

THE BENEFITS OF BOOK CLUB MEMBERSHIP

- You'll get your books hot off the press, usually before they appear in bookstores.

- You'll ALWAYS save more than 20% off the cover price.

- You'll get our FREE monthly newsletter filled with author interviews, book previews, special offers, and MORE!

- There's no obligation – you can cancel at any time and you have no minimum number of books to buy.

- And – if you decide you don't like the books you receive, you can return them. (You always have ten days to decide.)

ll..l...lll...lll.l..l.l..l.l..lll..l..lld..lll...l

Zebra Contemporary Romance Book Club
Zebra Home Subscription Service, Inc.
P.O. Box 5214
Clifton , NJ 07015-5214

with dismay. As though the flower's fragility had summoned up whatever caution she did possess, she glanced up at him with a mixture of wariness and defiance.

"I just have to know one thing. Are you still in love with your former fiancée?"

That was what worried her? Ryan shook his head.

"No," he said honestly. Emphatically. "To tell the truth, I'm not sure I ever was. Once her contraband carriage ride had turned the corner, I felt a little relieved. I know it sounds terrible, but it's true. I probably knew all along something wasn't right. But in the midst of the wedding, the planning, the being fleeced for my family fortune . . ." He shrugged. "It must have slipped my mind."

Thankfully, April grinned at his joke. *There was a God.*

"Well, I'm not interested in snagging your fortune," she said blithely. "I don't have *those* kinds of money issues."

For an instant, the way she'd phrased her denial made him wonder exactly what kinds of money issues April *did* have. But then Ryan pushed those thoughts aside. He was probably reading too much into her simple statement. Jackson, ever cynical and world weary, would have been so proud.

But he wasn't like Jackson, damn it. Not anymore, if he ever had been.

"And if you have to know" —her gaze roved over him, touching on his loosened borrowed necktie, his partly unbuttoned shirt, his suit pants— "I'm more of a 'booty, not bonds and stocks' type of girl."

He pretended to be shocked. "Then I'm just a sex object to you? A—a *boy toy*? Stud on a stick? Hunka hunka—"

"Only if you're lucky, big boy."

Her sassy grin shined again. He could have basked in the warmth of her smile all day, could have summered in the glow of her personality. Being around April just made him feel good. Somehow, he had to convince her to give him a chance.

"I want to be lucky with you," he said, keeping his voice low. "Very, very lucky."

Then he tipped up her chin with his knuckles, took her mouth with his own, and showed her exactly what lucky could feel like between them.

With a moan, April met his kiss gladly. By unspoken accord they stretched together across the truck's bench seat, vinyl and springs creaking beneath them. Sunlight slanted across their faces through the open window, chased by a breeze that did nothing to cool the heat Ryan felt building as their kiss went on. And on.

Their bodies met, pushing against the driver's side door for leverage. Their mouths angled and explored, a kiss as breathless as their first and as endless as their last.

Reveling in it, reeling beneath it, Ryan gave to her everything he could . . . and April could no more stop giving back than she could—apparently—kiss without wiggling and moaning and stroking him with wild up-down-all-over movements of her hands, which Ryan found incredibly sexy and impossibly arousing. Soon, he wiggled and moaned, too, driven at April's urging to pull her closer, to kiss her more deeply, to know her more thoroughly.

At last they parted, barely moving from their squashed-up position against the pickup's door. The handle jabbed Ryan's shoulder blade. The steering wheel contorted April's torso. Nevertheless, she remained semi-sprawled atop him, and he kept his arm around her to hold her there. Forever, if possible.

"Wow," he said. "Wow."

"Yeah," she replied. "*Really* wow."

He speared his fingers through her red curls, smoothing them back from her face. He smiled.

"Does this mean you're willing to take a chance on us?" Ryan asked.

When she didn't reply right away, he thought his heart might stop. April scrunched up her nose, thinking it over. What kind of wicked impulse made women deliberate so damned openly, when a straightaway answer was so much simpler? *Gah!* He should have kept kissing her, Ryan thought, until she agreed.

He ducked his head, intent on trying that very strategy. At the same instant, April nodded.

"Yes. Temporarily," she announced. She levered upward, leaving him bereft. "Given the tenacity you've demonstrated, I think it's the least we can do."

Hearing only her *yes*, Ryan felt a new grin coming on. But April's next words staunched it. A little.

"Until you leave town," she clarified, "let's go crazy."

Then she opened the passenger side door, grabbed the daisies she'd abandoned on the dash during their kiss, and jumped out of the truck.

Until he left town, April scoffed silently as she hurried around to the bed of the pickup truck and tried to look busy. Tried to look, really, as though she weren't contemplating turning cartwheels just because Ryan wanted her.

But *until he left town.* Come on! Where had *that* come from?

Dating Ryan, even temporarily, wasn't smart. Neither was kissing him—however wonderfully thrilling *that* had been. But honestly, coming along with him this morning hadn't been exactly Einstein-level thinking, either, and April had eagerly done that, too, hadn't she? It seemed her heart was getting the better of her . . . just the way she shouldn't let it.

And yet . . . *If Ryan is the one you want, don't wait,* Jamie had said this morning, looking as though she knew a thing or two about waiting, and regretting it. *Take a chance now.*

Don't turn me down, Ryan had said shortly afterward, holding out his hand to her and looking like everything she'd ever wanted in a man, wrapped up in Armani and served with a side of corny pickup truck charm. *At least not in front of all these people.*

And she hadn't been able to. It had been as simple, and as knotted-up, as that. April had taken one look at him, and she'd wanted him. Ryan had asked her to keep his pride intact, and she hadn't been able to say no. Then he'd asked her to take a chance on them both, and her pitiful Finnegan resolve had crumbled in the face of his appeal like an Oreo dunked in a cup of hot chocolate.

Weak. That's what she was when it came to him. In true shiftless Finnegan style, she couldn't resist anything ill-advised, potentially dangerous, and excitingly appealing. But it didn't have to be all bad, April told herself as her natural optimism asserted itself. Surely she could have a brief fling, enjoy herself *and* Ryan, and still protect her heart.

Couldn't she?

Sure. Falling for Ryan *temporarily* didn't have to mean falling in love for good . . . no matter how similar the two might feel.

Reassured, April touched one of the pickup truck's tied-on red bows. She would enjoy Ryan for as long as their time together lasted—which would be perfect, really, since that would allow her to hide her Finnegan-style "money issues" and preserve her *own* pride, too.

Drawing in her first relaxed breath of the day, she straightened the bow.

"Those were Kim's idea," Ryan said, watching her. He'd gotten out of the truck, and stood now on the opposite side. "Mark's sister-in-law. She seemed to think an ordinary pickup truck, all on its own, wasn't romantic enough."

"Skeptic," April joked. "The balloons?"

"Kim."

"The tie?"

He touched his yellow smiley-face tie. "Kim. She says it's good luck. Wouldn't let me out of the house without it."

"Mmmm." She peered into the truck bed. "The hay?"

"Ambiance. Gritty reality. And part of the bargain."

"Bargain?"

"My roadster for Mack's pickup," Ryan explained.

"You're kidding! Your convertible is worth way more than this—"

He shook his head. "Just a loan. Temporary. Like our wallet-free sponsorship bargain."

Like our fling, April thought, and although she'd set the limits of that fling herself, a niggling sadness still lingered at the edges of those boundaries. Resolutely, she pushed her melancholy feelings aside.

Instead of pining for everything she wanted but couldn't allow herself, she admired the flex of Ryan's forearms beneath his rolled-up shirtsleeves as he lifted a blanket and plastic cooler from the truck bed. She noticed the thoughtfulness inherent in the way he refused to let her carry a thing—not even the inexplicable camping lanterns—given the daylight—or the books—given all the kissing still to be done—he'd brought. She observed the attractive way his clothes were tailored to his body, right down to his . . .

"Sneakers?"

Ryan blinked, and glanced downward. He lifted a foot. "I traded my Kenneth Cole oxfords for our picnic lunch. Kim thought they'd look good with Mack's suit at the bowling league championship dinner, so she volunteered to swap. Sandwiches for shoes."

"Sandwiches? And here I thought a posh guy like you would bring caviar. Gold-plated cookies. *Something* spiffy." Grinning at the comical face he made in reply, April backpedaled a bit. "Mack has a suit?"

"He does now. Temporarily."

She caught his meaningful look, and nodded. "Oh."

He'd really gone all out for this, she realized, and was touched at the thought. Not only had Ryan adhered to the conditions of their bet, but he'd managed some worthy innovations, too. She'd never have believed bartering would have stretched so far, especially for someone like him.

"These are my racquetball shoes," Ryan went on. "I didn't have time to go back to Mark's place for another pair of dress shoes."

That got her attention. "Mark's place?"

"Yes."

Whoa. Talk about Felix and Oscar.

"I'm staying there until my lawyers straighten out the mess with my thieving former fiancée." Briefly, he explained something about unauthorized charges on his credit cards. April experienced a fresh wave of dislike for his gold-digging, minister-stealing, no-good, jilting former fiancée. Clearly, Ryan was better off without her.

"And just until I win our bet, of course," he finished, flashing her a cocksure look. "After which I'll pay Mark for the use of his sofa bed and approximately fifty gallons of coffee—I'm not used to getting up early—plus a nice bonus."

While April deliberated the wisdom of offering Mark

payment for a simple favor, Ryan hefted everything he'd brought, and came around to her side of the pickup.

"But there'll be time for that another day," he said. "Today, it's all about us. Shall we?"

At her nod of agreement, he set off toward the banks of the Willayump River, moving slowly until April fell into step beside him. After fifty yards or so, Ryan stopped. He looked puzzled.

"I see trees," he said, gazing at the jumble of mesquite and cottonwoods surrounding them. "I see grass and rocks. I don't see water. Where's the river?"

"You stepped over it, about five yards back."

He glanced over his shoulder. His eyebrows rose. "That little trickle—"

"—is the mighty Willayump River," April said.

He tilted his head for a better view. "I've seen more water in a bottle of San Pellegrino."

"Maybe. But not if you go this way. . . ."

Catching hold of his free hand, she led Ryan off the orderly park service path. Around the next bend, the grass thinned and the Willayump widened several feet, and boulders from baseball-size to pickup truck–size replaced the smooth dirt of the trail.

Stopping beside a waist-high clump of stone, Ryan looked around in surprise. "Wow. The things you find when you step off the beaten path."

She cocked an eyebrow. "You'll find lots of those things with me around."

"I can hardly wait."

Grinning over the note of masculine enthusiasm in his low-voiced reply, April squeezed his hand. She spotted a long, flat rock and guided them both toward it. There, they spread out their things, put April's daisies in a cup of water, and sat atop the picnic blanket, side by side.

The sun warmed them. Birds called nearby, and the

water of the Willayump splashed over rocks and against its gravelly banks on its way past. Overhead, a cottonwood's hanging branches added moving swaths of shade, along with the soothing sound of fluttering leaves. With Ryan by her side, the scene was as good as paradise for April . . . and twice as much fun.

He lit the camp lanterns—candlelight picnic, he explained—and read her poetry from library books by e.e. cummings and Walt Whitman—only the most romantic verses, he said. Ryan served appetizers of Kim's special peanut butter stuffed celery stalks and ice-packed deviled eggs, and they debated the wisdom of his having traded his shoes for either of those dubious delicacies.

April told him jokes and he laughed over every one, including the groaners she'd learned from Rainey. She told him about her time at the U of A, and about the first batch of chocolate chip cookies she'd ever made at the age of eight—and how, when they'd turned out too crunchy, she'd called them biscotti and served them anyway. Also, how her father, pre-divorce and always teasing, had called them "brickotti," but had eaten twelve of them, all the same. She told him about Ambrosia, and about her ambitions there. And when she was done, they pulled out their turkey sandwiches on Wonderbread, and Ryan took his turn in the spotlight.

He described his life in San Diego—and all over, really, since it sounded as though he traveled often and didn't spend much time at his own luxury town house on the Pacific Coast, unless he was throwing a party there. He described his parents and sister, jet-setters all. He described his days at Stanford, his initial disinterest in Forrester's Department Stores, his new plan to get involved in the family business. Through it all, Ryan smiled and shared and charmed her, making sure April always had iced tea in her plastic cup, a shady spot on their rock, a broad chest and strong shoulders to lean against while she listened.

It was as though they'd been together always, had been merely separated for a while and now needed to catch up. April found herself nodding in recognition at the things Ryan described. Even though they were far from the life she'd experienced, the emotions behind those encounters were as familiar as the feeling of flour on her fingertips when she baked. In the ways that mattered, she and Ryan were very alike ... both caring, both fun-seeking, both seeing their days through a necessary lens of humor.

Fiona Finnegan would have said that like begets like. She would have worried about wild, prank-pulling grandchildren and always-impending boredom, and advised April to make her match with someone more *un*like her. Someone responsible and dependable, who could curb her daughter's less-sensible impulses. Someone like Mark.

And while there might have been validity in such an approach, to April that didn't matter at all. Not while she fed bites of Twinkie to Ryan—who'd never tasted one—and laughed over his demonstration of a mambo—or so he claimed—and rolled up her pant legs to wade with him in the cool waters of the river nearby.

"Yikes!" Ryan said when he splashed in, barefoot, with his own pants rolled past his ankles. "This is colder than my wine cellar. Colder than my mother's fur-storage vault in La Jolla. Brrrr."

"Awww, poor baby." April waded closer, wiggling her toes against the rocky bottom. She put her arms around his neck, and pressed herself against him. "I'll warm you up," she murmured.

It was all the invitation he needed. At the first touch of her lips, Ryan took control of their joining, pulling her closer. He kissed her hungrily, his mouth stretching wide, his hands coaxing shivers and then a moan as he dipped his palms to her backside and snuggled her against him.

Her breasts grazed his chest. Their hips touched. His body pressed against her intimately, hard and full and eager. At knowing Ryan was as affected by their kiss as she was, April felt a new heat swirl through her. She buried her fingers in the close-clipped strands of his hair, and held him to her.

"You're amazing," he said, punctuating the words with a tweak of her ear and another gentle kiss to the side of her neck. Sounding breathless, Ryan smiled and shook his head. "And I might never have found you. I've never met anyone more honest—"

She thought of all the financial Finnegan skeletons in her closet, and stilled.

"—more determined—"

She thought of how awful he'd feel when she won their bet, and looked downward at the water eddying past their feet.

"—more ready to try new things."

She thought of her private resolution to lock away her heart while she enjoyed her temporary fling with him, and felt like the biggest liar who'd ever guided a man off his own well-ordered park service path.

"I'm glad you came with me today," Ryan went on. He cupped her jaw in his hands and stroked her cheek with his thumb, looking earnest and gorgeous and much too wonderful to be toyed with. "I've never had a nicer picnic."

"Me, either."

Aggh. Guilt was a jagged tortilla chip in the spinach dip–loitering story of her life. Silently cursing Jamie for goading her into the very thing she most wanted, April shoved it aside. There was nothing wrong with having fun while she and Ryan were together. Hadn't he said, this very afternoon, that he'd always kept the things in his life temporary, and easy to leave?

Doubtless, she fit into both those categories. Easily.

"Nice picnic," April said again. "And it's about to get even nicer."

She reached for his smiley-face necktie, feeling fairly certain that, given a few minutes, she could put smiles on *both* their faces—temporary, or not. For distraction's sake—and because she really, really wanted to—she slowly pulled the length of yellow fabric from around his neck. She flung it backward onto their picnic rock, and started in on his shirt.

Looking dumbfounded, Ryan stopped her hands as she hit the fourth button. *Damn!* She'd just gotten to the good parts. The fascinating width of his broad shoulders. His nicely sculpted chest muscles. His perfect smattering of golden chest hair, inviting her to spread open Ryan's shirt still wider, and start exploring.

"Are you sure about this?" he asked.

She gazed at all she'd uncovered. At all she had *yet* to uncover. "Oh, yeah. I'm sure."

His smile was magical. Intoxicating. "Come on, then," Ryan said, and led her out of the swirling water. "Let's go crazy."

Chapter Twelve

Arizona was, Ryan decided several sloshy steps and one long, flat rock later, quite possibly the most scenic place he'd ever visited. There was, for instance, the dazzling view as April lowered herself onto their shared picnic blanket, her hair spreading around her shoulders and her clothes sprinkled with splashed-on wet spots. There was also, for another instance, the wondrous sight of April smiling at him as she knelt astride him and attacked his shirt buttons again. There was, against all expectation and hope, the further vision of April's smile blinking from view and then reappearing as she pulled off her dancer-style, draped dark shirt and tossed it aside.

Unbelievably, her pants followed next. Both items landed atop his castaway shirt, beside their shoes and socks, everything mingling happily in the sunlight. Torn between applauding, drooling, and getting on his knees to thank whatever good fortune had sent him a woman like April to love, Ryan settled for simply staring, raptly, at the beauty she'd revealed.

If he'd expected her to turn suddenly shy, he'd expected wrong. Or he'd expected a personality transplant. Because the same April who'd dressed as a chipmunk, crafted anatomically correct chocolate Adonises—her story of Mark's reaction had cracked him up—and had personally begun more Little League spectator "waves" than he could count was the same proud, free April who straddled him now. And Ryan was glad for it.

God, she was terrific. He could only hope he was worthy of her. Pushing his doubts aside, Ryan nodded toward her leopard-print bra and matching printed panties. He waggled his eyebrows. "I think I hear the call of the wild."

"I hope so." She paused in the act of wrestling his recalcitrant belt into submission to deliver him a cocky grin. " 'Cause it's calling for you, and only you."

"Lucky me."

More clothes flew. More kisses followed, these roving lower and lower. Ryan knew the hard surface of their picnic rock jutted against his back, knew their free-for-all position wasn't very prudent—out in the open, as it was—knew he should have waited to love April until he could take her someplace romantic and wonderful and see the job done properly. He was also pretty sure his recently removed pants had just floated down the Willayump.

But he couldn't wait. Didn't care about discomfort. All he knew was need, and want, and April.

Evidently, she agreed. Breathlessly she caressed him; boldly, she whispered that she wanted him. Only a few minutes after leading them both from the Willayump's chilly waters, Ryan found himself sprawling on a blanket almost naked beneath the wide desert sky, dressed only in his boxers and holding a wriggling, writhing, incredibly sexy, bra-and-panties-wearing April.

Could a guy *get* any luckier than this?

April's breath panted past his ear. "Could a girl *get* any luckier than this?" she asked.

Their synchronicity didn't surprise him. What happened next, did.

"Ouch!" Ryan said.

Feeling a sudden fierce pinch near the back of his knee, he twisted away from its source. Then he gave a mental shrug, and turned his attention to more important things. Like discovering if the soft rise of April's cleavage tasted as wonderful as it felt in his hand.

"Mmmm. You feel so—ouch!"

Another pinch, stronger this time. He frowned, and twisted again.

"So good," he continued. "So—ouch! Damn it!"

"What's the matter?"

"I don't know." But now he felt tiny pinches all over. On his big toe. His forearm. His thigh. His—*hang on just a damned minute.* Pulling April into his arms, he surged upward to avoid a pinch in more sensitive places.

She squinted down at their blanket right along with him. "Ants," she announced. "They must have invaded our leftovers when we went wading. Did you get bitten?"

"Bitten? By *ants*? Teeny, tiny harmless ants? Ants don't bite."

"Oh, yes, they do. They do if they look like that one." With a casual gesture, April brushed something away from his bicep. "They're not bugging me. *You* must be extra delicious."

Her teasing grin didn't reassure him. Scowling, Ryan reached down to brush away the uncivilized little munchers before they—

"Ouch!"

"Let me help." Patiently, she circled around him, examining here and brushing there.

"Can't somebody come spray for these ants, or something?" he asked, feeling aggrieved. "This is the twenty-first century. Don't you have exterminators in Saguaro Vista?"

"Yes, but the ants *live here*. It's their home. We can't just stomp in and obliterate them."

"We can if they're going to destroy our romantic mood."

Why hadn't somebody addressed this problem before? The comfy, king-size, down comforter–covered bed at Ryan's town house was looking a likelier and likelier seduction spot all the time. Hell, a few phone calls and he could have a private plane waiting at the airport in Phoenix to take him and April anyplace they—

"Did you hear something?" April froze.

He listened. "Only the sound of killer ants. Sharpening their fangs for a second course."

She gave a small smile but didn't laugh. Instead, April slipped behind him and grabbed his shoulders. "I heard something. Something *human*."

"Something human?"

And them, nearly naked atop a hunk of rock. Staked out for all to see. Feeling protective of April, Ryan scooted them both sideways. He picked up their picnic blanket and handed it to her. It swooshed past his back in a woolen swath as she draped it around herself.

"Something like . . . ?"

And then he heard it. Singing. Off-key singing. Specifically—

"Shake it, shake it, shake it," sang a male voice loudly. "All you can, baby, shake it, shake it, shake—yo, Ape! And Darla's Maytag booty-knocker! How's it hanging?"

Mickey Finnegan emerged from downstream, holding a plastic trash bag in one utility-gloved hand and, if Ryan didn't miss his guess, a portable metal detector in the other. He gaped up at them both, looking cheerful and clueless.

"I got sunburned one time doing that," Mickey advised, nodding toward Ryan's semi-clad body and April's partly shrouded figure. "You don't even want to *know* what my—"

"Mickey!"

"—looked like," he finished, unperturbed.

"What are you *doing* here?" April asked her brother. She clutched the picnic blanket beneath her chin as she stepped out from behind Ryan. "Aren't you supposed to be looking for a new job?"

Mickey shrugged. "Job, schmob. *This* is where it's really at." He hefted his semi-filled bag, making its contents clank. "Forty cents a pound for these babies. By the time I work my way down the river, I'll have made—"

"About two fifty." April smacked her forehead with the heel of her hand. "What's the matter with you?"

He looked wounded. "I'm an entrepreneur now. I've had enough of working for 'the man.' After I take these cans down to the recycling center, I'll be on my way to financial independence. Just like they say on the infomercials."

"Financial independence, my ass," April muttered. "That's Mickey, always chasing the greener grass on the other side of the fence."

Ryan raised his eyebrows, feeling slightly more comfortable now that he was partly shielded by the blanket's folds. "The greener ass?"

"Har, har." She turned to her brother. "Did you even look at the classifieds I left out for you again this morning?"

Mickey sighed and rolled his eyes. He dropped his

metal detector and bag of aluminum cans near one sneakered foot and dragged a pack of cigarettes from his tattered shirt pocket. He tapped the pack's bottom sharply against his utility-gloved palm.

" 'Course I *looked* at them. How'd you think I found my smokes underneath 'em? Sheesh."

Squinting, he withdrew a cigarette and prepared to light up. With a whoosh of blanket, April vaulted from their picnic rock. She snatched both the unlit cigarette and the crumpled pack from Mickey's hands.

"Remember Granny Finnegan," she admonished.

Mickey looked chagrined. Ryan felt confused. And increasingly, publicly, naked. He had to do something.

"I think I saw a pile of beer cans about a quarter mile down the road," he told Mickey, pointing toward the trail he and April had first taken—and *away* from their compromising position. "Maybe a dollar fifty's worth."

Mickey brightened. He grabbed his metal detector and slung his bag over his shoulder. "Thanks for the tip, Maytag Man. See you 'round, Ape."

Just as Ryan had hoped, Mickey ambled down the path. The off-key strains of the "Shake It Baby, Shake It," song echoed behind him. A few minutes later, the last note drifted into stillness.

Thank God.

Ryan glanced down at April. She gazed back up at him, one hand on her cocked hip. Somehow, she'd arranged the picnic blanket around herself toga-style. Surprisingly, she managed to make the look work. Wool had never been sexier.

She winked. "So, where were we?"

"Heading back to town," Ryan said, already returning their things to the plastic cooler and gathering up the lanterns and poetry books. He handed April her daisies, then retrieved his pants—which had gotten snagged on an outcropping of rock on their way down to the

Willayump—and yanked them on. "I don't know about you, Ape—"

She made a face over the nickname, which Ryan found fairly endearing.

"—but seeing your brother and my boxer shorts within fifty feet of each other pretty much killed the mood for me."

She had to do something about her family, April decided on Tuesday morning, the day after the Mickey-style debacle at the Willayump picnic. Otherwise, she and Ryan might never finish what they'd started.

Because clearly, Ryan didn't understand Finnegans. His reaction to Mickey's can-scavenging appearance had made that much plain. Upon seeing her brother, Ryan had stiffened up like an overbeaten meringue, and April's hopes of satisfying the curiosity they'd aroused atop that rock had gone straight out the window. Or down the Willayump. Or whatever.

Once Mickey had wandered off in search of that elusive dollar-fifty find, April had been ready to pick up where she and Ryan left off. She'd arranged her blanket, given him a big smile . . . and found herself rebuffed.

In favor of packing the cooler and hurrying back to town.

Even now, the memory embarrassed her. There she'd been, trying to look toga-style sexy for Ryan. There he'd been, obviously appalled by Mickey's untimely reminder of what her family was like. There they'd been, gear-shifting and grinding all the way back to Saguaro Vista, not twenty minutes later.

It wasn't that April was ashamed of her family. Not exactly. She'd been a flighty Finnegan herself too long for that. She understood them and loved them, despite their faults—which she adamantly did *not* want applied, automatically, to *her.* But Ryan's family, she was sure, was nothing like her own carefree, unconventional, check-bouncing brood. No doubt his family was responsible and sensible and dependable—and didn't consider ten pounds of dirt-encrusted soda cans a fresh financial beginning.

So she vowed to, as much as possible, avoid any further reminders of her shiftless Finnegan background. And to let Ryan see only the best of her, during their few remaining days together. After all, he was used to the finer things in life. If she tried really hard, April figured she could convince him *she* was one of those finer things.

How tough could it be to pull off, for less than a week?

Damned tough, she realized as Ryan slid across from her into their usual shared booth at the Downtown Grill. Because Ryan was *fine* without even trying.

She looked up in appreciation as he offered a warm greeting. He reached for his coffee cup and turned it over. Her gaze was drawn to his hands, large and nimble and exactly the right shape to stroke her, to caress her, to awaken every tiny sensation in her ... *ahem.*

" 'Morning," she returned, clearing her throat. "Sleep well?"

Ryan's gaze fell upon her, brilliantly blue and much too perceptive. Had he noticed her scanning the width of his shoulders in his open-collar shirt? Ogling the slight pull of fabric over the front of his khaki pants as he sat down? Fantasizing about pulling off his upscale lumberjack boots to go wading in the Willayump again?

"Not as well as I ... might have," he said. "I wish you'd considered coming back with me to Mark's place yesterday, after our picnic."

Smiling, he waggled his eyebrows with teasing lasciviousness. April shook her head. *Woo-woo at her boss' apart-*

ment, with Mark downstairs at the bakery all the while? Impossible.

"No way," she said. "It wouldn't be fair to Mark."

"Your place, then?"

"Reserved for *non*-temporary craziness," April said, dunking her mint tea bag for the second time.

It was hard to keep her tone light, to keep the longing from her voice. It would be nice to let Ryan a little closer, to let him get to know her and her life—and even Calypso—a little better. But she had to resist. Her heart was at stake.

"I never bring casual dates back to my apartment."

"Which explains why you didn't invite me in when I dropped you off there the other day."

He looked down, running his fingers over the rim of his empty cup. His movements slowed, then stopped. Ryan drew in a deep breath.

"Let's abandon our bet," he said suddenly. "I still have resources. Untouched bank accounts. Friends in high places. One phone call and we could be together in a luxury resort hacienda with nothing to do except—"

"Nice try, buster," April interrupted. "But our . . . relationship . . . has nothing to do with our bet."

That's what you think, said Ryan's gaze, in the one startling moment when he glanced upward. Then he frowned and resumed his thoughtful examination of his cup, and April decided she'd imagined the whole silent exchange.

"Hey," she said to change the subject—and hopefully, brighten the mood. "I brought a surprise for you."

She pulled a packet from her purse and slid it across the table. "I saw this when I was grocery shopping the other day, and thought of you."

Ryan picked it up. A smile edged his lips. "Hollandaise sauce mix."

"Just add water!"

"Thanks."

He reached across the table with his free hand and clasped her fingers in his. The sappy, romantic look in his eyes confused her, but made her feel happy, too.

"I can't believe you remembered," Ryan said.

"Two eggs, lightly poached, rye toast, and bacon," April recited as their waitress approached. "With a side of hollandaise sauce. A glass of orange juice. And a large chocolate milk."

Ryan nodded. "I'm impressed."

"*I'm* gettin' aggravated," the waitress said, casting them both an I-don't-believe-this look. "I told you two, eggs come fried or scrambled, not poached. No rye toast. No hollandaise sauce. No special orders! Our cook hasn't been on the job very long and he doesn't—"

April and Ryan tried not to laugh. "We know, Mona," April told the server. "We're sorry. I know you don't have all that stuff. It's . . . kind of a private joke, is all."

"Well then, keep it private." With a "*hrrumph*," the waitress took Ryan's runner-up breakfast order of a short stack and coffee, then scooped up their menus. She took a few steps toward the diner's counter. Then she stopped and turned back.

"Say, you want some hot water for that hollandaise sauce mix?"

After a day packed with sponsorship-scrounging visits to local merchants, April was tired. She was hot. She was even prone to reminiscing about the halcyon days when all she'd had to worry about had been whether or not the Ambrosia cinnamon rolls were rising properly, and how best to scrub spilled cupcake batter from a stainless steel professional range. And that last—the reminiscing—was what worried her most of all.

The community-relations manager position was something she'd been working hard for. Really hard. How could it be less than satisfying?

Probably because of her competition with Ryan, April decided as she stepped out of a video rental store and spotted him leaving the flower shop across the street. They waved to each other, both of them near the end of their day's merchant visits. Once she'd secured Ambrosia's place in the community with the sponsorships she'd earned, nostalgic yearnings to be up to her elbows in flour and sugar would be a thing of the past.

She hoped.

Fifteen minutes later, April shook off her worries with a hollered "Hiya!" to Ryan, who was loading Forrester's Department Store displays into his borrowed pickup truck. She pedaled toward him on her bike, her T-shirt and Hawaiian-print miniskirt fluttering in the late afternoon breeze. Just for the hell of it, she honked her Schwinn's rubber-bulb horn.

He smiled at its cheery *aoogah* sound and shut the truck's door with a clang. Dust scattered onto his streetside parking space. Just as April brought her bike to a stop near him, Ryan snatched a parking ticket from the truck's windshield and tucked it into his pocket with good-natured resignation.

"Can't feed the meter with no cash," he said in reference to their bet. He shrugged. "I'll just have to make good with Wanda before I leave town."

Before I leave town. No amount of knowing that was his plan was enough to take the sting from the words. Determinedly, April refused to dwell on the inevitable. If she kept her heart secure, she reminded herself, everything would be fine.

"You'd better, you renegade driver," she teased. " 'Til then" —she pulled several quarters from her purse and plunked them into the meter— "allow me."

"But I'm headed back to Mark's place," Ryan protested. "I don't need—"

"Oh, no you don't. And yes, you do." Feeling a fresh surge of anticipation at the idea she'd come up with, April reached for Ryan's hand. She nodded toward the bows and balloons still attached to the pickup's bed. "The truck 'o love stays here. You're coming with me."

Waiting in the magical light that only arose in the high desert at sunset, Ryan watched as April strolled toward him. All around her, people milled past, drawn to the swap meet she'd brought him to at the edge of Saguaro Vista . . . but Ryan had eyes only for April.

Carrying a napkin-wrapped hot dog in each hand, she left the food vendor's cart and came closer, a miniskirted vision with killer legs and an even better smile. Her ease, with herself and with others, drew him to her in ways Ryan didn't understand—and didn't care to analyze. All he knew was that April had suggested they spend the evening together. Her treat. And that he hadn't been able to resist the invitation.

Resist? Hell, he'd hoped for it. Dreamed of it. And now, Ryan intended to make the most of it, too.

So far, he wasn't sure his just-Ryan seduction strategy was working. He couldn't tell if April was impressed with the wallet-less him. Truthfully, he wouldn't have blamed her if she wasn't, which was what had led to his last-ditch effort to abandon their bet at the Downtown Grill yesterday morning.

I can help you, boomed the James Earl Jones voice of his wallet, in his imagination. *Use me!*

Unfortunately, that strategy hadn't worked, either. Not even with the added lure of a resort hacienda. She'd turned him down flat, not knowing how their bet was hampering Ryan's efforts to impress her. Damn it.

"Two dogs, one with mustard" —April held back one relatively plain-looking hot dog— "and one with the works."

Ryan eyed the condiment-laden hot dog she offered. Spicy-smelling chili spilled onto the napkin. Ketchup and mustard and relish oozed from beneath. Jalapeño rings dotted the whole mess.

"Thanks," he managed. He'd never, to his recollection, eaten a street vendor hot dog. But the most macho method of ordering one had seemed to be with "the works," so that's what Ryan had done. *Let the consequences be damned,* he decided as he raised his impromptu dinner to his lips. *I'm a reckless babe magnet.*

Fifteen seconds later he was a reckless jalapeño and chili victim, desperately seeking something to quench the fire in his mouth.

"Try this." With a knowing look, April handed over a carton. "It'll take away the burning sensation."

Ryan took a sip. "Ugh. Milk?"

"It works." Hiding a smile, April watched as he gulped some more. "Better?"

He nodded.

"Good. I want you conscious for the rest of this. Come on."

She took his hand, and led him on a voyage of discovery. They passed through vendor booths, browsed swap meet sellers' tables, and examined artisans' displays. They held hands and tossed coins to a couple of teenage boys with guitars, who strummed and sang their way through a terrible rendition of a recent hit pop song. And as the last of the sun's glow faded and the electric lights strung from pole to pole overhead snapped on, April guided Ryan into a world he hadn't known existed.

Sure, he'd heard of swap meets. Garage sales. Tag sales. Estate sales. Ryan had even had a Martha Stewart junkie girlfriend who'd spent every Saturday combing out-of-the-way places for a find that would turn out to be A Good Thing. But he hadn't accompanied her on those Martha-approved expeditions, and he hadn't wanted to. Shopping was bad enough—a necessary evil, tolerated only long enough to acquire the latest high-tech stereo DVD player or a replacement Beemer. "Shopping" through other people's cast-offs had to be, Ryan reasoned, even worse.

Except with April, it wasn't. To her, exploring the goods offered for sale at the swap meet was an adventure. Ryan could see the thrill of the chase in her animated expression, could feel her excitement as she negotiated for a reduced price on the antique apothecary jars and the secondhand pieced quilt. Her sense of fun was contagious. It wasn't long before Ryan found himself swept up in it, too.

He stopped at a table piled with books—books arranged in tidy stacks, books sorted library style, books jumbled in boxes. Scanning the titles, he grabbed one.

"A vintage John Denton!" Ryan looked from the gaudy pulp-fiction cover to the bored seller sitting in a molded plastic deck chair on the other side of the table. "Do you know how much this is worth?"

Suddenly, April was beside him. "About fifty cents, I'd say," she told him, peering at the book and ignoring the handwritten price tag sticker. She glanced at the seller. "Got anymore like it? We'll take two for a dollar."

"You don't understand," Ryan protested, running his fingers over the book. "Denton was one of Raymond Chandler's contemporaries—you know, *The Big Sleep, Double Indemnity*. Denton's books didn't get the acclaim they deserved when they were first published, but—"

Darting a glance toward the seller, she made a dismissive gesture. "That book's over fifty years old. The spine's cracked, too."

Ryan cradled it protectively. This book was a collector's item. It was worth much more than fifty cents to the right buyer. *To him.* He began considering what he could barter for it.

The seller leaned forward in his chair, looking interested. "I'll let you have that book for fifty bucks," he said.

"Fifty bucks! The price tag says two-fifty."

"Forty-five. Final offer. You want it? Take it or leave it." The seller waved to a passerby. "Hey, lady—vintage John Dentons, here. Interested?"

"No!" Ryan said. He'd seen it first. Maybe the seller would consider a trade of some kind. "It's mine."

"No, it's not." Gently, April pried the book from Ryan's hands. She put it back in its box, amid the other jumbled paperback editions. Then she shook her head at the seller. "Forty-five dollars. I wouldn't give you that much for the whole box."

The man looked abashed. And stubborn.

Feeling his find slipping out of his hands, Ryan reached for the book again. Surely he could work out something. He might not have cash, but he did have ingenuity. And damn it, he wanted that book.

April spotted his movement and linked her arm with his. She turned to face him, blocking his view of the box.

"Come on," she said, smiling up at him. "There's something else I want to show you. You'll like it."

"But—" He couldn't believe there was actually something he wanted . . . and couldn't have. *Ever,* possibly. "I—"

As though sensing his conflicted feelings, she arched her eyebrow. "Ready to cry uncle?"

Their bet. Because of that damned bet, Ryan couldn't impress April properly. And he couldn't buy a simple forty-five dollar collectible book, either. That bet was ruining his life. It was, quite plainly, putting a serious crimp in his sense of well-being. It was—

It was something he wasn't ready to give up on, Ryan realized. Although their wager had begun as a challenge, it had grown into much more than that over the past week. Now, sticking to his side of their bargain had become a point of pride for Ryan. A new urban-businessman's badge of honor, if you will.

It had become important to him that he succeed here—that he succeed without his wallet, and his family connections, and his safety net of wealth to back him up.

"No," he said. "I'm going to win that bet."

"Then you don't need that book." April shot a dagger-eyed glance at the seller. "Especially at such a ridiculous price."

"Right," Ryan said emphatically.

He gave the John Denton a wistful look.

April tugged at his arm. "Be strong," she said.

That snapped him out of it. Straightening his shoulders, Ryan mentally dismissed the book, and all the deprivation its lack represented to him. He could do this. He could. Friday, the day of reckoning when the Saguaro Vista merchants chose their sponsorships, was only two days away. He could make it until then.

Especially with April by his side.

"So what's this thing you want to show me?" he asked. "It had better be good."

Chapter Thirteen

Jamie teetered on the ladder in the Better Apparel section of Forrester's Department Store, a length of glittery crepe paper strung around her neck and a roll of tape in hand. At nearly eight o'clock on a weeknight, business was slow. She had the store nearly all to herself.

Concentrating on the decorations she'd already hung for the upcoming prom-and-bridal show HairRazors had agreed to cosponsor, she listened to the Muzak piped over the store's speakers and deliberated how best to achieve the effect she wanted.

"More streamers," suggested a familiar voice just below her. "You can never have too many streamers."

Jamie looked over her shoulder and down. "Mark!"

The sight of him filled her with good cheer. And then, as remembrance of her disastrous confession sunk in . . . with regret. She clutched the ladder a little harder.

"And you can never have too many friends." Mark held up a pink cardboard bakery box, tied with string.

"I'm sorry about . . . the other night, after the Little League game."

Jamie's spine straightened.

"I'm sorry, too," she said, hoping the flippant tone to her voice would hide her true feelings. She descended the rungs to stand beside him. "Sorry you were too closed minded to give us a chance. Sorry to have mistaken camaraderie for something more."

Whoops. Sorry to be babbling about this, as though you broke my heart two days ago.

"Sorry I don't have any more streamers," she finished with an airy wave and an extravagantly bad French accent, "to complete your artistic vision."

If Mark could tell how much her effort to lighten things between them cost, it didn't show. He only smiled in recognition of her joke, and offered her the box he'd brought.

With a quizzical look, Jamie accepted it. A few seconds' work—with Mark looking on—had the string untied and the box opened. What she saw inside made her heart give a little leap.

"Sorry," she said, speaking past the lump that rose to her throat, "to have not stopped by the bakery to get these in person."

Hope filled her as she gazed up at Mark. "Thank you."

He put his hands in his pockets and shrugged, examining the fashion show runway under construction in the midst of Better Apparel. "You haven't been to Ambrosia in two days. I missed you."

At his gruffly spoken admission, dozens of emotions zipped through her. Relief. Elation. Tentative acceptance. But Jamie had been too hurt by Mark's initial dismissal of her to cave in right then and there. Especially—merely—because of two measly *pains au chocolat* nestled inside the tissue paper–filled bakery box.

"You know," Jamie said, contemplating the chocolate-filled croissants—*he'd remembered!*— "self-denial is a real drag."

She peeked upward. Did Mark know she referred to more than the sacrifice she'd made to skip her beloved morning ritual over the past two days? If he did, he gave no sign of it.

She made an offhanded gesture toward the goodies. "Join me in utter self-indulgence?"

Too shaky to wait for his reply, she sat on the lumber-framed runway, bereft of the brilliant red carpet it would eventually wear. Humming nervously, she propped the open box on her knees.

The scent of chocolate wafted upward. It was only then, as she enjoyed its decadent fragrance, that Jamie realized her mistake.

Mark would never, in a million years of post-work jogs and banished chocolate Adonises, join her in *anything* even remotely hedonistic.

All the same, he surprised her by sitting down next to her. He surprised her further by offering one of the croissants to her, and choosing the other for himself. Then, companionably beside her, Mark raised his treat.

"To you," he said.

They tapped croissants, like partygoers tapping champagne flutes in a celebratory toast. They each took a bite. Mark smiled as his croissant scattered crumbs over his shirtfront, and left a smudge of chocolate at the corner of his lips.

Fighting back an unreasoning optimism, Jamie thumbed the smear of chocolate away. This time, Mark didn't pull away from her touch. He only regarded her thoughtfully, and then took another bite of croissant.

"You'll need help with this prom-and-bridal show," he said when he'd finished. "Someone to hang the really high-up streamers. Hold the ladder for you. Walk you back to your car when you're done each night."

His voice was nonchalant. His expression was, too. But Mark's fingers trembled, just slightly, as he tore off another bite of croissant and chewed it. And his gaze, when he finally sent it her way, held a palpable hopefulness.

"Ambrosia is catering the show, right?" Jamie asked. *I'll see your nonchalance, buster, and raise you a dose of phony indifference.* "Since April is so busy trying to lock in her new community relations manager job, you'll probably need someone to help set up the preshow buffet."

They smiled at each other as the Muzak floated around them, carried by a chocolate-scented current of air-conditioned air. Fingers buttery with pastry, Jamie and Mark nodded in unison.

"Why not?" they asked. "It's only neighborly, after all."

Huffing with the effort of carrying her swap meet find through her open apartment doorway, April shook curly auburn tendrils from her eyes and tightened her grip. Ryan held the other side of the antique, four-foot framed mirror, and helped her maneuver it inside. Behind him, a moth winged its way into her living room, drawn from the early evening darkness by the glow of her table lamp.

Carefully, they set down the mirror, still holding onto its edges. Ryan looked around.

"I can't believe I'm actually entering the sacred shrine," he said. "Are you sure there isn't some Indiana Jones–style booby trap in here, rigged for unsuspecting temporary dates? A giant boulder, maybe, set to roll through your bedroom doorway? Snakes in the sofa? A

rickety rope bridge guarding the path to the refriger-
ator?''

April leaned the heavy mirror in Ryan's direction,
wordlessly urging him to accept its full weight.

''I only set the bedroom boulder on weekends,'' she
said, dusting off her hands. ''And the rope bridge only
caves under the weight of too much Concession Obses-
sion. It's a diet aid, really. Like one of those gadgets
that oinks when you open the fridge.''

Ryan smiled at her joke, but said nothing. She shooed
out the moth and closed the front door. Silence enveloped both of them. *An intimate silence.* It made her heart
beat a little faster. She hadn't expected to find herself
alone with him.

Clearing her throat, she hurried past Ryan to switch
on the kitchen light. ''Mickey? You here?''

The ''Yo, Ape,'' she expected never came. But there
was a note on the kitchen counter. *Dear Ape-o-rama,* it
read in her brother's scrawled handwriting. *Off to new
job.* . . . Encouraged, April smiled . . . *as fill-in DJ at the
country club. Disco Bingo night equals big tips.*

Her smile faded. Without a doubt, Mickey was king
of the opportunity-is-just-around-the-corner contingent.
Every new job—and this was his seventh in four
months—was going to be his best. His last. His most
fun.

Just for a moment, April envied Mickey his eternal
optimism. His adventurous spirit. His willingness to take
a chance. There were a few of those qualities in her,
too. What would it be like, she wondered, to hit the
open road like Mickey often did? To leave Saguaro Vista
and its skeptical busybodies behind, and—

''Nice place,'' Ryan said, his voice carrying from the
living room. There was a muted thud, probably caused
by his propping the mirror against the wall. ''I like what
you've done with it.''

April started. She backtracked into the other room, this time sans the rationalizations she'd used earlier. The ones assuring her that inviting Ryan to her place—strictly for the purpose of bringing home that fabulous mirror, of course—was a perfectly excellent idea. Now, those rationalizations had deserted her, sometime between coming up with them . . . and realizing Ryan had settled comfortably in her apartment.

She turned the corner leading to the living room, and found Ryan laying faceup on the living room floor.

"What are you doing?"

He held up a hand for quiet, his big body perfectly still—as though he were waiting for something to happen. Nonsensical as his actions were, April couldn't help but comply. As she did, she found herself appreciating the surprisingly appealing aspects of having six-plus feet of muscular male sprawled at her feet.

She also found herself considering the benefits of throwing caution to the wind and jumping him right then and there.

Yes, somehow Ryan managed to look that sexy. Even inexplicably laid out on the floor. He was patience and hunkiness personified. He was mysterious and good natured, and probably wouldn't complain a bit if she—just for example's sake—thanked him for his help with the mirror in a very *imaginative* fashion.

April had mentally tugged off Ryan's shirt and was all the way into figuratively admiring the six-pack abs she'd noticed at the Willayump River when something happened.

A tentative meow came from beneath the nearby table. Calypso poked her marmalade-colored head from beneath it. Her whiskers twitched. She eyed Ryan. Then, regally, she stepped all the way out from her hiding place and settled onto Ryan's chest. He pet her with long, careful strokes.

As April gawked, Ryan grinned up at her. "Somebody had to convince your cat, here, that this toy mouse wasn't going to attack."

He angled his head toward the stuffed jingle-bell mouse at the foot of the table, then picked it up with his free hand. "I heard her meowing and came over to investigate. I'll bet she hasn't been out from beneath that table all night."

April sighed. He was probably right, she knew. Calypso had been terrified of that mouse from the minute Mickey had brought it over during his part-time stint at Red's pet store. He'd probably forgotten to get rid of it, the way she'd asked.

"I'm pretty sure Calypso thinks the mouse is laughing at her," April explained, plucking the toy from Ryan's fingers and tossing it into the kitchen trash once and for all. "Because of its sewn-on grin. She's a little bit . . ."

"Neurotic? I recognize all the signs." Ryan nodded. "For your cat, it's a stuffed mouse. For my Aunt Sylvia, it's her ab roller. She swears it chuckles evilly whenever she puts on a bikini."

He was standing now, cuddling a contented-looking Calypso in his arms. April stared, dumbfounded, at the cozy picture they made. Her cat never permitted personal contact, especially on a first acquaintance.

Calypso was a little *standoffish*.

Calypso had never allowed anyone other than April to touch her—with the recent exception of Mickey. And *their* mutually simpatico relationship was obviously based on one thing: they were completely alike. Both followed the rules perfectly well as long as they were allowed to ignore them. Both liked to sleep twenty-four hours a day. And whenever April wasn't looking, both shredded the upholstery and ate the extra cookies.

But Ryan . . . well, *he* was . . . he was *getting along with her cat.* April boggled at the thought, an unprecedented development in the annuls of her dating history.

He'd have to get along with Calypso, she remembered herself saying on that long-ago day at Ambrosia, when she'd described her ideal man. *If he couldn't even nurture a cat, I'd be too scared to have kids with him. Someday, that is.*

Contemplatively, she watched as Ryan murmured something to the cat. He allowed a claw-clutching feline shinny down his side to the floor—Calypso was afraid of jumping. He even shook his head fondly as Calypso hit the ground and flinched at the contact.

Ohmigod, April realized. *Ryan was her dream man!* He had the taking-her-seriously thing, the sense of humor, the hand-holding, the whispered sweet nothings, and the nurturing ability. All he lacked was the kissing-in-the-rain slam dunk . . . and Ryan couldn't be blamed for the sunny Arizona weather they'd enjoyed until now, could he?

He. Was. Her. Dream. Man!

No, that was ridiculous, she told herself immediately. Preposterous. Crazier than wearing stilettos to cross a blacktop parking lot in August, or paying full price for . . . well, *anything.* But still . . .

Staring raptly at Ryan, April dodged Calypso's kitty garden filled with sprigs of catnip and grass—Calypso needed the roughage; she had digestive issues—and came closer to him. She had her hand out to touch him before she even realized what she was doing.

"What's this?" he asked at the same moment, moving before their bodies connected. Wearing a curious expression, he stepped toward her sofa.

April blinked. Ryan was looking around, she realized, as though he'd never seen an apartment before. And, quite possibly, he never had seen one like hers. Not in his hoity-toity country club–style life, at least. Time for the obligatory explanatory tour.

"It used to be a wrought-iron daybed," she said, suddenly glad for the distraction. She needed time to fully consider this new dream-man development . . . time to develop newer, hardier rationalizations. "I found it at the side of the road on trash day, had Pete Wykowski cut it down at his shop, and turned it into a sofa. A little paint, a few pillows . . . voilá."

Ryan nodded. "Ingenious. And this coffee table?"

She touched the pair of long, low, velvet upholstered ottomans she'd stacked to form a sort of table. "Another swap meet find, like the mirror."

Exploring further, Ryan complimented her decoratively hand-painted salvaged table and chairs in the kitchen. He grinned over the pair of reconditioned shutters April had bolted to the jamb in place of the bathroom door her landlord had stalled on replacing. He admired her assortment of books stacked in an old pie safe, and inquired about the origin of the dressmaker's dummy she used to hold coats near the door.

Finally, after April had led him all the way through her apartment, they arrived in her bedroom.

"Nice wagon wheel," he said, nodding toward her makeshift headboard. His hand touched hers, and a tingle shot from her toes to her nose. "I like it. Very creative of you."

His praise cheered her. His interested expression did a lot to further her, ummm, *creativity*, too. But her years of don't-mess-with-the-Finnegans pride smacked her down, all over again.

"It's easy to be creative when you have to be," April said with feigned indifference. "*Real* furniture costs money."

Ryan's gaze followed her, even as she turned her head to avoid his inevitable perceptiveness.

"This is the most 'real' home," he said, "filled with the most 'real' furniture, I've ever been in."

"Thanks." She gestured toward the rest of her apartment and away from the danger zone. After all, who knew when her most heartfelt wishes, a soft bed, and a hard man might suddenly collide? "Let's go hang the mirror. I've got a hammer in the kitchen drawer, and probably some wall anchors, too, so the—"

"I mean it." His arm blocked her exit from the bedroom. "There's a little bit of *you* in everything in this place. I could almost breathe in and feel your essence fill me."

"Oh, that. That *is* me. Drugstore perfume is pretty strong. I knew I shouldn't have spritzed so much. But it was a special occasion, being your first trip to a swap meet and all."

Grinning, Ryan shook his head. He turned, his body filling her vision and overwhelming her senses and making a complete joke of her efforts to resist him.

"It's *you*," he said. "I love—"

She panicked, and ducked beneath his arm.

"—it."

Arrgh. He was in her mind and in her apartment. It was only a matter of time now before he was in her heart, too. Galvanized by the thought, she headed for the kitchen counter where she'd dropped her purse.

Chivalry is dead, April remembered herself saying on that long-ago day. *Romance is dead, and true love is dead, too.* Ha! It was as though fate had finally gotten fed up with her spinach–dip loitering approach to life, and had set out to teach her a lesson. In the form of one chivalrous, romantic, one-thousand-percent wonderful man.

In the form of—let's be real, here—Ryan.

She needed distraction, April decided. And fast.

She scrabbled in her purse and came up with the

item she sought just as Ryan showed up behind her. His good cheer was in place. His expression was knowing. His shoulders were broader, his chest stronger, his hands more irresistibly competent than ever before. *Oh, boy. Was she in trouble.*

"Surprise!" she said, spinning around to offer him the thing she'd retrieved. "For you."

He accepted it, looking amused. Then, touched.

"The John Denton book," Ryan said. "How did you—"

"I went back while you were getting the pickup to transport my new mirror. You stink at driving a hard bargain, you know."

"Don't care."

"I got it for five bucks. Five, *not* forty-five. Not fifty." *Was it hot in here?* The way he was looking at her made her think—

"Don't care."

"My dad is a used and rare book dealer," April explained as Ryan carefully set the book aside. He reached for her, and pulled her nearer, hip-first. "He's the reason I discovered swap meets," she blathered on. "And garage sales. And bargain-hunting in general. I guess, when I go to a big, messy, free-for-all sale like that, it reminds me of my dad and I feel a little closer to him. And it's nice."

"Very nice." Ryan's voice was a mere murmur, all huskiness and promise—very little sweetness. "Thank you for the book."

"You're wel—"

His kiss cut off her words and stole her breath. Before she could blink, he'd backed them both against the kitchen wall. Flexing his fingers against her hips, he used his mouth to make April forget . . . well, everything that existed beyond the heat of his body, the solid strength of his arms, the consuming pleasure of their hearts and souls and needs coming together.

They separated at last. "Geez, that was some kiss," she murmured. Her clothes were rumpled, her heart was racing, her desperately needed sense of caution was nowhere to be found. "I think I hear bells."

His confident smile beckoned her nearer for more of the same. *"Ring a ling."*

She loved that about him, April decided as she lost herself in his arms again. Ryan made her laugh, could make her laugh even at the most erotic moments. Somehow, his easy ways only heightened the intimacy between them, made it simpler and simpler to get closer . . . closer.

"Mmmm, there they go again." Hazily, she began to reconsider the so-called dangers of inviting Ryan into her home. Into her life. She could handle it. Right now, April felt strong enough to manage anything, even unexpected true love. "Ring a ling, ring a—"

Abruptly, Ryan raised his head. "That's not bells you hear. That's a car horn honking. Or maybe a . . . Winnebago?"

Perplexed—and not really caring about the distinctions between modes of transportation—April kissed his earlobe. She moved lower to the side of his neck. "You taste good," she observed. "I'm glad you like your book."

They kissed. The bells—okay, the *honking*—grew louder. More insistent.

April pulled away, and frowned. She strode to her front door. Whoever was responsible for this would answer to her, damn it. She had a perfectly good make-out session going on here, and somebody was ruining it.

She opened the door. A new blast of noise made her cover her ears. "It *is* a Winnebago!" April said, over her shoulder to Ryan. She gawked at the thirty-foot vehicle blocking traffic in her duplex's small drive. "Hey, this is a private drive," she yelled. "You can't park there!"

The passenger-side door popped open. A shaggy-haired man leaned from behind the wheel and across the voluptuous, giggling blonde seated beside him. He gave April a good-natured party-boy's grin, then tossed something toward her.

"This fifty bucks says I can park wherever I want, doll," he said as the money fluttered to the ground in the glow from her porch light. "And there's another fifty in it for you if you can tell me where in this godforsaken burg I can find my buddy, Ryan Forrester."

Chapter Fourteen

By the time Ryan reached the Downtown Grill with Jackson and Lola in tow, it was nearly closing time. A couple of truckers sat at the counter with battered caps and bleary eyes, and three teenagers eating french fries filled the booth farthest from the door. A busboy lined up chairs to separate the "closed" area he was about to mop, and then went to work.

Mona was off duty. Instead, their waitress was a curvaceous brunette with a rose tattoo on her ankle and a ready smile for Jackson. She handed over three menus—including one for Lola, who'd vanished into the ladies' room to powder her nose—then sauntered away.

"Va va voom!" Grinning with typical good-time good spirits, Jackson leaned sideways to watch the brunette leave. Cheerfully, he straightened. "Is it me, or is our waitress like one of those glam trailer-park honeys straight out of the Guess! ads?"

Ryan raised his eyebrows.

"You know, the girl with too much eye makeup, too-tight jeans, and a dangerous attitude. Like she just might strip you naked, do the wild thing with you . . . and then steal your clothes and ride off into the sunset on her Harley?"

Ryan shook his head. "Madison Avenue has stolen your soul."

"Come on. What a way to go! Don't tell me you haven't thought about it." Jackson angled his head toward the waitress.

"With her?" Ryan asked. "No." He'd been . . . otherwise occupied. With April.

Jackson rolled his eyes. "Right."

"I've been busy. Working."

And falling for April.

"You. Working. Ha!" Jackson hooted. "A contradiction if I've ever heard one. You, my friend, work at finding the perfect martini. At snagging the best theater tickets. At scouting the most happening vacation spots. At throwing the wildest parties. That's your idea of 'working.' "

Remembering the times he'd done all those things, Ryan smiled. There were good things to be said for the bachelor lifestyle he was accustomed to. But still . . .

"Things are different now," Ryan said. "*I'm* different."

His friend looked at him skeptically. "Sure, I get it. You've cracked. Being here in the boonies has altered your sense of reality. Good thing Lola and I came to rescue you when we did."

Ryan couldn't help but laugh. Jackson seemed to consider that further proof of his small town–induced instability.

"Hey—is that tap water you're drinking?" Jackson narrowed his eyes. "And is that a Hanes T-shirt beneath your Calvin Klein button-down? Maybe we're too late!"

"You're not too late," Ryan said. Truth be told, he'd missed Jackson's life-is-a-party companionship. But not as much as he'd thought he might. "After our phone conversation, I didn't think you were coming at all."

And I almost wish you hadn't.

A shrug. "We would've been here sooner, but it took a while to get the Winnebago's satellite system and DVD player hookup working."

Pulling out one of the cigars he favored, Jackson took his time lighting it. The rich scent of Cuban tobacco swirled around their cracked vinyl booth. He looked around the diner.

"And this is it for fine dining?" Jackson shook his head. "No maître d' in sight. No wine list." He frowned down at the menu. "No prime rib, no risotto. I would kill for some of Henri's roasted salmon with shiitake relish right now."

"How about a nice grilled cheese sandwich?"

Obviously deeming Ryan's suggestion not worthy of serious consideration, Jackson went on.

"And this town is eerily silent, too. Have you noticed?" He puffed his cigar. "I swear the sidewalks actually rolled up for the night as we drove past. I don't know how you've been able to stand it here for this long."

"It's not so bad," Ryan told him. "There are things I like about Saguaro Vista."

Shuddering at the thought, Jackson turned over his coffee cup. Made a face. Wiped it clean with a paper napkin from the dispenser.

"I'm doing well here," Ryan added. "Small town life isn't for everybody—"

"Amen, brother."

"—but it has its advantages."

For an instant, Ryan considered telling his buddy about his wallet-free triumphs over the past week and a half. About his possibly pending sponsorship deals for Forrester's, which would cement his position in the family business once and for all. And—most importantly—about April.

But then he noticed the way Jackson yawned with weariness, heard his comment about having partied too much over the past few days, and reconsidered. A gap had opened, Ryan realized, between the life he'd lived before coming to Saguaro Vista and the life he'd discovered in the days since. That gap divided him and Jackson, even now.

Ryan had moved on to something new. Jackson hadn't. And he was happy that way. It wasn't up to Ryan to disillusion his longtime pal with concepts like effort. Ingenuity. Steadiness.

Commitment.

"Advantages, huh?" Jackson spotted Lola emerging from the ladies' room, and waved her to their booth. "Whatever. I don't see it. And after you get back to real life, I'll bet you don't eith—hey, doll! You miss me?"

Giggling, the blonde snuggled into the booth next to Jackson. Up close, Ryan saw that she was bubbly, braless, and beautified to the nth degree. Exactly Jackson's type.

"I'm pleased to finally meetcha, Ryan," she said. "Too bad your girlfriend couldn't come with us, though."

April. Ryan half-suspected she was still staring at the Winnebago tracks in her driveway, unable to believe what she'd seen.

Some instinct had driven him to do all he could to keep April and Jackson separated, and neither one of them had seemed to mind a bit. April had accepted Ryan's bid for a just-old-pals get-together at the Grill, and Jackson had accepted April's stiffly offered return of the fifty bucks he'd tossed at her.

"Passed that test with flying colors, didn't she?" Jackson had asked Ryan afterward, nudging him in the ribs. "Smart move, hooking up with her. A girl like that, who won't even take a friendly tip, sure as hell won't take you for a ride on the fleece-mobile. Baaaah!"

Now putting aside Jackson's reference to the wedding that wasn't, Ryan nodded at Lola.

"Yes, it's too bad," he said. "April's a very original woman. She's unlike anyone I've ever met."

He felt a mushy romantic grin cross his face. In reply, Lola smiled back at him. Beneath her flashy surface and showgirl body, she seemed like a nice woman. All of a sudden, Ryan was glad his friend had found her.

Jackson scoffed. "Did you forget what whatshername did to you? Jeez, Forrester. Catch a clue."

"That was a mistake," Ryan said. "I'm over it. I've moved on." He leveled a pointed gaze at Jackson. "You should, too."

Their waitress had returned. Capably, she poured three cups of coffee, then left them at Jackson's request to examine the menus a little longer.

"Just looking out for you," he muttered. He took out his pocket flask and doctored his coffee. "That's all."

He took a liquory sip. "Ahhh. Much better."

Watching him, Ryan wondered for the first time if Jackson's ever-present flask and constant search for the biggest and best parties were excuses. Cover ups. Expensive Band-Aids for something that was missing in his life. Could Jackson, twice-divorced from gold-digging ex-wives and never without a beautiful woman on his arm, actually be lonely?

"Jeez, the excitement here is killing me." With a sardonic grin, Jackson slapped his menu closed and looked at Lola and Ryan. "Who's up for getting out of here? Doesn't Hickville have a nightclub or something?"

"Only one," Ryan said. "The Roadhouse. It's closed on weeknights."

"So?"

"So this is a Thursday."

"That's a weeknight, hon," Lola pointed out to Jackson. "We working stiffs have to keep track, you know."

"Poor baby." Jackson gave her a commiserating kiss. With the air of someone evaluating their options, he gazed upward at the Grill's fluorescent strip lighting. "So, no nightlife. No edible chow. No fun to be had in Podunkville."

Ryan thought of April. She was definitely fun. "I wouldn't go that far."

"What say we head out to the Winnebago for cocktails?" Jackson suggested, perking up. "It's got a fully stocked bar and emergency rations. The concierge at the Venetian was really helpful about finding us goodies for the road before we left Vegas. He must have known it was a wasteland out here."

Expectantly, he waited.

"Drinks?" Ryan waved his hand. "Nah. Thanks, but I have to get up early tomorrow. For work."

"There's that *word* again!" Jackson said.

Ryan grinned. So did Lola.

"It's all right, baby," she crooned through perfectly lipsticked lips. "I'll make him wash his mouth out with cheap malt liquor if he ever says it again."

They all laughed. Ryan decided April would have enjoyed Lola's sassy sense of humor and almost wished he'd brought her along.

Almost.

After all, what if April got a sense of the life he'd lived until now . . . and realized Ryan truly *wasn't* "real" enough for her? What if she didn't realize he was changing for the better—because of her?

Watching Jackson and Lola coo baby talk to each

other, Ryan experienced an odd sense of urgency. He didn't want his relationship with April to be as temporary as Jackson's liaison with Lola would doubtless be. He didn't want to lose her.

But he didn't have much time to make April his, either. Only a couple of days remained in their wager. A couple of days before he left town. It was now or never.

"Well, I guess we might as well hit the road," Jackson said, breaking into his thoughts. "Ready, Ryan?"

"What, leave Saguaro Vista, now? *Tonight?*"

"Hell, yes." He put out his cigar. "Podunkville sucks."

Lola crossed her arms and nodded reluctantly. "I'm sorry, Ryan. I guess you like it here," she said softly. "And I thought it would be charming. I really did. But, well . . . the ladies' room doesn't even have potty protectors."

Her sorrowful gaze made her opinion of that missing amenity very plain. No potty protectors equaled no Lola.

"I'm not leaving yet," Ryan said. "I have work to do here."

"What, that community building thing?" Jackson shook his head, giving Ryan a regretful look. "Come on. What are the odds the Forrester's board will go for that, in the end? Face it. You're just a name at the top of the letterhead to them."

Just a master of idiot savant retailing, Ryan thought. Still smarting at the board's assessment of his scheme, he tightened his hold on his coffee cup. "All the same, I'm staying. At least through the weekend."

By then, he'd have triumphed in his bet with April. He'd have won rights to the town sponsorships. He'd have staged his prom-and-bridal fashion show at the department store to a successful conclusion.

And, with a little luck, he'd have won April's heart, too.

Jackson squinted across the table at him. Dubiously. Then, with obvious reluctance, he shrugged. "Your call. Lola and I will head back to Sin City tomorrow, then. In case you change your mind overnight. Okay, doll?"

Lola nodded and snuggled closer.

"You want to do the Winnebago swap now, or in the morning?" Jackson asked. He peeled a twenty from his money clip and tossed it onto the table to cover their coffee and a tip. "You probably don't want to spend another night in that cheesy motel room you told me about . . . but Lola and I just might be up for a walk on the wild side. One of those round beds and a ceiling mirror just might be a hoot."

Ryan thought of the Saguaro Vista Motor Court Inn's orange and purple decor. The hot and cold running water from rusty pipes. The velvet Elvis.

No. He couldn't do it to them. Besides, although his staying in the Winnebago wouldn't technically be a violation of his bet with April—given that Ryan hadn't actually paid for his accommodations-on-wheels yet— morally, it would definitely qualify as cheating.

"You take the Winnebago tonight," Ryan said as the three of them stood. He went on to describe the overnight RV park campground just at the edge of Saguaro Vista, a potential Forrester's Department Store partner. "I've got other plans."

They emerged outside the Downtown Grill into the deserted late-night parking lot. Through the darkness, stars shined twice as brightly overhead as they did in the city. In the lack of traffic sounds, cicadas could be heard whirring nearby. Ryan breathed deeply of the clean air, and smiled.

"We'll swap in the morning, then," Jackson said, striding with his arm around Lola toward the Winnebago.

"We towed one of those Miata convertibles behind this thing—"

"It's so cute! You'll love it!" Lola squealed.

"—for the drive back to Vegas, so it's no problem for us getting there." Jackson paused. Looked backward. A curiously thoughtful expression edged onto his usually jovial face. "Sure you won't change your mind now? Get the heck out of Mayberry before you crack up for real and start wearing overalls?"

Ryan smiled, pulling out the keys to the borrowed pickup truck he'd driven to the diner. "I'm sure."

"Hey, whatever floats your boat." With a wide grin, Jackson snuggled Lola a little closer. She giggled.

They said their good-byes and walked to their separate vehicles. Just as the door to Ryan's pickup screeched open, Jackson turned.

"Oh, and bring your checkbook tomorrow, willya?" he asked. "This thirty-foot geezermobile set me back about . . . awww, hell, how much was it, doll? You know I'm terrible with money."

"A hundred and fifty thousand. Give or take a few thousand."

"Yeah. So bring your checkbook, like I said," Jackson called to Ryan. "After you pay me back, there's a certain blackjack dealer I plan to make a return visit to at the Bellagio. Heh, heh, heh."

Ryan nodded. With a delighted-sounding chuckle, Jackson said another good-bye. He and Lola stepped into the Winnebago, leaving Ryan alone beside his temporary pickup truck.

Bring your checkbook, he thought. *As if.* He couldn't so much as request his accountants issue a check without falling down on his bargain with April. Feeling naked all over again without his wallet, Ryan got into the pickup.

He put the key in the ignition. Just as he was about to give it a turn, the unmistakable *pop!* of a champagne bottle being uncorked nearby came through the rolled-down window. Laughter issued from the Winnebago.

The sound left him lonely. Wrapping his fingers around the steering wheel, Ryan rested his forehead on his clenched knuckles. Briefly, he closed his eyes.

It was possible he wasn't strong enough for this. Wasn't real enough for April, after all. She deserved the best.

A few minutes later, Ryan made his decision. He opened his eyes, whipped out his keys, and got out of the pickup. Within moments, he was at the Winnebago's side door, hand poised to knock.

"I don't know, Jamie," April said on Thursday afternoon. "Do you really think Ryan will like it?"

She peered at the choice she'd just made, then at the remaining selections racked at Spicy Girl lingerie. The silky white chemise in her hand was sexy, but the black bra-and-thong-panty set three hangers down was downright hot.

Frowning, April mulled it over. It was the classic sneakers-or-stilettos question: comfort or combustibility? How was a girl to choose?

"If he has a pulse, he'll like it," Jamie said. "Now hurry up. My lunch break's almost over."

Making her decision, April grabbed both items—hey, variety was the spice of life, right? Resolutely, she headed for the cash register.

Halfway there, she stopped. Jamie did, too.

"What's the matter?" she asked.

"Re—re—retail," April stammered, gesturing vaguely with the lingerie in her hands. A weird sensation clogged her throat and made her heart beat faster. "I'm about to pay full retail price. I don't believe it."

"This guy means that much to you, huh?" With a kindhearted smile, Jamie gave her a hug. "Lucky Ryan."

Suddenly, salvation loomed into sight.

"Hey, the discount bin!" April spotted it, and lurched toward the rear of the store. She pawed through burnt-orange bras. Mud-colored panties. Pinchy neon bustiers. Feeling panicky, she held up a teddy with flashing Christmas lights tipping its cone-shaped cups. "Look! This one's eighty percent off! It might work."

"Oh, God." Muttering to herself, Jamie pried loose April's grasp on the hideous garment. "You're delirious. Snap out of it."

"How about this one? It's a second, but you can hardly see the flaw." Sure she'd gone glassy-eyed, April surged upward from her renewed bargain hunting with a pair of gauzy purple harem-girl pants and a multicolored spangled bra top. When she shook the ensemble toward Jamie, the bells embedded in the bra gave a wheezy jingle.

Gently, Jamie removed the unambiguously titled "fantasy wear" from April's grasp. She dodged sideways, blocking her next lunge for a fringed blue satin cowgirl outfit—complete with white Stetson—too.

"Just say no to giddy-up glamour," she said sternly. Putting both hands on April's shoulders, she guided her to the checkout. "The things you have are fine."

"But, but—full price. *Full*—"

"Ryan will *love* them."

Ryan. Ryan would love them. At the thought of him, some of April's panic receded. Taking a deep breath, she slid the chemise and the bra-and-thong-panty set onto the Spicy Girls counter. A store worker straightened from behind the counter.

"Hey," he said casually. "May I help—"

"Mickey!" April gawped. "What are you doing here?"

"Yo, Ape." Oblivious to April and Jamie's surprise,

Mickey ran his fingers through his ruffled bedhead hair. He blinked. "Collecting recyclables is for suckers. Totally. I met the manager of Spicy Girl at Disco Bingo night—"

"What is she, ninety years old?" Jamie asked. "Ewww."

"—and she offered me a part-time job. And no, Natalie's not ninety. She's twenty-seven. And cute."

"Cute?" April and Jamie exchanged glances.

"She was helping out her grandpa, the bingo caller. He lost his bifocals."

Thrusting his chin in the air, Mickey began ringing up April's purchases. All she could do was give in to the inevitable . . . and, for the first time in her life, hand over her hard-earned cash for a full-priced purchase. After years of penny-pinching and covering her mother's bad checks, it was a bewildering experience.

Geez, she hoped she wasn't making a mistake. Afterward, stepping out in the sunlight to walk Jamie back to HairRazors, April clutched her purchases and reminded herself that Ryan was worth it. He was worth it, she was head over heels for him, and she had less than two days to show him how much she believed it.

Any sane woman would have resorted to a thong. Right?

Right.

Now all she had to do was come up with an occasion to make the most of it.

Chapter Fifteen

Fashion shows weren't completely unheard of in Saguaro Vista—rural as it was.

For instance, the Wal-Mart at the edge of town had staged a grand opening extravaganza during its first week in business. People still talked about the employees who'd been chosen to parade down the center aisle modeling the best in discount casual wear, home appliances, and detergent. And Red's pet store had once held a doggie fashion show to promote a new line of pet apparel. Unfortunately for April, seeing her aunt's Chihuahua in a bright yellow slicker and matching rain hat still gave her the creeps.

Seriously . . . if dogs were meant to wear coordinated ensembles, would they really be color-blind?

Shaking off the memory, April unpacked a fresh bakery box of chocolate chunk macadamia cookies and went to work arranging them on a table at the edge of Forrester's Better Apparel. Ryan had agreed to let her man a mini Ambrosia refreshment stand during his prom-and-bridal fashion show tonight, and she meant to make it a complete sell-out.

With the cookies arranged atop a doily-covered plate—her contribution to Ryan's fancy-schmancy sensibilities—April looked up, searching for Ryan himself. All around her, spectators swarmed the cleared space, chatting about the upcoming show. A few Kool-Aid mustachioed kids raced up and down the newly constructed runway, chased by frazzled Forrester's employees. A microphone sound check boomed over the speakers set up at the perimeter of Better Apparel.

Anticipation was high, and so was that runway. April was glad she wouldn't be called upon to stride swivel-hipped up and down it, wearing something stupid like a bikini and heels. Was that realism? Hello? Who went to the beach hoping to spike themselves into a sand dune?

Granted, April's ideas of fashion shows were primarily based upon the aforementioned Wal-Mart and pet couture galas, and the Miss America pageant—which she never missed on TV each year. But it seemed likely Ryan's show would be similar.

Somewhere backstage—the dressing rooms behind Resort Wear—Jamie was working to glam up the volunteer models—high school students, local soccer moms, even a few hunky firefighters from the Saguaro Vista crew would be modeling tuxedos. Mark was circulating among the spectators with a tray of petit fours samples and a sign reading, "Indulge Yourself at Ambrosia." Mickey was canoodling with the Spicy Girl manager at the edge of Men's Unmentionables—April hoped that wasn't an omen. And Ryan was . . . he was nowhere to be seen.

A movement at her table's cloth-covered edge caught April's eye. A rustle, a hand moving stealthily closer to the triple fudge brownies—

"Uncle Bobby! Stand up and come out from behind there."

Sheepishly, Bobby Finnegan straightened. He brushed away the tablecloth edge clinging to his clothes. "What's the matter, April, girl? I was only making sure you had enough goodies for your customers."

"Mmmm-hmmm." Making a face, April picked up a napkin and rubbed a blob of chocolate icing from Uncle Bobby's shirt. "I have a feeling I'll have plenty of goodies, if only *you'll* stop guarding them."

"Ahhh, there goes your friend Mark." Uncle Bobby brightened. "I wonder if he needs help with those little cakes on his tray."

"Uncle Bobby, those are for paying customers on—"

It was too late. He'd already left, dogging Mark's heels.

In the next few minutes, April sold twelve of the chocolate chunk macadamia cookies, fourteen triple chocolate brownies, several lemon bars, and a miniature fruit tart. There was still no sign of Ryan.

"Sweetie!" Her mother popped into view, emerging from behind April's last two customers.

She gave her daughter a hug. "I just saw that *nice* Mr. Wright of yours. Did you know he's invested in the advance rental program at the video store? One prepaid video rental a week for two years. Smart planning. And," Fiona went on, leaning closer, "he got two percent off for those guaranteed rentals, too. You could do worse than a man like that."

She ought to resist, April knew. She ought to show some self-restraint and not rise to the bait.

Oh, heck. She was only human. "Mom, on a three-fifty rental, that's something like seven cents off."

Fiona glowed with pride. "I know!"

"What if Mark doesn't want to rent a movie one week? Then what?"

Her mother was undeterred. "A man who plans ahead knows what he's doing," she said staunchly. "A man who plans ahead is what a girl like you needs."

"*I* plan ahead."

"Since when?" Fiona picked up a lemon bar and took a bite. She saw April watching, and hunched her shoulders defensively. "I'll write you a check for it, okay?"

"Okay." April made a mental note to stash two dollars in the till herself.

"When do you plan ahead?" Fiona asked again.

Her obvious skepticism hurt. April searched her memory. "Just this afternoon, I picked out clothes for tomorrow. That's planning ahead."

Really, she'd chosen between her new lingerie, and had laid out the hot-to-trot bra-and-thong set with hopes of finishing what she and Ryan had started in her kitchen last night . . . but did her mother really have to know the details?

"Big whoop." Fiona finished her lemon bar and perused the remaining selections.

"Okay, okay. And last Thursday, based on my confidence about my new position at Ambrosia, I split my passbook account at the bank into two CDs and two money market accounts. How's *that*?" Feeling proud of herself—and wonderfully fiscally responsible—April grinned.

Fiona frowned. "Now, you know I don't talk Bank. Speak in English, sweetie."

"I'm saving for the future," April explained. "Ryan gave me some financial advice. He really knows what he's talking about when it comes to money."

"When it comes to everything else, I'm a total wash, though." Turning up just in time to hear April's last comment, Ryan stopped at her table and greeted Fiona with a smile. "Nice to see you, Mrs. Finnegan. The green in that halter top really brings out your eyes."

Fiona blushed and gave an "aw-shucks" wave.

Ryan tucked his hand at the small of April's back and tugged her closer for a hello kiss. It lasted just long enough to stir up memories of the other, hotter kisses they'd shared . . . and just briefly enough to make April wish for more.

She let out a breath she hadn't been aware of holding. Somehow, seeing Ryan was a relief. She'd actually begun to wonder if, well . . . something had happened to him. Like he'd been irresistibly drawn to his Winnebago-driving friends and had decided to bail out on Saguaro Vista for greener, hoity-toitier, pastures. After all, by now Ryan *had* to be missing the luxe life he'd temporarily left behind.

"A total wash?" she repeated, admiring the fit of his perfectly tailored suit. Boy, but that man could make Armani look positively sexed-up. "No. I didn't mean it that way. I think you're very smart. About lots of things."

"And I think *you're* very smart. Also beautiful, witty, charming, and—"

"Okay, break it up." If Fiona had possessed an umpire's whistle, no doubt she would have used it. "For the love of Pete, if you're going to get all mushy-gushy, get a room."

"Mom!"

"What? People are trying to eat, here."

Fiona elbowed her way closer, handing out cookies to curious onlookers before April could stop her, obviously intent on having the booth all to themselves. With the crowd dispersed, she cleared her throat.

"Now. Before this goes any farther, Mr. Forrester—"

"Ryan. Please."

"—I have to know a few things." Fiona straightened

and fixed him with a sharp look. "First, do you have an insurance plan?"

"Annuity or short term? Accidental injury, housing, auto, marine, or equine?"

"Equine?" April asked.

"I own a string of polo ponies."

"Oh." April pictured Ryan in tight riding breeches, and felt a charge that had nothing to do with the lingerie surprise she had planned for him.

"Oh. I didn't think of that." Pursing her lips, Fiona blinked. Then she stampeded onward. "Do you own a car?"

"Yes."

April's mother narrowed her eyes. "Does it run? Because six different cars up on blocks in the yard doesn't cut the mustard with me, sonny."

"Mom!"

"Yes, it runs. Quite well." Ryan regarded Fiona curiously. "It's currently parked outside the Saguaro Vista bowling alley, waiting for Pete Wykowski's championship dinner to wrap up."

"Ryan loaned his car to Pete," April explained, wanting her mother to be as impressed with Ryan as she was. He was being a good sport about this interrogation so far, but if the questioning went much further . . . well, frankly, most men who met Fiona Finnegan didn't survive The Inquisition.

Fiona pursed her lips. "A house?"

"Three, counting condos," Ryan answered. "Plus a summer share in the Hamptons."

Crossing her arms over her chest, Fiona looked Ryan up and down. A new interest lighted her eyes. She was nothing if not cautious, though. "How dependable, *exactly*, is this corporate raider business of yours?"

"I'm a Forrester's vice president. The corporate raider thing was a joke."

"Phony employment isn't funny. Just ask my Mickey."

Looking chagrined, Ryan backpedaled. "Did Mickey have trouble with a—" He caught April's frantic *don't-go-there* wave, and stopped. "Uh, hey! Look, there's Mickey now. And he's with a woman. I'm *sure* her blonde hair isn't natural."

Fiona looked, eyes narrowed. She snatched a brownie. Taking a bite, she stalked away toward her son.

With a sigh, April dug twenty dollars from her purse and added it to the till. She'd have to wait until the end of the night to tally up all the free baked goods her mother had given away to ensure privacy—the better to cross-examine Ryan with.

"Whew," he said, pantomiming wiping his brow.

"You're diabolical," she told him, shaking her head as she watched Fiona barrel toward an unsuspecting Mickey.

"What? I have it on reliable authority there's nothing mothers hate more than wannabe blondes going after their sons."

"Really?"

"No." He grinned. "But your mother needed a new target. And it was all I could come up with on the spur of the moment."

April couldn't help but grin back. "Your self-protective instincts are quite good. A person would almost think you could survive in this 'burg.' "

Ryan frowned, looking puzzled.

Burg.

As in, *And there's another fifty in it for you if you can tell me where in this godforsaken burg I can find my buddy, Ryan Forrester.*

April winced. She hadn't meant to make an open reference to the things his Winnebago-driving friends had said. And her remark had definitely come out sounding more barbed than she'd intended. But April had been curious about Jackson Hart and Lola since last night. It had just slipped out.

Silence fell between them.

Okay, not silence, exactly. People were still milling about, the show's sound system was spitting out static, and in general, chaos ruled. But between April and Ryan . . . silence.

" 'Burg?' " Ryan asked.

"That's what I heard your friend say. Right?"

He looked away. "Jackson can be a little too much," he said, seeming suddenly uncomfortable. He shrugged. "Like he says, small-town living might be right for some people, but—"

"—but not for you. Or your buddy. Right?"

He stared at her. April held her ground, even though Ryan *almost* managed to look as though he were actually considering daily life in Saguaro Vista. Then his expression changed.

I'm not staying here, she imagined him thinking. *Not for you. Not for anyone.*

All the same, she didn't want to hear him say the words out loud. Better that she come out with the awful truth herself, April decided, than to have it straight from Ryan . . . the man she'd begun fantasizing about spending the rest of her life with.

It was bad enough knowing the truth about Ryan and his big-city ways. April didn't want to be walloped with them. Especially right after having invested in full-retail-price lingerie. And Ryan didn't, she noticed, contradict her, either.

Damn it.

"I never said anything about that," Ryan told her, rubbing the back of his neck. "And you don't know Jackson."

No, she didn't, April agreed silently. And if he was the one who'd zipped into Saguaro Vista and reminded

Ryan of all he was missing by spending time with small-town *her,* she didn't want to, either.

"No, I guess I—" April stopped as two money-wielding soccer moms approached. "Excuse me."

He stood by, watching, as she helped customers purchase an assortment of goodies. Obviously, he was preparing a rebuttal. As soon as April had finished, Ryan went on.

"Jackson and Lola drove back to Vegas this morning, sans the Winnebago," he said. "Which *I* won't use until our bet is finished, by the way. It's still sitting at the RV park down the street. In case you were wondering."

"I wasn't wondering. I know you're a man of your word."

"Thank you." He looked pleased, and a little relieved as some of the tension between them faded. "Anyway, Jackson said to tell you he and Lola hoped we could all get together sometime. For drinks, maybe. If we—"

April held up a hand to stop him. Having a temporary fling was one thing. Pretending it could go further was something else. Something, given the circumstances, unkind.

"Maybe. Um, look. I really have to get some work done here. Can we talk about this some other time?"

Like, never?

Ryan blinked in surprise. "Uh, all right."

"Good. See you around."

She rearranged the fruit tarts. Glanced up. He was still there, looking bewildered. And damnably gorgeous.

"Good luck with the show," April added briskly, desperate to make him leave before she burst into tears—or did something equally embarrassing, like beg him to change his mind about staying.

She brushed her hands on her bib apron and came around the table, forcibly pushing him toward the backstage area. "Go on. Break a leg. Knock 'em dead. Win one for the Gipper."

"The Gipper?"

"Giffer? Gripper? Flipper? Whatever." April blew out a breath and shook the hair from her eyes. "Just go get 'em."

One more push had Ryan headed, still looking perplexed, toward the dressing rooms. He glanced over his shoulder, frowned at her, then disappeared around a corner. Watching him go, April felt a momentary loss . . . a premonition, even. A sense that someday soon, she'd see Ryan walking away from her *for good*.

Her Granny Finnegan would have said her feelings were real. She would have urged April to take action now, before the events she feared came to pass. But then, Granny Finnegan had believed in all sorts of kooky things. Like crocheted toilet paper covers. Melted-together lumps of hard candy ribbons. Ben-Gay as an aphrodisiac.

April knew better. She knew, most of all, that she could hardly force Ryan to stay in Saguaro Vista. Not if he wanted to be someplace else. And it looked as though he did.

Reining in her disappointment, she trudged back to her Ambrosia baked-goods table. She still had a few good days left with Ryan, April reminded herself. She'd darn well make the most of them.

Standing in a corner at the far side of the Forrester's Better Apparel department, Mark watched the fashion show. The portable spotlights came on, highlighting the various glittery decorations he'd helped Jamie put up. Subdued music played. At the microphone, a Forrester's employee held a stack of note cards and read gushy, adjective-laden descriptions of the clothes being shown.

A celebratory mood prevailed as Saguaro Vista was treated to a real, city-style preview of the latest in formal gowns for women.

Now, fifteen minutes into the show, the newest in a parade of prom-dress–wearing local "models" strutted down the makeshift runway.

"Ooooh," the crowd murmured. *"Ahhhh."*

A futuristic "bride" dressed in a bubble-shaped gown that seemed to be made of papier-mâché strutted down the walkway.

"Ooooh. Ahhhh." Wild applause.

A contingent of tuxedo-wearing firefighters escorted blushing soccer mom models—wearing bridal gowns—and their giggling high school daughters, wearing prom dresses.

"Ooooh. Ahhhh."

At the crowd's latest exclamation, Mark shook his head. He flipped his empty petit fours tray sideways and tucked it beneath his elbow against his waist. Didn't *anyone* see what was wrong here?

Down to the littlest model—a preschool "flower girl" with a bouquet of carnations—every person on the runway had an outlandish hairstyle. Spikes stuck straight up. Ends flopped over eyes and cheeks. Braids bounced willy-nilly. Colors were all over the rainbow. And what were those multicolored twisted things called? Bozo dreadlocks?

Jamie was responsible for all of it, Mark knew. *His Jamie.* She'd created unique "formal" hairstyles for each of the show's models, and every one was more outrageous than the last. Their spikes and twists and shaved initials made his own daring application of styling mud this morning seem downright pedestrian by comparison. Mark didn't understand it. Didn't Jamie know how many people in town would be appalled—even horrified—by her experimental styling?

She'd be shunned, he realized. Ostracized. Possibly, no one would come to HairRazors anymore. Jamie wouldn't be able to make her rent. She'd be thrown onto the street. She'd starve, and resort to panhandling tourists for "Hairstyles While U Wait." She'd grow pale and gaunt. The zestful enthusiasm that accented everything Jamie did would be blunted forever by the weight of Saguaro Vista's scorn . . . and by having been forced to go cold turkey on mousse, styling pomade, and gel.

He couldn't let it come to that, Mark thought. *He had to do something to save Jamie. He cared about her, maybe even lo—*

A new fanfare caught his attention. The spotlights swung wildly, then refocused inward at the curtained entrance to the runway. The hostess announced the final gown of the night, then stepped away from the microphone, applauding.

The crowd held its breath.

Suddenly, a vision in white emerged at the top of the runway's red carpet. This model wore a wedding gown so pale and pure, it sparkled faintly in the glow of the lights. Blinking, Mark watched her, mesmerized.

She stepped forward—no, glided, really—graceful and sure. Her short dark hair framed her face, offsetting intelligent eyes and a serious expression. Closer and closer she came, the crowd breaking into applause as she neared the end of the runway.

The bride stopped. She contemplated the bouquet of white flowers she held, as though stricken suddenly shy. Then, as the music reached its crescendo, she looked up. Her seeking gaze found Mark. She smiled.

Jamie. His heart lurched. His breath stopped. He would have sworn he floated a few inches toward her, but when she inclined her head to him and then turned to walk back up the runway, Mark realized he'd only stepped forward a little, as though to reach her.

She glided away, beautiful and feminine and—in a sense—unknown to him. The curtains closed behind her. The crowd stamped its feet, roaring its approval. The show lights turned off, leaving the space lit by its usual fluorescents.

Mark felt stunned. *Jamie . . . ?*

Before long, models began drifting from the backstage area, most dressed in jeans and T-shirts but with their showy makeup and wild hairstyles still in place. Their families greeted them. Mark saw one teenage girl hug her mother, then bend down so her little brother could pat the purple spikes in her hair. Everyone smiled.

Mark boggled. Could it be that Saguaro Vista was not as staid and judgmental as he'd feared? The idea flew in the face of everything he'd been raised to believe, and some of what he'd encountered in his day-to-day business dealings at Ambrosia. But still . . .

Setting down his tray, Mark went to find Jamie. Whether she'd suddenly become a purple pomade pariah or was the toast of the town, Jamie would need someone by her side. Mark hoped it would be him . . . if he could only find the courage to make it so.

Jamie was struggling out of the corset and petticoats required of the grand finale wedding dress when she heard someone calling her name. More than likely, she decided, that masculine voice belonged to one of the firefighter volunteers. Probably one who wanted to book an appointment with her.

To her amazement, until a few minutes ago when everyone else had left, Jamie had been inundated backstage with requests for her stylist's services. At first she'd tried to accommodate everyone with on-the-spot appointments. Eventually, though, Jamie had been forced to tell people to just call HairRazors in the morning. But there was no denying it—being in demand had been gratifying.

"Jamie?" came the voice again, sounding nearer down the corridor dividing both rows of dressing rooms. "Are you back here?"

Mark. Instantly, she froze. Everyone else had already changed and left . . . what was *he* doing here?

Probably, he'd come to harass her about having the audacity to actually participate in the show, Jamie thought. About making "a spectacle of herself."

A nervous hum burbled up from inside her. Frantically, Jamie wrestled with the yards of tulle that made up her petticoats, unable to prevent her humming from growing louder. Oh, boy. If she didn't get a hold of herself before she spoke with Mark, she would never—

The curtain was yanked aside. Her humming squeaked to a stop. Mark stood in the dressing room's opening, wearing a suit and tie and a forbidding expression she couldn't quite read. Even stranger—he'd actually loosened his tie.

"Mark!" Jamie slapped her hands over her chest. The motion did nothing to restrain her breasts, which had been corseted to the point of overflowing. Shocked by his appearance, she backed up. "Look, if you've come here to lecture me about being in the fashion show, you can just save your breath."

He stepped inside, his gaze intent. On her. On her breasts. On her face. On her breasts again. Oh, boy. The air between them heated, and so did Jamie's body temperature. What the . . . ?

"I didn't plan it this way," she babbled, still wondering what was going on but determined to play it cool. If she could. "One of the girls sprained her ankle in those stupid shoes. It wasn't that bad, but nobody could convince her to put on those stilettos again. And the dress was too long to go barefoot."

Silently, Mark whipped off his tie. She wasn't sure she'd ever seen him without it, for Mark Wright was nothing if not proper and traditional.

He flipped it over her head. The cool silk lassoed her shoulders. Jamie jerked in surprise. Holding the ends, he tugged her closer.

"—and, and they needed someone to fill in," she continued, waving her arms helplessly. Maybe he would think those gestures were nonchalant. *Yeah, right.* "With the grand finale wedding dress, that is."

An overwhelming urge to hum struck her. Jamie looked from side to side at the necktie inexplicably strung around her shoulders, and released a few notes of a song she couldn't name.

"The dress just happened to be my size, and so I—"

"It looked beautiful," Mark said. His voice sounded gravelly. Intense. "*You* looked beautiful. In fact, there's something I've been meaning to tell you."

"Oh?" Jamie wrinkled her brows. She folded her arms, as though they were having a simple conversation about chocolate croissants, or the latest Diamondbacks game. "What's that?"

"This," he said, and kissed her.

The necktie lasso tugged her closer, their bodies leaned together, their mouths met in a union so welcome and so surprising that Jamie could do nothing but gawk when it was over with. *She'd kissed Mark!*

She cleared her throat. Looked up at the dressing room's ceiling, which suddenly didn't seem nearly high enough to hold the sense of jubilation she felt. Summoning up every ounce of savoir faire she could, Jamie gave Mark a contemplative look.

"I have something to say to you, too," she said.

The kiss they shared next rocked her to her toes. It pushed her against the wall. It made her petticoats fly off to land in a jumble against the dressing room's dinky bench seat, and her corset fall to the floor. It made Mark's clothes follow suit, piling beneath the mirror that showed the most unexpected sight Jamie had ever expected to see:

Mark, making love to her.

Okay, so actually it was she and Mark who flung clothes willy-nilly across the room, not her kiss. And it was she and Mark who leaned against the wall and tried to be quiet as they indulged everything that had been building between them for so long. But it was Jamie alone who stopped mid-proceeding and frowned down at the mess surrounding them.

"Are you sure about this?" she panted. "We might be discovered. We might tear the dress. We might—".

"I'll buy it," Mark said, gallantly unrolling the second of her white silk stockings down her thigh. He kissed her knee, then straightened. "And I don't care who knows about us."

He tossed the stocking over his shoulder, exhibiting a remarkable quantity of machismo. "Now shut up and let me love you."

"Oooh, I love it when you talk tough."

"You'll love *this* even more," Mark promised. And then . . . he made it so.

Chapter Sixteen

"Well, today's the day," Ryan said on Friday evening.

"Yep. Today's the day," April agreed.

They stared at the pile of envelopes on April's ottomans-turned-coffee table. Each of those envelopes contained a sponsorship decision from a Saguaro Vista merchant. After their days of visiting local businesses to secure Ryan's community-building program and April's Ambrosia-awareness program, the moment of truth had finally arrived.

During those visits, Ryan and April had asked each merchant to deliver their sponsorship decisions in a sealed envelope by Friday at five o'clock. Now, looking down at the pile, Ryan felt unaccountably nervous. What if his program really *was* an example of "idiot savant retailing"?

"You go first," he told April. "Go ahead."

"No, you."

"I insist."

She ignored his gallantry. "What are you, chicken?"

He tried to look offended. "Are you?"

"Of course not." Shaking her head, April released a pent-up breath. "Are you?"

"No." Silence. "Let's do it together," Ryan suggested.

They each picked up an envelope from the pile. April hesitated and bit her lip. Ryan ran his fingers over his envelope's seal, acutely aware of the fact that its contents could completely change his life . . . or, at least, his standing at Forrester's Department Stores, Inc.

"Before we do this," April blurted, "I have to say— you've really surprised me, Ryan. You rose to the challenge of a wallet-less two weeks, and I'm . . . I'm proud of you."

He looked up in surprise. Her smile seemed shaky, but it warmed him all the same. More than likely, April was as nervous about the sponsorship decisions as he was. And still she had the generosity to compliment his efforts.

It was, Ryan realized suddenly, no less than he would have expected from her. April had helped him—and challenged him—nearly from his first moments in Saguaro Vista, despite knowing his success might mean fewer opportunities for Ambrosia. She truly had a generous spirit.

He breathed in. "Thank you. I—I wasn't sure I could do it, you know," he admitted. "Stand on my own two feet. Ditch the Forrester family safety net. Go it alone without the help of James Earl Jones."

April wrinkled her forehead. "James Earl Jones?"

"Someday I'll tell you the whole story." A smile edged onto his face, and Ryan scooted closer to her on the unconventional sofa. "The important thing is, you're proud of me. And I'm proud of me, too. I proved something to myself these past two weeks. I have you to thank for it."

Her expression brightened. She squeezed his hand. Then, as though mere hand-holding wasn't enough, April wrapped both arms around him and hugged. Two suspicious-sounding sniffles came from the vicinity of his shoulder, where she'd laid her head.

"You're welcome," she said, her tone hoarse.

Clearing her throat, April straightened. Moisture gleamed in her eyes, but she swiped it away with the back of her hand. She gave a self-conscious–sounding laugh.

"See?" she said. "A few words from you, and I'm a complete mushball."

"You were already a complete mushball."

She shook her head, but Ryan wasn't fooled. He'd never known anyone more kindhearted than April— however much she tried to hide it behind flashy vintage clothes and a sassy attitude. He counted himself lucky to have met her.

Suddenly, a new thought struck him. What if reading these sponsorship decisions changed things between them?

He didn't want to lose the camaraderie they'd found, the attraction they shared . . . the easy laughter that flowed so warmly between them. April had come to mean a lot to him. He didn't want to lose *her*.

They looked at each other. With a jerk, Ryan put down his envelope. April put down hers, too.

"What do you say we have dinner first?" he asked.

"These can wait a little while," she said at the same moment.

They laughed. All at once, the mood between them lightened. April sniffled and squeezed his hand again. Ryan slung his arm around her shoulders and tugged her close. A few minutes later, he nuzzled her temple and spoke.

"So, how does grilled fajitas sound for dinner? My treat."

"Your treat?" She arched her brows. "Since you're temporarily wallet-less, I presume you mean your treat as in, you cook, we eat, I rave?"

He nodded, and couldn't resist kissing her neck.

"Mmmm." April looked cheered. "I've never had a date who cooked dinner for me before."

"You might not have one now, depending on your definition of 'dinner.' I'll try to make it edible, but . . ."

She rolled her eyes. "I'm sure it will be scrumptious. And I did wonder what was in the bag you stuck in the fridge when you got here."

"Chicken, peppers, tortillas . . . I bartered my Diamondbacks season tickets to Coach Haffy for some groceries—*and* his tutelage at the barbecue grill."

April nodded toward the portable hibachi and bag of briquettes Ryan had stashed just inside her front door. "And for the use of his grilling equipment?"

"That was extra. Our first couple of lessons went . . . awry. After the flambéed pork loin and the curly charred hot dogs, Coach Haffy needed a little extra assurance."

"In the form of . . . ?"

He glanced away. "A ballroomdancelesson."

"What?"

"A ballroom dance lesson," Ryan repeated reluctantly. "Coach Haffy and his wife are going to a wedding in Scottsdale next month. Jason was worried he would embarrass himself by not knowing how to dance at the reception. So I taught him a few ballroom dance moves."

April grew silent. She gazed around the living room, as though imagining Ryan and the burly coach waltzing through it. She grinned. "Awww. That's so sweet of you."

"Yeah, well." *It will be worth it, if my cooking skills impress you.* "It got the job done. Now I make a mean chicken fajita, believe me."

After only seven tries, too.

Her smile broadened, as though April found barbecue lessons unbelievably endearing. Ryan elected *not* to tell her about the tequila marinade he'd mistakenly served up as mixed drinks. The shrimp kebab torches. The exploding baked potatoes. Instead, he got up and got busy.

He was carrying the hibachi and briquettes toward the sliding glass doors leading from April's kitchen to her tiny backyard patio when she called his name. Ryan stopped.

He glanced over his shoulder. She still sat at the sofa, contemplating the pile of sealed sponsorship-decision envelopes. Thoughtfully, April tapped one of them against her chin.

"You know, technically these should all belong to you," she said. "After all, you went a whole two weeks without pulling out your wallet for anything. You won our bet."

He shook his head. "The stakes weren't fair."

"But you won! And I'm not a welsher."

"You can't just hand over those sponsorships to me," Ryan insisted. "They're not yours to give. Some of those merchants undoubtedly chose Ambrosia."

April shrugged. "I'll tell them our community-building program is taking a little longer to get going than I expected. And then I'll suggest they partner with Forrester's in the meantime." Her expression turned stubborn. "So, see? We don't even need to open these envelopes. Congratulations!"

Ryan let the bag of briquettes sag against his chest. "April, some of them should be yours. You did a terrific job representing Ambrosia. I—"

"No excuses," she interrupted brightly, holding up

her palm. "You won fair and square. I insist. After all, it's" —her face paled and her hand trembled, but she forged onward— "it's not as though my job depends on these sponsorships. *Yours* does."

Looking at her, he felt confused. Her voice sounded a little uneven, but her expression was a curious mix of determination, pride, and . . . and *love?*

Surely he had this wrong, Ryan told himself, suddenly awash in a jumble of emotions he couldn't begin to label. Surely, despite his feelings for her, April hadn't fallen for him, just like that. Surely—

"We'll open them after we eat," he said, taking refuge in something certain. The rest, they'd deal with later. He angled his head toward the sliding glass doors in an invitation for April to join him outside.

"Now, come on," Ryan said. "I need someone to make sure I don't set my eyebrows on fire."

From the backyard, the sounds of Ryan singing while he toasted marshmallows for s'mores drifted in through the patio doors. Inside, April strode through the cool dimness of her living room, having snuck away to floss bell peppers from her teeth. She cupped her hand against her mouth and blew into it, testing the effectiveness of her minty mouthwash.

All good. With flutters of nervousness whirling inside her, she strode past the TV, headed outside again. Dinner had been delicious, if a *teensy* bit overdone, the s'mores for dessert would be even better, and afterward . . . well, Mission Thong was a "go."

The heated looks she and Ryan had shared over the spicy fajitas still had April feeling revved-up. By all indications, her *chef du jour* felt the same way. She'd never wanted a man the way she wanted Ryan. Wholeheartedly. Enthusiastically.

Nakedly.

Spurred onward by the thought, she picked up the pace. As she passed the ottoman coffee table, her gaze happened upon the pile of sponsorship-decision envelopes. Just like that, April's spirits fell. *Why* was Ryan insisting on opening them? She'd done all she could to convince him that wasn't necessary, but he'd refused to listen.

For a man who'd accomplished things he'd never thought himself capable of before coming to Saguaro Vista, Ryan Forrester could be remarkably dense sometimes, April decided. Couldn't he tell when a person was trying to do him a favor?

She wanted to see him kick booty with the Forrester's board, those cretins who'd called his plan to enter the family business "idiot savant retailing." She wanted to reward Ryan for persevering when he'd undoubtedly felt a little ... well, naked without his wallet. She wanted—and really, everything came down to this—to make him happy.

But how could she, if he refused to win?

Tilting her head toward the back door, April listened. Strains of a sappy love song drifted inside, interrupted briefly by a curse and a soft, charred-marshmallow-on-concrete *plop*. It sounded as though Ryan was still manfully struggling with the s'mores.

His efforts touched her. And now, looking back over the time they'd spent together, April recognized all the other things, large and small, he'd done to woo her. The flowers. The picnic. The jokes and the kisses. The putting up with her oddball family. Everything Ryan had done meant so much to her.

Being with him meant so much to her.

How could she let him be crushed by the inevitable outcome of those sponsorship decisions?

Biting her lip, April sat on the sofa. She scanned the

pile of envelopes. Undoubtedly, she figured, she—on behalf of Ambrosia—would win most of the bids. After all, she'd worked hard. Her presentations had been good. And when it came right down to it, Ryan was an outsider. Given the choice, Saguaro Vista would support their own.

Even if "their own" was a flighty Finnegan.

Another chorus of Ryan's song—and the scent of burnt marshmallows—wafted inside. And in that moment, April realized the truth: she loved him. *She loved Ryan.* Loved his thoughtfulness and his good cheer, his sexy sizzle and his knack with a gourmet breakfast. During their time together, meeting with him throughout the mornings and afternoons had become the highlight of her days.

She couldn't hurt him with the truth, April decided as she picked up the first of the envelopes. And she couldn't bear to see Ryan brought low, when he'd tried so hard to succeed. She knew now that achieving great things with his community-building plan meant more to him than she'd realized. Much more. Ryan *needed* that success.

I proved something to myself these past two weeks. I have you to thank for it.

When she'd first suggested their wager—impulsively, April would be the first to admit—she'd never expected it to come to this. She'd been certain she would win— certain she'd *want* to win. But now . . . well, things had changed. *She'd* changed.

Remembering everything Ryan had told her earlier this evening, April glanced toward the patio again. He deserved nothing but the best. He deserved to feel he'd accomplished his goals.

She slit open the first envelope and read the decision

inside. Frowning, she opened another. Another. Soon, the sofa pillows beside April were piled with two stacks of sponsorship decisions—Forrester's Department Store on the left, Ambrosia on the right. The piles teetered unevenly as she leaned forward to pick up the last envelope. They righted again.

April held the envelope, running her fingers over its seal the same way Ryan had earlier. They'd both been equally reluctant to learn this decision—that much had been obvious. Now, April found herself even more reluctant to have things change between them because of it.

Well, that won't happen, April assured herself as she opened the final envelope. *I simply won't let it.*

She scanned the short message. Stunned, April read it again. Then she crumpled it against her heart, and blinked to hold back the tears welling in her eyes.

She'd done it. The Ambrosia stack was taller than the Forrester's stack. Despite everything, Saguaro Vista had chosen *her.*

It was almost too much to take in. Too much to believe. And it meant even more to April than she'd expected, to know she could have succeeded.

Could have . . . because picking up several envelopes from the Ambrosia stack, April carried them to the kitchen and hastily stuffed them into a cupboard until she had time to hide them properly. If Ryan saw them, he'd never accept his victory—and he'd never be happy, either. And no matter what else happened, April meant for him to be happy. Even if that meant temporarily giving up her first community-relations victory—and it looked as though it did.

Well, so be it, April decided as she shut the cupboard door and headed outside again. It was the least she could do for Ryan's sake . . . for the man she loved.

The first raindrop caught Ryan by surprise. It fell from the darkening evening sky, and landed on his wrist as he handed April her second s'more.

"I *love* these," she said, thanking him as she accepted it.

She took a bite, inadvertently shattering her graham crackers and sending crumbs flying onto the dimly lit patio underfoot. After chewing and swallowing, April swiped at a blob of melted chocolate with pure enjoyment and licked her finger clean. "Delicious."

"I aim to please," Ryan said. He squinted at the fast-moving gray clouds swirling overhead. Several more raindrops sizzled onto the hibachi's hot wire grid. In a few minutes, they'd have to move inside. "I'm glad you like them."

"I do." She grinned. "Almost as much as I like you."

"I win out over chocolate?" He nodded toward the discarded Hershey bar wrappers wadded on the plastic table in the patio's corner. "Not every woman would go that far. I'm impressed."

"So am I. *Obviously.*"

He finished his s'more in three bites, inordinately pleased with the dessert Coach Haffy's wife had suggested for tonight—and with April's reaction to it, too. It had taken him a few tries to get the hang of toasting the marshmallows—and not turning them into miniature blowtorches—but Ryan had prevailed. In the end, the expression of delight on April's face had been worth every minute.

Because really, all he wanted was one thing: to make April happy. That was what this night was all about.

If he was lucky, she'd never realize how many of the super-puffed marshmallows he'd accidentally dropped onto the patio—and scraped off with the long-handled spatula afterward. And it looked as though he *was* lucky, because April had stayed inside during much of that time, doing, he guessed, whatever primping things women did between dinner and dessert.

Thoughtfully, he looked at her. Something *was* different about her, but Ryan couldn't pinpoint what it was. Her face fairly glowed with ... *something*. An inner knowledge. A certain surety. And her eyes—well, April had the most beautiful, the most expressive eyes he'd ever seen. They were beautiful because of the warmth behind them, he thought. That, and something more.

Several curly strands of her hair were lifted in the breeze. They swirled around her shoulders, sparked by the porch light's glow. Although their barbecue spot was only a simple concrete slab a few steps down from her apartment's back door, April inhabited it as though it were the most romantic party spot ever.

As he watched, she finished her s'more and gave a little "mmm" of contentment. Then the raindrops suddenly increased. She yelped with surprise as several plunked onto her head and shoulders.

"Yikes! Rain!" she cried.

As though she'd cued it with her words, the downpour really got going. Ryan braced himself for the inevitable flap of arms over her head to protect her hairdo, for the shriek of dismay as her clothes got wetter.

To his surprise, neither came. Instead, April laughed out loud with childlike glee. Arms spread, palms up, she stepped deeper into her apartment's small allotment of yard space. She twirled. Then suddenly she stopped, peering at something through the dusky light and continuing downpour.

"Coach Haffy's grill!" she said, lunging for it. "We can't let it get ruined."

April grabbed the hibachi by its stay-cool plastic handles and hefted it upward, wincing at the tendrils of acrid smoke that rose from the rain-struck coals. Carrying it, she hurried toward shelter.

It was just like her, Ryan thought as he stowed the leftover tortillas and graham crackers safely in a plastic bag, to be more concerned with her friend's hibachi than with her own well-being, or her coiffure. He watched as she nudged open the sliding glass doors with her elbow, then leaned over to set the grill down inside the small dining area. He barely had a moment to admire the perfect shape of her derriere before she whirled back again, obviously intent on rescuing more of Coach Haffy's barbecue supplies.

Ryan intercepted her just as April straightened with the open bag of briquettes in her arms. Their bodies collided, crushing the bag between them. Rain showered them both, coming faster now in true, late spring–storm fashion.

Blinking, April looked up at him through the silvery light. A raindrop slid down her nose. He felt a ridiculous urge to lick it off.

So he did.

"Wha . . . ?" she asked.

"I want to kiss you," Ryan said, blinking against the downpour. He cradled her cheek in his hand, unable to reach the rest of her because of the briquette bag. He'd meant to help her, to take the bag from her, but the minute their bodies touched, all rational thought was lost to him. "I need to kiss you."

Her smile was awe-inspiring. "You need to kiss me?"

He nodded. Rain slid down the back of his neck, and glued his clothes to his body. It felt warm, and a little soothing—like the old-fashioned rain showerheads at his favorite resort.

"I *need* to kiss you," Ryan repeated. "Now."

"Okay." Just like that, April dropped the briquette bag.

It landed with a thud on the rain-soaked concrete patio. Chunks of charcoal rolled around their feet.

Neither of them cared.

Putting his other palm to her face, Ryan urged her closer. He lowered his mouth to hers, and discovered a heat that existed wholly separately from his body or from hers. It was a heat generated only by their coming together, and it spread through him with a speed he wouldn't have thought possible.

With a moan, April returned his kiss. Her hands roved over his shoulders, his waist, his backside, and still she crowded closer. Sensations rushed at him all at once, too welcome and too myriad to categorize immediately. The sexy curve of her hip. The taste of her mouth. The soft slap of her wet curls against the backs of his hands. The fresh scent of the soap she'd used, amplified by the drizzling rain. The mesmerizing sound of her pleasure, as April responded to his kiss.

It was all too much ... and Ryan couldn't wait for more.

But he'd have to, he realized. He couldn't breathe.

Gasping, they broke apart. He looked at her. She looked at him. Both of them panted as though they'd run a mile uphill, just to arrive at this moment.

The rain pelted them. It pinged against the adobe exterior wall, snaked in rivulets around the edge of the patio, was eagerly sucked up by the dry ground beyond. It showed no sign of stopping, but by now they were both too wet to care.

Ryan glanced at the scattered briquettes, which were currently dissolving into black streaks on the concrete. The bag lay on its side nearby. He looked at April.

"You dropped everything to kiss me," he said. *"Literally."*

"You kissed me in the rain," she said at the same moment.

Staring, they both backed up a step. Ryan didn't grasp the significance of her "kissed me in the rain" comment, but April didn't sound at all displeased by having experienced it, so he chose to let that go. Besides, he had more pressing things to think about. Because he *did* know what *he'd* meant.

All I've ever wanted, he'd told Jackson on that long-ago day while describing his ideal woman, *is a woman who will drop whatever she's doing, no matter what it is, when I want to kiss her.*

April was that woman.

She dropped everything when he kissed her. She smiled hugely when she saw him. She fit every hoped-for qualification for the woman of his dreams, including remembering what he liked for breakfast. And looking at her now, Ryan hoped April would have an opportunity to use that last skill. *Soon.* He hoped to wake up with her tomorrow, after a long night of—

He kissed her again, driven to it by an urge he couldn't resist any longer. Their mouths met, hungry and eager. Their wet bodies pushed together, sharing warmth despite the rain that continued to fall. April's hands were everywhere—on his back, his chest, at the hem of his shirt. Her palms slid inside, past his abs and upward, pushing up his clothes with their movements. Cooler air and rainy drizzle whisked over his exposed skin, but Ryan didn't care. April was in his arms, and that was all that mattered.

She kissed him back with a fervor he found wildly exciting . . . and incredibly moving. Heart and soul, April gave herself to him, and he could do nothing but take the gift she offered—and hope he had as much to offer her. No matter what, Ryan vowed, he would make this night a memorable one for April. He would love her and pleasure her, and they would both—

"You are one incredible kisser," she murmured. "I never knew—I never realized—I mean, *wow.*"

Urgently, she wrapped her leg around his, trying to get closer still. The motion sent sprinkles of rainwater from her sarong-style skirt to the patio underfoot, and parted the colorful, rain-spotted fabric to reveal a sensuous length of her bare thigh. Groaning, Ryan wrapped his hand around it. His fingertips grazed the back of her knee, and edged higher.

Their joining deepened, as intimate as his dreams and twice as hot. Holding April close, Ryan tasted rain and need as he kissed her. He'd wanted this for a very long time, he realized; possibly since he'd first spoken with her, and definitely since he'd first felt her casually touch him.

There was nothing casual about her touch now. April's caresses were deliberate, and sexy, and just aggressive enough to thrill him. She continued exploring beneath his shirt, wedging the fabric beneath his arms as she stroked him. She pressed tiny bites to his neck and sensitive earlobe, rubbed her chest against his.

"Mmmm. That feels amazing." Panting, Ryan used his free hand to trail over her neck, past her shoulder, lower to her breast. There, he hesitated. The view, he decided after a moment's hazy contemplation, was simply too good to miss.

He looked. Leisurely. And wasn't disappointed.

Rainwater molded April's skirt and skimpy midriff-baring T-shirt to her body, revealing the subtle curve of her waist. The delicate rise of her breasts. The rigid points of her nipples. It struck him suddenly that April was living proof a woman didn't need to be built like a centerfold to look feminine—and wildly exciting. She was . . . perfect. Exactly as she was, right now.

Exactly as she would be, Ryan decided, forever.

"You're beautiful," he murmured.

"I'm dripping," she confided.

He smiled at her matter-of-fact rebuttal, knowing exactly how wrong April was. She *was* beautiful to him. And in the midst of this electric moment, she'd managed to draw him even closer, in a uniquely April way. Ryan rested his forehead against hers, and looked deeply into her eyes.

"So am I," he said. Raindrops parted his hair in new and plastered-down styles. "I don't care."

She dragged a hank of hair from his brow. "I couldn't *be* any wetter."

He paused. Slowly, Ryan flexed his fingers and raised her thigh a little higher against him. Her sarong fell open farther.

"Oh, yes," he said, gazing at the sleek bare skin his movement had revealed from mid-thigh nearly to her hip. *"You could."*

April's eyes widened. Then darkened, as she realized what he meant. A wonderful sassy smirk edged onto her lips. "I didn't mean *that.*"

"I did."

She trembled, not moving from their intimate position. It was a close-knit mambo for two, a shower-soaked vertical tease, and no matter how much of it he enjoyed, Ryan wanted more.

He wanted *her.*

"I might have to ask you to prove that claim," April said, breathlessly.

"Happy to demonstrate." He kissed her, then flexed his fingertips against her thigh. Her skin felt silky, her muscles long and resilient and strong. "In more private circumstances, of course. I don't intend to share you. Not even with curious neighbors and their binoculars."

She jerked up her head, opening her eyes wide. Squinting through the rain as though she'd just at that moment remembered where they were, April gazed at the patio, the briquette streaks, the remaining stories of the drenched apartment building looming above them.

"Inside," she commanded, and Ryan felt himself being pulled, dripping and eager, through the patio doors to the apartment beyond.

Chapter Seventeen

Stepping from the rain shower into the . . . well, the *shower* shower made sense at the time April thought of it. She'd hauled Ryan inside her kitchen. Shut the patio door behind them. Flung herself onto his soggy, mostly-dressed body in an effort to keep their sexy groove going. And the results had been remarkable.

Until.

Until the air-conditioning turned on, catching them both in a seventy-two-degree artificial cold front. April's teeth had chattered. The impressively developed muscles in Ryan's arms and shoulders and chest—revealed now that she'd cast aside his pesky shirt—had developed goose bumps. They'd both shivered.

One and a half minutes later, April had turned off the A/C and implemented her solution. Which was how they came to be in her tiny bathroom's shower, semi-dressed and kissing as luxurious hot water poured over them both.

"Ahhhh, this is better," Ryan said when their kiss ended.

With his back to the spray, he spread out his arms, looking like the sexiest water god imaginable. If, that is, water gods wore nothing but plastered-on khaki pants— they'd kicked off their shoes before jumping in the shower—and a devilish smile. Water sparked from his skin toward the slippery wall tiles and bounced onto April's head.

Ryan pulled her close and swiveled, thoughtfully putting her into the showerhead's path—despite April's insistence that he, as the guest, should have the most pleasurable spot. As the water's touch replaced the chilly air, warmth poured over her.

It felt heavenly. *He* felt heavenly. Ryan was a considerate seducer, a friendly lover, a hunky fantasy-in-the-making. And just for tonight, April thought, he was *hers*.

She couldn't ask for anything more—except more. Couldn't dream of anything more perfect—except more. Couldn't possibly hope for anything, she reminded herself, beyond this night—except she did.

Damn it! There was no point in wishing Ryan loved her. He wanted to *love her*, and for now, that would have to be enough.

In the spirit of that thought, April put her hands on his water-slicked shoulders and pulled him into the spray along with her. Warm water sluiced over their bodies. Their moans and sighs echoed from the tiles. Her soaked sarong glued itself to her legs, making movement difficult. She persevered anyway, distracting herself from her lack of easy mobility by focusing on Ryan. And on getting rid of his pants.

"Your zipper's stuck," she murmured, panting past his ear as she wrestled with the fastening. They kissed. Moaned. Exploratively, she moved her hand lower.

Stroked him. "There's something . . . huge and hard in the way, I think."

At the feel of him, excitement swirled inside her. A gentle pulse took up residence between her thighs, and throbbed further as she discovered the full breadth and length of the, er, *obstacle* at hand.

"I hope it doesn't come as too much of a shock," Ryan ground out in a low voice. His hips arched forward an inch, the movement seeming wholly involuntary and completely sexy. "I'd hate for you to be disappointed."

"Disappointed?" April scoffed. "I'm disappointed like a spoon is disappointed to dive into a pint of Chunky Monkey. That's how 'disappointed' I am."

He paused. Looked straight at her. A puzzled frown appeared between Ryan's brows. "Chunky Monkey? That's good, I hope."

She couldn't believe he'd never tasted—had apparently never even *heard* of—Ben & Jerry's super-premium banana nut ice cream, and told him so. "You have a whole *world* of things to explore with me, don't you?" April asked.

Or at least, you would . . . if you were staying.

Which, of course, he wasn't.

To divert herself from that troubling thought, she kissed him again, and discovered Ryan tasted better than any ice cream imaginable. *He* was her favorite flavor.

"Let's start right now," she said. "Discovering those things, I mean."

And then I can keep them close to my heart, after you've gone.

Damn it! Stop that!

"I have an idea." Thoughtfully, Ryan looked at her. A slow, promising smile edged onto his mouth, one that distinctly caused her knees to weaken. "Let's pretend you're the ice cream. And I'm the spoon. And I can't *wait* to taste you."

He kissed her in demonstration, beginning with her mouth and moving lower. By the time he'd reached the scooped neckline of her black T-shirt, April was already trembling with need. She clamped both hands on his head and stopped him long enough to catch her breath.

"Spoons don't kiss," she said as an excuse. "Or lick. Or give those little love bites you're so good at, or—"

"Stop poking holes in my metaphor," Ryan ordered with mock sternness. He lifted the hem of her T-shirt and nodded for her to raise her arms. "It's working for me."

It was working for her, also. *Boy, was it working.* That's why April obediently raised her arms. She might have danced a cha-cha, too, if he'd asked her to. Anything. Everything.

Her T-shirt sailed over the curtain. Shower water cascaded past her shoulders, flowing over her breasts in a way that made her acutely aware of the fact that she was now dressed from the waist up in approximately— merely—eight square inches of fabric. In front of her, Ryan stared at the two black silk triangles covering . . . no, revealing . . . no, *featuring* her breasts. His gaze darkened.

"Very nice," he said.

His voice was thick. The raspy sound of it made her no-discount, full-retail-price-only bra *completely* worthwhile.

"You think so?" April raised her arms overhead and struck a brazen pose, doing her best to affect an airy casualness. Unfortunately, airy casualness was utterly at odds with the lust thrumming its way through her. She wasn't sure she could pull it off, but she tried.

She gestured toward her bra. "This is just something I bought the other day. You know, a little—"

"Not the bra." He looked into her eyes. *"You."*

"Oh."

She was lost. *Lost,* she realized as Ryan took her into

his arms again. His spoon technique continued, until even April had to admit his metaphor was worthy. They kissed. He kissed. She clutched him tight against her and kissed him until she was breathless. *More, more, more* was all she could think. And Ryan provided it.

He solved her zipper problem by quickly shedding his clothes. Then, with a "Just so we're approximately even," he untied her sarong. Given the distraction of his newly revealed nude lower body to contemplate, April didn't complain as he unwrapped her skirt and draped its colorful fabric haphazardly over the curtain rod. Splaying one hand against the tile for support, Ryan pulled her against him again.

Gladly, April came. His direct look all but commanded it. She felt free—free and daring and in love. No matter that she was dressed only in her new bra and panties. No matter that she was hardly supermodel material, and her man magnet ta-tas had never arrived. She didn't care. Not when Ryan's kiss made her dizzy. And definitely not when his free hand, moving leisurely from her breast to her waist and lower, made her moan.

"A thong?" A rakish grin lit his face as his fingers encountered the T-shaped strip of black panty and then, bare skin. "Sexy. Turn around."

A thrill raced through her. She did.

He looked. For a moment, the only sound was water falling from the showerhead, swirling past their feet. Then there was a low rumble of appreciation, and Ryan captured her hips to pull her against him. April encountered the thick weight of his erection against her backside, felt the searing heat where their wet skin touched. Suddenly, she wanted, wanted—

Wanted to turn around, first of all. She wiggled.

"Did you wear that for me?" he asked, holding her fast. Sounding breathless.

"Yes," she said. "Yessss, I—"

He cupped her breasts from behind, making her gasp. Okay, so maybe staying put had its advantages, April decided, writhing beneath his loving touch. Maybe she'd just—

"I love it," Ryan said against her ear, letting his fingers slide past her rib cage. They marked a slow trail, each touch a tiny caress. His thumbs traced her risqué panties' satiny side strips, teasing her.

"You do?" she managed. "You love it?"

She felt him nod. "Almost as much," he promised, "as I'm going to love seeing you out of it."

Happily, April pivoted, kissing him as the water continued to pour over them. She felt soaked to the skin, drenched in desire and heat. Driven by those feelings and more, she reached for her bra's front clasp. Unfastened it. Savored the heightened interest in Ryan's eyes as she flung the scrap of black satin past the curtain.

"Yep," he said, indulging himself with an unhurried look. "I *love* seeing you out of it."

He smiled wickedly, and her heart turned over. Her inner sex goddess applauded. Feeling sultry, and more than a little crazy about him, April smiled. She gave her shoulders a little shimmy.

His eyes nearly crossed. Geez, but she loved this man.

"There's still more to go," she said, gesturing toward her panties. "But let's see how halfway suits you."

Wasting no time in accepting her invitation, Ryan touched her bare breasts. Reverently. Expertly. And with, April discovered, an absolutely maddening sense of leisure.

Long minutes after baring herself to him, April found herself quivering in Ryan's strong grasp, silently arching her back in a plea for him to lower his mouth to her breasts and . . . *ahhhh*. With a guttural moan, she buried her fingers in the sodden strands of his hair, and held him to her as he fulfilled her unspoken desire.

"You taste delicious," he murmured much later, tilting his head sideways to look up at her.

She caught the affectionate glimmer in his eyes, the sexy assurance of his water-spangled half-smile. Looking like a man wholly devoted to her pleasure, Ryan circled her taut nipple with his tongue, then sucked. "Mmmmm."

His eyes closed. His cheeks darkened, suffused with a passionate flush that doubtless matched her own. If their shower had cooled after these long minutes, April didn't notice it—their bodies more than made up for any lack of heat.

In the moments that followed, Ryan drove her mad with wanting; April felt determined to return the favor. With eager hands she explored the man before her, testing the breadth of his body, the masculine texture of his skin, the wonderful feel of his carefully honed muscles.

There was no doubt about it, she decided—Ryan was magnificently built. Wide in the shoulders and strong all over, he had perfect proportions, and exactly the right amount of wiry golden hair to embellish them. Naked, he was only more gorgeous . . . more manly, in every way.

Focusing on a favorite of those *manly* attributes, April brought her hands from the solidity of Ryan's chest to the intriguing indentations near his hipbones, then lower. Drawing in an anticipation-filled breath, she wrapped her fingers around the steely length of him.

His body pulsed in response. Unbelievably, he grew even larger, even harder, in her grasp. Groaning, Ryan shivered at her touch, his mouth momentarily stilled on her breasts. He straightened as though enraptured, his eyes closed in concentration. Too aroused to miss his intimate kiss for long, April seized the opportunity to indulge her other senses, too.

She inhaled a deep, steamy breath. The scents of soap and man filled her. Her gaze focused on the rivulets of water running past Ryan's shoulders and snaking sinuously down his chest. Raptly, she followed one bead of water on its journey south, watching as it passed over well-defined abs and slipped into the darker hair at his groin.

She looked lower.

His penis jutted from her fist, large and thick and excitingly aroused. There could be no doubt that Ryan wanted her as much as she wanted him. The knowledge both thrilled and scared her. Loving Ryan was a temptation April would have been wiser to avoid; now, with the weight of his interest solid against her palm, she could no more deny herself than she could stop touching him. Casting aside her fears, she stroked him lovingly, stepping even closer so their bodies could glide together fully beneath the shower's spray.

"You look amazing," she told him, the words nothing but truth. "You *feel* amazing. So sexy and strong. Nothing has ever felt better to me, *ever*, than your body against mine."

With a self-conscious half-grin, he looked away, surprising her. It was obvious Ryan was pleased—and equally obvious he hadn't expected her praise. April would have sworn a man as unabashedly gorgeous as Ryan would have known it . . . but if the way he grasped the nape of her neck and hauled her nearer for a kiss was any indication, being openly adored embarrassed him.

Her water god, it seemed, was a little on the shy side. *Imagine that.*

She decided to address the issue.

"You'd better get used to being admired," April told him when they parted. She swept her tongue over his lower lip, then delved inside again. "Because I intend to *admire* you all over."

A tremor shook him. Thrilled to know how strongly she affected him, April tried another kiss. "All over," she repeated. "All over, all over, all—"

"Good," Ryan rasped. Their gazes met, his both loving and filled with promise. "Because I intend to return the favor."

"Good," she teased, tingling. "Because I *want* you to."

"Oh, God, April." Releasing a long sigh, Ryan tangled his fingers in her hair to tilt her head back for another, hotter kiss. "I *need* you. I've needed you forever."

As though her murmured assent had the power to make wishes real, Ryan maneuvered them both against the shower's wall. With an aggressiveness April welcomed, he pressed her against it, still kissing her. His hands were everywhere . . . on her breasts, her belly, her hips. Wet satin slipped past her thighs and calves as he deftly removed her panties, letting them fall to the tile.

April parted her legs. She curled her toes against the shower floor, seeking purchase. Twining her arms around Ryan's shoulders, she gave herself to their next kiss. It went on and on, sweetened by his murmured praise and by the continued touch of his hands on her hips. His fingers delved lower, slipped between her trembling thighs, discovered the heat within—and an excited slickness that owed nothing to the shower and everything to Ryan.

Closing her eyes, April let her head loll to the side. Water spilled over her shoulder and scattered droplets onto her cheek, then cascaded down her body in a sensuous fall. Erotic tension wound her tighter and tighter . . . the whole world narrowed to the gentle stroking of Ryan's fingers, the subtle swelling and pulsing his movements caused.

They moaned in unison. April grappled for a tighter hold, feeling her legs weaken. Ryan whispered loving words, somehow finding every slick, sensitized part of her. It was as though he sensed exactly what she wanted, what she needed—and then devoted himself to giving it to her. Trembling beneath his touch, April felt her breath coming faster and faster.

"I love the way you feel," Ryan murmured, sounding all but undone with desire and need. "So soft, so hot, so *good.*"

His words compelled her onward, spiraling her orgasm ever closer. Desperate to have him, she closed her fingers around his heated body and guided him nearer. His penis's slippery head rubbed intimately against her, and they both groaned aloud.

"Please," April begged. "I need—I need—"

"I need you," he said.

His head tilted backward, exposing the powerful column of his throat. Water trickled over his skin, trailing downward to the place where their bodies were nearly joined. Gasping, Ryan guided both big hands to her derriere. He cupped her, raised her, braced her body against his lean, strong hips . . . entered her.

Their union was ecstasy. Nearly overwhelmed by it, April felt her body shudder uncontrollably. She pulsed in secret welcome, beyond anything but the feel of this man inside her and the joy in her heart as she loved him. Blissfully, she tilted her hips forward.

Ryan stilled the motion. "Wait . . . wait," he whispered. "I want to feel . . ." He kissed her, urgently. "I— it's you. I need to remember, because it's you."

It's you. Tears prickled her eyes and scratched her throat. Holding him close, April felt their hearts pounding together, felt their bodies expand as they gasped for breath.

"I'll always remember," she murmured. "Love me. Please."

Their foreheads touched; their gazes met. In Ryan's, she glimpsed a deep affection, a growing need . . . and knew that those same feelings must be reflected in her eyes, too.

His smile flashed, anticipatory and wholly male. "Hold on."

His warning still echoed from the shower walls when his first thrust came, long and slow and incredible. Again and again Ryan filled her, then withdrew, then came into her again. April rocked her hips against his, arousal sparking higher than before. She couldn't believe how he held her in his hands against him, how he took care to make sure she felt good, how he kissed her amid the downpour of water, in a way both seductive and romantic.

"Yes . . . yes!" she cried, raking his back with urgent fingers. "Oh . . . *ahhh*."

Ryan's moans sounded with hers, throaty and needful. His thrusts increased, pinning her decadently between the tiled wall and his hot, hard body. April clutched at him as the first waves of her orgasm shook her; sensing her release, Ryan let his movements grow increasingly frenzied. Blissfully, she urged him onward.

His grasp on her backside tightened. With a roar of pleasure, Ryan stiffened. Even as April's tremors began to fade, he quaked in the throes of a powerful release. Then, together, they slumped against the wall, spent and gasping.

Ahhh. Rumbling with contentment, Ryan buried his face against the damp curve of her neck. Several moments swept past, during which April was aware of nothing but the satisfied feeling of having loved—and having been loved—thoroughly and well. A wide smile slipped onto her face, and she kissed Ryan's shoulder.

Slowly, he released her, helping her stand on the tiled floor. Their bodies wobbled uncontrollably; for some reason this struck them both as hilarious.

"I may never stand unassisted again," April said, grabbing for Ryan as her knees buckled. Her goofy grin never left her. "What have you done to me?"

"The same thing you've done to me." Ryan's grin matched hers, goofy meeting goofier. "My ears are ringing."

"Mine, too! I thought that was the phone."

"If it was, it can wait. Awww, April." An expression of intense caring warmed his face. Ryan cupped his hand loosely and ran his knuckles over her cheek, his gesture tender. "I don't know what I did to deserve this night. To deserve *you*."

She took a breath, trying to restore her tilt-a-whirl equilibrium. At the edge of the shower, some of their discarded clothes eddied in the overflow, a shameless testament to their hurried need for each other.

"All you did was be you," she told him. "And that was enough. You're all I need."

Something uncertain darkened his eyes. Hoping to chase it away, April rose on pruney tiptoes and kissed him.

"You, and several aphrodisiac s'mores, of course," she amended playfully. "A girl's got to have her priorities."

Ryan nodded seriously. "You're right."

He turned. Grabbed the shower curtain as though to pull it aside.

"Hang on!" April said. "Where are you going?"

His over-the-shoulder grin was seductive. "To blowtorch more marshmallows, of course. When it comes to his dream girl, a guy's got to have his priorities straight, too.''

She hauled him back in, *dream girl* whirling crazily in her head. If she was his dream girl, and he was her dream man, then together the two of them were . . .

Impossible, April decided sadly. Wishing for a future with Ryan was like wishing Hershey bars were calorie-free: understandable, but useless.

Still, while he was here . . . "I'll get your priorities straight," she said with a wink, grabbing the bar of soap nearby and working up a bubbly lather with her hands. "But first—"

"First, *you'd* better get ready for round two."

Ryan slipped the soap from her hands, leaving April with nothing to do but spread suds all over his studly, sexy, naked-and-hers-for-the-night body. Not bad work, if a girl could get it. Just watching the bubbles slither down his chest and slide toward his groin, her heartbeat kicked up a notch.

So did Ryan's, apparently. He soaped her from head to toe, diligently and seductively. He sculpted a foam bikini for her, then pivoted to model the soapsuds G-string April fashioned for him. And by the time they were both squeaky clean and the shower was running cold—and making scary enough-is-enough type creaks—they were indeed ready for round two.

After they'd toweled off, April took Ryan's hand. She led him into her bedroom, fully intent on showing him what kind of temptress she could be—while fully dry. Instead, Ryan tumbled her onto the comforter-covered mattress, thoroughly mussed up the pillows and sheets . . . and made her fall even more deeply, more wonderfully, more hopelessly in love—with him.

Chapter Eighteen

Ryan wasn't sure he could move. And he wasn't entirely certain he *wanted* to, either. After all, an entire weekend's worth of lovemaking tended to take its toll on a guy.

Beginning Friday night, he and April had spent every blissful minute together. They hadn't left her bedroom for anything except the necessities—showering, ordering take-out pizzas, laughing over cheesy movies on TV, and devouring midnight bowls of Cap'n Crunch. It had been silly. Wonderful. World-changing. And exhausting—hence Ryan's reluctance to get up and, say, boogie.

But when April leaped up from bed late on Sunday night and padded toward the bedroom door through the wavering light of the stubby candles she'd lit, he seriously considered it.

Moving, that is. Not boogieing. Moving from the bed, to chase April down.

He didn't want her to get away. Not even for a few minutes. Not if it meant losing the head-over-heels, blissful feeling being with her gave him. Not if it meant doing without her. Besides, he was comfortable in April's bedroom. In her space. *In her life.* Everything about her fit him remarkably well . . . except her current getaway plans.

"Hang on," Ryan called. Weakly, he raised his out-flung arm from the mattress. "I think I can go for one more."

Her sassy smile lightened his heart. "Later, He-Man," April said. Candle glow burnished the white satiny chemise she slipped over her head, and deepened the fire in her red curls. "First, I have something to show you."

"Show me? That sounds promising." With a lusty, eager smile, Ryan edged higher in bed until he reached the jumble of pillows. Naked except for a wayward swath of sheet, he waved her onward.

She turned to the door again, leaving him to admire her sleek, endless legs as she left the room. Waiting impatiently, he raised his arms overhead and rested his nape in his cupped palms. "Hurry back," he called.

"Insatiable!" she teased. "I will."

She did, moving with a suppressed eagerness, hugging something against her chest. Not sure what it was, Ryan squinted through the dimness. His body ached pleasantly from loving April, and the languid, satisfied heaviness in his limbs made him reluctant to exert himself further. Unless . . .

"Is that the leftover marshmallows?" he asked, glimpsing a flash of white in her arms. "I could use a little sustenance. I think my blood sugar dropped after that last acrobatic move, and I—"

"Hey, is that a complaint?" Giving him a teasing smile, April knee-walked her way toward him across the mattress. Her mysterious burden made her movements unsteady as she took care to hold onto it. "Because *I* thought that acrobatic move was a big hit. One of my favorites. And nearly as innovative as the one you showed me. In fact, I thought of a variation. After we've looked at these—"

She dropped her bundle. Envelopes scattered over the rumpled bedclothes.

"—we can get started."

Her face glowed with happiness. Gazing at her, Ryan felt an answering gladness fill him, too. Being with April, loving her ... well, it gave him something he hadn't known he was missing, until now. Their weekend together had shown him, more certainly than anything before, that *he*, just as he was, could be enough. Enough for anything.

April had gifted him with that knowledge. She'd kissed it onto his lips, hugged it into his heart, caressed it onto every inch of his body. Without her, Ryan knew, he would still be living life as an empty, endless party. Because of her, from here onward, everything would be different.

He would be different.

"What's this?" he asked, looking at the pile of envelopes in their midst. "Fan mail, already?"

"Nah." She grinned. "I give my kudos in person."

In demonstration, she leaned nearer, bracing herself on her forearms. Her lips touched his, sparking a new heat Ryan wouldn't have thought himself capable of— especially at this point. Helplessly yearning for her, he raised his arms to pull her closer. His palms met silk and skin; his mouth found passion.

Too quickly, April leaned back, sitting on her heels. Her eyes sparkled. "See? That was a 'bravo.' If you want to see a 'yahoo,' just stay where you are and keep smiling at me that way. I'll be yours for the taking."

Ryan lost interest in the envelopes.

" 'Yahoo?' Hah," Ryan scoffed. "*I'm* going for zip-a-dee-doo-dah."

He rolled them both onto the comforter, crushing pillows as he pulled April tight against him. He kissed her, running his hands along the outstretched length of her body. As responsive and exciting as ever, she arched beneath his touch.

Before long, though, she made a reluctant quelling motion with her hands and pulled away. "Actually, if I zip-a-dee-doo-dah one more time, I'm not sure what will happen. Parts of me may go numb with exhaustion," April teased. "It would be some kind of record, for sure."

He waggled his eyebrows. "So we'll call up the Guinness Book people afterward."

"Very funny. But we Finnegans have enough notoriety in this town already, thanks."

Realizing she was serious about stopping—for now—Ryan sat up against the pillows again. April gathered the envelopes she'd brought and snuggled beside him. He watched idly as she sorted through them.

"What kind of notoriety?" he asked.

She stilled. Then concentrated—very obviously, he thought—on squaring the envelopes against her satin-covered lap. "Hmmm?"

"You said the Finnegans had enough notoriety in this town. What kind of notoriety?"

Her cautious gaze shifted toward him. As though deliberating something, April bit her lip. Then she shrugged.

"You've met lots of Finnegans by now," she said offhandedly. "I'm sure you can figure it out. Now" — she held out the envelopes— "it's time for your big moment. Are you ready?"

Glancing at the stack she offered, Ryan recognized at last what those envelopes were. "Those are the sponsorship decisions! I thought we were going to open them together."

"I couldn't wait." She hesitated, a *please understand* look in her eyes. "I opened them on Friday night, and I meant to give them to you then. But I've been a little, um, distracted. By mind-blowing passion. You know how it is."

He loved her teasing. "Oh, *I* know how it is."

Grinning, April waggled the envelope stack. "Go ahead—take them."

He did, but made no move to examine them. "Why didn't you wait?"

Ryan had wanted to be there to comfort her, in case she didn't win the majority of sponsorship decisions. He'd wanted to explain, to offer to share any business opportunities that were relevant to them both. Because despite April's crazy insistence on Friday that he accept all the sponsorships as his prize for winning their wager, Ryan didn't seriously expect to come away from Saguaro Vista with a clean sweep.

"I had a feeling about them. I had to open them." She hugged his bicep between her breasts and cuddled nearer. Her hair spread across his naked chest. "And when I remembered them tonight, I couldn't keep you in suspense any longer."

Suddenly, he *wanted* to be in suspense. Looking at the envelopes that might change his future, Ryan wasn't entirely certain he was ready for the decisions they contained.

What if April had had similar softhearted feelings toward him? What if *she'd* decided to soften the blow of his idiot savant retailing scheme's failure?

Hesitantly, he shuffled through the stack. It had seemed larger, he thought, piled on April's ottoman coffee table two days ago. Or maybe it had just grown in importance in his imagination.

"Well?" Beside him, April gave an impatient bounce. She blew out a breath. "Okay, fine. I'll help you, then."

Before he could react, she slipped the first envelope from the stack and withdrew the note from inside. "Forrester's Department Store!" she read, grabbing for two more. "Forrester's. Forrester's."

Ryan felt too stunned to move. The decisions piled up all around them, increasingly in favor of his community-building plan. A few specified Ambrosia. But again and again, April read "Forrester's." By the time she'd finished, business decisions littered the bed—the majority of them overwhelmingly in favor of Forrester's . . . and Ryan.

"I don't believe it," he said, looking at them now.

"Believe it! You're a winner, *baby*!"

That brought forth a smile. "Your Dick Vitale imitation is terrible."

"Hey, it gets the job done." Grinning, April tossed the last few envelopes in the air. As they rained onto the mattress, she levered herself upward and straddled him. "Congratulations."

Congratulations. He—Good-Time-Guy Ryan Forrester—had actually earned congratulations. On something work-related. Incredible.

"Thank you," he said, feeling dazed. A thought struck him. "And now that our bet's officially over, I guess this means I can finally pay back Jackson for the Winnebago."

Ryan explained about the time he'd spent with Jackson and Lola at the Downtown Grill, about feeling discouraged that he couldn't reimburse his friend the hundred and fifty thousand for the RV . . . about knocking on the Winnebago's door afterward to reveal the truth about his wallet-free two weeks.

"Although what I'm going to do with the Winnebago now, I don't know," he mused, running his hands along April's thighs as she continued to straddle him. "I won't need it back home in San Diego."

"Back . . . home?"

Her voice quavered. Beneath his hands, her body tensed. Ryan decided April must be reacting to their intimate position, and happily expanded his stroking to include her hips. Hey, never let it be said that a mere business achievement turned Ryan Forrester into a less considerate lover.

He nodded.

"Well, now when you go back to San Diego," April said firmly, "you'll be a huge success. Good for you!"

Back to San Diego. Ryan had envisioned the scenario enough times—him, returning triumphant to present to the board of directors; the board applauding his ingenuity—but until this moment he hadn't quite believed in it. His mind whipped into motion, calculating drive times and meeting dates, dictating memos and moving toward the next phase of his business plan.

Feeling increasingly excited, Ryan smiled at her.

"It would be nice to be a huge success," he admitted. "Especially at something besides throwing a terrific opening-night party."

April's smile wobbled. Shadows darkened her eyes, but her voice sounded cheery enough when she spoke. "Well, your wish is my command. Nice job, Mr. Forrester."

She kissed him congratulations. Ryan held her close, still feeling amazed, and happy.

Something new occurred to him. Running his hands up and down her arms in a careful, thoughtful way, he looked up at her.

"What about you?" he asked quietly. "What does this mean for your position at Ambrosia?"

April hesitated atop him. Her solemn look warned of a serious explanation to come, despite the fact that she still straddled him in a celebratory, sexy way. Already missing the lighthearted mood between them, Ryan gave her an encouraging nod.

"Tell me," he said.

Early Monday morning, April was still thinking about Ryan's question—one of the last he'd offered and definitely the last she'd hoped to hear.

What does this mean for your position at Ambrosia?

Now, standing at her kitchen stove with a cookbook propped beside her and a carton of eggs at her elbow, April still wasn't sure she'd handled things correctly. Sure, she'd dissuaded Ryan from prying any further into her job prospects . . . but she hadn't been entirely truthful, in the process.

"My job as community relations manager was a trial run," she'd told him with a dismissive shrug. "A fluke, really. I started at Ambrosia as a baker, and that's what I really do best. I guess I'll go back to it. Full-time again."

If Mark will have me, that is. April wasn't at all sure he would. Those chocolate Adonises had pushed him pretty far.

"And you're happy baking?" Ryan had asked.

"Yes." *Mostly. At least I was, before I sampled a little extra responsibility.* "I am."

His all-too-perceptive look had nearly pulled the whole story from her then. Beneath the lure of Ryan's sympathetic expression, April had almost admitted everything. Her quest to become reliable, responsible, and dependable. Her hopes that her community relations manager job would lead to un-Finneganlike financial security. Her attempts to convince Saguaro Vista that she *wasn't* just another flighty Finnegan.

But then Ryan had pulled her closer, hugging her against his chest. He'd put his arm around her shoulders, and tenderly smoothed the tangled hair from her face. He'd practically vibrated understanding and empathy and caring.

And he'd echoed her thoughts uncannily with his next statement.

"Okay. If you're happy, I'm happy," he'd said . . . and her confessional moment had passed.

In the bright light of the morning after, April figured it was better this way. She wouldn't have Ryan burdened by thinking she'd wound up a failure—and, after all, she *would* bounce back. Finnegans always bounced back. They'd had lots of practice at it.

Doing her best to shore up her resolve, April adjusted the heat beneath her pan. The hollandaise sauce needed butter, egg yolks, and lemon juice. If she could just hunt down a lemon in her nearly empty fridge—

Suddenly, Calypso meowed. An instant later, Ryan was there behind her, freshly showered and wrapping his arms around her waist. He eased her back against him. The unlikely scent of mango shaving cream—hers—combined with the sleek feel of a wonderfully close shave—his, courtesy of a spare Lady Bic—as he nuzzled the side of her neck.

"That smells delicious." He shuffled them both toward the stove, neatly avoiding April's sprawled cat, then peered over her shoulder into the pan. "What is it?"

"Poached eggs." April squinted toward her cookbook. "I think. I'm a baker, not a cooker."

"So *that's* how they do it," Ryan marveled. His wrinkly pants and shirt rustled as he edged nearer. "Looks like egg soup."

She surveyed the frying pan. It was filled to within an inch of the top with simmering water, into which she'd slid the eggs, one at a time. Each one had held together in a roughly oval-shaped mass as it cooked, and they looked nearly done.

"There's coffee over there" —April gestured toward the drip coffeemaker, wishing she'd had some of that gourmet Motor Court Inn stuff to brew for him— "and some powdered creamer, so help yourself. I'm afraid I don't have any rye toast, but I'm about to tackle the hollandaise sauce."

"No need." Looking happy, Ryan tweaked the haphazard ponytail she'd tucked her hair into. He poured coffee into the mug she'd left, then carried April's mint tea to her. "Despite the ferocious appetite we worked up—"

His grin was followed by a steamy kiss.

"—I don't have much time to eat, anyway. I've got to get going."

April abandoned her plans for hollandaise sauce. Now that she knew what went into it, it didn't sound all that appetizing, anyway. But his words were alarming. *Really* alarming. She set down her teacup.

"Going?" she asked, then realized what he must have meant with a burble of relief. "I guess Mark must be wondering what's happened to his temporary roommate, huh? In fact, *I'm* wondering what's happened to *my* temporary roommate. Mickey's never stayed away this long without giving me a call first."

With an absentminded smile, Ryan looked up from his coffee—or from contemplating his first fully lit view of her full-retail-price chemise. April couldn't tell which. But he seemed pleased, all the same.

Definitely the chemise.

She put a little extra sway in her hips as she went to the toaster and popped in two slices of bread. This was cozy, being here with Ryan in the morning. She could almost imagine it happening again and again . . . happening every day, forever.

"Well, Mickey's a grown man," Ryan said.

"In a sense."

"And Mark can probably guess where *I* am."

"Probably."

"But that's not what I meant. I meant, I've got to get going as in, I'm headed back to San Diego today. Remember?"

His announcement stopped her. "What?"

"Like we talked about. To make a presentation to the Forrester's board." Ryan nearly levitated with boyish excitement. "Board meetings are held Tuesdays at nine. It's about seven hours from here to San Diego, so if I spend today driving—and tonight putting together a presentation—I can just make it."

She'd never heard him speak so quickly, or so enthusiastically. Or so *much*. Listening, April fought against a rapidly growing sensation of dread.

"After my success setting up the community relations program here in Saguaro Vista, I'm almost guaranteed to be granted additional funds," he went on. "I'll be able to expand the program to other Forrester's stores. Maybe in the order of the dates they were opened, as a nod to the history of the chain."

His face glowed. "I can't wait to get a look at the board members' faces when I describe how well the community relations program has been received here!"

She nodded. Cheerfully, Ryan crossed the room, still talking.

"Mind if I use your phone? Now that I have full use of my wallet again" —he winked— "I can pay you back for the call. I need to get in touch with my secretary— yes, I actually have one now—and ask her to reserve a spot for me on the board meeting's agenda."

Numbly, April waved toward the phone at the end of her kitchen counter. "Sure, go ahead."

He was leaving. Right *now*.

Despite their weekend together. Despite their feelings for each other. Despite . . . everything.

Disappointment nailed her to the floor. Slotted spatula in hand, April let the sound of Ryan's phone call—the sound of his arrangements to leave her—wash over her. Interminable minutes passed. She'd known this was coming. Had thought she was prepared for it. But still—

A knock sounded at her front door. Turning off the burner beneath the eggs, April frowned and went to answer it. *Great,* she thought. *Just what she needed this morning—company for her misery.*

"Hello, sweetie." Fiona Finnegan barged inside, chattering about her morning and bearing shopping bags. She dropped them all onto the vintage barcolounger, then fished around in one until she emerged with a round, transparent plastic cat toy. "For Calypso," she announced, beaming.

April snatched it away. "Mom, you know Calypso can't handle these Race 'N' Chase things." Awash in sudden exasperation, she turned over the toy, which featured a noisemaking fish inside a trick cylinder. "Every time she thinks she's caught the fish, it goes spinning out of reach again."

"That's the whole idea!"

"It makes Calypso feel inadequate." Wearily, April stuffed the toy back into the bag. "Thanks anyway, but you'll have to return it. Use the money for a padlock for the laundry room instead."

"What?" Darla appeared in the doorway, tottering on wedgies and evidently trailing Fiona. Behind her, her car was parked in the duplex's driveway. She crossed her arms, the gesture seriously at odds with the fit of her skintight spandex tube dress. "Exactly what are you insinuating about Aunt Fiona's laundry room?"

"Nothing. I—"

"Mornin' Mom. Ape." Mickey Finnegan pushed his way past Darla, dressed in bedraggled clothes and looking as cluelessly cheerful as ever. "Hey, Darla. Maytag anybody yet today?"

Their cousin pouted, and didn't answer.

"Maytag?" Fiona asked. She looked to April for an answer.

Dumbfounded, April watched as Mickey ambled to the sofa. He lifted the remote and turned on the TV. The high-pitched audience screams of a rerun edition of MTV's Total Request Live filtered toward the group at the doorway.

"New Britney Spears," her brother said. "Cool."

Darla glared. If looks could have killed, Mickey would have been a puddle of goo.

"Anyway," Fiona said, after a sorrowful glance at her eldest child, "I just came by to see if you'd co-sign for cell phone service with me, April. Those bozos at the phone company have turned off my service again."

Deliberating, April glanced toward the kitchen. Ryan's voice still drifted from that end of her apartment, steady, and by now, beloved. She ought to be memorizing that sound—and everything about the man who went with it, while she still could—instead of dealing with her family.

She sighed. Duty called. "They turned off your service? Did you pay the bill, Mom?"

Fiona sputtered. "Of course I paid the bill!" An elaborately innocent look came into her eyes. "I may have switched it with the electric bill by mistake—"

April wasn't fooled by her mother's cherubic expression. "That old trick *never* works! By now, everyone at the utility company knows you put your checks in the wrong envelopes to buy time on the bills. You've got to stop doing that."

"Fine. After I get hooked up again, I'll call Debtor's Anonymous. But first, I need a phone." Stubbornly,

Fiona regarded her daughter. "I've never had a cell phone, so I have a clean slate there."

"And a great instant-credit offer," Darla put in, examining her manicure. "No payments for thirty days!"

She and Fiona exchanged an eager look. April fought back an urge to scream. Why did they always come to *her* with these harebrained ideas?

"It won't kill you to help your mother, just this once. After thirty-six hours of labor—and they didn't have those cushy epidurals back then, either, missy—oh, hello, Ryan." Fiona's gaze turned speculative. "Fancy seeing you here so *early* this morning."

"And so . . . rumpled," Darla purred. Eyes fixed on Ryan's deliciously relaxed-looking self, she stepped forward.

April elbowed her backward. Possibly with more force than she should have.

"Dude." Mickey gave Ryan a swift up-and-down assessment. He grinned. "Glad I could oblige with the weekend at Natalie's place. *If* you know what I mean. Welcome to the family."

Groaning, April smacked her forehead. Could this day *get* any worse? Ryan was leaving, her family was insane, Ryan was leaving, Ryan was leaving—

"Mark broke in on your call waiting," Ryan said, turning to April after offering hellos all around. His voice was low, and meant for her alone. "He says if you don't tell your Uncle Bobby the bagels are off-limits, he'll call the police." His eyes were curious, but his expression was only sympathetic. Helpful. "He said you'd know what he meant."

She did. Oh, God. Uncle Bobby had grown an instant bagel potbelly again, and Mark had caught him. She would, April realized, never work in this town again.

"April, about the cell phone—" Fiona butted in impatiently. "I hate to pester you, but the special offer is only good for today. And Darla and I want to get to the Payless before all the good shoes are gone.''

"Wedgies are on sale today," Darla clarified.

"A sale?" Suddenly, something inside April burst free. She couldn't contain it any longer. It was loud, proud, and aggravated. "Mom, you've been overdrawn on your checking account for the past seven months. *When* are you going to stop spending?"

Fiona gasped. Darla scowled.

"And *you*," April continued, rounding toward her cousin. She trembled now, fully at the end of her rope. "The last thing you need are more wedgies to go Maytagging in. You're better than that, Darla. Have some self-respect."

The room felt silent, except for the squeal of teenage girls applauding a new boy-band video. Looking shocked, Darla backed up a step. "You—you—"

"April, maybe you should hang on a minute," Ryan said.

His hand touched her arm, reassuring and wonderfully steady. Ordinarily, his presence would have comforted her—or at least brought her back to her senses. But today, on the day he was leaving . . . well, today, April couldn't take it anymore.

Tears clogged her throat, squeezing off her breath. She tried to gulp in more air, and only succeeded in releasing a tiny, pathetic-sounding sob.

They all stood by, obviously not knowing what to make of her outburst.

"Hey!" Mickey said, his eyes glued to the TV. He pointed with the remote. "Check out this ad for XYZ Tech! I could totally become a certified dog walker."

"Mickey—" April tried.

"Or a professional landscape maintenance man."

"Mickey, I'm a little upset right now. I—"

"I am *definitely* calling Greyhound for a bus ticket to Phoenix. XYZ Tech, here I come!"

"Mick, shut *up!*"

He gawped at her, his mouth wide. "Geez, Ape. Bite my head off, why don't you? Nobody said *you* have to improve your professional qualifications in thirty days or less."

As though his rebuttal had let loose the floodwaters, her mother and cousin both leaped into the fray. Their voices rose, getting angrier by the minute. The phone rang. Ryan took one look at the mayhem surrounding him, and went to answer it.

"It's your Uncle Bobby," he called from the kitchen.

"Please ask him to call back," April begged. She wasn't sure how much more she could take. A rant from Uncle Bobby on how "narrow-minded" Mark Wright was just might send her over the edge.

A few seconds passed. "He says he only has the one phone call." A beat. "I'll take a message."

Weary and overwhelmed, April yelled a "thank you" to Ryan. Then she scooped up Calypso into her arms, and did her best to calm her cat's frazzled nerves.

Ryan came back. His hand settled onto her shoulder. "Uncle Bobby's bail ought to be set by noon," he murmured.

"What?" April wailed. All heads turned toward her, and her family quieted. "Mark said he wouldn't—"

"It wasn't Mark. Evidently, Uncle Bobby got a little worked up after Mark called you from the bakery." Ryan glanced at Fiona, Darla, and Mickey, as though unsure how they would react to this news. "He took Wanda's meter maid cart for a joyride through downtown."

"Oh, my God." April covered her face with her hands.

"Whoa." The crackle of cellophane came from Mickey's direction. His lighter clicked. The scent of burning tobacco wafted nearer. "Maybe Uncle Bobby's cracked for good."

A cigarette, April saw. He'd lit a cigarette. And after all her reminders about Granny Finnegan, all her worrying and trying to stash those Marlboros anyplace he'd never look. Now, Mickey had the gall to cop a smoke, right in the midst of her personal meltdown.

She must have tensed, because an instant later, April felt Ryan's hands kneading her shoulders. He stood behind her, silently offering his strength. His normalcy. His—let's face it—near-certain confusion at discovering exactly how screwed-up her family—and April, by extension—really was.

This could *not* be happening.

After a brief moment of silence, Fiona and Darla went right on talking. Their explanations grew louder and more strident, covering the subjects of shopping, Maytagging, stealing meter maid carts, and more. Standing in the middle of it was like being immersed in some bizarre Olympic event—synchronized sniping, maybe. Or competitive criticizing. Her mother and cousin were obviously both gold medalists.

"Stop!" April cried, holding up her hands. *Knead, knead* went Ryan's fingers against her knotted shoulder muscles. "Just stop, everybody. Please. I can't think."

Mickey held up his Marlboros. "Try a smoke," he suggested. "These always calm me down."

"Arrgh!"

"Okay, never mind." Sheepishly, Mickey put away his cigarettes.

Ryan lowered his hands. Maybe he was afraid to touch the loony woman. Feeling besieged, April drew in a deep breath. *First things first,* she told herself. *Just handle everything one problem at a time.* She turned to Ryan.

"I'm sorry," she told him, pausing to grab her handbag from the side table. "*Very* sorry. You should help yourself to breakfast. I really have to go deal with all this."

"I understand," he said.

His gaze met hers. It was, April saw, filled with the same kind of regret she was experiencing. Their weekend together had knit them even more closely together than before, she realized. That knowledge heartened her, a little.

"I have to get going, too," Ryan went on. "I've got a long drive ahead of me."

She gawped at him, at the cavalier way he could discuss his leaving. Ryan was already occupied, though, having pulled a wad of cash from his wallet. April's eyes widened at the size of it. Nearly all the bills, she saw, were hundreds.

"Everything will be all right," he said in a soothing, take-charge voice. He separated eight Ben Franklins from the pile. "Take this, spring Uncle Bobby from the clink, and try not to worry. I'll call you from San Diego with the name of a good lawyer."

Disbelieving, April stared at the money Ryan held toward her. Beside her, Fiona and Darla—and Mickey, on the sofa—lapsed into silence. More than likely, they were stupefied at the sight of so much cash in one place.

"I can't take this," she said.

"Why not?" Ryan asked.

April hesitated, searching for a way to explain. Instead, *spring Uncle Bobby from the clink* reverberated through her thoughts. *The "clink?"* Ryan made it sound as though her life were a cartoon—and he, the broad-shouldered, cash-wielding superhero. Macho Millionaire Man. The Super-Spendthrift Kid. The Caped Cash Crusader.

"Whoa!" Mickey broke in, craning his neck. "The only place I've seen that much cash is tucked into a stripper's G-string. And those were all ones and fives. Wow."

Fiona sent him a tight-lipped look. "Since when have you seen a stripper, Mickey Francis Finnegan?"

"Why don't you ask Darla?" Mickey settled back for a sulk, still smoking his cigarette. "She moonlights as one, you know. Down at the Hotsy-Totsy Club on—"

"I do *not!*" Looking outraged, Darla teetered toward him on her wedgies. "How dare you?"

"Well, you *could*. 'Specially in those clothes."

"Jerk."

"Hussy."

"Couch potato."

"Laundry lover."

"Stop!" April yelled. Couldn't they see how serious all of this was? Feeling increasingly desperate, she looked up at Ryan again. "I'm sorry. For . . . everything."

She gestured futilely, indicating her family, the money, the perfect romantic morning-after breakfast she'd had to abandon. She should have known it would come down to this, sooner or later. She and Ryan were just too different.

"Take the money," he urged again, reaching for her hand. Gently, he laid the cash—enough to help Uncle Bobby *and* get her car out of Wykowski hock—across her palm. He began closing her fingers over it. "I want to help."

April gazed at the money. At Ryan's earnest expression. At the money again.

She shook her head. "You don't get it," she said quietly, slipping her fingers away to leave the money in Ryan's grasp. "This is real life. *My* real life. Money won't fix it."

He frowned. "Sure it will."

"No. You don't understand." Tenderly, April closed

his fingers around the cash. "I don't think you ever will."

Ryan fisted his hand, staring at her helplessly. "I want to," he said, his eyes fierce. "That's what I've been doing all week. 'Real' life. 'Real' work." His voice lowered. " 'Real' love."

Around them, everyone hushed. The word *love* seemed to hang in the air.

A sob hitched in her chest. Desperately, April held it back. She had to be strong, for both their sakes.

"Pretending isn't enough," she said. Emotion stretched between them, wistfulness and yearning nearly tangible enough to touch. "A bet isn't enough. And neither is something ... temporary. Even though I hoped it would be. We both knew it would come down to this, didn't we?"

"Come down to—" Obviously befuddled, and a little angry, Ryan raked his hands through his hair. He blew out a breath, staring at her. "Okay. Fine. Have it your way."

Miserably, April watched as he swept everyone assembled with one last, dark look. Knowing she couldn't help but remember this moment forever, she drank in the sight of him, too. Ryan's familiar features hurt to look at ... and it hurt even more to know she wouldn't have the chance to see him again.

Even furious, even confused, he would always have a place in her heart. Always.

He headed for the still-open front door. There, Ryan stopped. "I wrote down my number in San Diego on the notepad by the phone," he said. "Call me if you change your mind."

And with that, he was gone.

Chapter Nineteen

Arriving back at work after lunch on a Monday afternoon was so much nicer, Jamie realized, when you had somebody to share the ride—and the lunch—with. She knew this for certain, because *she'd* shared both with her new love. Mark.

Unbelievable.

Now, smiling, she watched as he hefted her tote bag from the backseat of his sensible, mint-condition used Volvo. He shut the door and came around to her side of the car, steadying her wedding magazines with his elbow when the tote bag's stack slid.

He smiled back at her. At the gesture, Jamie was ninety percent sure she actually felt her heart go "pitty-pat."

"You'd look beautiful in a gown like that," Mark said conversationally, nodding toward the topmost issue of *Modern Bride* as they began walking through the shared parking lot behind Ambrosia and HairRazors. "And that headpiece, too. Have you considered a circlet of silk flowers instead of a veil?"

He reached out with his free hand as he spoke, tenderly ruffling her cropped cut. "It would look amazing with your hair."

Her hair. Her dress. Her headpiece. And this morning when he'd driven them both to work, Mark had offered a compliment on her Sam & Libby shoes, too. Adding all those things together, Jamie could only conclude . . .

Oh, no. She'd fallen in love with a gay fashion designer wannabe! Panicked, Jamie stopped a few feet from their destination. *Hold on a minute,* she ordered herself, *and think.*

Minus time occupied this morning by their respective jobs, she and Mark had spent the last seventy-two hours together. They'd spent roughly a third of those hours making love—having decided together that pacing themselves was only sensible. At worst, she decided, Mark was a *bisexual* fashion designer wannabe.

Trying to decide if she could come to terms with this new development, Jamie regarded him quizzically.

"Jamie?" he asked, obviously puzzled by her scrutiny.

"Mark?" she replied. "Have you—" She gathered her courage and started again. "Have you considered how unusual your interest in bridal wear is?"

He shrugged. "It's not as though I'm wearing a wedding dress."

Suddenly, she was more worried. "Do you want to?"

"Only on my head."

Okay, even *more* worried. "Huh?"

"On my head," Mark repeated, "because I've just taken the gown off you on our honeymoon, and have to stow it someplace while I carry it safely to the closet for safekeeping. I'd imagine those long trains make carrying a gown without tripping on the hem a little tricky."

Honeymoon? Relief filled her. Then: "Preceding this honeymoon, would you by any chance have been ogling the groomsmen and ushers at the wedding? Thinking they look 'hot' in their tuxedos?"

He looked at her as though she were crazy. "And I would do that because . . . ?"

"I knew it! You're just experimenting with me! You're bisexual," Jamie blathered, in full freaking-out mode. "Not that there's anything wrong with that, honestly, but I guess I'm more of a one-man, one-woman kind of person, and I—"

"So am I." With admirable steadiness, Mark put down her tote bag and framed her face in his hands. He kissed her. "So am I. Where do you get these nutty ideas?"

"The—the dress. The headpiece. The hair." Feeling increasingly silly the longer she went on, Jamie gestured wildly toward her spiky cropped cut. "The shoes!"

Mark smiled, shaking his head fondly. "Even *I* know better than to buy into every cliché about men who discuss fashion," he said. "Those things are important to *you.* So they're important to me. That's all. I want everything to be perfect for you."

Jamie's heart turned over, all over again. "I want everything to be perfect for you," she whispered, reassured.

"And I knew I wanted that, forever," Mark went on, "from the minute I saw you on that runway. I had to do something. Right then. I'm so glad I didn't let you get away."

Now she was getting choked up. "Me, too," she whispered.

They looked at each other. Then, through an unspoken accord they'd always shared, but had only recently understood, they came together for a kiss in the shadow

of Ambrosia's back door. Breathlessly, Jamie lost herself
in the man she'd yearned for, hardly able to believe the
happiness she'd found.

"Then you're not . . . ?" she asked when they separated.

Mark shook his head. Patiently. "Not a chance.
Besides, I'm *yours.*"

That settled, he unlocked the bakery's back door and
held it open for her. Jamie picked up her tote bag. She
started in.

She paused, thoughtfully, in the entryway. "So . . . do
you have any aspirations toward fashion designing?"

"Jamie . . ." he said warningly.

"Okay, okay." Jamie held up her palms, unable to
resist a laugh. "I'm done."

But as she entered the bakery with Mark by her side,
Jamie knew she would never be done. Not when it came
to this man. This love. This opportunity, so longed-for,
to show him how much he meant to her.

A girl just couldn't *get* any luckier. Really, her story
belonged in a bridal magazine, Jamie decided. It truly
did.

April was dusted in flour, weary all the way through,
and trying to bury her heartbreak in maple-frosted–
cookie baking, when she heard a thump at Ambrosia's
back door.

She jerked her head upward. Already today she'd
weathered Ryan's leaving. She'd spent twenty grueling
minutes discussing cell phone contracts with her
mother. *And* she'd trooped down to the city jail to assure
Uncle Bobby she'd cash in part of her savings to post
bail the minute it was set. After all that, April wondered,
should it really be so surprising she'd be called upon

to—she could only presume—foil bakery burglars at the back door?

Resolute, and alone in the kitchen because the other Ambrosia employee was manning the bakery's shop area, April selected a marble rolling pin designed for pastry making. She faced the passageway connecting Mark's rear office and the kitchen. She got ready.

Actually, April told herself as adrenaline raced through her, a good self-defense related pounding might release some of her pent-up frustration. She could practice some kick-boxing moves, work up to her cardio-vascular capacity, and call it a day. Sure. Multitasking. Who needed a gym, when crime-fighting workouts offered it all?

Another thump. Then, the sound of the door creaking open.

Yikes! The door was actually opening! At the realization, April's common sense returned. Only lingerie-clad bimbos in horror movies faced off against the bad guys alone—and they usually wound up creatively killed for their trouble. Clutching her rolling pin, she raced toward the phone near the cash register, mouth open to yell a warning.

Partway there, she glimpsed the open back door from the corner of her eye. Then she saw Mark, standing within the entryway. And Jamie, standing beside him.

Whew. It wasn't bakery bandits, come to divest Ambrosia of cookies, mixers, baking pans and wedding cake toppers. It was only her boss—her boss and his . . . Jamie?

Mark hadn't noticed April yet, and although she knew she should have tiptoed away quietly, she couldn't do it. Mark and Jamie? Jamie and Mark? She'd thought there was something between them, but . . .

They murmured a few words. Then they kissed. Not just a friendly buss or a peck on the cheek, but a real, groping, move-in-for-the-movie-close-up-style lip lock. April felt her eyes bug out. Jerking her arm upward, she moved to shield her vision from this private moment . . . and conked herself in the forehead with the rolling pin.

"Ooof." April staggered beneath the impact, seeing stars. Luckily, the blow had been a glancing one, but still . . . "Ouch!"

Jamie and Mark broke apart. They gasped.

"My God, April!" Jamie hurried to her side and assessed the situation. She removed the rolling pin of doom from April's grasp and set it aside on one of the worktables. "Are you all right?"

"Sure, I'm fine. I'm—" Still a little dazed, both by the unexpected sight she'd seen and the head-clonk, April wavered. She waved her arm, trying to seem unaffected. "I'm fine."

"No, you're not. You look terrible."

"Gee, thanks."

"I mean—" Jamie urged her toward a chair and sat her down— "you don't look like yourself. Did something happen?"

"She just bashed herself in the head with a rolling pin, Jamie," Mark said. "She's bound to be a little unsteady."

"It's not just that," Jamie told him. "Although we probably did give her a shock." She looked back at April, her expression worried. "What's the matter?"

"Nothing. It's not like the sight of the two of you kissing was grotesque, or anything. You were probably both enjoying it, so that makes it—" At their jointly horrified expressions, April backpedaled. "I mean, I didn't mean to see you. I thought you were burglars. I was on my way to dial 911 when I realized it was you."

Mark paused on the way to his desk. "Burglars? Maybe that knock on the noggin was harder than we thought."

Jamie scoffed. "You're obviously not a woman."

"Thanks for noticing." He gave a grinning leer.

"Because a woman always thinks every weird little noise is a burglar. Or worse. We're vulnerable. We have to be constantly vigilant."

Explaining this, Jamie went to the sink to wet a towel. She carried it back to April and gently held it to her forehead.

"That's kooky," Mark said.

"No, it's not!" Jamie and April said in unison.

He shrugged. "Okay. I'm not arguing with both of you."

As he put down Jamie's tote bag and headed for his office, Jamie pulled up a chair across from April. She helped hold the cool cloth to her forehead, peering into her face with concern.

"Okay, be straight with me. Because I recognize the signs of therapeutic baking as well as anyone," Jamie said, nodding toward the coconut cupcakes and partially-mixed maple cookies April had managed to make so far. "Do you want to tell me what happened?"

Looking away, April shook her head. It was all so ... so painful. So raw. So utterly sad.

"Nothing," she whispered. "I'll be fine."

Jamie waited. A few minutes passed. Cautiously, April lowered her cool cloth and looked at her friend.

Her empathetic expression was April's undoing. Tears welled in her eyes.

"He left!" she wailed, knowing Jamie would understand whom she meant. A helpless sob burst free. "We had this wonderful weekend together, and everything was perfect, and the sponsorships were all set, and I thought we were in love and then—and then—and then my family showed up, and turned all flighty Finnegan on me!

"He saw them all. My mom with her credit issues, and Mickey with his job issues, and Darla with her nym-

phomaniac issues, and Uncle Bobby with his getting-
arrested issues, and me with my neurotic cat issues—
he doesn't even know about *my* money issues—and Ryan
couldn't get out of my apartment fast enough. He just
. . . left. Back to San Diego.''

April stopped, sucking in a breath. Misery wrung
another sob from her as Jamie leaned forward and
hugged her.

"What did he say?" she asked quietly. "Before he
left?"

Sniffling, still clutching the cloth, April spoke into
Jamie's shoulder. "He said to call him in San Diego if
I decided to let him pay Uncle Bobby's bail."

"Huh?"

Reluctantly, April straightened and explained the
events of the morning, ending with Ryan's attempt to
solve everything with cash.

"*And* family influence," she added, shaking her head
as she remembered it. "He offered to give me the name
of some fancy lawyer."

"Money *and* advice? The rat bastard."

At Jamie's exaggeratedly indignant tone, April
couldn't help but give a choked laugh. "We're just too
different, Jamie. Ryan thinks everything comes down
to who he is, as though being a Forrester is all that
matters."

Jamie gave her a pointed look.

"What? He does! And now that he knows about
me—"

"Hmmm. His philosophy sounds like it belongs to
somebody else I know. Somebody who thinks being a
Finnegan defines everything about *her*, too."

April stopped. Was that true? Did she think—

"It's not the same," she argued. "Ryan's proud of
being a Forrester. He's proud of the benefits it gives
him. And I'm—"

"A flighty Finnegan?"

She frowned. "You make it sound so terrible."

"Isn't that what you think?"

Jamie was confusing her. Everything had seemed so cut-and-dried when April had arrived at the bakery late this morning, ready to bury her sorrows in butter, flour, sugar, and eggs. Ryan had discovered the truth about her, and he'd left. Simple as that.

They were over, and she was miserable.

"I have a valid concern! Ryan's wedding didn't work out because of his fiancée's 'money issues,'" April pointed out. "He told us that himself."

"And also," Jamie put in, "that the scheming so-and-so kidnapped his minister and ran off with a groomsman. I dunno, I think those details may have had something to do with it, too."

April wasn't dissuaded. "We're different. Plain as that. Ryan found out the truth about me. And then he left. That's all there is to it."

Fresh tears stung her eyes. She blinked them away.

"Okay," Mark said from the doorway of his office. She had no idea how long he'd been standing there, listening, arms crossed over his chest. "Exactly what truth is that?"

Leave it to him to be aggravatingly rational. April drew in a breath. "Well," she said shakily. "That I'm unreliable. Irresponsible. And undependable. Just like all the other Finnegans in town. You've said so yourself."

Mark shook his head, walking toward them. With an affection even April could recognize in her dejected state, Mark stood behind Jamie's chair and casually dropped his hands to her shoulders. Their contact was comfortably intimate—the touch of lovers. Clearly, something had happened this weekend.

"You're not defined by your family, April," Mark said. "Once, when I thought I'd fallen for you—"

April wrinkled her brow in confusion.

"—I thought you were, and it worried me. How could I be interested in a woman who came from such a flaky background?"

Growing more confused, April sent a quick glance toward Jamie. Her friend nodded, as though she'd known all this already, and was perfectly fine with it being revealed now. At Jamie's peaceful expression, April felt ready to hear more.

"Because of that," Mark went on, "I may have been too harsh at times, when I spoke about your family. I'm sorry. Now that I've moved on" —beaming, he kissed the top of Jamie's head. They both glowed with happiness. "—I realize I treated you unfairly."

April boggled. "But—but—" This was too much to take in, all at once. "But my mother really did write you bad checks. And Uncle Bobby really did try to smuggle bagels! Today! How can you say—"

"Because," Mark replied patiently, "you're not them. Jamie helped me see a few things more clearly. And now I know you're not responsible for what your family does."

Jamie nodded at that, but April couldn't quite grasp it.

"Then why do they always come to me for help?" she cried. "Why do they always look to me to bail them out?"

Jamie and Mark both gazed steadily at her. She had the impression they were in complete agreement about this.

"When you figure that out," Jamie said quietly, "then you'll know what we mean."

A moment passed. April stared at them. Then she got up and hurled the wet cloth into the sink, untied her apron and dropped it onto her chair.

"Okay. Fine. Have it your way," she said. "I can't stay here listening to this. I have things to do."

Suddenly stricken with the fact that she sounded exactly like Ryan had this morning, when confronted with his lack of understanding about real life, April stopped. Then she pushed onward, grabbing the pile of envelopes she'd brought with her.

"You might as well know, Mark, that I blew it with the community relations plan. I didn't bring in the business I thought I would for Ambrosia."

"That's all right," he said, seeming befuddled by her sudden burst of movement—if not by her revelation of failure. "You gave it a shot."

"It's *not* all right!"

April looked at him, still standing behind Jamie. Now they were holding hands, their fingers clasped at Jamie's shoulder. Their instant togetherness was palpable . . . and painful to see. Although she wanted to be happy for her friends, right now April knew she'd have to do that from a distance. From a place where seeing them together wouldn't bring back memories of everything she'd lost with Ryan.

"But I'm sure it's what everyone expected," she went on. *Including me, maybe.* "So, I'm going to visit all these merchants" —April waggled the sponsorship-decision envelopes she'd hidden from Ryan— "and explain that our community-building program has been postponed."

"What? Why?"

"With Forrester's in this town, there's not room enough for both of us."

Mark frowned. "They're a department store. We're a bakery. Surely we can coexist with—"

"Look, who's the community relations manager, here?" April snapped, pushed to the edge of her self-control by frustration and sadness and confusion. "It won't work."

Jamie blinked, obviously surprised. Mark straightened.

Desperate now, April plunged onward. "After that, I'd like to request a few weeks' vacation time. I have the time built up, and I need to get away. Out of town. *Someplace.* Mickey's thinking of going to Phoenix to enroll in technical school, and I thought maybe I'd—"

"Leave now," Mark interrupted, stone-faced.

"Mark!" Jamie said.

Giving her a reassuring pat, Mark came around her chair. He nodded toward the envelopes April held.

"You're in no shape to discuss business with my customers, anyway," he said. "Leave those with me, and do whatever you have to do."

April's fingers froze on the stack of envelopes. "Are you *firing* me?"

He looked away. "I didn't say that."

"But that's what you meant." Disbelieving, April looked from Mark to Jamie, and back again. Everything she'd feared was coming to pass—she'd proven herself a shiftless Finnegan, and now she was paying the price. "Mark, wait. I—"

Gently, he slipped the envelopes from her grasp. He frowned down at them. "Go. Do whatever you have to do. When you figure things out, come see me."

As if *that* would ever happen, April thought, stunned. Figuring things out was not her strong suit, evidently.

She couldn't think, couldn't speak. Of all the ways she'd imagined this day would play out, this scenario had not been among them.

"Okay," she whispered. "I understand."

Mark and Jamie watched as April gathered up her few personal belongings from the kitchen. They watched as she paused at the back door, reluctant to leave. They watched as the realization struck her that nobody was going to jump in, happily ever after–style, and make everything okay.

A few minutes later, April was gone.

Chapter Twenty

Bright and early Tuesday morning, Ryan arrived at the Forrester's offices in downtown San Diego, ready to do battle. His presentation was polished. His display materials were prepared, his space on the board meeting's agenda reserved. All that remained now was actually speaking with the board—and making an end run past the company's overeager security guards.

As he had almost exactly two weeks ago, he rode the elevator to the top floor. Its doors "dinged" open, sliding sideways to reveal his nemeses—two blue polyester–wearing Terminator wannabes.

"Excuse me, sir," the first one said. "Visitors aren't allowed on this floor. You'll have to leave."

"I'm not a visitor," Ryan said. Visions of his butt landing—again—on a concrete sidewalk whirled through his head. "I'm a—"

"It's you!" goon number two interrupted. He thumbed open his walkie-talkie's belt holster and came forward. "Look, pal. We already threw you out once. What are you, a glutton for punishment?"

"No. I'm a vice president" —smiling, Ryan flashed his new ID badge, Fed-Exed to his Pacific Coast town house by his equally new secretary— "in charge of community relations."

Both security guards scrutinized his badge. Then their shoulders slumped. They sighed.

"Go on through, Mr. Forrester," they said in unison.

"Cheer up, fellas," Ryan said as he stepped from the elevator. "Maybe you'll get some real action soon. I happen to know a person's life can change completely in a matter of weeks."

Thinking over all the ways *his* life had changed—for better and worse—over the past two weeks, Ryan strode down the carpeted hallway to the posh, glass-enclosed Forrester's reception area. As he passed through, various employees sent greetings his way. Having learned a thing or two from April, Ryan took his time chatting with everyone.

It didn't get more "real," he thought, than making genuine contact with people.

In the boardroom, though, he found himself in hostile territory. When he entered for the meeting, the greetings he received were cursory—and occasionally smirking. Several board members openly shook their heads as Ryan settled into his place at the table.

Idiot savant retailing, he read in their eyes. *You don't stand a chance.*

Well, their derision was "real," too, Ryan told himself. He'd just have to learn to live with it. And then he'd have to prove them wrong.

He sat through the requisite reports, presentations, and motions listed on the agenda. Most items were familiar to him, thanks to his study of past meeting minutes. To his delight—and very much to others' surprise—Ryan was able to contribute several forward-thinking suggestions to the discussions at hand. Then, it was time for his presentation.

He gathered his materials and stood. At the head of the table, he faced eleven hostile faces.

Inwardly, he balked. What the hell had possessed him to try this in the first place? Ryan wondered. He could have been lounging poolside at the OceanView resort. Admiring the view at Girls-A-Go-Go with Jackson. Answering the piles of party invitations that had awaited him upon his return to San Diego. He didn't need this. He didn't need—

Suddenly, he remembered something April had said to him. *You rose to the challenge of a wallet-less two weeks,* she'd told him, only a few days ago. *And I'm ... I'm proud of you.*

She was proud of him. Or had been.

He couldn't let her down, Ryan realized, squaring his shoulders. He could be the man April believed he was—or at least the man she'd *believed* he was, before he'd whipped out his cash again and all but proved her wrong. He could do this. And when he was done, he would return to Saguaro Vista ... and prove her right.

"Ladies and gentlemen," Ryan began, focusing on the board members before him as he introduced himself. "Some of you don't know me. Even worse—some of you do."

A smattering of reluctant laughter rose from the board members.

"Or *think* you do. Because you've been to my cocktail parties, my New Year's Day brunch, my Fourth of July blowout, my annual opening night masquerade. But there's more to me than meets the eye. And there's more to the small town of Saguaro Vista, Arizona, than meets the eye, too."

Ryan nodded toward his secretary. On cue, she

pressed the remote to lower the lights, and began his visual presentation. On the screen behind him, an archival photo of Saguaro Vista glowed in nostalgic black and white.

"Saguaro Vista is a town of around thirty thousand people," Ryan went on. "Those people are grocers, industrial workers, accountants. They're schoolteachers, mechanics" —a vision of Pete Wykowski wearing Ryan's suit for his bowling championship dinner popped into his head, and Ryan had to smile— "and doctors. They're hairdressers. Bakery owners. Bakers."

He thought of April, and misery fisted around his heart. He'd ended things badly between them, Ryan knew. At a critical time, he'd reverted to his old ways of coping with things, and he'd regretted it ever since.

The screen behind him flashed as it changed, bringing him back to the discussion at hand.

"In short," Ryan said, "they're a lot like you and me. And they want certain basic things out of life. Health. Happiness. Security. Loyalty."

One of the board members shifted restlessly. Drawing in a breath for patience, Ryan continued.

"Forrester's department stores can't offer its customers a cure for the common cold. But we can offer them happiness, in the form of a pleasurable shopping experience. And we can offer them security, in the form of a community relationship that will only grow and broaden with the passage of time."

The screen flashed, displaying a montage of photos from the Saguaro Vista prom-and-bridal fashion show. Watching as the board members smiled over the images, Ryan felt encouraged.

"Sometimes it takes a fresh eye to see the best solution to a problem," he said, echoing the words April had said to him on their second day together, while canvassing Saguaro Vista for sponsorship contacts. "I am that 'fresh eye.' And I'm here to tell you, our old ways of doing business are only accomplishing one thing—driving Forrester's *out* of business."

Grumbling was heard around the table. The Idiot Savant Retailing glares came back out in full force.

Ryan held up his hands. "I recognize and appreciate the experience gathered in this room. And in the face of the challenges presented us by ever-expanding big box chain retailers, we'll need that experience to guide us. But Forrester's can't compete with those mass market merchandisers on their terms. We need a new approach. And that's where my community-building program comes in."

He nodded, and his secretary changed the screened image again. This time, prospective partnership graphs filled the screen. Looking at the representation of all his work in Saguaro Vista, Ryan felt a new and wholly unaccustomed surge of pride.

"Customer loyalty is earned through relationships," he said, noticing a flicker of interest in some of the faces gazing up at him. Gaining momentum because of it, Ryan went on to describe some of the merchant contacts he'd made in Saguaro Vista. "Forrester's can't match mass market retailers for discounts," he said next. "But we can meet—and beat—them in earning customer loyalty. Through my plan, every Forrester's store will become closely knit within the community. Each store will form unique alliances with local businesses— alliances that will work to strengthen both Forrester's and the community it serves."

Now, his secretary was smiling, too. Ryan made a mental note to offer her a raise. Maybe a nice Swarovski crystal paperweight for her desk, too, or—*no, that was old-Ryan-style thinking,* he realized. Frowning briefly, he thought harder. Maybe, after the board meeting, he would simply tell her how much he appreciated her hard work and assistance.

He smiled back at her, his decision made. After all, there was more to life than the things money could buy. Ryan had had seven long hours of driving to contemplate that fact, and it was finally beginning to sink in.

"Real life" meant really thinking about what was important. And doing all you could to safeguard it.

Turning his focus back to his presentation, Ryan went on talking. He described how warmly Saguaro Vista had welcomed him. How enthusiastic the residents had been in their participation in the fashion show. How, afterward, he'd lost count of the number of people who'd sought him out to tell him, happily, that they'd never felt more connected to a company than they did to the "new" Forrester's.

"This program will work," Ryan said in conclusion. "It will bond Forrester's with the community, create new opportunities for expansion, and strengthen our position in this difficult market. I propose immediate implementation in the Saguaro Vista test market, with plans for an additional two test markets next quarter. With your support, Forrester's will once again be unmatched in our retail sector. Thank you."

The lights came on. His presentation ended. For the next few minutes, Ryan fielded questions. Then, anticlimactically, it was over. The fate of his program, he was told, would be decided after further discussion by the board members, with a decision pending at the end of the day.

Nodding, Ryan sat stoically through the rest of the meeting. Now that his presentation was finished—now that he'd done all he could to step toward the new life he wanted—all that remained was April. He couldn't wait to straighten things out between them. Even if it meant driving all night, Ryan meant to be back in Saguaro Vista by morning.

Nothing could stop him now.

At Pete Wykowski's shop on Tuesday afternoon, April waved her checkbook, staring at Pete in disbelief. She'd come to ransom her VW Rabbit. Now, she'd just discovered, she couldn't. The way her life had been falling apart lately, she guessed she shouldn't be surprised there was a hitch in the process. But still, she'd been optimistic.

Evidently, not even heartbreak was enough to obliterate her tendencies toward pointless hopefulness. For instance, April still hadn't been able to stop looking for Ryan every time she stepped outside her front door, as though he might actually have come back. The streets of Saguaro Vista seemed empty without him.

"What do you mean," she asked, " 'the part's not in yet?' "

Pete shrugged. "It's not in. These foreign parts take a while, sometimes. You could prob'ly pick one up while you're in Phoenix. I'll write down the specs for you, if you want."

As though intending to do exactly that, he moved toward the cluttered desk in one corner of his grimy shop's office. April stopped him.

"Pete! I can't get it in Phoenix if I can't *get* to Phoenix!" The city was only about eighty miles away—but her jogging program really wasn't coming along *that* well. And her Schwinn wasn't that sturdy. Fighting for composure, April searched her mind for an alternative.

"Do you have a loaner car I can use? I'll only be gone a couple of weeks" —*unless I give up on Saguaro Vista completely*— "and I really, really need some help here."

"Well . . ." Thoughtfully, Pete scratched his head.

"That old Chevy over there runs pretty good. Can't take it up over forty-five in this weather, though, or it'll overheat. And I'd have to charge you extra to put on a door."

She examined the beat-up compact car he indicated. It sat on four flat tires across the shop, hood open to reveal an incomprehensible, greasy engine. An air of complete dejection seemed to emanate from it—a side effect, possibly, of the car's missing driver's side door. April felt sorry for it. Kind of.

But she didn't feel desperate enough—yet—to try taking it out on the open road.

She sighed. "No. Thanks, anyway, Pete. Maybe I can come up with something else."

"No problem." He nodded, ushering her toward the shop's front door. Its bell jangled as he opened it for her, his hands conspicuously clean-scrubbed for their meeting. "Good luck."

"Thanks," April said. "I think I'll need it."

Then she went to find Mickey, and tell him of this latest glitch in their flighty Finnegan getaway plan.

Ryan was scrutinizing his office's unfamiliar plush carpet, wondering if he'd worn a tread in it with his pacing, when his secretary buzzed him to announce Jackson had arrived.

That was a surprise.

"Send him in, please," he told her.

At the same moment, the door opened. Jackson came in, wearing summery shorts and a deceptively plain four-hundred-dollar T-shirt.

"I've been waiting down at the club for you for almost an hour," he began. "When are you" —he doffed his sunglasses to peer at Ryan— "Christ, what happened? You look like hell."

"Nothing," Ryan said, resuming his pacing. "*Nothing* happened. That's the damned problem. It's" —he glared at his Rolex— "almost five thirty. The board promised a decision at the end of the day. What the hell is taking them so long?"

He stopped, staring at Jackson as though expecting his friend to come up with a reasonable excuse. Or the decision he was waiting for. Or *something*.

"That's not what I mean." Frowning slightly, Jackson peered into Ryan's face. "I mean, I've never seen you look this way. Not even when whatshername bolted with the Grisham clone. You look like I do after a fifth of Johnny Walker and a night out with the Montblanc twins. This could be serious."

Ryan started walking again. "It is serious. I said I'd stay here until I heard the board's decision. But I really want to be in Saguaro Vista. But if I break my word to the board members, won't I look like a jerk to April?"

Jackson tilted his head, as though considering all that. Then, "If you don't go back to her, you'll look worse."

"If I do—if I leave now—I'll never bring the board members over to my side. I won't get another chance."

"Do you want one?"

Ryan stopped, his thoughts even more tangled than before. He looked at Jackson, the epitome of good-time friendship. They'd been through a lot together. Yacht races. Ski trips. An ill-advised jaunt to the tattoo parlor where, at the crucial, painful moment, Jackson had asked to hold Ryan's hand, and Ryan had let him. No, Jackson wasn't anybody's idea of perfect. But he understood the inescapability of *im*perfection, and that made him a good person to have around, sometimes.

"Do you want a second chance," Jackson asked again, "with this thing you told me about—this *real-world work* thing?"

Ryan looked at him. "You say that as though it tastes bad."

"Strange," Jackson amended with a grin. "Not necessarily bad. Sort of like sushi."

Blowing out a breath, Ryan strode to his office window. He gazed out at the view of the harbor, with its docked sailboats and milling tourists. Waiting for the board members to make up their minds about his program was hard. But being away from April was harder.

He turned. "To hell with this. I'm getting a decision. *Now.*"

And then Ryan strode through his office, past his startled-looking secretary, and down the hall to the conference room where the board members had been deliberating their decision.

Wednesday morning, April watched as Mickey stuffed the last of his Budweiser T-shirts into the Army-surplus duffel bag he traveled with. He tucked his cigarettes into his shirt pocket, cast a wistful glance at TRL on MTV, and then clicked the remote to shut off the television.

"You don't have to go with me, Ape," he said for the tenth time in three days. "I'm a grown man. I can handle enrolling at XYZ Tech without my little sister holding my hand."

"I want to go!" April said brightly. "It will be an adventure. And what's a Finnegan without an adventure?"

"A Smith, Jones, or Wallace?" Mickey guessed halfheartedly.

"*Exactly*! Finnegans are adventurous. Carefree. Modern-day gypsies with no worries about dependability, reliability, or responsibility."

"And no clean underwear most of the time."

"Huh?"

He frowned. "I dunno. Stability has its advantages. Your apartment has its advantages. Like a laundry room. And besides, you don't seem the type to—"

"Of *course* I'm the type!" April interrupted. Hadn't she proved already that being steady, serious, and dependable wasn't for her? In the wake of the debacle with Ryan—and since getting fired from Ambrosia, although Mark insisted on calling her absence a vacation—April had decided the only thing to do was embrace her family's eccentricities. "I can be as wild and crazy as the next Finnegan. You'll see."

"Wild and crazy, huh?" Jamie nudged her. "I guess that's why you're bringing Calypso" —she raised the pet carrier in her hand, indicating the tabby inside— "along with her complete battery of allergy medicine, soothing cat toys, and special blanket, for a two-week trip to Phoenix."

"I said *I* was wild and crazy, not my cat. Calypso has needs." April nuzzled her cat through the carrier's air vents. "And I couldn't leave her behind. What if I decide to stay?"

"Stay? In Phoenix?" Jamie asked. "What for?"

"For the adventure of it!"

They both gawked at her. April felt driven to explain.

"Mickey does things like this all the time. Why not me? I'm a Finnegan, too. A flighty Finnegan." She cast a defiant look toward Jamie. "The *prototypical* flighty Finnegan. Look out, world! Here I come!"

Mickey shook his head sadly. "I think she's cracked," he said to Jamie. "This morning, I found her deliberately ordering a genuine paraffin spa treatment kit—"

"And a motion-sensitive trash can!"

"—at full price on QVC. And then she poured sugar all over a bowl of Lucky Charms and tried to pass it off as breakfast for me."

Looking aggrieved, Mickey crossed his arms and shook his head at his sister. "All I wanted was the nice piece of wheat toast with natural peanut butter she usually forces down my throat. And the multivitamin she makes me take with it. But *nooo*. Miss Wild and Crazy over here would rather see my teeth fall out between now and next Tuesday."

April saw Jamie gawping at her, and frowned.

"Live on the edge, Mick," she said. "Oh, and by the way—I canceled your dental appointment. You won't have time for namby-pamby details like having a cavity filled when we're living our Finnegan-style life of adventure."

Jamie set down Calypso's carrier. She came nearer. "Are you feeling all right?" she asked quietly. "Because sometimes heartache can make a person—"

"I'm fine!" April fibbed. Just because she spent every other minute wondering how Ryan was doing didn't mean she wasn't fine. Just because getting involved with him—and thinking she could keep things casual—had been the flighty Finneganiest thing she'd ever done didn't mean things weren't hunky-dory. "Don't worry about me."

Reminded of something, she pulled out her wallet from her handbag, and extracted her checkbook. She handed it to Jamie.

"Say, could you do me a favor, though?" April asked. "Just rip out a few pages from that. A few from the check register, maybe a couple of actual checks, too. I'm working on the art of an unbalanced checkbook, but I think I need a little help. I keep automatically writing things down. At this rate, it will be months before I catch up to my mom's expertise."

Mickey groaned. "On second thought," he said, "maybe it's a good thing you're going with me, Ape. So I can keep an eye on you."

Jamie caught his eye, and nodded in agreement. "Phone in reports," she suggested to him, pantomiming dialing a phone. "Daily."

"What is the *matter* with you two?" April asked. "You'd think I was running away to join the circus or some . . . hey! I've never met a carny before. Now *that* would be an adventure." At the least, it would be distracting. And distraction was what she needed, now that Ryan was gone. "Do you think they let beginners join up?"

Silence fell. Jamie and Mickey shook their heads.

"Hourly reports," Jamie amended. She gave April a hug, her gaze suspiciously teary. "Take care of yourself. When you get over this, I'll be here for you."

" 'Get over this?' What do you mean?"

Jamie sighed. "Doesn't the fact that you're having to pursue wild and crazy Finneganness with such . . . *zeal* tell you anything?"

April wrinkled her brow. "Like what?"

Another hug. This time, for Mickey. "Don't worry," Jamie told him. "Your sister will be back to her old self soon."

"I hope so," he said, hugging back. "Yesterday, she wanted to head down to the railroad tracks and hitch a ride to Phoenix in a boxcar. I barely talked her down. She's totally turning into some tragic, real-life country-western song."

"What song?" April scoffed. "April's Hobo Hoedown? *Puhleeze.*"

She squinted at the packed vintage Samsonite luggage she'd scouted at a yard sale. Deliberately, she scuffed one side of the smallest suitcase. One small step for woman, one giant leap toward Finnegankind.

"You two are too much," April said into the gloomy silence. "I'll be fine. Just as soon as I'm on the road *out* of here."

But as she and Mickey piled into Jamie's Escort, then

said their good-byes to her at the downtown Greyhound
bus station, April wasn't so sure. She *hoped* she'd be fine.
But somehow, without Ryan in her life . . . well, April
didn't see how anything could ever feel truly right, ever
again.

Ryan squealed into Saguaro Vista at half past nine on
Wednesday morning, laying skid marks onto Main Street
in his quest to move his roadster as quickly as possible
toward April.

Toward his future.

Those skid marks, as it turned out, were a problem,
though. Ryan had nearly reached the corner housing
Ambrosia when his screeching tires attracted the kind
of attention he *didn't* need. A horn blared behind him.
The vehicle trailing him edged up beside him, all but
forcing his Beemer off the road.

Irritated, Ryan glanced sideways. Then he boggled.

It was Wanda, driving her meter maid cart with Indy
500–style gusto. The cart's engine raced. The tires gob-
bled pavement, edging closer into Ryan's lane. She saw
him looking, and gestured fiercely toward the curb.

For one irrational minute, Ryan considered ramming
Wanda's cart and making his getaway for April's apartment, à la "The Fugitive." After being delayed in the
California–Arizona border town of Yuma with engine
trouble and a flat tire, and then finding himself forcibly
detoured from the highway because of road construction, he was feeling none too patient. But then Wanda
honked again. He glimpsed the Road Warrior determination in her freckled face. And he—wisely—relented.

"I've been lookin' for you," Wanda said when they'd
both parked down the block from the Pins 'N' Strike,
and she'd come to stand beside his convertible. She
consulted her handheld ticketing device, and shook her

head. "Do you know how many unpaid citations you have in this town?"

"Well . . ." Given that his roadster's glove compartment would no longer fully close on the traffic tickets shoved inside, Ryan guessed it was probably . . .

"A *lot*," she told him.

"I'm sorry, Wanda," he said. "I meant to pay them. Really. But I had this bet going, and I couldn't exactly—"

"Too late for excuses now. You'd better come with me." She nodded toward the municipal complex at the center of Saguaro Vista. "Don't want to take a chance on your skippin' town again."

"I won't. I promise." *I'm staying as long as April is here.* Ryan tried his best, most charming smile. "I'll pay you for those tickets right now, in fact. How about that?"

He leaned forward at the wheel, reaching for his wallet.

Wanda slapped her arm across his chest. "No funny business, city boy. I'm wise to your tricks. We're headed downtown. Right now."

Longingly, Ryan looked toward Ambrosia's retro sign, down the stretch of road remaining between him and April. If he could just get back to her, explain what had happened, beg her to take him back . . .

Well, he would. Just as soon as he wasn't a fugitive from parking ticket justice. With a reluctant nod, Ryan agreed to follow Wanda to the municipal complex.

He started his roadster and pulled out in the wake of Wanda's meter maid cart. Just as they edged onto the street, a gigantic rumble rose from behind him. Tapping the brake, Ryan glanced over his shoulder— and was blasted with a hot *whoosh* of exhaust-scented air as a dusty Greyhound bus passed them. Ryan blinked through the smoke the vehicle left behind, feeling strangely bereft at the sight of it. He felt almost as though he'd just lost something, had just witnessed something important. Something sad.

Why a Greyhound bus leaving town should matter to him, though, Ryan didn't know. He didn't even travel coach. So he shrugged and hit the gas again, then caught up with Wanda and went to face his vehicular destiny.

The sooner he settled things here, Ryan told himself, the sooner he'd be reunited with April. And that was what really mattered, wasn't it?

Chapter Twenty-one

April's plans to embrace her shiftless Finneganness began to dissolve the minute she crammed herself into her Greyhound seat beside Mickey—and realized that her seatmate across the aisle was having a conversation with his duffel bag. It sounded as though the duffel bag were making some excellent points, too.

They receded further as the bus jolted and swayed its way out of the station onto Main Street, passing by Wanda's meter maid cart and a convertible that reminded her powerfully of Ryan's roadster. Ryan. *Ryan.* It looked as though April would never stop thinking about him . . . wishing for him.

Loving him.

And those wild-and-crazy plans of hers unraveled completely when the bus drove past the RV campground at the edge of town, and April glimpsed Ryan's Winnebago parked in one of the spaces. It had to be his, she knew; it was the only one that was sparkling new . . . with a deluxe satellite dish on top. Despite its newness, though, the Winnebago looked a little forlorn as they zoomed past it.

Probably because, April thought morosely, it had been abandoned by Ryan, too. More than likely, he'd sold the Winnebago to some bored itinerant gazillion-aire, who now planned to outfit the vehicle with mink seat covers and solid gold hubcaps. After all, Ryan didn't need it anymore. He'd gone back to his luxury life. And she was alone.

Alone. The realization of everything she'd been through struck April all at once. She'd lost the man of her dreams, and what was she doing about it? Running away. Believing the worst of herself. Giving up.

Defiantly anti–flighty-Finnegan now, April hugged Calypso's pet carrier to her middle. She bounced up and down as the bus struck a highway bump. She turned to Mickey.

"I want to go home!" she cried. "Let's go home, Mick."

"What? Ape, the bus is in motion. We can't go home now." Patting her forearm, Mickey gave her a reassuring look. "If you've got motion sickness, there's a bathroom in the back of the bus. You'll probably make it in time."

"No. You don't understand—I've got to go back. This" —April's frantic wave encompassed the grimy bus, its passengers, and especially Talks With Duffel Bags to her left— "isn't for me. I'm not like you. I'm not. Really."

"Oh, I get it." Nodding wisely, Mickey leaned forward. "Listen pal, can you keep it down?" he asked Duffel Bag. "My sister here is having a personal crisis."

The man looked up. "A crisis? That's too bad."

"Mick—"

"Yeah, she just got dumped by this guy. Billionaire type. Cool car, though."

"Mickey!"

"Bummer." Duffel Bag nodded toward his debate partner. "We'll keep it down."

"Thanks." Satisfied, Mickey smiled at April.

So did Talks With Duffel Bags. *Arrgh.* Now she was garnering sympathy from loony strangers on the bus. Burying her face in her palms, April gave a muffled groan.

Mickey nudged her. "I told you, the bathroom's in the—"

"I'm not sick." She looked up. "I'm sad. I think I found true love. Did you know that? I think I found *true love* with Ryan. And what did I do? Throw it away. Just" —April pantomimed hauling out the trash— "throw it away. I let him walk right out that door. Oh, my God."

Duffel Bag shook his head sadly. "Hey, you weren't kidding," he said to Mickey. "She sounds on the edge. Look, don't jump, sister. True love is worth it."

April swept her hair back and gazed at him. "Do you think so?" she asked in a small voice.

Nodding, Duffel Bag regarded her seriously. "Horn tootin', I do."

Okay, so maybe the guy was a little . . . unusual. And maybe he thought the Nike swoosh on his "luggage" was a little smiley-er and more interactive than the average person. But he practically radiated empathy, and hopefulness. Right now, April needed both.

She sniffled. "Then you don't think it's too late?"

"No way," Duffel Bag said.

"Heck, no!" Mickey chimed in. Looking relieved, he patted her hand, which still clutched Calypso's carrier for security. "In fact, if I had a cell phone like Mom does, I'd give it to you to call Ryan, right now."

"Aww. That's sweet, Mick." April sighed. "But Mom's new phone only works inside the city limits, anyway.

Even with instant credit, you really can't get something for nothing.''

"See?" Mickey beamed at Duffel Bag. "That's my sister for you. Totally smart. Ape always knows what's what. My whole family relies on her."

Taken aback by his words, April frowned. "Relies on me?"

"Sure. Who does Uncle Bobby always ask for bail? Who does Mom come to for help when her rubber checks bounce? Who does Darla count on for a fresh supply of Maytag candidates?"

Grrr. April thought about the last few dates, Ryan excepted, she'd taken to the weekly Wednesday barbecue. To a man, they'd succumbed to Darla's spin-cycle charm.

"Me!" she said with surprise.

Her brother nodded. "And you don't see me crashing at just anybody's place when I hit town, either. I stay with *you*. Because I know you'll always have stuff."

"Groceries?" she guessed.

"Yeah. And other stuff."

"A sofa to sleep on?" she asked.

"Sure. And other—"

"I get the picture, Mick."

"Other things, too," he said stubbornly. "Like, you'll always watch out for me. You care about me. I like that."

"Oh!" Blinking back tears, April twisted sideways to hug her brother in the narrow confines of their seats. His skinny shoulders felt surprisingly solid beneath her palms. "Thanks. I—I'll always care about you. You know that."

There was a loud sniffle beside them. When she pulled away again, Duffel Bag was hugging "someone," too. He'd clutched his bag to his chest, eyes screwed shut. He opened them and saw her looking.

"That's beautiful, sis." He wiped his eyes.

Mickey agreed. Drawing in a breath, April considered all he'd said. In a sense, it was true—she did come to her family's rescue sometimes. They seemed to . . . need her. But did that mean . . . ?

"Okay, *maybe* I'm reliable," she admitted grudgingly. "For a Finnegan. But Mark fired me. And Ryan left me. Where does that leave me?"

"On a Greyhound headed for Phoenix," Talks With Duffel Bags said prosaically. The bus slowed, and swerved into the next pick-up stop, where a few passengers got on. "But, hey—at least your constant companion isn't rip-stop nylon, with a broken zipper."

April and Mickey looked at his duffel bag. She guessed she ought to count her blessings. "You have a point there."

"And Mark didn't fire you," Mickey put in. "He let you go on vacation. That's different."

"I told him it might be a permanent vacation. I told him we flighty Finnegans 'couldn't be tied down.' I told him I might not come back!"

Duffel Bag shrugged. "Born to be free."

The bus pulled out again. Even though it was only late morning, the seats were crammed full. The temperature inside rose, despite the air-conditioning, as they chugged down the highway to pick up the final batch of passengers at the casino on the outskirts of Saguaro Vista. Staring out the window at the desert landscape and distant mountains passing by, April fought back a rising sense of panic.

"I could have worked things out with Ryan, if only I'd taken the time to talk with him," she said. "He was wrong to offer me that money—but people don't change overnight. He was only trying to help."

Mickey nodded.

"And I was wrong, too. I should have leveled with him about my real life." With a regretful twist of her lips, April gazed down at Calypso's carrier. "All that time, I lectured Ryan about being 'real.' When *I* was the one who was afraid to show him the real me."

Softly, Mickey spoke: "It's not too late."

April turned to him. "Yes, it is! He's gone, and I—"

"Do you have his phone number?" Duffel Bag interrupted gently. "Because there's a pay phone at the casino up ahead."

She stared at him. "A pay phone? I could kiss you!"

He reddened. "Hey, whatever paddles your canoe."

Blowing an air kiss toward his puckered lips, April grasped the ray of hope he'd offered. She grabbed her handbag from the floor and dug into it, searching for the scrap of paper Ryan had left. She'd looked at it dozens of times, had wanted to call but had convinced herself Ryan wouldn't want to hear from her. But now . . .

Now she was braver. And wiser.

She found the paper. It was soft from having been handled so much, and the bold, inked-on numbers had gotten creased, but she had it. Her link with Ryan.

As soon as the bus arrived at the casino, April vowed, she'd call. She'd call Ryan, and she'd set things right. And then . . . and then, if they were lucky, they would have another chance.

"Thank you very much," Ryan told the clerk at the municipal center. He'd just shelled out hundreds of dollars in parking fines, but he didn't care. The fact that he was free to go to April was all that mattered.

"Bye, Wanda," he called.

"Watch your back, Forrester!" she yelled with a grin.

They waved to each other, Ryan making the gesture as he passed through the doors leading outside. There, he headed for his roadster at a near run. At this time of day, April might be out visiting merchants, but if what she'd said about returning to baking was true, his best bet for finding her was Ambrosia.

Once he arrived at the bakery, though, Ryan couldn't believe what he heard.

"So that's where all these came from," Mark was saying, nodding toward the stack of sponsorship envelopes in his hands. He'd been on his way to discuss them with the relevant merchants, he'd explained, when Ryan had arrived.

"April thinks there's not room enough in this town for Forrester's and Ambrosia to both have community-building programs," Mark said. He gave Ryan an assessing look. "What do you think about that?"

Astonished, Ryan motioned for Mark to hand over the envelopes. He scanned each one. He'd never seen them before. And a quick tally told him the number of sponsorship decisions they contained was roughly equal to those Forrester's had earned—maybe greater.

April had sacrificed these for him, Ryan realized. She'd opted not to compete, rather than beat him. She'd given him what she thought he wanted most—his Forrester's partnership program . . . when all he really wanted was her.

"I think she's too generous," he said, his heart filled with the realization of all April had tried to give him. He glanced upward to see Mark watching him carefully. "And I think I'll need to return these to April as soon as possible."

He turned from the counter, determined to do exactly that—and nearly ran over Jamie and Fiona Finnegan.

"That'll be easier said than done," Jamie said. She held up both hands, nearly touching Ryan's casual knit shirt. "Seeing as how I dropped April and Mickey off at the Greyhound station about an hour ago."

Shock jolted him. "You did what?"

"Dropped them off." Jamie looked at him seriously. "They had tickets for the nine forty-five bus to Phoenix."

Nine forty-five. Roughly the same time Ryan had seen the Greyhound bus whip past him on Main Street. Roughly the same time he'd felt that odd sensation of loss.

Roughly the same time his dream woman had left him, possibly for good.

"I've got to stop her," he said.

"Now you're talking!" Jamie cried, beaming.

She glanced at Mark. He smiled at her. Something passed between them, something intimate and fresh. Ryan realized he'd missed more than April's departure—he'd missed a new love between old friends.

"I'll drive you!" Fiona said, dragging him forward for a small but feisty hug. She released him, blinking back tears. "If we hurry, we can probably catch them when the Greyhound stops to take on passengers at the casino."

Ryan shook his head, already stepping onto the sidewalk outside with Fiona, Jamie, and Mark in his wake. The bakery's door swooshed shut behind them. "Thanks, but my car's faster. Which way does the bus go?"

They gave him directions to the casino, describing in turns the route the bus typically took to Phoenix. Listening hard, Ryan nodded.

"Okay. I'll be back. And I'll have April with me."

"Go get her!" they yelled, cheering. "Good luck!"

Ryan strode toward his roadster. A few seconds passed as the group on the sidewalk watched him. Then a feminine voice rang out.

"I'd better go, too," Fiona yelled, scurrying to meet him at his Beemer's passenger-side door. She glanced upward, smiling mischievously. "What can I say? A gallant, movie-style chase for true love always brings out my urge to play the quarter slots.''

At the casino, April listened dispiritedly to the sound of Ryan's recorded voice on his answering machine. She hung up the phone, and turned to face an expectant Mickey.

"No dice," she said. "He's not home."

"Hey." Noticing her doubtlessly downhearted expression, Mickey moved closer. He enveloped her in a quick hug. "That doesn't mean he *won't* be home. That doesn't mean you won't get a hold of him. Hang in there."

Sucking in a deep breath, April nodded. But tears pooled in her eyes, all the same. She'd so hoped things would be different. During the last several miles on the bus, she'd imagined the whole scenario. Her, calling Ryan. Him, overjoyed to hear from her. Her, finally seeing everything turn out all right.

All around them, just beyond the alcove housing the bank of pay phones, the small casino glittered and flashed, packed with shiny slot machines and millions of lights. Jackpot alarms shrieked from the machines, and coins plunked rhythmically into their bins. Voices rose as early bird gamblers gathered around the blackjack and poker tables. Music played over all of it, adding to the general sense of festiveness.

Except for April, it wasn't festive. Not when she couldn't find Ryan. Where was he?

"You go back to the bus, Mick," April told her brother. "The driver said he wouldn't wait, and you need to get to Phoenix. I'll—I'm going to stay here. I have to keep trying."

Mickey shook his head. He began piling up their luggage in a corner of the alcove, creating a seating area with April's ancient, hard-sided Samsonite bags. He put Calypso's pet carrier carefully beside them.

"I'm staying with you," he said, not looking at her as he worked with deceptive casualness. "You're my sister, and you need me."

"Awww. Thanks." She needed him, too, as it turned out.

Warmth filled April as she watched Mickey settle stubbornly atop one of the bags. He gazed at the bank of phones, his whole demeanor patience personified. He'd sit there, his expression said, if it took all day to get Ryan on the phone. No matter what.

It looked as though shiftless Finnegans *could* change their ways, April realized. If Mickey could abandon his latest get-rich-quick job scheme for the sake of staying by his sister's side . . . well, anything was possible.

Feeling heartened, April picked up the pay phone again. Maybe this time she'd get lucky.

Ryan jumped out of his roadster at the casino, his gaze fixed on the Greyhound bus idling near the gaudy, light-embellished entrance. *April*, he thought. *Please be there.*

No sooner had his feet hit the parking lot blacktop than several more cars screeched to a stop beside him. Mark and Jamie got out of Mark's reliable Volvo. Uncle Bobby got out of his battered Buick. Darla wiggled from behind the wheel of her used Corvette.

Trailing them all, Fiona Finnegan eased herself from the passenger side of Ryan's roadster. She smoothed down her pantsuit as she squinted toward the smoke-chugging bus.

"You'd better hurry," she told Ryan. "Those things don't stop for long."

He did hurry, running toward the Greyhound. The

rest of his romantic rescue crew trotted behind, although Ryan was only peripherally aware of them.

Fiona had cheerily used her new cell phone to call the additional Finnegans on the way out of Saguaro Vista, and had encouraged them to join in on the chase. And Mark and Jamie had taken instant time off from work, their excuses running toward the "What? You think I'm missing *this*?" variety.

All in all, Ryan was sure they'd made a wacky caravan, chasing the Greyhound down one of Arizona's bumpiest highways.

But now, they'd found it. And now—

He braced his arms on the Greyhound's sides and leaned into the entrance, addressing the driver. "I'm looking for a passenger," Ryan said. "A beautiful red-head, about this tall—" He held up his hand to collar height, feeling a rush of affection as he remembered holding April against him there. Cherishing her. Loving her.

He couldn't wait to do it again.

"—with a terrific sense of humor, sexy vintage clothes—probably sequined or spangled or brightly colored—and a smile that just brightens up your whole world."

The driver looked at him blankly.

"Have you seen her?" Ryan asked hopefully. "She's supposed to be on this bus."

"I'm not allowed to discuss the passenger manifest," the driver said. Then he turned away, examining something on his clipboard.

"Hey!" Ryan said. The driver glanced up, reluctantly. "Please. I'm not asking for the moon, here. Just a girl."

There was a pause. Encouraged, Ryan waited.

"A beautiful, redheaded, sexy, smiley girl?" the driver asked. His mouth twisted to hold back a grin. "Trust me, pal. You *are* asking for the moon."

"No, wait" —Ryan levered onto the bottom step—
"I have to find her. Please."

"Sorry." The driver checked off a few things on his
clipboard, then stowed it. He looked out his enormous
windshield, as though preparing for the drive ahead.
Then he gazed pointedly at Ryan's feet, poised on the
step. "I can't help you. And I've got a schedule to keep."

Miserably disappointed, Ryan shoved back from the
bus's entrance. He thrust his hands in his hair. Looked
around. Checked each of the Greyhound's long glossy
windows. But the glass was tinted, and he couldn't see
a thing.

A short distance away, the rest of his caravan stood
together. Fiona, Mark, Jamie, and the rest shook their
heads sympathetically. No one seemed to know what to
do from here.

For one crazy instant, Ryan considered throwing his
head back and bellowing *"April!"* in true, Brandoesque
Streetcar Named Desire style. He considered forcing his
way onto the bus, and searching every seat. He considered how difficult it would be to woo and win April
from the jail cell such a maneuver would probably result
in.

What the hell was he going to do?

Ryan didn't know. Then someone tapped him on
the shoulder. A skinny, long-haired man stood there,
hugging . . . a duffel bag?

"Dude, that woman you're looking for?" the man
said. "I know where she is."

Chapter Twenty-two

April sat on one corner of her Samsonite set, elbows propped on her thighs and chin in her hands. Her hair drooped. Her jeans and purple vintage disco top drooped. Her spirits drooped.

Where was Ryan?

She had to tell him how much he meant to her. She just *had* to. But would she get a chance?

Beside her, Mickey unwrapped a piece of Nicorette and popped the smoking cessation gum in his mouth. He chewed thoughtfully.

They both stared into the casino, waiting out the requisite five minutes that had seemed reasonable between phone calls. April's waiting time was filled with misery. More than anything, she missed Ryan.

She regretted the way things had ended between them; regretted not asking him to stay. Regretted, most of all, not telling him how she felt about him.

"Hey." Mickey's head came up. He quit chewing. "Isn't that Ryan over there?"

"Probably a mirage." With a decided lack of hopefulness—after all, Ryan Forrester probably wouldn't set foot in a cheesy casino—April tilted her head sideways. She looked in the direction her brother pointed. "We've been trying so hard to call him our minds have snapped."

"No, really. Look closer."

Halfheartedly, April did. The man, having obviously just come in from the casino's entrance, stood scanning the gaming floor.

"Nope. That guy's wearing jeans. Ryan *never* wears jeans. They're probably not allowed in the San Diego Country Club, or something."

She swiveled toward the pay phone and punched in the numbers she'd long since memorized.

"He's buying flowers from that casino worker," Mickey remarked. "No, wait a minute. Hang on. He's buying *all* the flowers from that casino worker." He whistled. "Somebody's girlfriend is going to be pretty happy when she sees those."

Glancing sideways, April glimpsed the man as he cradled an armload of red roses against his chest. The flowers were so plentiful, they partially obscured his face. Wistfully, she remembered the less-glamorous yellow daisies Ryan had brought her for their picnic. She'd loved them. *Loved him.*

She never should have let him go.

Closing her eyes, April concentrated on the recorded sound of Ryan's voice. It teased her with deceptive closeness. He could have been right there, she thought. Not two feet away from—

A massive bouquet of red roses was thrust in front of her. Their perfume filled the small space between April and the pay phone. Drawing in a confused breath, she trailed her gaze from the lush blossoms to the leafy stems. Up to the cellophane wrapper, and past it. Over the masculine hand holding the roses, and along the mystery man's muscular arm. To his shoulders. His chin. His face.

She dropped the phone.

"Ryan!"

At the sight of him, joy filled her. She smiled, hugely. Somehow, he'd come for her. And he'd found her, *here* of all places, just as though he'd known how much she needed to see him. Just as though . . . oh, it didn't matter.

He was here.

Her heart pounded, beating out a happy-to-see-you rhythm. Her eyes misted, and her fingers shook. If this was the product of an overactive imagination—and too much pay phone dialing—April didn't care. Just so long as Ryan didn't disappear.

"Remind me to tell you the one," he said gruffly, "about the doofus who left town . . . and forgot to tell the woman he loved he was coming back for her."

"You—back—me—" Desperately, April cleared her throat. "Here—now—please."

Arrgh, she was literally incoherent with gladness.

Ryan smiled. His whole being was a wonder to her— tall and broad and strong and remarkable. His blue eyes were kind, his golden hair tousled, his presence warm and necessary.

He *was* the blue jeans man, she realized, adding yet another surprise to the impossibility of his being here at all. His denim clung where it was supposed to, skimmed loosely where it needed to, coordinated nonchalantly with his defiantly nonbusinesslike shirt. He'd finally mastered the casual look. And on Ryan it was, she decided, manly and sexy and *very* hard to be diverted from.

His voice, slightly husky and filled with emotion, successfully managed it.

"I feel the same way," he said. "Here—now—please."

"Yes," she said breathlessly.

Ryan gave her the flowers, pulling her into his arms in the same motion. Being held by him—holding him—was bliss. Better than fifty percent off. Better than an unexpected garage sale. Better, even, than a chocolate croissant.

"I've missed you," she said. "So much."

"I've missed you," he said. "Without the duffel bag man, I don't know how I would have tracked you down."

April remembered Talks With Duffel Bags from the bus, and offered a silent thanks to him for sending Ryan her way. By now the Greyhound must have left, but she figured karmic kudos couldn't hurt.

"I'm so glad you did," she murmured, unbelievably comforted by the solidity of Ryan's chest against hers, by his arms around her shoulders. Still, her roses quavered in her grasp at what she had yet to tell him. "I have a lot to tell you, and I wasn't sure I'd get the chance."

"Oh, you'll get the chance." With a sexy semi-smile, Ryan angled his head nearer. He touched his lips to hers, softly. They both *mmmm*-ed. "If you think I'm letting you get away again, you're nuts."

"Maybe." Maybe she was. Because, suddenly, all April could think about was how much worse all this would be if she confessed everything to Ryan—if she showed him her "real" self—and he turned away. "But here goes, anyway."

Handing her flowers to Mickey for the duration of her explanation, April watched as her brother solemnly retreated to the far side of the phone alcove with Calypso, offering them more privacy. Then she gathered her courage. Squeezed Ryan's hands in hers. And began.

"I love you," she said. "I think I started falling in

love with you from the moment I looked out from my chipmunk suit and saw you smiling at me. I started falling in love with you from the moment you thought I was a serious competitor, and wagered with me. I started falling in love with you from the moment you first touched me . . . and I've never stopped. Never."

Silently, Ryan listened. Her heart pounded even more frantically.

"I don't think I'll ever stop. I fall in love with you again every time you look at me. When you walk into a room, I feel so buoyant I could dance on air. When you speak, my whole body listens."

His thumb rubbed over her hand, gently. His gaze remained fastened on hers.

"But" —April gulped, struggling for the courage to go on with what she knew now had to be done— "but there are things about me. Things you don't know. My family—"

"Some of my favorite people are Finnegans." He smiled.

"—they've had their share of troubles. And they don't always handle them very well. But I'm one of them, and I'm not sorry for it. We help each other, and we care about each other. And that's what a family is all about."

"I agree."

"I'm *not* just a flighty Finnegan. I'm more."

"And I'm not just a playboy Forrester. *I'm* more. You showed me that, April."

They were both more than they'd thought, she discovered, and April was glad for it. But looking at Ryan's understanding expression, she realized her confession needed to move along. If Ryan was ever to understand things, she needed to get to the heart of the matter— difficult as it would be.

Cutting straight to the point, she said, "Four years ago, my Granny Finnegan was diagnosed with lung can-

cer. She just couldn't do without her 'cigs,' you see."
April drew in a pain-filled breath, remembering. "We
did all we could. Hospitals, at-home nurses ... but in
the end, it just wasn't enough."

"I'm very sorry," Ryan said. "You must miss her."

He tugged her closer. With a shuddering exhalation,
April laid her head against his shoulder. Just for a
moment.

"I do," she whispered. Then she gently pushed away,
and grabbed for whatever levity she could. "Nobody
could comb a yard sale like Granny Finnegan. She could
haggle a fifty-cent collectible plate into a two-for-a-penny
bargain, and leave the seller happy about it. I learned
a lot from her."

"Obviously. Or you wouldn't have this nifty luggage."

Taking his cue from her deliberate lightheartedness,
Ryan grinned and toed the corner of her Samsonite
case.

"And you wouldn't have that nifty John Denton
book," she reminded him, feeling a little lighter already.
"But getting back to what I was saying ..."

His face sobered. He held both her hands tenderly.

"After all that time with Granny, my family was
broke," April told him bluntly. "The hospital bills took
their toll. The family's finances—my mom's and Uncle
Bobby's, especially—have never been the same. So
that's why—"

"Your mother bounces checks, your uncle helps himself to freebies, and your brother is always looking for
a new and better job?"

She stared at him, agape. "You *knew* all that?"

"Of course." Ryan shrugged. "And what I hadn't
already guessed, Fiona filled in for me on the way here.
I know they're trying. They're doing their best, and
that's good. But April, they're not what's most important

to me." He came nearer, framed her face with his hands. "*You* are what's most important to me. Only you."

"But I'm not a debutante! I'm not a sophisticated socialite!" Confused and hopeful—and filled, she'd admit, with no small quantity of relief now that her secret was out—April flung out her arms. "I live on Ramen noodles and store brand Lean Cuisine. I pamper my cat. I'll probably continue to step in every time some family problem comes up. I think I'm unemployed! I— I—"

"Those are things I love about you," Ryan interrupted in a quiet voice. "You're compassionate. You're giving. You plan ahead. And as for being unemployed" —he withdrew something from his rear jeans pocket and handed it to her— "I think once you agree to work on these, that won't be a problem."

She gawped at the sponsorship envelopes in her hand. *He knew?* "You knew?"

"I found out." A wide smile spread over his face, making him even more handsome. More beloved. "And thank you, but I can't accept. I want your happiness more than I want any job. Any company."

"But—"

"We'll share the sponsorships," Ryan said. "The town obviously wants it that way."

"Well ..." Dumbfounded, April handed the envelopes back. She'd think about them later. Right now, there were more important things to consider. Like Ryan. And Ryan. And *her* with Ryan. "We can't disappoint Saguaro Vista, now can we?"

"Hell, no."

"And we can't disappoint each other, either."

"No."

"So when are you going to kiss me?" April asked, immeasurably cheered and ready to move forward. Everything had turned out wonderfully, and she was ready—more than ready—to claim her dream man for her own. "Typically, when a woman confesses her love, she gets a kiss."

"Typically," Ryan said, "when a woman confesses her love, the object of her affection gets a chance to reciprocate. Or do I have that wrong?"

Excitement burbled inside her. Pretending nonchalance, April quirked her brow. She nodded. "That sounds about right to me."

"But in this case, I have something a little different in mind."

"You do?" Some of that excitement fizzled. "How different?" she asked cautiously.

"Different." Smiling, Ryan touched her cheek, her hair, her neck. "I, for example, do not have a declaration to make right now. Instead, I have another wager in mind."

"A—another wager?"

"Yes. Like our no-wallet two weeks. Only this time, you're the subject of it."

He seemed to be holding in a secret. A sizzling, exciting, can't-wait-to-tell-it secret. Unable to guess what it was, now that everything between them was out in the open, April looked up at him. "Me?"

"Yes. I'll bet," Ryan said, "that you can't go another day without hearing that I love you, heart and soul. Because I do, you know. Your smile makes my whole world brighter. Being with you makes me happy."

She couldn't resist kissing him. Their mouths met, lingered . . . reluctantly separated.

"I'll bet," he continued, sounding even huskier now, "that you need me just as much as I need you. And I'll bet—"

Pausing, Ryan got to one knee on the dingy casino floor. He gazed upward with his hands holding hers. At the gesture, April nearly sighed with romantic appreciation.

"I'll bet," he said again, "that if I ask you very nicely, and if I throw in those roses over there—"

Ryan angled his chin toward an avidly watching Mickey . . . who'd been joined, April saw, by her family and friends. Somehow, it felt perfectly natural to see them there.

"—that maybe, just maybe, my favorite Finnegan will consider becoming my bride."

She gasped.

Undeterred, Ryan smiled. There was a nervous edge to his smile now . . . but there was a certainty, too. A certainty that April loved.

"I love you so much. Will you marry me, April?" he asked. "I know we haven't known each other long, so our engagement can be just as lengthy as you want." He squeezed her hands. "But I need to know we'll be together. Forever. From here on out, no matter—"

"Yes!" April cried. Laughing, loving, she dropped to the floor beside Ryan and threw her arms around him. He felt wonderful. Amazing. Like everything she'd ever wanted. "Yes, yes, yes!"

"Yes?"

"Yes!"

"Wahoo!" With a fierce exclamation, Ryan surged upward again, bringing April with him. He pulled her into his embrace, lifting her off her feet and into the air. She felt herself swinging, swinging . . . and laughing with joy. "She said *yes!*" he yelled.

Heads turned their way. Speculative murmurs trailed April's downward descent, until she felt her toes touch the floor again. An instant later she was surrounded by her mother, Uncle Bobby, a squealing Darla, Mark, and Jamie.

"A wedding!" Jamie exclaimed, rushing forward to

hug April. "Dresses, showers, invitations ... you are going to need *so* much help planning. Yippee!"

"You," Mark said with a smile, "are going to need so much wedding cake. I'm thinking French vanilla, with white chocolate icing. A spice groom's cake. Maybe petit fours for the children's table ..."

"You are going to need so much advice," Fiona said when she stepped in. She rubbed her hands together, as though relishing the thought. "Come to me *any time*, darlings."

April covered her eyes. Ryan laughed.

"You're going to need someone to taste test the menu for the reception," Uncle Bobby said, rubbing his belly.

"And someone to help with groomsmen's fittings," Darla added, utterly unrepentant. "I volunteer."

Mickey came nearer, setting the roses atop Calypso's pet carrier so he could get something from his pocket.

"You are totally going to need someone to scout out honeymoon locations," he said, popping another piece of Nicorette. "As long as Natalie can get time off from Spicy Girl to come with me" —he grinned good-naturedly at them both— "I totally volunteer."

April looked at her groom-to-be. Love filled her, leaving her so happy it was almost unfair to the rest of the world.

"Are you sure you're up for this?" she asked him, nodding toward her friends and family. "It will probably be like this all the time, you know."

Ryan smiled. "With you? I wouldn't miss it."

He turned to everyone waiting. "Jamie, you're a born wedding planner. We'd be fools to turn down your help."

She grinned, and executed a perfect curtsy.

"Mark, we wouldn't think of using another bakery. Ambrosia it is."

He nodded, looking pleased.

"Fiona, we'll be sure to cook up some real potboilers to ask you about. Your expertise is appreciated."

April elbowed him. Her mother only preened.

"Uncle Bobby and Darla, how could we refuse?"

They linked arms and left—presumably to visit the buffet.

"And Mickey . . ." Ryan turned to her brother, shaking his head. "I don't know about you. Now that the Forrester's board has approved and funded my test program, do you think you could stand taking over my Winnebago for me?"

Mickey's eyes grew big. "Really?"

"Sure. You can scout all the land-based honeymoon spots you want in that thing. Or find some interesting jobs."

"Cool! You're on!"

"And *you*" —Ryan turned to April, his words nearly a growl of delighted masculine possession— "what shall I do with you?"

She couldn't help but laugh. Languidly, she wrapped her arms around his shoulders and pulled him closer. Their bodies touched, sharing space in a way that defined intimacy.

"Well, love me, of course," she said, kissing him. "As much as I love you."

"Forever and ever, Red," Ryan said, kissing her, too. "I may not be a betting man—"

April scoffed. Ryan grinned.

"—but I'd bet everything I have on us, together."

"I think," April said, "you already did."

Then they turned toward her luggage, picked up all the pieces and Calypso's carrier, and headed away together—into a future where everyone won on both sides of a bet . . . and true love always proved victorious.

Dear Reader,

One of the things I love most about being a writer is meeting new characters. Sometimes they're brash, sometimes they're wacky. Sometimes their vulnerabilities make me misty-eyed at the computer, and sometimes their outrageousness makes me laugh out loud. When April and Ryan came on the scene in *Falling for April,* they were no exception. I couldn't wait to get these two together, and help them find their happily ever after. And I *really* couldn't wait to share their story with you.

I'm currently working on my next Zebra Books contemporary romance, *Reconsidering Riley,* and I hope you'll look for it when it hits the shelves this October. Until next time ... I'd love to hear from you! Please write to me c/o P.O. Box 7105, Chandler, AZ 85246-7105, send E-mail to lisa@lisaplumley.com, or visit my website at www.lisaplumley.com for previews, reviews, my reader newsletter, sneak peeks of upcoming books, and more.

In love and laughter,
Lisa Plumley

<u>BOOK YOUR PLACE ON OUR WEBSITE</u> <u>AND MAKE THE</u> <u>READING CONNECTION!</u>

We've created a customized website just for our very special readers, where you can get the inside scoop on everything that's going on with Zebra, Pinnacle and Kensington books.

When you come online, you'll have the exciting opportunity to:

- View covers of upcoming books
- Read sample chapters
- Learn about our future publishing schedule (listed by publication month *and author*)
- Find out when your favorite authors will be visiting a city near you
- Search for and order backlist books from our online catalog
- Check out author bios and background information
- Send e-mail to your favorite authors
- Meet the Kensington staff online
- Join us in weekly chats with authors, readers and other guests
- Get writing guidelines
- AND MUCH MORE!

Visit our website at
http://www.kensingtonbooks.com

DO YOU HAVE THE
HOHL COLLECTION?